Romancelandia, #2

Billionaire with Benefits

Anne Tenino

Riptide Publishing
PO Box 6652
Hillsborough, NJ 08844
www.riptidepublishing.com

Cover art: L.C. Chase, lcchase.com/design.htm
Editor: Carole-anne Galloway
Layout: L.C. Chase, lcchase.com/design.htm

ISBN: 978-1-62649-197-7

First edition
October, 2014

Also available in ebook:
ISBN: 978-1-62649-196-0

Romancelandia, #2

Billionaire with Benefits

Anne Tenino

This book is for Alec, just for being there.

Table of Contents

Prologue

Fourteen Years Ago

One night in October, Tierney discovered an honest-to-fucking-God glory hole. He'd been on the way back to his room from a midweek party and stopped at Cambridge Hall to visit the facilities, going all the way to the basement restroom for a little (drunken) contemplation.

As soon as he sat on the throne, he spied the opening in the stall wall. His palms went sweaty. He'd watched enough porn on the internet to recognize it, but still thought he might be hallucinating. Any moment it would disappear.

It didn't.

No way.

He leaned sideways—barely keeping his wasted butt on the john—to look through the hole.

Shit! There was a guy in there. Tierney's pulse really took off then, all the blood draining from his head. Instinctively he leaned forward, putting his face between his knees—and into his briefs, hanging between them—to keep from fainting.

Tap tap tap. For a split second he knew it was his mother's habitual knock on his bedroom door, and he jerked his head out of his underwear, eyes opening so wide they strained his lids.

Tap tap tap. It was a shoe. In the stall next to him. The shoe of the guy in there. And he was tapping. Like, knocking. Like he wanted to send a signal or wanted—

Tierney gasped.

"Dude." A voice floated through the hole. "You okay?"

"Yeah," Tierney squeaked. "I just, you just. Surprised. Me. Um . . ."

The guy didn't answer, but his foot moved. He was standing now, taking a step. Tierney heard the door lock opening over the drumming in his ears. *He's leaving.* "Wait!"

The shoes stopped. "Yeah?" the anonymous voice asked after a second.

"Uh . . ." His heart thumped so hard he shook with it. Something he hadn't experienced since realizing that, as a Terrebonne, he'd never be allowed to kiss a guy or touch someone else's dick or feel male hands touch his.

Or get an anonymous blowjob through a glory hole from a man.

"Dude," the anonymous man in question said, sounding twitchy, calling Tierney fully back into his current situation. In a men's room stall that happened to have a hole to another dimension where a guy would suck his dick.

Next thing Tierney knew, he was hugging the wall like a gecko, hips straining to push even farther into the opening, the rough edges of particle board and laminate biting into the skin of his thighs, and then—thank fuck—someone's breath on his cock. Tierney grunted when he felt the heat of the dude's mouth on his skin, taking him in, no playing around like girls did because they didn't really want to taste dick.

This isn't a girl.

The guy's lips wrapped around him and sucked hard, and seconds later Tierney was coming. Groaning, then panting so loudly he nearly drowned out the dude bitching about how fast he'd shot before slamming out of the stall. Tierney closed his eyes and rested his cheek against the cool surface, listening to the door to the restroom swing open, and then footsteps fade away.

Oh God. He'd done it. Anonymously. The Terrebonne family name would never even know.

Weeks later, lying in bed the night before Thanksgiving vacation, Tierney let his mind revisit his most recent trip to the glory hole. He'd pictured his friend Ian in the neighboring stall. Ian was so butch and blond and built-all the good "B" words. He kept his hair trimmed short and didn't go for the sloppy grunge look like the other guys in their dorm. All the guys but Tierney.

Ian was like him in other ways too. They had similar backgrounds in emergency services, except Ian's family was blue-collar. They were all firefighters, while Tierney's were all ambulance company owners. Ian smelled like engine oil and saltpeter—not that Tierney knew what saltpeter really smelled like. Sounded masculine, though.

They weren't roommates—Tierney paid extra to have his own room—but they lived on the same floor. Ian liked his dad about as much as Tierney liked Grandfather, and somehow that led to the two of them hanging out a lot.

Like with other friends over the past five years, Tierney knew his desire to be with Ian was a little different than the normal straight guy's impulse to chill out with dudes. But he mostly ignored that, until the day Ian had said, "Chicks are more trouble than they're worth."

That made Tierney start to wonder. He had no other reason to think Ian might lean his way, just a feeling. A strong one. There had to be other guys around like him, right? Ones who were into dudes, but not exactly *gay*. And maybe . . . Ian could be one?

There was only one way to find out.

The night after Tierney returned to school from the holiday, he had Ian in his dorm room, drunk on bourbon he'd brought back from home. The dude's eyes were glassy, and he was working to focus them. But was he drunk enough for The Plan?

Tierney swallowed down a hysterical giggle with another swig from the bottle. *One more test.*

"So, like, you feel horny, man?" he asked, slouching against the side of his bed. *Look casual.* He was just a regular guy who talked about sex. Yep, nothing freaky here.

Ian's eyes went wide, showing the whites all around his irises. Then he mirrored Tierney's slouch. "Well, yeah. Always."

"I can fix that for you, dude."

Ian froze for a second before squinting. "What're you talking 'bout?"

"Just, you know." Tierney shrugged. "When I'm hurting, there's a place I go to get taken care of." He wanted to take another pull off the bottle, but his hands felt shaky. He didn't need to showcase that.

"Like, you mean hookers'r something? 'Cause I'm n—"

"No, dude. No money changes hands. Just, there are people out there who like giving head as much as others like getting it, and I know how to find them."

Ian's tongue flicked out across his lower lip.

Oh yeah, he was into it.

After that, everything unfolded in flashes of activity. *Are we really doing this?* Must be, because he and Ian were going together across campus, moving in sync. Tierney watched his foot land on the asphalt path at the same instant Ian's did, orangish in the glow of the security lights.

"Where are we going?" Ian's question came out on clouds of breath, puffing into Tierney's peripheral vision.

"Cambridge," he answered, because one word was all he could manage.

Then they were there, and he yanked the door open, swinging it wide so nothing could block Ian's path to the glory hole. *Glory.* The sound of their feet pounding down the stairs echoed in his ears. "It's in the basement."

"What is?"

He ignored the question, pulling ahead once they reached the hallway, footsteps keeping time with his heartbeat.

What if there isn't anyone here? Had to be. Too important. He shouldered the men's room door open, forcing swagger into his walk, only glancing into the mirror for a split second to make sure Ian was following him.

He was.

There were feet in the left stall. As far as he could figure glory hole etiquette, the guy who wanted to get sucked off stood in the one on the right.

He opened that one just as the lower half of a face appeared in the hole. He and Ian halted, and Tierney stared at the whiskered, dimpled chin and plump lips waiting there. *So obvious it's a man.* The guy's breathing echoed around the bathroom, or maybe just in Tierney's ears. Fuck, what if he'd been wrong and Ian was about to freak? *Too late to wimp out.* He shoved his buddy inside. "Open your jeans and stick your dick through, dude. He wants it."

Ian shifted his stance a couple of times, hands resting on his package, but his fingers hesitated on his fly button. "You gonna watch?"

Thank fuck, he was really going to do it. "No," Tierney scoffed, moving far enough away to seem like he wasn't looking, but keeping Ian in his peripheral vision. Tierney heard the sound of unzipping, and saw a flash of flesh as Ian untangled his cock from his pants. Tierney *couldn't* not see that—turning his head, he caught a brief view of the tight skin and protruding veins of a raging erection before it disappeared through the hole.

Oh fuck. He could *hear* it. The slurp and suck, and then a *hmmm*, like the other guy enjoyed Ian's flavor, and it was all Tierney could do to just stand there and let it happen. For the first time, he wanted to be in the left-hand stall but *only* because Ian was in the right. Only totally gay guys *sucked* dick. *He* wasn't into that.

Except, if *Ian* was into it, Tierney would offer. On his knees, with lips parted.

The slam of a palm hitting the stall wall made Tierney flinch, but the moan that accompanied it—low and throaty and quickly cut off—told him Ian wanted this. More than liked it, because that noise had been laced with the same ache Tierney had had every time he'd been here.

He's into it. He's into guys.

Ian stumbled out, jeans still open, lurching forward, and hit the tile wall next to the sink, then slid down to sit on the floor, facing the glory hole.

Tap tap tap. The sucker wanted more, and Tierney was right there, as hard as he'd ever been. The whole time he was being blown, he watched Ian. The dude barely blinked, gaze fixed on the action. When his hands crept toward his groin, and the bulge in his briefs, Tierney came almost as fast as he had the first time. But this guy didn't bitch, maybe because he'd had two loads. Tierney faked cool, doing up his jeans and stepping out to offer a hand up to Ian, who seemed too freaked to see it shaking. "Ready to go, or you want more?"

Ian shook his head, and pushed himself up to standing under his own power. "Let's go."

The whole way back to the dorm, Tierney kept having to remind himself to breathe. Ian was silent, walking rapidly with his hands shoved in his coat pockets. Tierney's nerves stretched taut, waiting for him to say something, but Ian didn't even look his way.

Had he fucked up?

Tierney stumbled, lurching into Ian's side, brushing elbows. Ian jumped away, like contact with Tierney sent a thousand volts of revulsion right through him.

Oh fuck. Going up the stairs behind him, Tierney didn't even watch the guy's ass like he normally did, too caught up in internal panic. *He's never going to speak to me again.* What the fuck had he been thinking? He'd exposed his own desires to someone else. Someone who *knew* him, who'd seen his face, unlike the guys in the Cambridge Hall men's room.

Someone he *liked*.

What if he tells everyone I'm a homo?

"Later, dude," Ian muttered when they reached their floor, hunching his shoulders around his ears and walking down the hall. Away from Tierney. It was late, the dorm was quiet, but the common areas were still well lit. Anyone who looked Tierney's way could see it all right there in the glaring brightness: his fear and his insecurities and his stupidity. Maybe someone could even see the sinkhole that opened up in his gut. But no one was watching him; he was all alone, standing there long after Ian had reached his room and gone in.

Tierney didn't sleep all night, totally wired and steeling himself for the imminent public shaming. So preoccupied that, at five when he crept out to piss, he didn't see Ian in the hall until he nearly ran into him.

"Hey," Ian grunted, then yawned and ran his hand through his hair.

"Hey," Tierney echoed.

As Ian passed, heading back toward his room, he added in a mumble, "See y'at breakfast."

Tierney slumped, resting his weight against the wall until his leg muscles firmed up again.

Ian isn't going to tell everyone.

The relief Tierney carried for the next couple of days made him feel light, and vulnerable to other positive emotions, like hope. Hope that maybe, just maybe, Ian *was* into guys, but he'd somehow missed the message that Tierney was too. Tierney had no reason to think so—they were nineteen, most guys their age would take any blowjob they could get even if the mouth came with a mustache—except for one thing: Ian was *too* careful to act "normal." Before, if Tierney showed up for breakfast and there wasn't a seat at the table, Ian wouldn't have done shit, but now he told the other guys to shove over and make room. Things like that kept hope alive, like a small candle flame in Tierney's heart. But it wasn't until Ian searched him out in the common area the morning before they went home for Christmas that Tierney's hope drove him to act.

"Wanna hang out tonight?" he asked, faking interest in a letter from his mother. She was always sending him stupid shit, reminding him of social obligations, or simply wondering how he was. Why couldn't she call and leave a message he could pretend he never got?

"Sure." Ian shrugged. "You care if I bring my girlfriend?"

Skid marks on my heart. He totally got the song now. But the deflated lungs got left out of the lyrics, so did the sputtering, dying flame of hope in his chest and the ringing in his ears.

"T? You okay, man?"

"Fine," Tierney forced out. "I didn't know you were seeing someone." Muscles in his jaw wanted to clench and grind, but he fought them off.

"Yeah, uh, just started." Ian licked his lip. "Her name's Sherri."

"Huh." *Mother. Fucker.* "Guess I shouldn't mention what happened the other night in front of her."

And there it was, a flicker of emotion just before Ian's face went completely blank. It told Tierney everything he needed to know: as far as Ian was concerned, that blowjob never happened.

"Our first date was the day after," Ian told him in a monotone.

Part of Tierney wanted to stay and hit the prick. Punch him right in one of those opaque eyes of his. But a much bigger part of him was injured, hemorrhaging pain, and had to get the fuck away. "I forgot, I have shit to do tonight," he choked out before turning and walking blindly down the hall to the exit. Outside, the cold hit him, scraping his internal organs with shards of ice. He needed a coat, but he wasn't fucking going back. He might see that traitorous dick and do what-the-fuck-ever to him. Punch Ian until he loved Tierney back.

I love him?

I must. His eyes were blurring with tears, and his lungs were doing a weird shuddering thing, almost like sobs, except he wasn't crying, just trying to survive. That *had* to be love, right? A black hole opened up inside him. He recognized it from a night five years ago, when—like his father and brother before him—he'd been required to have dinner with his grandfather on the eve of his fourteenth birthday. That night, Milton Terrebonne had made a point of telling Tierney that giving in to any *deviant physical longings* was not done. "As a Terrebonne," Grandfather had intoned gravely, "it's your duty, to yourself and the family, to master any *unnatural* urges. Not only because of our social standing, but because of *your* financial future. Am I clear?"

He'd been clear then, and many times since. And this situation with Ian, that was just another kind of reinforcement. Another message to Tierney's secret self that it had to stay hidden. In the closet. Sex with guys had to be anonymous, and love . . .

Love sucks the big one.

Fuck this. Tierney went back to his room and finished the bottle of bourbon he'd shared with Ian *that* night. Then the tequila he'd brought as backup.

He wasn't crying then, either.

The next day, he drove home hungover as fuck. When he arrived, he only told Agatha, managing to completely avoid his family before crashing in his bedroom.

Hours later, something woke him. He lay on his stomach, hugging his pillow, trying to figure out what it might have been.

Tap tap tap. His mother's knock. Knuckles on wood, not a foot on linoleum.

"Yeah?" Tierney called, rolling over onto his back

"Darling," Mother began before she'd even fully entered the room. "We don't say, 'Yeah,' when we answer the door. You should say, 'Come in,' or, if you're feeling brusque, you could say, 'Enter,' the way your grandfather does, but only rarely."

"Sorry, Mother," Tierney answered on autopilot, rubbing his eyes with the heels of his hands.

"Your grandfather is expecting you to join him for an early dinner."

Tierney froze. "Huh?"

"Tierney, we *don't* say 'huh.' You may beg my pardon or, on occasion, even ask, 'What?' like your Grandfather Milton, but 'huh' is unacceptable."

He sat up, watching his mother settle into the chair she'd insisted he have next to the window. "Um, what?"

She fixed him with a firm eye. "I beg your pardon?"

"I beg your pardon?" he parroted. He must not have Grandfather's chops yet. *Excuse me, we say "gravitas," not "chops."*

"I said Grandfather is expecting you to join him for dinner." She arranged herself, adjusting the folds of her dress. "In an hour."

Fuck. He'd hoped his years of private dinners with the old guy, full of veiled comments and probing inquiries into his activities, were over. "Do I have to?"

Mother tilted her nose up slightly, but made no correction to Tierney's "inelegant" question this time. "I'm certain I don't need to answer that."

Tierney swallowed his sigh. No way he was getting out of it; he should've known that already. *Sucks.* "Thanks, Mother. I better get dressed, hu—right?"

"Yes." But she sat there a second, regarding him. "Don't worry, darling. You haven't done anything to make your grandfather disappointed in you . . ."

He could hear the *have you?* she didn't tack on to the end of that statement hanging in the silence between them. "Nothing he knows about," Tierney muttered, too low for her to catch.

"Don't mumble," she admonished him, then went on in a gentler tone. "Is something wrong, darling? You look a bit *rough*."

Heart thumping, he nearly said it. That little candle of hope started flickering again, encouraging him. Could he actually tell her? What would she do? What was it he even needed to say? Or ask. *Are Terrebonnes allowed to like dick?* He opened his mouth, ready to try.

"Drinking is no way to get through college," she said before he could let free whatever words wanted out of him. "Remember, even at a state school, you'll make friendships that can turn into valuable contacts in the future. You don't want them thinking you're only interested in partying. If there's some *reason* you've been imbibing so much, some sort of problem . . .?" She lifted her brows.

Tierney snapped his jaw shut, shaking his head. *Thank fuck*. How could he have thought she'd understand?

"Well, darling." She sighed, pushing up out of her seat and clasping her hands. "Please try to remember how important this period of your life is. Drinking is fine, but not in such excess. Not *all* the time." She smiled briefly, but then her lips turned down again. "If there *is* a problem, maybe you could have yourself examined by a professional?"

A professional what? Homo-exterminator? Could someone just gas or cut it out of him? He nearly laughed, but then Mother would want to know why, and Tierney was still too close to the edge. If he got into an argument with her it would all come spilling out. That'd be just like him.

"Fine, Mother," he said. "If I have a problem, I'll get it taken care of." *By the guy in the left-hand stall.*

That was good enough for her. Her expression read pure relief as she excused herself and left. God fucking forbid he have a problem *she* had to deal with.

He scooted his butt to the edge of the bed and got up, heading for his bathroom. To the bourbon he kept stashed in his medicine cabinet. Alcohol was necessary when he needed some extra backbone.

The problem with taking a couple belts of booze, just enough to feel it but not enough to really catch a buzz, was that it made him all *contemplative*. While shaving, tilting his jaw sideways and stretching his skin taut, watching the long stroke of the disposable razor gliding along his neck, he got all caught up in thinking. About how Mother had almost offered some support, but then bailed.

Made sense. Wasn't as if she could help him, anyway—she was as much under the Old Guy's thumb as everyone else in this fucking family. The dude ruled through fear and uncertainty, kept them walking on eggs, never sure quite what the bastard's expectations were or how they were failing to meet them. Like, with Tierney, he never came out and *said* anything, just made sidelong references to unnatural urges and hinted that deviating from "The Terrebonne Way" would negatively affect Tierney's inheritance. Grandfather had never once said "homosexual," but it didn't matter what words he used, the meaning was clear: Terrebonnes weren't gay. Period.

"Ouch!" He'd nicked his Adam's apple, bad. Blood was seeping out, dribbling down from the cut. Staring at the growing red line, Tierney had one of those moments of clarity he usually tried to avoid. *Slit my own throat. How fucking Freudian.*

That's what he was doing by listening to Grandfather, wasn't it? Abiding by the dude's rules, like the spineless fucker he was. Because the old guy knew his one weakness: Tierney couldn't stomach being cast out. Every time he thought about defying Grandfather, he *felt* the truth of it—the yawning emptiness that would rip him apart, an intense ache of nothingness in his gut. That's what he'd *be*. Nothing. An abomination.

Snatching up the towel and pressing it against his wound, Tierney yanked the door of the medicine cabinet open, getting rid of that fucking reflection of himself. Of his self-inflicted wound. He grabbed the bottle of bourbon, because alcohol was good for cuts, right? A few more gulps and sense began to return as the burn slid down his throat and into his gullet.

Mother had shut him down because she didn't want to face it, just like Ian had. It was another message to his hidden self. *No one* wanted him to be gay. Not his family and not the guy he was in love with. He had no one to be gay *for*.

It's not me. *It's him. Them.* They were *making* him be straight.

Thank God, because for a minute there, he thought he might have some of his own expectations to live up to.

Chapter 1

Present Day

Sunday was a day to play a game commonly called "rugby" but which Tierney thought of as "bloodletting and beer with a ball." *Sometimes* he remembered the ball. Tierney'd always looked forward to Sundays, but when Ian had moved to the city and started playing on Tierney's team, Sunday became the best day of Tierney's week.

For a couple of months. Until Tierney figured out that, while he'd always thought of Ian as his closest friend and backup plan, Ian pretty much saw Tierney as not much more than an old college buddy.

Then, last week, when Tierney'd gone to pick him up for their scrimmage, Ian had been freshly showered and seemed too fucking *loose*. Relaxed.

Sated. As if he'd been banging some chick all night long.

A chick he had, like, *feelings* for.

Knocking on Ian's door this particular Sunday afternoon, Tierney couldn't shake his foul mood. So foul he was ready to quit playing rugby if his friend was going to be a dick. Last week, Ian had taken forever to answer. If that douche took too long to answer this week, Tierney'd—

Ian opened the door. "Hey man."

Tierney's anger switched gears. "Nice of you to show right away this time." Stepping forward into the entry, he started forming his plan of verbal attack. "You ready or—"

A nearly naked guy stood in Ian's bedroom doorway, blinking like he'd just woken up.

Christ. Tierney's mouth was an uncharacteristic beat or two behind. "Dude?"

"Just a sec," Ian said from the end of an echoey tunnel. "Almost ready."

Sam. That was his name, the guy in Ian's place. That skinny, flaming waiter Ian had met a few weeks ago. Tierney couldn't breathe, blackness creeping into his vision from the sides, narrowing his focus down to a pinprick. Until all he could see was his closest friend in the world, the guy whose image he'd jacked off to a million times and who he'd fucking been *holding out* for, walking up to that emaciated pale twink on the other side of his living room and—

Jesus fucking Christ. Tierney's palm hit the wall, holding him steady.

—Ian kissed Sam.

Halfway to their rugby game, during the tense, silent ride, a thought surfaced out of the white noise in Tierney's head: that kiss was for show—Ian's way of coming out to him. He'd figured out a while ago that Ian was, at least sometimes, into guys, and since he'd figured that out about Ian, the guy must know about *him*, right? And if Ian *did* know about Tierney, but hadn't ever done anything about it . . . *Motherfucker.*

Fourteen years.

For fourteen years Tierney'd waited for a sign from Ian that the dude was interested in him, and it never came. Never an indication that he was ready for them to be together. Nothing. And now Sam happened along and stole Ian away before Tierney even knew he was a threat. Couldn't the dude see that Sam was too femme and too gushy and too dorky and just not *right* for him? It was pretty fucking obvious to Tierney.

Except Ian had *chosen* Sam. *Because he doesn't want me.*

When they neared the field, Tierney jumped out of Ian's truck as soon as the dude had slowed enough to make it safe. Ish.

He'd make a much more appropriate partner for Ian. Couldn't the dude fucking see that? "Obviously not," Tierney muttered to himself just as he reached the group of players. One of his teammates gave him some side eye, but Tierney bared his teeth, and the guy averted his attention. Or at least his eyes. But the dude had to be perking his ears up, because Tierney was making a spectacle of himself, pacing and gesticulating.

Fourteen years.

This morning, Ian had killed the future Tierney'd waited for all this time. Hadn't even thought about how it would affect *him*, had he?

"Goddamned coward." He jerked around to find the pansy himself heading toward him. Tierney glared, trying to wither his friend where he stood, but Ian kept coming, until he stood almost toe to toe with Tierney. Close enough for spittle to fly in his face as Tierney let loose. "You motherfucking traitor!"

The gasp clued him in that the other rugby players were slowly circling them, rubbernecking.

Ian had the balls to fucking *laugh*. "Traitor to *what*?"

"To *men*." Tierney's fingers bit into his palms as he tried to hang on to his temper. "*Straight* men." Guys who didn't admit their secret longings.

Ian's face went expressionless in that way he had. Cutting him out. "Why's that, Tierney?" he asked. "'Cause I never told you? Maybe I thought you'd act just like this."

"So it's true? You're fucking that fairy?" he half yelled, but he didn't need an answer. "Just tell me one thing." He could hear that little note of achiness in his voice. Hope that this could somehow be salvaged. "Why *him*?"

"Why not? Me being with him should mean fuck-all to you."

He body-slammed Ian and knocked him on his ass, and something broke inside him. An internal organ he hadn't even known he had, full of pus and bile he'd been storing up for the last twenty years. It hazed his vision with sickly green and plugged his ears so all he could hear were the things he was screaming to his best fucking friend, as Ian lay on the ground, gasping for breath. "Get up you fucking faggot! Bet you can't fight a real man since that little nellie boy got you up his ass, can you? How is he, huh, Ian? Does he squeal like a pig when you—"

Ian hooked Tierney's legs at the knee, taking him down and shutting Tierney up with his fist. Then it was all about fighting dirty. "Fourteen years. *Fourteen* years." He couldn't stop saying it, in between getting whaled on by Ian and doing his share of damage in return. He got in one good punch to Ian's eye and was rewarded with a fierce surge of joy, burning away some of the sickness filling him. He redoubled his efforts, took his fourteen years of pain and fed it to Ian via bodily harm, cleaning himself out a little more every time his fist connected with flesh.

He'd never felt rage like this, or wanted to hurt another person so much.

Then he was being pulled away, up to standing, fighting the arms pinning his behind his back, unable to focus on anything but Ian's face and his own desire to cave it in. Make Ian fully pay for those lost years.

Make him pay for caring about someone else enough to come out.

By the time the guys had let go of him—after Ian'd left—Tierney had gone numb, except for the parts of him that hurt from Ian's fists. But that was physical pain, which was fine. He could deal. The emotional pain would kill him once he started feeling it again.

He had to get home before that happened. To the oblivion bourbon offered. One of the guys on the team gave him a ride back to his car, right in front of Ian's place.

Whatever.

Before taking off, he had to rest his head on the steering wheel for a minute, squeezing his eyes shut and fighting off the first wave of his returning emotions. The little creatures he'd learned to keep trapped inside. The inmates he kept under lock and key so he could fulfill the role he'd been assigned. The role he'd thought he'd escape only if the stars aligned and Ian gave him the out.

Fourteen years of sacrifice and avoidance in his past and never letting himself look for another man because he had his fallback. Fourteen years of glory holes and women he didn't really give a fuck about. Fourteen years of hiding, and being a lying, homophobic dick.

Fourteen fucking years.

Yeah, he was *done* with rugby.

It was a little over an hour until Dalton would meet the guy his boss, Ian (and Ian's boyfriend Sam) had set him up with. He'd been unable to think of anything else since lunch, and now that it was the end of the day, he'd finally given himself busywork and let his mind dwell on his first real date in five years. While working his way through college, he'd only had time for casual encounters of the sexual kind and the occasional friend with benefits, so he was a little out of practice in the dating department. Thank God Ian and Sam were going to the Exposed Innerds concert too, so it wouldn't just be him and the unknown guy named Miller.

Except, judging by the phone call he'd overheard earlier—Ian really didn't understand the concept of a "private voice"—Sam and Ian might not be going. Not unless Ian apologized for whatever he'd done.

What *had* he done?

"I need to see Ian Cully. Now."

At the sound of the voice behind him, Dalton dropped the forms he'd been tallying. *Oh no.* He was the face of the office, the first thing people saw when they walked in, and it was important to give the proper impression. Sucking in a quick, calming breath, he spun his chair around, fixing his most professional smile on his face.

"May I help you?" Even as he said it, the guy's body language was answering, telling him he *couldn't* help. This man considered himself a Very Important Person, and Dalton a Lowly Receptionist (somewhat like Lowly Worm, but gainfully employed). Forget that he *wasn't* one—his official title was Office Specialist Two—he *looked* like a receptionist. Visitors like this saw Dalton sitting behind a faux-wood-decaled desk in the entryway of an institutional suite in a state government building and made the assumption. The man's dismissive gaze flickered over Dalton, then focused on Ian's door.

Ian's not-quite-closed door.

Dalton immediately shifted gears, knowing from previous experience as an *actual* receptionist what was about to go down. Just as the visitor stepped forward, he stood, moving to block the man's path.

Which allowed Dalton to really see him for the first time.

Troglodyte chic.

It just figured he'd find this guy attractive, didn't it? Designer suit, artfully disarranged hair, muddy green eyes, and beard scruff. Not to mention beautiful bone structure, albeit under a slightly puffy face.

Ignore.

"I'm sorry, sir, but Mr. Cully is on a very important call at the moment, and can't be disturbed. As a matter of fact, he's booked for the rest of the day. May I schedule an appointment for you next week?"

The visitor stopped and narrowed his eyes, then took a step forward, invading Dalton's personal space.

Oh, please. He'd become immune to that intimidation tactic long ago. He smiled pleasantly and held his ground.

So did his opponent, for another half minute. Long enough for Dalton to get a whiff of stale sweat and alcohol. Then the man stood down, losing his suspicious squint and revealing how bloodshot his eyes were. He backed off and ran a hand through his hair, turning his head to reveal a mashed, sticking-up section.

Ah. Not artfully disarranged. Dalton's inattention cost him.

"How come none of the phone lines are lit up?" the visitor asked.

"I'm sure he just ended the call. Why don't you sit down and I can buzz him and see if he might have time for you, Mr. . . .?"

"Tierney." The man tried to sidestep Dalton. "I don't think he's busy; it's four thirty on a Friday, and his door isn't shut." He maneuvered the other way, forcing Dalton a little closer to Ian's office.

Time for a pity gambit. "Mr. Tierney, I'm new and it would make me look incompetent if I let you just barge in on him when—"

"Tierney's my first name, and I know you're new. You weren't here two weeks ago when I came in." He stopped trying to make Dalton give more ground and checked him out instead. A furtive, quick up and down Dalton knew very, very well.

"Mr. Tierney—"

"Terrebonne."

Dalton unleashed his shyest smile, cocking his hip just slightly and biting his lip in fake—yet suggestive—insecurity. "Mr. Terrebonne, I'd be grateful if you'd just let me buzz you in first."

Tierney Terrebonne stopped for a couple of seconds, blinking, focused on Dalton's mouth.

Gotcha. His deduction about their visitor's orientation was correct.

But Mr. Terrebonne shook off the effects of Dalton's display within a second. "Why don't you just tell him I'm here? You're practically in his doorway."

Dammit.

He gave in. "*Please,* just wait right here and let me at least announce you." He placed his palm on the man's shoulder.

Mr. Terrebonne froze at his touch. Dalton took advantage, whirling around and taking the last step to Ian's doorway just as his boss's voice floated out. "Hey, Dalton, you're fine driving yourself, right? I need to pick up Sam for dinner and—"

"Ian? There's someone here to see you." He couldn't stop himself from shifting his weight. "He seems *anxious.*"

His boss stared at him a second. "I can't see anyone *now*. Tell him he has to make an appointment."

Dalton lowered his voice. He could hear Ian's visitor pacing behind him—a couple quick steps to either side. Any second and he'd shove past. "I said that, but he keeps *insisting.*"

Mr. Terrebonne was now peering over Dalton's shoulder. "Dude, I really need to talk to you. I'm, um, I'm sorry. For last weekend."

Dalton stayed put, providing his boss with the small amount of shield he still could, but his ears perked up in spite of himself. Ian had come in with a black eye on Monday. Judging by his boss's expression right now, Mr. Terrebonne had something to do with that. Ian glanced at his watch, all his jaw muscles flexing. "You have a half hour, dude. That's it."

A half hour? That would be cutting it really close for dinner with his boyfriend. Especially to meet with some guy who'd punched him. Had Ian given Tierney any injuries? Dalton had to steel himself against the urge to turn and search the man's face for fading bruises. Hopefully not on that perfectly angled jaw.

Oh shut up.

While he'd been lost in his imagination, Mr. Terrebonne had made some kind of reply. Ian shook his head, obviously to himself. "Gimme a minute." He glanced back up, and whatever he saw made his face go hard. "Just go sit out there and wait for me," he barked.

After a second, Dalton felt their visitor move off, and Ian lost his tense, jaw-ticking expression.

"Can you go a little early and wait for them? Then if I'm a couple minutes late . . . Please?"

Dalton tried to stay out of his employer's personal business. Really, he did. But that look and request confirmed the suspicion he'd developed today: Ian and Sam *were* having some kind of problem or fight, and Ian desperately wanted to make up.

Dalton smiled, hoping to reassure. "Of course. I'll leave in five minutes." He could wrap things up enough for the weekend in that amount of time. "Don't worry," he added when Ian's face didn't relax.

Finally, Ian's shoulders eased down below his ears, so Dalton turned to go.

For midautumn, the weather was unexpectedly clear, with streaks of pink across in the sky as the sun set when Dalton arrived at the Monte Carlo club. A streetlight began to eke out a glow across the road from him, near the mouth of an alley. At the other end, he could see Simpson Avenue and the drugstore where he'd once bought condoms in an emergency.

Okay, twice. Or more. They had an impressive selection.

Being here, surrounded by all things LGBT, was comforting. Taking a deep breath, he inhaled the essence of the neighborhood, then took a second to glance around, wondering if he could afford an apartment here, now that he had a job but no tuition anymore. Probably not, since having a roommate wasn't an option, at least not if he could help it. He was currently still living with four guys who he'd been in college with, and he was sick of it. He'd *never* really lived alone, not when he was paying his own way. At twenty-seven, it was time for him to take full responsibility for himself. If that priced him out of this neighborhood, he was okay with that.

The streetlight had finally gotten strong enough to illuminate this end of the passage, and two guys walking toward him down the alley caught his eye. He didn't know what either of the guys he waited for looked like, but he had a feeling he'd recognize Sam from his sister's description. According to her, Sam didn't measure up to Ian physically. Andrea had called him a "flaming geek" and then went on and on about how cute he and Ian were together.

One of the guys was very tall and thin, with light hair. The other was more of a traditional bear shape—barrel-chested and stocky. They *could* be the guys he was here to meet . . . or maybe they were on a date? As they got closer to the well-lit part of the alley, he caught himself holding his breath, waiting to see their faces. *Just a couple more feet.*

The stocky guy said something that made the tall one laugh so hard he had to lean against the brick wall for support. It was cute, but Dalton needed them to get it over with and keep moving toward him. He leaned a couple of inches closer, onto the balls of his feet, as if that would help.

It didn't. The guys had twisted around, and were looking back at the other end of the alley. Dalton shifted to see what they were seeing.

Five men were advancing on them, one of the group carrying a bat. They weren't here to play baseball, that was obvious from the way they walked.

No.

Yes?

Could he be reading this right? Could something *violent* be happening? He was paralyzed, half bent to the side. *Five guys, baseball bat—*

"Sam, these guys could kill you!" the stocky guy yelled at the thin guy.

Sam. Dalton's insides went to ice. He *knew* it was Ian's Sam. As the group of men attacked, knocking Sam down, Dalton ran unthinkingly into the street. Fortunately, a car's honking brought him out of his panic.

Forcing himself back to the sidewalk, in spite of the instincts making him want to go hit and fight—not to mention the liquid feeling in his gut—he tried to figure out what to do. He was supposed to be able to deal with this; his brothers had *insisted* he take self-defense classes.

Those classes and reality were very different.

Stop overthinking. He ran to the door of the Monte Carlo, blurting "Call the police," as soon as he spied the host. "Someone's getting beat up in the alley. I think it's a bashing!"

Dalton dashed across the street, checking for cars, then paused to text Ian—*911 I think Sam's getting bashed behind the club*—before continuing to creep toward the scene, hiding in what shadows he could find.

Oh God, Sam's friend was down and they were circling around, kicking him over and over. Dalton's body revolted, forcing him to stop a few seconds behind a dumpster for some dry heaves. *So not safe.* But he couldn't just watch. He texted Ian again while assessing the situation as well as he could manage. What was the best approach? If he jumped one guy, the others would just attack him, right? He wasn't good at this fighting thing, in spite of all his brothers' practical instruction when they were kids, but maybe—

The guy with the bat lifted it over his head, about to slam it into the head of the man on the ground.

Dalton was most of the way down the alley before Sam struggled up and jumped on the batter's back. Dalton stumbled in surprise, halting only a few feet away as the guy shook Sam off, then started taunting him. Pretending to swing, while the rest of the bashers watched and laughed.

Oh God. Dalton took a deep breath, sliding his shoulder along the brick wall, and inched closer, looking for an opportunity. *Almost there.*

Sirens.

"Sam!" From the other end of the alley, two more people were running toward them. Distracting Dalton, so that too late he turned back to see the basher swing at Sam with real intent this time, bat slicing through the air.

Sam was already falling, even before being hit. Avoiding it? Dalton tried to stop the bat's arc, jumping the attacker, using his body weight and momentum to take the guy down. A jolt shuddered through his skeleton as the wood connected with Sam's head. Then they were all three on the ground.

He couldn't check on Sam, because the guy he'd knocked over squirmed under him, trying to punch him, and Dalton remembered enough of self-defense to avoid *that.* Or so he thought until the guy's fist connected with his jaw. His neck made a snapping noise, stopping his head from flying back any farther. *My brothers really* weren't *hitting me that hard.*

Shake it off. Except he couldn't because he'd never been hit like that in his life, and it *hurt.* Disoriented, he rolled onto his side to curl into a ball and found an ankle right in front of his nose. His hand shot out and grabbed it, yanking back until everything connected to the ankle—the batter's whole body—came down again with a thud he felt reverberate in his gut.

Yay me. Fuck you.

Then police were swarming everywhere, and they grabbed the batter when he jumped up once more. Dalton stayed where he was. It seemed safer. His muscles wanted to dissolve right there, but his eyes flickered around frantically, watching everything: the police cuffing someone, and two of the attackers being dragged back toward them by a big blond guy. Meanwhile, some black-haired guy was kneeling next to Sam, looking panicked.

Ian. Dalton needed to tell him. He still had his phone in one hand. It took some concentration to make his fingers hit the right letters. *They hit him in the head with a baseball bat.* If that didn't get a response, Ian wasn't the boyfriend Dalton thought he was.

An officer was suddenly talking to him, ordering him to stand up slowly, keep his hands in plain sight.

"I'll cooperate. It wasn't me. I'm not one of them." Dalton gave up the security of the pavement, getting to his feet without using his hands, which wasn't easy.

It took a few minutes to straighten things out, but soon Dalton ended up waiting next to a patrol car for a detective to come and question him. He felt almost normal, in a hyper-real kind of way. Totally still as everything bustled around him. An observer of the scene but apart from it.

When Ian arrived, Dalton's heart nearly melted. Face pale, fingers trembling, he clung to Sam's hand until the very last second, just before the ambulance doors closed on his arm.

"Sam, please, just be all right, okay?" Ian begged.

It was so sweet, Dalton forgot about what was really going on for a second while watching them.

"Hi there, Dalton? I'm Detective Johnson, and I'd like to ask you a few questions."

Oh yeah. I'm a witness to a crime. Dalton turned to see a guy in a rumpled pair of cargo pants and one of those department-issue nylon jackets. "I'm Dalton Lehnart." Oh, maybe he needed to show some identification?

"I hear you did pretty well against one of those guys."

"I did?" Dalton's brain scrambled to catch up. "My brothers insisted I learn self-defense."

The man nodded. "I know one of 'em, your brother Peter?"

Of course. Peter was a detective too. "He's the oldest." As if it mattered.

"Good guy," Johnson said, sounding satisfied. Did that mean he didn't need to see Dalton's driver's license? "Okay, why don't you tell me what happened. Start from the beginning."

Chapter 2

What a bizarre fucking night.

First he'd dragged Ian to some bar to apologize, then nearly confessed his feelings for the guy. But Ian had saved him—when Tierney had choked out that he was jealous of Sam, Ian jumped to the wrong conclusion. Except it was right.

"Shit," Ian had said. "It's true? You're gay?"

Fessing up to that was easier than telling him what he'd really been saying.

Right after that, Ian had gotten a text, gone white as a sheet, and run out of the bar.

Tierney was still staring after the dude trying to figure out what was going on when his cell rang. It was his brother, Chase, and he almost didn't answer.

He kind of wished he hadn't. Because now he was sitting in a small private waiting room at the hospital, waiting for someone to come tell them that Grandfather had kicked it. For sure the old guy *was* going to croak—they didn't put people in private waiting rooms unless the reaper was already knocking on someone's door.

This had to be either karma or irony, but he couldn't decide which. Now that he'd finally confessed to Ian about liking dick, Milton Terrebonne had had a massive and unexpected heart attack.

When the doctor eventually did come in and told them Grandfather had been pronounced dead at 7:03 p.m., Tierney felt nothing. Or everything. His emotions were chaotic, and it was all too confusing to make sense of, so he gave up and went numb.

While they waited for someone to show them to the emergency department so they could "spend some time with the deceased," he sat next to his mother. She kept dabbing at tears—real ones, he could tell from long experience—and clutching his hand, her grip alternately loosening and tightening.

Father stood near the door, pale and tense, and Chase sat with his head hanging down and his fingers interlaced tightly between his knees. His wife Emily sat next to him.

How do I look to them?

"I don't know what to do," Mother said in his ear.

"Um, I think what we're doing is fine." They may own and operate an ambulance company, but none of them had ever worked as paramedics. Still, Tierney'd been on enough ride-alongs, and in enough hospitals, to know the drill. "Um, there might be quite a bit of cleaning up to do in order to make Grandfather look, you know, presentable."

"Yes," she whispered, pressing the side of her fist over her lips for a moment before continuing in a shaky voice. "What I meant is that your grandfather didn't *anticipate* this."

Who the hell anticipated having a massive heart attack after being declared healthy as a horse a month before?

"He didn't leave any *instructions*." Her voice rose, and her fingernails were starting to dig into Tierney's hand. "I'm just not sure what the appropriate memorial—"

"Hyacinth." Father sat across from her. "A social worker . . ." He adjusted his still-knotted tie. "Someone will be along soon to help us make the arrangements. In the absence of guidance from my—" he swallowed "—f-father, we'll have to rely on their expertise."

"But . . . will it be what Milton would want us to do?"

Father took a deep, quavering breath. "We'll simply have to do our best. We have no other choice."

"Oh no." Mother's voice broke, and she began ugly crying. Tierney patted her hand while his father and brother inspected the room for features of interest.

Finally, thank *God*, Emily moved to sit on the other side of Mother, putting her arm around the woman and murmuring to her. When his mother let go of Tierney to clutch at her daughter-in-law, he fled to a chair near his father.

"I'm sure we'll be able to muddle along without him," Father said, but he didn't *sound* sure.

Tierney considered moving again, to sit next to Chase, but he and his brother couldn't get along on a good day.

"A wake?" Mother asked, lifting her head and peering at Emily. "You think he would approve?"

"Of course," Emily assured her. "I recently read in *Forbes* that the family of the Whitewash Consulting Group CEO held a wake in *his* honor."

Forbes covered wakes? Not likely. The quick grimace Emily shot at Chase and then him told Tierney it was a lie, anyway. She *got* them, didn't she? Emily understood that what his parents needed most in this moment was for someone to tell them what to do and how to behave as a proper Terrebonne.

I need a drink.

"Mr. Terrebonne?" A man appeared in the now-open doorway. Chase and Father stood. "If you're ready . . ."

It wasn't until Emily got out of her seat and helped Mother up that anyone moved. Then, like good little Terrebonnes, they all trooped off to go say their farewells to their overlord.

Standing in the emergency cubicle, surrounded by his silent family, Tierney looked down at the old guy's disheveled body and it hit him.

He could never disappoint Grandfather again.

He *could* disappoint his parents, but if Grandfather Milton was the old God who turned people into pillars of salt for disobeying him, Father was the less frightening, less vengeful and largely absentee dude in the New Testament. Tierney didn't know who that made Jesus, or what role his mother played in his analogy—she wasn't the Virgin Mary, that was for sure—but it mattered less and less as he searched his grandparent's slack, gray features for signs of condemnation.

He found none. The old bastard really *was* dead, unable to pass judgment anymore. For a brief second, everything changed inside Tierney, like he was viewing the scene through a kaleidoscope and it had switched patterns on him. Shifting and colliding with other things. Changing.

I could . . .

What? He couldn't come *out*. Grandfather was dead, and Ian was in love with someone else. Tierney still didn't have anyone to come out *for*. Or against.

No point in doing it at all. And with that, everything inside him settled back into its rightful, repressed place.

Monday evening after work, Dalton stood on Sam and Ian's porch, casserole in hand, waiting for someone to respond to his knock. He'd been raised right—in case of tragedy, deliver a filling, throw-in-the-oven meal a few days later. He'd had to buy a Cheesy Chicken Noodle Bake at a trendy, nouveau home-style delicatessen on the way over, because he had no idea how to make something like that himself. His cooking skills were subsistence level at best, even after being kicked out of his parents' house at eighteen.

It was taking a long time for someone to answer the door. Maybe they weren't home? Ian had called in sick today, but everyone knew it was because of his injured boyfriend. Maybe they'd had to go to urgent care; Sam's concussion might have gotten worse. But no, when Dalton checked behind him, Ian's truck was at the curb.

Just as he turned back around, the door opened.

"Yes?" Ian stood there in jeans and a black T-shirt, barefoot, as hot as usual. "Dalton?"

"Uh-huh." He nodded.

Ian yanked him inside, took the foil baking dish out of his hands, and gave him a one-armed, choking hug. "Thank you so much for helping Sam. Detective Johnson told me what you did and fuck I'm so glad you were there."

Okay. *Shock.* His boss didn't generally seem the type to hug anyone, or babble gratitude, but these were unusual circumstances. Dalton patted his shoulder. "You're welcome."

Ian let go of him so suddenly it knocked Dalton off-balance. "Sorry, didn't mean to freak you out."

"It's okay." He patted some more before stepping back.

They stared at each other for another few moments.

"I should put this in the kitchen. You want to see Sam? I mean, is that why you came over?"

Dalton jumped on the offer. "It is. I thought since, you know, we survived the, um, *incident* together, I should introduce myself."

Ian led him a couple of steps into the living room, announcing, "There's someone here to see you, kiddo."

Sam's upper body appeared over the back of the couch, his eyes wide, a book in his hand. He tilted his head. "Oh." A line grew between his brows. "Hi?"

"This is Dalton," Ian said.

"Oh. *Ooooh*. Oh, hi!"

Dalton pasted on a smile, suddenly jittery. "Hi. Sam."

"Hi."

"You aren't really showing your vocabulary to its advantage," Ian said.

Sam turned pink, ducking his head and grinning. "I guess not, huh?"

"It's nice to meet you," Dalton blurted. *Awkward*. So of course then he started with the inappropriate laughter, trying to stifle it behind his hand, which resulted in snorting.

Thank God Sam busted up too, giggling and honking, squeezing his eyes shut and rocking with it.

"Dalton brought us food," Ian said when they'd quieted down enough to be heard over. "I'll let you guys get to know each other while I put this away." Maybe he said more, or rolled his eyes, or started laughing at them, but Dalton was still caught in the grip of his emotions and the release of tension he'd been carrying around for days. He leaned against the couch, trying to catch his breath. God, he'd needed that, hadn't he?

"It's nice to officially meet you too," Sam said, calmer but still smiling. "Want to sit down?"

"I really want to." Dalton flopped onto the chair next to the sofa, letting his body sink into it. "This is a nice chair. I need one like it when I get my own place." It had beautiful lines, although Dalton would prefer a solid color.

Sam shrugged. "I don't know where Ian bought it, you'll have to ask him. Maybe in California."

Dalton wasn't sure where to go from there, because it was the first time it occurred to him that Sam didn't live here. But obviously he stayed a lot, or at least he did when he had a head injury.

Sam cleared his throat. "I need to—I *want* to thank you. For what you did the other night." He waved a hand in the air. "You know, helping me."

Dalton lurched forward, sitting upright. "I'm *so* sorry I didn't stop him from hitting you."

"You tried," Sam said. "It means a lot. And you caught one of those guys—Jurgen couldn't have done it all himself."

"But you got a *concussion*. If I'd been able to st—"

"Oh my God, do *not* get your guilt all over me. Ian's shed his everywhere in the last three days. I mean, *thank* you, but it's not like you were the one who hit me."

Again, not sure where to go now.

Eyeing him, Sam said, "I forgive you. Does that work?"

"I guess. Um, how's your friend?"

Sam blinked. "My *friend*? He's in the kitchen."

"Uh, no. I meant the guy who was with you that night. My, well, date. Miller."

"Oh God, it's awful. He's in the hospital still—he had to have emergency surgery because he was bleeding internally. One of his ribs, like, *broke* and punctured a lung. He had other cracked ribs and lots of contusions, whatever those are, and stitches."

More guilt—he'd done nothing to help Miller. "I feel nauseous."

"He's the one those guys came after. I was just, like, collateral damage. They didn't even know my *name*."

"I'm sorry," Dalton said, uselessly.

Sam chewed on his lip for a few seconds in silence. "I don't want to be a dick, but can we talk about something else?"

"Please." *Thank God.* "What are you reading?" He turned his head, trying to see the title of the book Sam had set on the coffee table. Were there really two bare-chested, headless male torsos on the cover?

"A romance novel," Sam said.

Dalton looked at him.

Sam tilted his chin up. "I read them, and I've stopped attempting to justify it to people."

"You mean they try to tell you that reading them is wrong or something?"

"I know, right?" He threw his hands in the air. "It's always someone who's never read them, either, so they have no clue what they're talking about. It's prejudice informed by ignorance, and it needs to stop." He wrinkled his brow and cocked his head. "I've been thinking about starting, like, a pro-romance nonprofit that educates people about their literary value. Skillful wielding of genre tropes is an underrecognized art form."

Dalton nodded politely.

"You don't read them, do you?"

"No." And he'd never felt badly about it before. Or thought about it. "Maybe you could recommend—"

"Oh! I'll make you a list. Do you think you'd prefer gay romance or straight?"

Duh. "Gay, for sure."

Dalton learned more about romance novels in the next ten minutes than he had in his entire life up to that point before they moved on to other subjects. Ian never came back into the room, and after initially suspecting he wasn't going to in an attempt to let them "get to know each other," Dalton forgot about him. Sam was interesting. Chatty and gossipy and not at all reserved. He started telling Dalton stories about his friends, Nik and Jurgen, who'd shown up that night after Dalton had. Nik—"my best friend"—was the guy who'd been so freaked out about Sam, and Jurgen—"Nik's boyfriend. Oh, and he's also Ian's cousin"—was the one who'd caught some of the assailants. Then Sam wandered on to other people's business.

He'd just finished telling Dalton about Ian coming out to his father—in a hushed tone, since, as he admitted, he probably shouldn't be—when the doorbell rang.

Sam sighed. "We've been really popular since I got myself bashed." He started to stand, but Ian materialized from the kitchen, ruffling his hand through Sam's hair on his way past.

"I'll get it."

"He thinks I'm broken," Sam whispered loudly. "He won't let me do anything, just makes me lie on the couch all day and read. It's awesome."

"If my boyfriend had been beaten up, I'd do the same thing."

Sam wasn't listening, he was craning around to see who was at the door.

"Hey, man," Ian said from the entryway, just as Sam's eyes went impossibly wide. Dalton tried to surreptitiously look, but he wasn't willing to half fall out of the chair. He probably wouldn't even know whoever it was anyway.

"Can I come in?"

Oh, but he recognized that voice. *Mr. Terrebonne.* It sounded raspier than before, but it still had a quality Dalton could almost feel, like fingernails trailing up his spine. *Totally bizarre.* He turned to ask Sam—quietly—what *he* thought of Tierney's voice, but Sam's body language was weird. Stiff. Even his face muscles had set.

Then Tierney Terrebonne walked into the room, coming up short just inside the door. "Um, hey." He fumbled his hand out of his pocket, lifting it to acknowledge Sam, then dropping it.

"Hello."

He looked even worse than he had three days ago. His suit was crumpled, like he'd been sleeping in it, but Dalton knew it wasn't the same one—definitely a different designer. Maybe he'd put it on over the weekend and not taken it off since.

Ian glanced at Dalton from behind Tierney's shoulder, giving him a look he'd already learned from the office—the grin-and-bear-it expression, but without the grinning. He came up alongside Tierney. "You've met Dalton, right?"

Tierney tore his eyes away from Sam to tip his head at him, but he wasn't truly paying attention. He turned back to Ian right away. "Dude, can I talk to you? In private?"

"Yeah, let's go in the kitchen." Dalton caught the quick grimace Ian flashed Sam on his way out of the room, but Tierney didn't. The man was so wrapped up in his own head he probably couldn't see anything.

Sam frowned, but waited until the two other men left before he said, "Tierney's got *issues.*"

Well, yeah. "He's pretty much wearing them for everyone to see."

"Not all of them." Sam snorted.

Dalton raised his eyebrows because it would be rude to outright ask.

Sam's glance darted off to the side. "It probably isn't something I should talk about," he mumbled.

The guy had shared his boyfriend's painful coming-out-to-his-father story, what else could there be that he wouldn't feel comfortable shari—

Oh duh. "Tierney's gay."

Sam bit his lip, looking all around the room, possibly for an exit. Then he leaned forward and nodded quickly. "Totally in the closet. He hadn't even told Ian until the other night. The night I was . . ."

"The night of the incident."

Sam pointed at him, or what Dalton had said. "Yeah, that. But I already suspected, of course."

Of course. "So *that's* why he wanted to talk to Ian last Friday?"

"I don't know if that's the real reason." Sam scrunched up his brow. "I think he only meant to apologize. You know," Sam waved at his own face, "for the black eye, but the part about him being gay just came out. I think Ian kind of guessed. Because, you know, I'd already told him I thought it was possible."

"You're very perceptive," Dalton said, nodding.

Sam beamed, making it clear what had attracted Ian to him initially. "Thank you. Anyway, now that I know that . . ." Sam shrugged. "I feel sorry for Tierney."

Dalton's gut tightened up, rejecting that unpalatable morsel. Pity was a horrible thing to inflict on someone like Tierney. He was a walking textbook example of low self-esteem. "Don't tell him that."

"I know, right?" Sam tilted his head. "You're very perceptive yourself."

That *was* a nice thing to hear. "Thank you."

Sam smiled. "You want to hang out sometime?"

Dalton was brought up short. Not because he didn't want to—he did—but because he hadn't expected this. He hadn't thought about it at all beforehand, but it hit him now that he'd expected this to be a courtesy visit, and then he'd go back to being Ian's employee.

When he saw Sam's smile slowly turning into a frown, Dalton blurted, "I'd love to. Maybe we could go to the gym?"

"The *gym*? Do I look like a guy who works out?"

"Uhhh . . ." How should he answer that?

Sam shook his head vigorously. "Let's just do lunch sometime."

"I can do that." He was eager to, even. And that was his cue to leave. Dalton stood, digging in his hoodie pocket for his keys. "I should go. I don't want to tire you out."

"Yeah, 'cause my constitution is so delicate and all." Sam stood too, walking Dalton to the door while reciting his cell number and then typing Dalton's into his contacts. Just before leaving, Dalton turned to give him a hug. He didn't know if it was living through a trauma together, or if they would have clicked anyway, but he really liked Sam. Sam hugged him back, so maybe the feeling was mutual.

The raised voices sort of ruined the moment, though.

Make that raised *voice*—Tierney's only. And judging by the stomping, he was headed toward them. Dalton let go of Sam, both of them turning as Tierney stormed into the entryway, then rounded on Ian and pointed at him. "I *trusted* you, dude."

"You can trust me as much as I can trust you," Ian said calmly, reaching past Tierney to open the door. A muscle flickered in his jaw, regardless of how mellow his voice was.

Neck cording with tension and fists clenching, Tierney growled.

Ian stepped back. Not a retreat, but a move toward Sam, wrapping an arm around him and pulling him close.

Tierney gasped, so quietly Dalton wasn't sure he heard it, until he saw the man's face in the second before he left. Deep lines were etched across his forehead. Pained ones. He turned, shouted "Fuck!" then slammed out.

"He really knows how to make an exit," Sam said conversationally.

Ian snorted a laugh. Then he leaned close to kiss Sam on the temple. "You should rest, kiddo. Don't let that asshole bug you."

"I'm not the one he was yelling at." Sam laid a hand on Ian's chest. "And I've rested enough."

God, they were having a moment in the aftermath of Tierney's very different kind of moment, and all Dalton could do was stand here watching them. "I should go."

Ian nodded, not even bothering to look at him. "Probably."

Sam whacked his boyfriend on the shoulder, then said to Dalton, "This is such a surreal way to begin a friendship, isn't it?"

Uh, yeah. "Totally."

If you sit here any longer, I will kick your ass, Tierney threatened himself. But it didn't do any good. Five minutes later, he was still on the curb in front of Ian's house, staring between his knees at the asphalt. The only difference now was that his butt was cold and it was a little closer to sunset. Fucking October.

He really should get the hell away from this place. The emotions he kept locked down inside him were staging a riot, and he needed to get out of the public eye before one of the inmates got control and caused problems.

Well, more problems. Life would be easier if he didn't have to live through it in his own skin.

He hadn't even managed to tell Ian about his grandfather's death. But seriously, he'd had to convince Ian to not out him first. After what went down with Sam and the bashing the other night, he'd thought the dude would be more understanding. Ian's assurance that Sam was the only one who knew didn't fill Tierney with confidence. He knew how shit happened—Sam would share it with just one person, who'd just share with one person, and so on. Before long, everyone would know. Ian had apologized, but then he'd come up with some crap about Sam having already figured it out.

No one could just *guess* Tierney was gay. Ian *had* to have told him.

They'd argued about it until Tierney couldn't listen to Sam's name one more time and he lost it. He might have said some stuff that was a little over the top after that. When his anger took control, it tended to make him talk trash, usually trash he couldn't remember very well later.

"Jesus Christ," he groaned, running his hands across his face and gripping his hair.

"Are you all right?"

He didn't need to lift his head; he knew it was the guy from Ian's office. Dalton. "Uh, *nooo.*"

The dude's footsteps came closer. "Can I do anything to help?"

Suck me off? "I doubt it."

Dalton didn't go away. He stood there a few more seconds before saying, "If you need to talk, we could go get coffee or something."

Tierney jerked his head up. "Are you always this annoying?" Persistent fucker.

Dalton didn't react the way Tierney'd expected—hoped, possibly. Oh, the guy got pissed, nostrils flaring and looking down his nose at Tierney, but he didn't try to flay him with words like Tierney would have. He simply said, "Probably."

"The last thing I need is some amateur head shrink, dude. What, you got an A in Psych 101 so now you've got mad skills?" See? The flaying with words.

Dalton arched his brows and crossed his arms over his chest, but he still didn't leave. It gave Tierney a chance to really study him. The dude was no Ian, but he had definite appeal. A slim but not skinny body that Tierney bet was nicely toned under that hoodie. He could see the swell of biceps just stretching Dalton's sweatshirt. *I'd let him blow me.*

He was on his feet before he realized where his mind had gone. Maybe *something* would work out tonight. Dude probably already knew Tierney was gay—he'd bet Dalton was Sam's one person. May as well get the most out of this queer clusterfuck.

"I'm sorry for being a dick. Let me buy you a drink to make up for it?" As he said it, panic reared up. *We don't do this. Try to pick up guys.* It was strictly outside the boundaries he'd set when he'd started playing the role expected of him.

Shut up. Grandfather's dead, and we've just never done it before. Until now, he'd been strictly restroom.

Dalton narrowed his eyes, until Tierney almost couldn't see their blue color in the shadows. "I don't drink much."

"It's okay, I can drink enough for both of us." *Smooth. You the man.*

"Well, that makes your invitation *very* appealing." Dalton shoved his bangs off his forehead, but they fell back within a second, flopping over his brow. How could such a blond guy have such dark lashes? Even in the dusk, his hair was so bright it almost glowed. His cheeks had little spots of color—Tierney had really annoyed him, hadn't he?

Sweet. He could work with that because he *was* the man. Time to kick the remorse into a higher gear. "I overreacted."

Dalton huffed. "Are you talking about out here with me, or in there with Ian? And Sam?"

Tierney's stomach seized up but otherwise he ignored the reference to his friend and his friend's lover. "If you'd rather get coffee, I can do that instead."

Finally Dalton met his eyes again, tightening his lips but giving him a brow lift. "I'm offering you a chance to talk if you want—or not, if you don't—not an opportunity to fuck me."

Sam *had* told him. He had to unclench his fist in order to keep his voice relaxed. "Who said anything about hooking up?"

Dalton's lip curled. "You're far more obvious than you think."

"You're pretty fucking obvious yourself. You flame almost as brightly as Sam. What's it like to be a stereotype?"

Before he could blink, Dalton was right up in Tierney's face, and yes, he was a couple inches shorter, but Tierney still found himself intimidated. And invigorated, because anger was seductive, and Dalton was much more than Tierney had originally thought, and he had those eyes and his hair was sexy with the long-in-front-and-short-in-back thing. What would his bangs feel like brushing across Tierney's naked skin?

Get a grip. He stepped toward the guy, until they nearly touched, like he'd fallen into Dalton's gravitational field. *I'd love to orbit you, baby.*

Dalton didn't back down, jaw set, eyes flashing in the twilight, and voice too controlled. "*Mister* Terrebonne. I get that you're a closet case—"

"I *knew* Sam couldn't keep that to himself!"

Dalton ignored him, even though Tierney had nearly yelled down his throat. "I even get that you're scared, but I *will not be* a handy punching bag for your existential distress, and I won't apologize for being who I am. I've been there and done that, which is more than you can say."

Tierney swallowed, trying to unstick some kind of response, but his throat clogged up on him, strangling his words.

Dalton leaned forward, and now their chests *were* touching, his hoodie sliding and catching against Tierney's coat, and his lips so close Tierney could feel them move just below his ear. "And in the future?" he whispered. "Anytime you start thinking you're better than me because you pretend to be straight? You just remember you wanted to tap this."

Tierney couldn't breathe. Fuck, what if it was an allergic reaction to too much reality? Dalton stepped off, releasing Tierney from his field. Enough so he could sip some air.

But of course the dude wasn't done slicing and dicing him. "I'd recommend not taking it out on other people either, if you want to have any friends left." He started to go, then stopped, pointing his finger at Tierney. "And if you try to do anything to ruin Sam and Ian's relationship, I'll make sure you regret it."

Panic had filled his gut and petrified his diaphragm, and the rest of Tierney's emotions began their eddying dance. They were starting to really whirl by the time Dalton shoved past him, leaving.

Don't let him go. In his addled state, the guy suddenly looked more like a life preserver than the cause of Tierney's internal rough seas. He whirled around. "I could drink coffee," he croaked, then cringed. He may as well have sliced open his torso and invited Dalton to have a peek inside the asylum. Jesus fucking Christ, he was pathetic.

But the dude had stopped. "Are you saying you *do* want someone to talk to?" Dalton stood there, still within inches. Waiting for Tierney to answer.

What's my answer? He stared at Dalton's ear, right in front of his face, and the dude's hair where it had been clipped short over the curve of it.

It seemed like a trustworthy ear. "I do." Tierney cleared the frog out of his throat. "Want someone to talk to."

Fuck. Dizzy spell.

"Enough to not be a dick?"

He swallowed. "Um, could you define that for me?"

Dalton sighed, turning to him. "Can you try *not* to pick me up?"

"I can try that."

"Just platonic." Dalton pointed at him, index finger an inch from Tierney's nose. "And don't make me regret this." He dropped his hand, giving Tierney a warning look. "I'm taking my own car."

"Of course." Tierney nodded. "I'll follow you. Lead me where you want me to go."

Chapter 3

Tierney had been endearingly unkempt, with his head in his hands and a defeated slope to his spine as he'd sat on the curb outside Ian's place. That was Dalton's thin veneer of an excuse for why he'd offered to listen to the guy's woes.

Groan. Completely shameful that he still had a weakness for guys like Tierney. Wounded, self-hating assholes who needed reforming. Guys who had flash and cash, but no substance. What he needed was to meet an attractive, wounded, self-*healing* asshole, then he could trick himself into liking the guy but wouldn't have to deal with the drama of the guy not liking himself. In his experience, men who didn't like themselves made selfish boyfriends, and that was the most polite thing he could say about them.

Not that he considered Tierney potential boyfriend material. Dalton was simply being kind, and the *slight* twinge of emotional pain in his chest was simply the sympathy he'd have for any human being in the man's position.

Giving himself a firm nod and ignoring pangs of empathy, he gripped the steering wheel tighter and drove in a straight line until he had to turn at an intersection, randomly going right when—*ta-da!*—a coffee shop appeared. They were on the west side of the city, which Dalton wasn't very familiar with, but he'd be damned if he'd ask Tierney whether he knew of a place nearby.

"We roast our own beans," a sign proclaimed, and Dalton could smell the truth of it—the typical scents of sour and burnt—before he turned into the asphalt parking lot. Tierney's car was pulling in behind him when Dalton glanced in the mirror. His own gaze caught him for a second, a bright strip of Tierney's headlight reflected onto his face. "I cannot *believe* I'm doing this."

As he parked and got out, then watched Tierney do the same on the other side of the lot, the man's car registered for the first time. The color was a dirty cream, and in the low light of dusk and streetlamp, he mistook it for a Jaguar. It had that *sports car in sedan's clothing* look that high-end automobiles had adopted recently.

He felt less derisive when he remembered noticing the signature BMW headlights in his rearview. Beemers weren't as pretentious, if just as poorly designed in recent years.

Then he realized how much time he'd spent dwelling on Tierney's choice of ride and he lost all derision.

Sigh. This was going to be such a trial, battling his own susceptibilities and Tierney's douchebaggery. But standing there, watching the man approach, he began to revise that thought. Tierney's swagger was missing. He walked toward Dalton with his hands shoved in his pockets, head down, and shoulders hunched in. It was windy, blowing through Dalton's sweatshirt, but not so cold he shivered, so he doubted Tierney was chilly. *Nervous*, and possibly a little cowed. Exposing a hint of the soft underbelly that Dalton had been secretly (and traitorously) hoping the man had.

Someday, empathy would be the death of him, wouldn't it? "Is this place all right?" he asked, as if it mattered what Tierney thought. But it did, even if he tried to deny it.

Tierney stopped in a pool of yellowish light right in front of Dalton. The buzzing of the bulb made a very appropriate soundtrack for the man's fidgeting. He licked his lip in quick movements, shifted his weight, and avoided Dalton's gaze, or answering his question.

He stood there so long Dalton reached out to touch him, a quick brush of fingers across his arm. "Are you okay?"

Tierney swallowed. Then again. "Did you . . ." He took a huge breath and blew it out, straightening his shoulders and looking Dalton in the eye at last. "When you said that about not doing anything to ruin Ian and Sam's relationship, what did you mean?"

Oh no. He'd been angry and he shouldn't have said it, but it had all fallen together in his head in that instant: Tierney's expression when Ian put his arm around Sam, and the way he'd come into the office last Friday and to Ian's place today, wanting to talk. Dalton would lay money on Tierney being in love with his friend. No wonder he was such a douche bag. The guy was in horrible pain, wasn't he?

Dalton was silent too long, or his expression gave him away, because Tierney croaked like a frog: wordlessly, mouth hanging open, face paling. Dalton grabbed the man's shoulder as he swayed, then pulled him toward the car where he could prop himself upright until he regained enough equilibrium to do it on his own.

"It's okay," Dalton soothed.

"What?" Tierney panted. "What's okay?"

Um . . . "It's okay about Ian." *Cringe.* Not really, but he had nothing else to offer.

Tierney slumped against the car so hard it rocked. Dalton gripped his arm and stepped closer, trying to shore him up. Physically or emotionally, he didn't know. "I'm sure I'm the only one who's noticed. Ian hasn't, I'm positive." *Please let that be true.*

Tierney began wheezing. Too bad Dalton didn't still carry Xanax with him everywhere, but he hadn't needed it for years, not since the months after he'd been kicked out of his parents' house and reality had slapped him in the face.

"K-kinda—" *wheeze*, Tierney said.

Dalton leaned forward to hear better, close enough to see how clammy Tierney's skin was.

"Pathetic," Tierney spit out, barely louder than the buzzing of the lot light. "Kinda pathetic."

"It's not." Dalton shook his head. "It just . . . it just *is*. You can't help how you feel sometimes, no matter how wrong it is." He had the personal experience to back it up.

They stood there forever like that, Dalton inches from Tierney, breathing in a regular pattern as if he could get Tierney's lungs to settle down just by setting a good example. Either that or time worked and eventually Tierney calmed. He was less pasty and the sweat that had popped out on his forehead had disappeared.

Dalton sighed silently, backed off, and glanced around. Someone was watching them intently from the window of the coffee shop. An employee judging by the apron.

Dalton was just about to suggest they go in or leave when Tierney muttered, "What a fucking mess."

Oh, he totally concurred. "I'm sorry."

Tierney snorted halfheartedly. "It's not your fault; you didn't get them together, right?"

"I mean I'm sorry for saying anything. For even trying to talk to you outside of their house. I should have left you alone." Maybe other guys wouldn't feel guilty for breaking an ego this fragile, but Dalton couldn't help it.

Tierney shoved his hands in his pockets, looking up from under his brows. "No, it's okay. I feel better." He swallowed. "At least someone else knows, now. I'm not alone." He flinched, closing his eyes.

Dalton pretended not to notice that Tierney'd admitted to loneliness, glancing away, toward the window again. The employee was gone—maybe she'd decided they were harmless. "Do you want to go inside and get that coffee now?"

Tierney's eyes popped open. "I guess." He took a deep breath and straightened up. "Oh, good. A Klunhausen's."

Of course. Of course Tierney would be one of those guys who liked Klunhausen's. The chain was the "it" coffee purveyor in the city. If Dalton had noticed earlier, he would have driven on by and found someplace else. Except not, because they really did have fantastic coffee. How else would they get away with charging nearly twenty bucks a pound for their regular roast? Not that he ever bought it, but sometimes he let himself have a latte there.

This time he indulged in a mocha because Tierney insisted on paying for it. Dalton let him. The way the guy wouldn't meet his eyes and his fidgety body language convinced him there wouldn't be any more "I'm such a big dawg you should be into me" crap.

He hated to admit it, but humility did make the man a little, tiny bit more appealing. God, he was *such* a sucker for damaged men. Coming here was a horrible idea. "I can't believe I agreed to have coffee with Tierney Terrebonne," he muttered to himself while they waited by the barista's counter for their drinks.

Tierney took a step closer to him. "Did you just say my name?"

Cringe. He hadn't thought he'd said it loud enough to be heard over the espresso machine and other ambient noises. Dalton turned to him, forcing his eyes wide. "No. I *was* talking to myself, but I don't think I said anything that sounded like 'Mr. Terrebonne.'" Oh, seriously, that just sounded *wrong* now. He knew the man's darkest secret, after all.

Tierney squinted. "Are you ever going to call me by my first name?"

"Um . . ." *Too intimate.* "If you insist, I suppose I'd have to." *Oh,* that *was gracious.*

"I insist." Tierney tipped his chin, and his nostrils flared. But then he shifted his weight and his air of command disappeared. "Please don't call me that anymore."

Did he *have* to look at Dalton that way? "Okay. Tierney."

Zing.

Oh no.

Tierney compounded Dalton's small attraction problem by smiling suddenly and brilliantly. "Thank you."

"Tall mocha with whip," the barista announced. Thank God for impeccable timing.

Dalton led them to a dark, semisecluded corner of the shop, and Tierney couldn't help wondering why. Because he was sensitive to Tierney's being in the closet, or because it was a good atmosphere for a serious talk between near strangers? Whichever, they sat down at a rickety table with thin, scrollwork iron legs that were all a different height. Every time either of them set their cups on the marble top, the whole thing rocked in a new direction, creaking.

That was the bulk of their conversation for the first few minutes. Dalton sipped and looked around, but didn't say anything, just occasionally glanced across the table.

I need a drink. "I love the coffee here," Tierney blurted.

Dalton nodded. "It's good."

"Yeah. The quality of my coffee's almost as important as the quality of my bourbon." Tierney took out his flask, tipping some liquid gold into his vanilla latte.

Dalton didn't say anything, just tilted his head and watched.

Tierney put the flask back and gripped his mug between both hands, taking a few drinks, one after the other, letting it scald him a little but not to the point of real pain. "Yeah, I love coffee. Especially when I'm hungover. I buy beans here and make it at home. I have one of those machines that grinds the—"

Dalton's fingers landed on Tierney's forearm, and the babble pouring out of him stopped. The heat of the guy's touch rolled over him, relaxing Tierney's shoulders and loosening his chest enough to let him take a deep breath. "Thank you."

"For what?" the dude asked.

Tierney turned his mug around by its handle. "Isn't it obvious?"

"I don't know, is it?" Dalton's fingers slid away, back across the table.

God, did he have to say it? "For not telling Ian."

"Well, I haven't had a chance, but why are you so sure I won't?" When Tierney jerked his head up, Dalton was blowing on his drink, as if the subject wasn't important.

"You won't." Tierney swallowed. "Will you?"

Dalton arched his brow.

Tierney was familiar with anger in all its subtle shades, but it still took him a minute to puzzle out the source of Dalton's irritation. "It's not that I don't trust you, I mean, I don't think you'll tell him, but . . ." He couldn't come up with any more explanation. "I didn't plan on telling you at all." Lame finish.

Dalton made a face at him, the adult version of sticking out his tongue. "Of course I won't tell him. I wouldn't *do* that. It would be like outing someone."

Tierney blinked. "There are people who'd do it."

"Would *you*? If it was me in your shoes?"

Tierney licked his lip. "I don't really know you," he hedged. It was true—they'd only seen each other twice and both times were weird circumstances. It didn't matter that Tierney *felt* like he knew the guy better.

Dalton pursed his lips. "You know me as well as I know you."

Tierney dropped his gaze, running his fingers up and down the sides of his cup. "I might." He swallowed. "Out you."

Dalton didn't respond.

Tierney took a whack at explaining. "You gotta understand, I'm in charge of government affairs and PR for the company, and for us, PR means making sure the local politicians are indebted to us. I use every advantage I have over someone to get what I need. I manipulate people. That kind of attitude bleeds over into my personal life, I guess."

Dalton eyed him, pinning him like a bug. "Do you *have* to do your job that way?"

"It's how *I* do it." Tierney shrugged nonchalantly. He hoped. "It's how I was trained to do it, from freaking birth." Nice. He'd sounded plenty bitter there.

"I don't understand." Dalton's nose scrunched up, and Tierney found himself fascinated by the tiny details of his expression. The small lines and the way Dalton's brows pulled in, and how blue his eyes were even in this light.

"Um, Metropolitan Ambulance is a family company," he explained absently.

"So you were, what, groomed for this position?" More of that nose wrinkling, and now he'd tilted his head so shadows slipped into the hollows of his cheeks and the line of his chin, while the light glinted in his hair.

Dalton had to be the hottest guy he'd ever sat across from. Totally different from Ian, but sexy as hell.

"Tierney?"

Fuck, he was *stunning*. "Huh?" The shadows shifted again, sliding around to highlight other features of Dalton's face, like the slight but graceful curve of his temple. For a brief second, Tierney recognized the sensation—kaleidoscopic. Just like the other night when he'd seen Grandfather's body, things fragmented and changed, showing a new perspective or something like that. A different way to see his world. "Grandfather's dead."

Dalton leaned forward, his expression changing into one of concern. "Did you just say your grandfather died?"

"Yeah." He sat back, shaking himself out of his fog. Christ, he must seem like a huge dork. "Yeah," he repeated. "I did."

"Oh." Dalton's face went wide—eyes opening farther and his lips parting. "I'm so sorry."

"'S okay," Tierney shrugged. "I hated the bastard anyway." The dude—Dalton, not Grandfather—had a beautiful mouth. Sculpted. His fingers twitched, wanting to feel it and see if it was as smooth as it looked.

But Dalton was pulling back from him and closing up. Crossing his arms over his chest and hardening his jaw, the way he had earlier when Tierney'd pissed him off. What other reactions could he get out of the dude? Happiness? Sympathy? Desire? Affection? *I want affection,* something whispered inside him, so quietly Tierney could pretend he hadn't heard anything.

"You do realize that makes you sound like a monumental prick?" Dalton asked, one eyebrow lifting.

"What?" Then it hit him, what he'd said. He squeezed his eyes shut for a second, as if that would reset this conversation. Like he could get a do-over. "Just . . . lemme explain?" His mind raced, trying to get a handle on exactly what reason he'd give for hating his grandparent, searching Dalton's face for clues. Little hints of emotion that might tell Tierney which way to spin this.

Dalton regarded him steadily from under his light brows, lips in a tight, straight line.

Tell him the truth.

No way. He couldn't do that, could he? He'd never told *anyone* . . . but Grandfather couldn't touch him anymore. Tierney may not have a reason to come out, but he could do this much, couldn't he? Tell someone why. Tell *this guy* why.

Don't wanna do it.

He opened his mouth to say something else—pretty much anything—and Dalton was leaning toward him again, wrapping long fingers around his drink.

I care what he thinks.

"Um," Tierney began, then had to clear his throat. Oh shit, he *was* going to tell him the truth, wasn't he? "Um, see, a long time ago, like, before I was born, Grandfather started the ambulance company."

Some people who said, "I hated my grandfather," could be given the benefit of the doubt. Dalton would assume they had a justifiable reason for their feelings. In his experience, losing family was too painful for casual hatred, so someone who had personal integrity wouldn't say that carelessly.

An hour ago, he never would have credited Tierney with having personal integrity; he was only here because the man needed a sympathetic ear. And Dalton's sympathetic ear had heard something in the time they'd been here. Not words, per se, but hints of someone other than a two-dimensional guy with a skanky libido whose entire self-worth was tied up in designer clothes and a flashy car.

That kept Dalton seated, listening to Tierney talk about how his grandfather had gone from mechanic to ambulance company owner.

As Tierney told his story, more clues fell into place, painting a picture of his past—what had made him the man he was today. It didn't take long to figure out the grandfather had had a lot of control over Tierney's life, and that was the root of the hatred.

"So, see, Grandfather had specific ideas about how we should run the business and, like, conduct ourselves, and he wasn't shy about ordering us to do what he thought we should, you know?" Tierney waited, as if he needed Dalton to confirm he'd followed this much.

"Mm-hmm." Dalton nodded.

"He lived in the 'guest house' on our property. You know, I never met my grandmother?" Tierney spun his empty cup around, but didn't seem to need a response this time. "She died before I was born, and he only had one painting of her in the house. No photos or anything; guess the old guy didn't like her much." He flicked a glance toward Dalton. "Is this boring?"

Not at all. "Not really." He shrugged, not sure why he was pretending nonchalance. Maybe it had to do with his sense that Tierney didn't normally share this much, and if Dalton overreacted, he'd shut down. "If you want to talk, I'll listen." *Too much encouragement or too little?*

Tierney sank into himself, shoulders pulling toward his ears.

Too little. "What did he do to you to make you hate him?" *Oh no.* Now he'd gone too far in the other direction. "Um, if you want to tell me."

Tierney tucked his chin into his chest. "It's kind of a long story."

"I'll listen."

Swallowing, Tierney straightened up, revealing his pale face and the tightened muscles around his eyes. It made him look haunted. Or hunted. "He had lots of expectations, and he'd manipulate or bully me or whatever to make me live up to them." He fiddled with his empty cup, turning it by its handle, then took a deep breath before continuing. "He grew up poor. I'm not even supposed to know that, you know? But Mother slipped up one night and mentioned it. So, he got rich and that meant, like, keeping up appearances. He married a socialite, and did everything he thought a guy of his station should do. And then his son came along, and he made sure his son did everything necessary to maintain the reputation of the family. Then his son married a socialite and had kids, and those kids had to live up to the family name."

All at once Dalton knew where this was going. It was so *obvious.* A full-blown ache for Tierney bloomed in his chest as he leaned across the table. "A gay grandson wouldn't be acceptable."

"It's not done by Terrebonnes," Tierney whispered, staring into his mug. Then he moved, a blur of motion as he reached into his inner suit pocket and grabbed his flask, unscrewing the cap with a practiced twist of his fingers and dumping some more of the contents into his cup, then taking a drink. Not a gulp, but far more than a sip. "Fuck, I can't believe I'm telling you this." He swiped his sleeve across his mouth, everything changing with the motion and the words. His eyes narrowed and some of his mask fell back into place. "You already know too much about me and now . . ." He shook his head, frowning.

"I'm sorry." Dalton took a chance, touching Tierney's hand briefly, his fingertips brushing across the long bones on the back of it. Offering comfort, but also trying to reach that other side of him again. The real man.

"Dude." Tierney sat back, pulling away, taking another drink as he glanced around the coffee shop. "I don't— I've never told anyone that. *Anyone.*" His frown had grown into a glower that he trained on Dalton. As if Dalton had *made* him confess.

"I won't repeat it." But maybe *Tierney* should, because it would help everyone understand him so much more. See why he could be such a douche bag, and how much of his psyche was at stake. *Trained from birth.* Tierney'd said that about his career, but clearly acting the part was a habit ingrained into his whole being. The public facade was all about self-defense, which Dalton had already assumed, but now that he knew why, it didn't seem so abhorrent. Or weak. Tierney was struggling to deal with his situation... or had Dalton read that wrong?

"I would've done it," Tierney asserted. "If I'd had a real *reason* to come out, I would've defied the old guy. Told him to shove his trust fund up his ass," he continued, thrusting his chest forward in that way men who were trying to prove their masculinity did.

Dalton picked up his stir stick from the table and put it into the dregs of his mocha, swishing it around, giving himself something to focus on besides Tierney. His hands held steady, but he jittered inside. "You have a reason now."

"What?" Tierney jerked in his peripheral vision. "What reason?"

He glanced up to see the man's face had gone pale again. "Well, it's more that you no longer have a reason to stay in the closet now that your grandfather is dead."

"What about the rest of my family?" Tierney's machismo deflated as the words spilled out. He ran a hand through his hair, gripped it for a second, then released it. "Grandfather brainwashed them too."

Dalton dipped his chin, in concession to the note of panic in Tierney's voice rather than his words.

"Besides, it's too fucking late for me."

He laid down his stir stick, resting his hands faux-carelessly on the table. "If you don't mind my asking, how old are you?"

"Thirty-four."

That's about what he would have guessed. "That's a lot of your life left to stay in the closet." He shouldn't be pushing this. He believed each person had to come out in their own way; personal experience told him it was best. But it just seemed so obvious that Tierney could be an okay guy—maybe even a *nice* guy—if he'd drop the act.

"Yeah?" Tierney was back to glowering. "It's *my* life. I thought we were here talking so you could, I dunno, express your sympathies, not psychoanalyze me. Or, like, fix me." He shoved away from the table, chair legs scraping on the tile floor, but stayed seated, eyeing Dalton from the increased distance between them.

"I'm sorry," Dalton said, even though he didn't mean it. "I'm not trying to fix you. I just thought you might not see the situation clearly. Sometimes when people are too emotionally involved—"

"I'm *not* emotionally involved." Tierney sliced his hand through the air and continued through clenched teeth. "Didn't you hear what I said? I don't have any *reason* to come out."

Dalton blinked, trying to follow the logic.

"I don't have *any* emotional involvements. Not now," Tierney went on, then suddenly his glare became a sly twist of his lips. "Unless you wanna be my reason to come out?"

"I barely know you." He winced on the inside. *Could've come up with something more concrete.*

Tierney brushed off that defense. "So? I haven't known any of the guys who've sucked my dick as well as I know you." He leaned forward, his mocking smile getting downright mean. "Besides, you think you know me well enough to tell me what to do."

"That's not what I—"

"Is that your game? Are you one of those dudes who're on a crusade to make everyone come out?"

"No!" How did this happen so fast? Thirty seconds ago Tierney was the emotionally vulnerable one and now he'd turned the tables. The difference was that Dalton hadn't been trying to twist the knife in the other man's wounds. He took a calming breath. "I shouldn't have said any of that earlier. It really is none of my business. I wanted to . . ." He couldn't fight his nervous energy anymore, so he picked up his empty cup and held it between his palms, curling fingers around like it gave him warmth. "I thought I could help."

"Oh, so that's your angle, huh?" Tierney sneered. "You get off on giving 'help.' Is it a power thing, or are you a guy who needs to feel superior?"

Tierney's words made sense, but Dalton still couldn't quite grasp them, because the attack was so off base. "Is it really so hard for you to believe someone would be sympathetic to your situation and simply want to give you support?"

"Uh, yeah," Tierney scoffed. "In my world? People don't do anybody any favors unless they're getting something out of it."

"So, in your world, I'm getting an emotional payoff from exploiting your pain?"

One corner of Tierney's contemptuous smile crumbled, like his defenses weren't holding up, but he recovered, smirking. "Exactly."

"I'm so sorry you think this way. *Live* this way." Dalton leaned forward as he pulled his coat off the back of the chair, touching Tierney's arm one last time. "I understand that you think no one is capable of being kind to you, but I'm not sitting here talking to you because I'm getting anything out of it." He squeezed Tierney's arm so hard he could feel the bone through the man's suit jacket, then he let go and stood. "I just saw another human being in pain, and tried to make things better. I won't make the mistake of thinking you want to escape your miserable existence again."

As he walked away, he thought he heard Tierney mutter, "Better not, dude." At the door, when Dalton checked the man's reflection in the glass, he could make out Tierney's sulking, slouching self, arms crossed over his chest. All alone in his personal emotional stew, which was apparently how he intended to stay.

Dalton had to tell the ache under his ribs to give it up numerous times as he drove home, but it didn't listen.

Chapter 4

Heh. Blotto. Such a good word. Perfectly described the way alcohol could blur out the rough edges of life. Tierney didn't care that Ian would never be his, or that he'd never get to be gay, or that he'd totally acted like a four-year-old with Dalton right after spilling his guts to the dude—none of it mattered if he was drunk enough. Plus it brought other things into focus: like how sexy Dalton was. Anytime he closed his eyes, he saw the guy across the table from him in the coffee shop, with that hair and the way his face was so symmetrically perfect or whatever it was that made him so hard to look away from.

He'd like a little dose of that scenery right about now. Since he'd finished the bottle of bourbon he'd cracked open as soon as he walked into his condo this evening, he'd take a break, check out the view in his head again, then find more booze.

He came to at 3:33, still wearing his suit, wristwatch glowing in front of his face, head pillowed on a couch cushion, and disconcertingly wide-awake with dread jumping up and down on his ribs. A sure sign that he'd had way too much to drink. This particular event only happened after he'd really tied one on.

Self-recrimination hour.

Tierney groaned, and it echoed in his ears. *Ouch*. Carefully, he rolled off the couch onto the floor and started crawling across his condo to the bedroom. Trying not to think. But it was impossible. Like a psychotic, disjointed movie, flashes of the night before—only a few hours ago—played through his head.

Fight with Ian.

Dalton knew.

Dalton was stunning, and Tierney'd done everything possible to disgust the dude. Talked a bunch of shit he didn't mean and totally shamed himself. Exposed all his weaknesses.

And—*oh God*—he'd drunk-dialed Ian and left a message. *"You're right, y'know, I haven't earned your trus' and 'm a lousy friend. Didn't mean to be a dick 'bout your boyfriend. He's a good guy, Sam is. Deserves you . . ."* He couldn't remember the rest, but he knew there was more. Fuck, what if he'd confessed—

Lurching to his feet, Tierney barely made it to the bathroom before he puked. Totally at the mercy of his body and his emotions. He was pretty sure the tears streaming down his face weren't from retching.

When he was finally done, he flopped onto the bathroom floor, shuddering and gulping air.

He couldn't vomit out this kind of illness. And he'd done it to himself. Waited too long to talk to the guy he wanted, then gone rogue and let some other guy see the mess inside him.

Loser.

Later that morning he tried to call in sick, but his assistant, Gina, made him go to work. "You have a meeting with your father and brother that you *cannot* miss." Her voice was so strident he had to hold the phone away from his ear.

"I can talk to them anytime," Tierney whined.

"Yes, you *can*, but apparently you don't, like, *ever*. That's why they scheduled this meeting."

He rubbed his eyes, considering sitting up in bed. Probably shouldn't risk it. "Why do I have to be there?"

"Your brother offered me a raise if I get you here."

"*I'm* your boss; I'm supposed to give you raises, not Chase."

She huffed. "Your meeting is at nine thirty. Be here by nine fifteen and I'll brief you."

"Okay, suppose I show up for this thing—"

"*Tierney . . .*"

"What are you going to do for me?"

"What did I tell you the last time you made an inappropriate request?"

"I had all the inappropriate I could handle last night," he muttered.

"You did?" Her voice switched to interested rather than censorious.

Christ, why had he said that? She'd assume the wrong thing; he'd trained her to think of him that way.

Gina went on. "I figured you were calling in because you were hungover, but if it's because you have some wom—"

"I'm hungover," Tierney blurted. "Never mind, I'll be there by nine."

At 9:18 he presented himself to Gina, standing at attention in front of her desk—he couldn't avoid walking past it to get into his office—blinking against the light, considering the ethics of asking one of the paramedics to hang a saline drip from the ceiling and put in a line to take the edge off his hangover.

Gina rose from her seat to come around the front of her desk and look down her nose at him, mouth prim. "I thought you were going to be here by nine."

"I like your new haircut." It was cute, sort of pixieish.

"Thank you." She patted her head and smiled. "I've had it for weeks."

Ooops. "Um, I like your shoes?"

"Oh, shut up." She turned and picked up a manila envelope off her desk. "Here, this is from your brother, and I'm not allowed to read it."

Tierney groaned. It could only be one thing: projected earnings for the fourth quarter. "How bad is it?"

"Believe it or not, when it's sensitive financial information, I keep my nose out of your paperwork."

"If I give you a raise, will you look at it for me?"

"No."

"C'mon," he whined. "You're letting Chase bribe you with a raise, why not me?"

"Because if I let you bribe me every time you wanted me to do something *you* don't want to do, the company couldn't afford my salary."

No argument for that. Tierney inspected the envelope in his hand while Gina went back around her workstation and pulled out her chair. "Go sit at your desk and look at it. You have ten minutes until you need to be at your father's office."

"I want to look at it here," he said.

She sat down, flicking a hand at him. "Whatever, just don't bug me. I have things to do."

Well, fine then. He turned and opened the door to his office, grateful for the soft carpeting that muffled noises and the relative dark—his blinds were mostly shut. Gina must have done that. He probably wouldn't be as nice to him if he were in her shoes.

They *were* cute shoes.

Tierney didn't look at the projections, other than opening the envelope and finding the graph that showed income falling. Again. Fortunately, he had a possible assist for them. He spent his ten minutes sending careful inquiry emails to a couple contacts and poking around a certain county commissioner's website.

Which was how, a half-hour later, he was able to say to Father and Chase, "I have one new potential revenue stream."

"Go on," Father said. He sat sideways behind his desk with his arm propped on his blotter, tapping his fingers in random patterns. It seemed like he wasn't paying attention, which he reinforced by leaning back and mostly focusing out his window, but it was all vanity—he liked visitors to his office to think he was a Very Important Captain of Industry, so he affected an air of bored superiority to cover up his shortcomings. Reality was, he was going deaf in his left ear, so he needed to keep the right one toward the conversation.

Well, at least Tierney knew where he got his own worst trait. "Marlyle District One isn't going to bid to renew their ambulance contract, so the county will issue an RFP at the beginning of the year."

"Have they announced it yet?"

"No, I found out through Jerry Brown, but it's supposed to be kept under wraps."

For one moment, as they chuckled at the idea of anyone in their little community successfully keeping a secret, Tierney felt like they were a family.

Then Chase said, "Well, do your job and make sure we're in a position to turn in a bid they'll accept."

Tierney scowled at him. "I'll do my job, if you do yours," he snapped.

"What's that supposed to mean?" Chase sat forward, glaring.

"It means the last time we bid for the city contract, I had to come up with an explanation for why *your* response rates were out of compliance more than twelve perc—"

"Boys," Father barked. "Try to remember we're on the same team."

"I will if he will."

Chase rolled his eyes. "Grow up."

Father rubbed his forehead. "Go back to work, for God's sake."

"Your friend called," Gina said when he got back to his office. She was typing away at her computer, focused on her screen.

Dalton. Tierney halted, dizzy for a second, not sure where the idea had come from, but— "Um, who?"

"You know the one." She lifted one hand off her keyboard (cutting her seventy words a minute typing speed to, like, sixty-five) and flapped her hand at him. "Your college friend. Ian."

Jesus. The clenching of Tierney's gut totally distracted him from objecting to her implication that he only had a single friend.

"Wants you to call him back," she continued, squinting at her screen, then holding down the delete key.

Some craven part of him nearly didn't return the call, but he *had* to. Forget the dude being the love of his life or whatever the fuck, truth was, Ian *was* his only real friend. If Tierney didn't phone, that'd be over, wouldn't it? But if he did, there was a pretty good chance Ian would forgive him. Tierney'd been a big prick in the past and Ian had gotten over it, so . . .

He dialed the guy's cell before overthinking, because that shit always got him in trouble. Sitting at his desk, one hand fisted on the surface and the other smashing his receiver against his ear, he listened to it start to ring.

"Dude," Ian answered immediately. "Your grandfather died."

"He did?" *Christ.* "I mean, I know, but how'd you know?"

Ian's voice went bone-dry. "You told me in the message you left. In the middle of the night."

His drunken apology. "Okay, yeah. I'm a douche bag, man. I'm sorry." But had he said anything about—

"How long are you going to keep doing this?"

"Doing what?" he asked through a suddenly cotton-filled mouth.

"Being an asshole, drinking, hiding in the closet. Apologizing to me and expecting me to forgive you. All of it."

Tierney swallowed twice. Once in relief and once in fear. "I guess until it stops working."

Ian half snorted. "Whatever, T. You know, I should tell you to fuck off. Cut you out of my life—"

"But work—"

"You don't think I could work with you? I manage to deal with that fucker Sheriff Fowler, and his son was one of the guys that attacked Sam and Miller."

Tierney'd heard that through the grapevine, but he'd assumed Ian wouldn't put up with that homophobic prick again. "You're saying you could be in the same room with that asshole?"

"Yeah. I am. And that's my point. *I* could handle dealing with you if we weren't friends. It'd be *you* that couldn't, and that's another clue in your big mystery of life. The way you're running it now isn't *working*, you giant dumbass."

His head was pounding so hard the building shook with it. "Um, so you don't forgive me?" He *had* said that out loud, right?

"I don't fucking know *why*, but yeah I do—"

Tierney collapsed against the back of his chair.

"—I'm just getting sick of this, T, and I don't know how much more I can take before I give up on your shit." Thudding in Tierney's eardrums nearly drowned out what Ian said next. "If I didn't know you were gay? I probably would've bailed already."

Wait. So it was *pity* that kept them going? The blood pulsing through him halted, then reversed direction. Clockwise for despair, counterclockwise for anger. He'd wanted sympathy from Dalton, but getting pity from his friend *blew*. He could feel words he'd regret rising in his throat like lava, but Ian continued.

"We've been friends too long. You know something? It's because of you I even figured out I was gay."

Only his white-knuckle grip on the edge of his desk kept Tierney from falling out of his chair. Did Ian mean— Was he saying—

"That night when we were freshmen and you showed me the glory hole? That's when I first knew."

Are you fucking kidding *me?*

"So, your grandfather—you wanna get together and talk about it or anything?"

"No," Tierney half yelled into the phone, shaking his head. All he wanted in the world was for Ian to stop toying with him like this. "Really. If you need to express your sympathies, do it to my parents. Mother's planning some wake and she's expecting you to come."

"Me?" Ian's voice rose in pitch much like Tierney imagined his eyebrows were raised. "I could've sworn she thought I was too 'blue-collar.'"

"Yeah, well, now that you have a bunch of grant money to disburse, you're the kind of business contact Terrebonnes like to cultivate, you know." He ran a shaky hand through his hair, trying to regain some calm after all the fucking hits he'd taken from this little chat. First the shame, then the anger, then the hope and then a loop-de-loop and the straight drop to the bottom of the pit.

"Your family," Ian muttered. "I don't know how you live with them."

"Alcohol." Which he'd need some of soon, at this rate. "Uh, so, I've got an appointment . . ."

"I'll let you go—"

Thank fuck.

"But don't forget about the big meeting here next week, man, or you'll never get any of that grant money your parents have pinned their hopes on."

Tierney managed a fake laugh, said his good-bye, and watched his trembling fingers return the handset to its cradle.

Considering all he'd been through this morning? A three-drink lunch was totally justified.

The rest of the week, every time the door of the Interagency Disaster Relief office opened or the phone rang, hopeful apprehension infused Dalton. It wasn't a pleasant feeling, but when whoever walked in or called turned out *not* to be Tierney, he was disappointed.

And guilty. He couldn't believe he'd let himself react like that when the man had lashed out at him, because—*duh*—Tierney was just trying to protect himself the only way he knew how, by pushing Dalton away. Worse, Dalton knew deep down inside that he'd been doing some lashing out of his own. Tierney's comments about him getting an emotional payoff had hit a little too close to the truth, once Dalton had time to reflect on it.

In spite of no contact from Tierney, he did hear from Sam within a few days. They made plans to meet for lunch the following Sunday, during Ian's rugby game. After checking with Sam, Dalton picked Murray's Bistro, right in the heart of Simpson. It was his first trip to the neighborhood since *that* night, so he thought it was appropriate to go with Sam, if Sam was okay with that.

"Oh yeah!" Sam had said when Dalton broached the subject. "I need to get my first trip back to the gayborhood over with, and Ian would be all, you know, *protective* if I went with him."

Murray's felt like an indoor atrium, with a tile floor, huge potted plants in between glass-topped tables and banks of floor-to-ceiling windows that let natural light flood the dining area. The chairs were all cast iron enamel with (fortunately) cushions tied onto the seats, and the acoustics were very European-bustling-café—clinking cutlery and chattering in the air that made one feel in the middle of the action. It reminded him of the restaurant in the boathouse at the Palace of Versailles, but he didn't tell Sam that because he might have to explain who paid his way to France and why.

Instead, he let Sam lead the discussion. "So at dinner one night my mom started talking about when I'd have my first boyfriend and that's how I came out," Sam said, continuing the conversation they'd been having before the waiter brought their meals.

He couldn't express surprise at Sam's family just knowing—it seemed pretty obvious—so instead Dalton asked, "How old were you?"

"I think about fourteen." He squinted up at the ceiling thoughtfully. "Young enough that I wasn't completely grossed out that my mom wanted to talk about boys."

"My mom would've talked about boys with me the same day hell froze over," Dalton said before taking a bite of salad. Lettuce wasn't his favorite food, but the parmesan cheese and Caesar dressing coating it elevated it to nearly scrumptious. If it wasn't for dressing, he might never get enough vegetables.

"So, she's not supportive?" Sam's eyes had gone droopy and sympathetic.

"It's okay." Dalton smiled reassuringly. "I'm over it. I mean, it'll always hurt, I guess, but I spent a while seeing a therapist and I learned how to accept it."

"So, like . . . you don't have a relationship with her at all?"

"No." He shook his head as Sam continued to give him that sad face. "Neither of my parents could accept me when they found out, and they've never tried since."

"What happened?" The broadest of questions—but of course he'd be that curious.

"Well." He picked at his lunch with the fork, using the tines to rearrange the leaves as he spoke. "Just after I turned eighteen, they caught me kissing my high school boyfriend and freaked. I thought Stephen and I were in love and we'd stand strong against our oppressors. Except when my parents called his, and they demanded *he* not be 'homosexual,' he agreed to their terms." A sad smile leaked out of him. "If I'd told my parents I was just experimenting, or maybe agreed to 'get over' my little problem, they might have let me stay, but I just . . ." He shook his head, because he still couldn't explain it. "I wouldn't back down."

"So . . ." Sam's brow scrunched up into his hairline. "They, like, kicked you out?"

"Uh-huh." Dalton sighed and sat back, but not so far that he'd have to raise his voice to be heard. He didn't have to share it with the world. Or their neighbors on the other side of the palm plant. "They said I could come back when I came to my senses. They thought it was tough love." He suppressed a shiver, remembering it all. "I thought my life was over. I walked out of the house with all the cash I could find, as many clothes as I could carry in my backpack, and my cell phone. It took me a while to work up the courage, but eventually I called my brother Peter. He's the oldest. I was afraid he'd agree with my parents, but his wife answered and told me to come over. She had Peter awake—he was working night shift—and up to speed by the time I got there. You know what they said when they answered my knock?"

Sam shook his head.

"Nothing, they just hugged me, both of them." Oh God, he was tearing up. But that part still got him. Maybe it was because they'd already had children or just the way they were that they accepted him, but Dalton hadn't expected it from his analytical, responsible, parent-approved older brother and sister-in-law.

"That's so sweet," Sam whispered, wiping his eyes.

Dalton nodded, swallowing hard around the painful lump in his throat.

"And you stayed with them while you went to college?"

Choke. His whole body leaped into awareness, adrenaline surging. He should have expected more questions from Sam, but he'd been caught up in reliving the love he'd felt then and not what happened after. Looking into Sam's very sincere, slightly teary gray eyes, Dalton went with his gut and confessed. "No. I found a boyfriend to move in with after I graduated. He pretty much supported me, and I . . . met his needs." Hugh had had a lot of them, beginning with requiring an outlet for his massive sexual appetite. Even at eighteen, five or six times a day, every day, was too much for Dalton for more than a few months. "He wasn't that much older, just thirty, but he was one of those dot-com millionaires. And when that relationship ended, I found another guy just like him. A guy who needed someone like me."

A few heartbeats of silence passed before Sam's whole face screwed up. "So, like, you were, um, financially dependent on them?"

Dalton suppressed the butterflies in his stomach by pressing against it with his palm, under the table. "Yeah."

Sam gasped, pulling back and covering his open mouth with his fingers, glancing around.

Oh no.

But when Sam dropped his hand, Dalton could see the titillated smile he'd been trying not to let out. "Oh my *gawd*!" The force of his exclamation propelled his body forward until his huge grin was nearly in Dalton's salad. "I've never met an actual *kept boy* before." Then he lurched back, "I'm sorry" floating out from behind the palm trying to hide his now-horrified expression.

Dalton blinked, totally disoriented. He'd always seen that period of his life as a serious blot on his past, but apparently Sam thought it was more . . . an adventure? "Sorry for what?"

"For calling you a 'kept boy,'" he said, leaning back across the table.

An indelicate snort slipped out. "It's okay, that's what I was. I'm not anymore," he hurried to add. "I never want to go back to that kind of life, but for about four years after being rejected by my parents, I sort of, well, survived that way. I'd find men who needed me and could, you know, meet my needs. When I walked out on the last one, I was twenty-two."

Sam's huge grin broke out again and he sat back in his seat, bouncing a couple of times. "So can I ask you all about it? If I get too, like, personal, just tell me to shut up."

Dalton couldn't possibly be offended by someone this cute. "Yeah, you can ask me about it, but, um, please don't tell anyone. Not even Ian."

Sam had been nodding along until Dalton said his boyfriend's name. Then he pursed his lips. "Oh, that'll be hard. Maybe you shouldn't say anything else. I mean, I really can't promise not to tell *him*. Well, I could promise, but, you know, I'd probably slip."

Dalton worked his jaw, but before he could respond—and thank God, because he really couldn't talk about it if it meant his boss finding out—Sam saved them from the awkwardness.

"Let's change the subject." He burst into enthusiastic motion, digging through his backpack under the table. "I have that list of recommended romances for you." He handed over a computer-printed sheet of paper that included the titles, authors, and even the ISBNs of a *lot* of books. "Some of them are electronic only."

"Thanks." Dalton folded it and put it into the pocket of his coat hanging on the back of his chair. He planned on reading at least a couple, because he had a feeling there'd be a test in the future.

"And now we should gossip," Sam announced.

"What are we gossiping about?"

"Tierney," Sam said, in a "duh" tone of voice.

Uh-oh. "Tierney?" he asked carefully.

Sam tilted his head. "I thought you'd want to discuss him."

"What?" Circumstances demanded he speak with food in his mouth. "Why?"

"I saw you talking to him out on the sidewalk in front of the house when you came over last Monday." His whole face brightened. Which was weird, since Dalton had been certain Sam didn't like Tierney.

"I wanted to make sure he was all right."

"Uh-huh," Sam agreed, nodding and smiling and watching him with avid eyes.

"Well, I mean, did he seem well to you when he left your place?"

"Nope."

"Okay. So . . ." Dalton turned all his attention on his lunch. He sucked at lying, other than polite social ones. That was the reason he'd learned to *be* polite and social—to make up for his tendency toward bluntness.

"*Sooo*, you find him attractive?" Sam's whole body bobbed up when he said "attractive," as if he'd scented his prey in the wind.

Dalton gulped down his lettuce before he was really ready. "Well, I mean he's not *un*attractive." Pointless to even try for the lie. *Prevaricate! Prevaricate!* "But he's got that personality. I mean, he's so *slick*. Too concerned with which profile he has turned to the camera."

"He reminds me of a train wreck."

"Or a porn star in a train wreck."

Sam nodded. "You can't not look at that."

"Exactly, but there's something . . ."

"When he's not being an idiot or a poser, Tierney can be, I don't know, sincere," Sam mused. "And also, he really cares about Ian. *Really* cares about him. Like, a *lot*."

Dalton jerked his head up, and saw in Sam's gaze what he'd been afraid he might: Sam knew about Tierney's feelings. Knew that Tierney *longed* for Ian. Possibly thought he loved Ian. "Please tell me Ian hasn't figured that out."

Sam shook his head. "Of course not. My boyfriend's not anywhere near as perceptive as you and I are."

Phew.

"Tierney's not a dick to me," Sam continued. "You saw that the other night. I mean, not a *total* dick. He greeted me civilly. I don't know if I could not be a bitch to him if he had Ian instead of me."

"Well, it is very . . ." *Understanding.* "Human of him."

Sam nodded enthusiastically, but then ruined it by frowning. "But he's no Ian."

"Not everyone can be an Ian."

Sam sighed happily. "Yeah, the Rainbow Gods were smiling the day they made him gay."

Seriously, the guy was so cute. "Where do you come up with this stuff?"

"I don't know." Sam shrugged and picked up a fry. "My overly fertile imagination. It's a curse. I have a habit of reading romance novel plots into everything. It's my fatal character flaw." He sighed and took a bite, eyes wandering around the room. "Anyway, back to Tierney. Ian wants to keep inviting him over and stuff since T admitted he's gay—"

"Even after that scene at your house? I didn't think Ian would ever want to see him again."

"Tierney apologized. He called, drunk, and left a message in the middle of the night saying sorry and that I was a good guy and he was happy for us and et cetera." Sam waved a hand in the air. "But see, that's what I mean."

No, actually, he didn't see. "*What's* what you mean?"

"Oh, uhhh." Sam wiggled a fry in apology. "Just, like, Ian told me about it, and he rolled his eyes and huffed awhile, but he *forgave* him. Repeatedly accepting someone's apology is kind of against my boyfriend's character. Well, I mean, not totally against his character, but you know—"

"I do." Dalton nodded, hoping the interruption would prod Sam to finish telling him whatever it was.

Sam hunted up a new fry before continuing. "So, he thinks Tierney needs some kind of support, and he has to stand by him if possible and provide some help. I said the kind of help he needs, we aren't qualified to provide." He refocused on Dalton. "But then it hit me . . . don't you think a guy like him would benefit from having a relationship?"

"And you're volunteering *me*?" Forget that stab of empathy when Sam described Ian's pity for Tierney; the last thing the man needed was a pity *boyfriend*. Dalton had inflicted enough sympathy on the man already.

Sam rolled his eyes—a motion that included his whole head. "No. I was just fishing. Seeing if he appealed to you at all."

God. How to explain his feelings about Tierney? "Well, I mean, I can see how someone might find him attractive. It's like he's . . . covered with a hard shell of chocolate."

Sam scrunched up his face, chewing thoughtfully before swallowing. "Chocolate. You really think chocolate? He's so, I don't know, much less delicious than chocolate."

"He's like deep, dark chocolate. The bittersweet kind, but some people have a taste for it. Deep, dark chocolate with a caramel center that oozes out when you bite into it. Sea salt caramel—very trendy, with an edge."

"Are you a fan of bittersweet chocolate-coated, trendy, oozing caramel?" Sam asked hopefully.

Dalton snorted. "I have enough flashy caramel men in my past. I'm so done with them."

For some reason, that made Sam smile.

Chapter 5

Working under the supervision of one's sister took some getting used to.

Dalton liked his job, and the benefits were great. He didn't want to be an Office Specialist Two for the rest of his life, but it was a good starting point for a career. Places could be gone to from where he was now.

Being in the same office with Andrea, though, just might kill him. He suspected she'd pushed him to apply for the position so she could keep an eye on him. She seemed to have a need to mother him at the best of times, but at work? She mothered *and* bossed. When he came in Monday morning, she asked him what he'd had for breakfast, told him yogurt with granola wasn't enough "fuel" to last him until lunch, then said, "Oh, Ian will want donuts for this meeting. You'll need to run down to the bakery on Fifth and get a couple dozen."

His irritation made him a little snippy when Tierney came in—the first time they'd seen each other after their weird coffee shop interlude. He knew within a second of the man walking into the office how it was going to go. Tierney couldn't meet Dalton's gaze when Dalton smiled in welcome. His eyes pinged around the room like this was pinball and Dalton's forehead read "tilt."

Sigh. Not surprising, but annoying. Dalton pretended to be focused on a stack of paperwork for the meeting while surreptitiously watching Tierney's feet sidle up to his desk.

When those feet were about a yard away, Dalton spun his chair a quarter turn and Tierney flinched. Dammit, he wasn't trying to intimidate the guy. *No sudden movements*. He nodded. "Good afternoon, Mr. Terrebonne."

Tierney coughed, or possibly choked on spittle. "Do you have to call me that?"

I'm trying to treat you like anyone else. "I feel it's disrespectful to address visitors to the office by their first names. Even if we had coffee together socially." *Ooooh. Could have handled that better.* And it wasn't true—he'd call them by name if invited to, and this man had not only invited it, but insisted.

Tierney's nostrils flared, and he poked his lip out. "I'll be waiting over there." He jerked his head toward the love seat in the corner of the entryway before stomping off in that direction.

Dalton stood up. "Tierney? If you like, you could wait in the conference room." The best he could do to make amends here and now. "We have donuts."

Tierney halted, turning, but then someone came into the reception area behind him. Two someones—one of the city's assistant chiefs and that hospital administrator who raised Dalton's hackles for no reason he could pinpoint.

Tierney's body language changed immediately: His shoulders dropped back and his weight shifted. One corner of his mouth curled up. Not exactly a smile, more the edge of a smirk. But it was his eyes that changed the most, somehow seeming to shrink and go hard, more brown. Walling the real Tierney inside.

"Hey there, guys. Aspell, Chief." He nodded at each as he said their names. "I see I beat you here, again. You two ride together?"

Dalton sat down, half his attention on compiling his paperwork and the other half eavesdropping on the group. The way the three men spoke to each other was revealing. Mr. Aspell and Chief Siriano were comfortable together, and the chief displayed that same business-jocular approach with Tierney that Tierney met him with. The same couldn't be said about how Tierney and Edward Aspell treated each other. If they were dogs, they'd be making stiff-legged circles, lips raised in proto-growls.

Strange how comforting Dalton found it that Aspell didn't like Tierney. Mr. Aspell was a douche bag, and everyone knew douche bags of a feather flocked together, therefore Tierney couldn't be a real douche bag.

Or he was a douche bag of a different feather.

Oh shut up. Dalton forced all his attention on assembling the information for the meeting. He'd spent far too much time in the last week thinking about Tierney, he didn't need to continue it now, when it was so obvious Tierney couldn't handle even the most rudimentary friendship.

So, that was that. He mentally wiped his hands of the man.

Yep.

God, wouldn't it be wonderful if dealing with inappropriate attraction was really that easy? *It's not attraction, it's something else.* Empathy. His susceptibility to wounded creatures.

The sound of his boss's door opening behind him startled Dalton out of his reverie. "Do you have those packets ready?" Ian asked. "Sorry I had to ask you to do it."

Mental eye roll. "It's my job."

"Yeah." Ian grimaced. "I'm not used to having a secretary."

Dalton gave him a look.

"I mean an office specialist," Ian corrected, smiling apologetically.

Dalton nodded. "I'll finish the paperwork and get it to you before you start."

"Hell," his boss muttered. He didn't want the packets? "Tierney's here already." Ian ran a hand through his hair and adjusted his tie, turning toward the men in the reception area and smiling. "I wish the dude would just hurry up and have his big, queer breakdown, then maybe it wouldn't take so much energy to deal with him," he said to Dalton out of the side of his mouth.

Dalton couldn't repress his snort. "You really think he'll come out of the closet one day?"

Ian gave him an odd look, but answered. "You've met him. He's a fighter, not the type to just passively accept shit. He'll struggle with this until it breaks him. He's already falling apart, you can tell by looking at him."

"It's going to be painful to watch," Dalton said, sighing and glancing at Tierney beneath his lashes. He was threadbare, in spite of his sleek designer suit and expensive haircut. "And to live through."

"Yeah. It's gonna suck to be him for a while."

There was no argument for that. "He'll need his friends."

"Yeah, well, I'll do my best, but the dude's good at pushing people away."

"Ian!" Aspell chose that moment to holler across the office. "How you doin'? Ready to hand over some of that grant money?"

Ian gritted his teeth in what might pass for a smile from more than a few feet away. "Nope, sorry. This is just the meeting where I explain how this process is going to work and what information I'll need from you. I must not have made that clear in the email invite."

"Oh, yes, you did," Dalton said, sotto voce. Then he ducked his head, because really, he should stay out of it.

"This is gonna be a horrible meeting," Ian said in a similarly quiet voice before stepping forward to greet more visitors. Dalton glanced at Tierney again and caught the man watching him, locking gazes with him before Tierney jerked away. Shortly after that, he wandered into the conference room, flashing a faint smile when Dalton glanced up just as he disappeared through the doorway.

Was that progress? He really didn't know.

He could hear someone coming. Dalton's car was almost the only one left in the state employee parking garage, so Tierney figured he had a good chance of those rhythmic tapping noises being his footsteps.

His feet twitched when he caught sight of Dalton's blond head shining in the parking lot light. He was looking down, bangs obscuring half his face while he dug through his leather messenger bag, probably for his keys or phone.

Straightening up from where he slouched against the compact white Toyota, Tierney fisted his hands in his pockets. *You can totally do this, dude.* "Um, hi." *Maybe should've rehearsed a better opening.*

Dalton stumbled, lurched to a halt, squinting and yanking his hand out of his bag. In it he held a can of mace attached to his key fob. After a second, he dropped his arm and the defensive posture. "In case you don't recall," he said, "I witnessed an assault a little over a week ago, and finding someone hanging out by my car in a deserted parking garage after dark is *disconcerting*." He walked up to the vehicle, nudging Tierney away from his door. His hair obscured his eyes from this angle, but Tierney had a very intimate view of his ear, again. He liked the swirling whorls of it and the way the darker-blond hair on the back of Dalton's head swept forward and just brushed the pale upper curve of it. Ignoring twitchy fingers that wanted to trace the shape, he licked his lip and said, "Sorry. My bad. That was . . . Sorry."

Maybe he should just get "forgive me" tattooed on his forehead.

"How did you find my car?" Dalton asked while unlocking it manually.

"Um, I searched for the one with my butt print on it?" Would he even remember Tierney collapsing against it the other night?

Dalton jerked his head up, shoving Tierney further out of the way to look at his paint job. There was nothing there, and Dalton turned to him, raising his brows.

Weak joke fail.

But Dalton smiled, rolling his eyes, and relief rained on Tierney's insides like water on the desert. "Wanna get coffee?" he blurted.

"Coffee?" Dalton wrinkled his nose. Either confusion or disgust.

"Um." Tierney straightened up, trying to look more respectable or something. "I kinda was thinking I should, like, apologize." Was there a limit on the number of times he could? "For the last time we went for coffee. How I acted and some of the shit I said."

"You *kind of* think you should?" Dalton yanked open his door and tossed his messenger bag onto the seat. "Wow. Your fervent sincerity is overwhelming." He tilted his chin, which gave him an air of confidence that Tierney really wished he could get some of. "Should I assume you have a favor you want from me? Or is there something you're trying to manipulate me into?"

Totally deserved that. A wave of dizziness swept over him, and Tierney had to brace his palm on Dalton's car. "Just . . . I need a friend. I mean—" Christ he was a dork. "I guess, you know, if you don't think you'd get anything out of it—"

"Tierney." Dalton sighed, sucking his lower lip into his mouth a second.

Why was that so hot?

"About what you accused me of at the coffee shop . . ."

The shit he said when he was mad always came back to bite him in the ass. Tierney smacked his brain around, trying to get it to pay attention to what the dude was saying and not the shiny wetness of his lip. "Which thing I accused you of?"

Dalton shifted, glancing around the garage a second. "That I'm getting some kind of, um, emotional charge from giving you a sympathetic ear. You weren't completely wrong. It's not a power thing," he said quickly. "Or a feeling of superiority. It's just sort of . . ." He wiggled his shoulders, as if warding off a shiver. "I get a little bit of a rush out of helping people. I mean, especially people who are like you."

Like him? *Messed up in the head.* Tierney shrugged. "I *am* kind of a fixer-upper." A momentary twinge of angry pride pinched his gut. How come it was so much less dangerous to admit this to Dalton? But fuck, anyone had to be able to see it. When he'd built this fake personality, he'd never planned to make it such an obvious facade. But he had, and now he didn't care enough to change it. Not anymore. *Too much energy.*

He suddenly found himself fighting a grin, because that was such a fucked-up reaction to all of this. Him being a douche bag and Dalton's pity and, like, condescension. But still. "If you wanna use me for the thrill of poking around in my psyche, I'm okay with that. I mean, I'd be using you too."

Dalton dropped his chin, trying to hide a small smile that Tierney couldn't miss. *So adorable.* Wait, had he really just thought that? "I guess you are kinda using me too, huh?" Dalton asked.

"Yeah. Using you to be my friend, or at least pretend to be."

"So cool, it's agreed." Dalton grinned. "We're using each other."

"Uh-huh." Tierney blinked away the effect the dude's smile had on him. "So, coffee?"

Dalton tilted his head, the smile dying. "I can't. I'm meeting my brother at the gym."

"Oh, yeah, well." Tierney shrugged one shoulder. "Whatever. Just thought I'd offer, you know." The guy had to meet his brother—it wasn't *really* a brush-off. Unless Dalton was lying. About everything, like using him— Why would he want to do that, anyway? If he didn't have a penis attached, Tierney wouldn't bother using himself.

"Seriously," Dalton said, reaching for him, briefly grabbing his arm to halt him. "I'm not blowing you off."

"Um, yeah." He nodded and just kept on nodding. Dalton really *did* want to use him? *Not the penis.*

"Do you want my number? In case you need to talk or something?"

What did *or something* involve? He stared at Dalton, heart speeding up.

"Tierney?"

"Why would you want me to have your number?" *I'm smooth. I'm the man.*

But Dalton didn't laugh at him, although he did smile more. "It'd be hard for us to use each other without access."

The inmates, who'd been mostly silent, listening intently, began clamoring for the number. "Um, okay."

"Give me your phone." Dalton held out his hand, wiggling his fingers when Tierney simply stood there.

"Oh, uh . . ." He found it in his coat pocket. His fingers brushed Dalton's skin when he passed it over.

Dalton entered himself into Tierney's phone. "Now call me, and I'll have your number."

Tierney took it back, and there was Dalton's name on the screen, so he touched it and held it up to his ear.

Dalton's pants rang—something catchy that Tierney couldn't place but he'd heard on the radio—and he lifted his jacket to get his cell out. Tierney was caught by the sudden sexiness of the way his khakis stretched across his hip. Watching him dig through his front pocket, bulging and grabbing and nudging up against things, reminded Tierney once again of just how stunning Dalton was. Everywhere.

"Hello," Dalton said once he'd liberated his phone, lips caressing the word, his voice echoing in one of Tierney's ears, then the other.

"Hi," he returned. *I think I'm in lust with you.*

One afternoon later that week, Mother came by Tierney's office to speak with him about Grandfather's wake. He hadn't thought she knew where his office was, but someone had narced him out. Probably Chase.

She sat in a visitor's seat, one ankle crossed over the other, adjusting the jacket of her pantsuit and regarding him over the desk. "Father and I thought that, considering all the extra attention Grandfather lavished on you—he always kept his eye on you, you know—*you* should give a short toast to him. A mini-eulogy, as it were. It will be a fitting, final tribute to your grandfather," she said, dabbing at her eyes with a handkerchief.

Wouldn't it be fun to tell her why Grandfather had kept tabs on him? *Right.* "Yes, Mother." He stood from his desk, hoping to signal the end of their little tête-à-tête. It wasn't, of course: she spent another ten minutes instructing him on various points of behavior before he managed to convince her he had an important text.

For the most part, Tierney didn't let the old guy's death get to him, but after a conversation like that, he deserved a drink after work. Or three. Whatever it took to forget.

Half a bottle of liquor into his night, well buzzed but not quite drunk yet, sitting on his couch and watching *Star Trek* for lack of anything more interesting to do, it hit Tierney that drinking alone was a sign of alcoholism.

But he wasn't an alcoholic, right? He was just using it to deal with a temporary period of stress.

What about tomorrow? Are we doing this forever?

Seriously, who asked you?

Loser.

If he were drinking *with* someone this wouldn't be so pathetic. All of "this": the being in love with his best friend but not able to have him, and the being in the closet shit, and what his life had become.

Fuck. Why had he thought about that stuff? Now one of the inmates, Morose, pulled up a barstool, not saying much but depressing the shit out of the place. Tierney stared into his bourbon on the rocks, feeling more alone than he ever had in his life. More so than after he'd found out about Ian and Sam. Or maybe this was just a different kind of alone.

Alcohol used to be his friend at times like this. It used to shore up his confidence and his defenses, and make all that lying possible. He used to never be alone with beer or bourbon by his side. Tequila he'd reserved for instilling courage.

"Not my friend anymore, are you?" He glared at his drink, then past it at Captain Kirk, macking on some alien chick. *Gross.* Weird how he used to think Kirk was such a stud, but now the guy seemed kind of pathetic. He took himself way, *way* too seriously, and he wasn't the hot shit he thought he was.

"Nice pecs," he told the TV. The Kirk currently inhabiting it broke off his kiss, gazing meaningfully into the eyes of Enemy Alien Chick, who of course he was about to bonk. "Sulu has abs, though," Tierney hollered at him.

Kirk ignored him in favor of the precoital fade-to-black.

Tierney pointed his glass at the TV screen. "You're a womanizer, Kirk, but you can't fool me. I've been there, man. You be careful, or you'll end up in the same place I'm in." He hit the Pause button, capturing Kirk in postcoital dishabille. (Dude didn't last long, did he? One commercial break and he'd shot his wad.) Squinting at the image, he tried to decide: could Kirk be gay?

And if so, would Tierney do him?

"Probably," he muttered, starting the show again. He'd pretty much do anyone, right? He was sex starved. Stupid, fickle male sex drive. He could think he loved one guy, but now spend all his masturbatory time imagining what another guy would feel like naked and pressed up against him.

I wonder what he's doing right now?

Tierney glanced at the next cushion over, where his phone was lying. Its screen was so blank and sad. "Let's be alone together." Picking it up, he brought it to brilliant life, mesmerized by the phone's cheery display of apps in sparkling, jewel-toned colors.

The text bubble looked especially promising. He stroked it, fingertip language for "hello there," and the program bloomed to life on his screen, cursor blinking, inviting him to reach out.

Only one person had recently invited Tierney to contact him if he needed a friend.

What the hell did he text? *What are you doing?* That seemed casual and non-needy. Didn't it?

While he waited for a response, his heart beat unsteadily, right up in his jugular. *Dalton probably thinks I'm pathetic.* Dude might not even answer.

Thirty seconds, then a minute, then Kirk fighting off Enemy Alien Chick's spurned love interest. But Tierney wasn't watching the show, he was staring at his phone's glaring white display, hoping. Knowing how the scientists who'd sent out those golden records in the *Voyager* spacecrafts must feel. Waiting for another being to notice and respond.

I'm reading, Dalton texted back. *What are you doing?*

Tierney collapsed on the couch, breath whooshing out of him. His screen rotated when he flopped over, making it hard for him to find the right letters, but he got a response sorted and hit Send. *Texting you.*

I figured that out. :-) How are you doing?

All right. He pushed himself back up on one arm, not sure where to go from here. He'd hoped to find other life in his universe, but now that he'd found it, what did he do?

Invite it back to earth, of course.

Would you like to come over?

Chapter 6

God, if Dalton hadn't been reading one of those books Sam had recommended, or if Sam had bothered to mention that all those books were so freaking erotic, or if Dalton hadn't been in the middle of a sex scene when Tierney texted . . . then he wouldn't be in this position. Standing in the fifth-floor hallway of the Welsea Lofts Building—*of course* Tierney would have a penthouse condo in the most expensive neighborhood in the city—in his new skinny-core, striped button-down, which was supposed to look like business casual but was really about showing off slim but toned torsos.

He'd actually changed into this shirt. And fixed his hair. And now he found himself hoping Tierney would *notice*.

"Oh my God," he whispered, his finger hovering over the doorbell. This was such a horrible idea.

What happened to avoiding this attraction?

He said he needed a friend. I can hardly reject him now.

Believe that if you want.

Tierney yanked the door open. "Are you gonna ring that or what?" In his hand was a glass of something alcoholic. People didn't drink apple juice out of highballs, and they didn't put ice cubes in.

It hadn't occurred to Dalton that Tierney might not be sober, though it should have. His voice on the intercom when he buzzed Dalton in hadn't sounded drunk, but the audio quality had been awful. Regardless, it was obvious now. Tierney was red-eyed and not quite steady on his feet.

Dalton smiled. First, because Tierney was barefoot, and dressed like a slob, which was oddly, unexpectedly charming. Second, because a drunk Tierney was something he could totally avoid being attracted to.

He pushed Tierney's button. *Ding-dong.*

Tierney frowned, looking half-angry and half-confused, watching Dalton's finger. Then he grinned. "You're funny."

Not really, but it was nice to be told so. "I'm here, as requested."

Tierney straightened away from the door. "Would you like to come in?" he asked, in that slow tone people used when they were working not to slur.

Dalton shouldn't, and possibly he should be censorious about the drinking too. He'd heard about it from Sam and seen enough from the man himself to suspect Tierney had a problem with alcohol. But so far *he* hadn't had any experience with a drunk Tierney. "Sure." He took the plunge, stepping into Tierney's apartment.

"Can I take your coat? Would you like a tour of the condo, or you wanna watch *Star Trek*?" Tierney took a step back, catching himself on the door, then rounded on it as if it had bumped into him.

"We can watch *Star Trek*. Give me a tour another time?" *Groan.* That had totally sounded like invitation fishing. Dalton shrugged off his black leather jacket.

Tierney looked over his shoulder. "You like *Star Trek*? I'd offer you porn, 'cause that's the only other thing I ever watch, but I already saw that t'night, if you know what I mean." He winked and faced Dalton again, taking the coat and hanging it on a hook hidden behind the door. At least Dalton assumed there was a hook because he didn't hear anything hit the ground.

"Take me to your television."

Tierney bowed low, sweeping a hand toward a large, open room with a wall of windows. "Right this way, m'sieur." He straightened and crooked his arm, holding it out. Was Dalton supposed to take it? He hesitated, but he'd never seen someone just stand still, waiting, elbow hanging in the air for any *other* reason before. He took it; Tierney's skin was warm and a little crinkly with body hair, which shifted against Dalton's forearm as Tierney led them toward the TV.

Dalton rolled his eyes, mostly at himself. "You're a ridiculously charming drunk."

"Why, thank you." Tierney guided him toward one of those long low couches in an L shape. The cushions were extra wide, lots of butt room. Two guys could lie down next to each other on it, if they were close. Dalton focused so much on that that he almost missed checking out the rest of the place. It was all one big room as far as he could see, but the lights in the living area were the only illumination, and that area seemed sort of . . . anemic. He'd bet a designer picked out the pale leather club chairs, the coffee table and matching, gilded end tables, not to mention those pleated-shade lamps. None of the furniture fit Tierney. He'd pick out dark stuff, with simple lines and splashes of red, or some other color. Maybe he liked yellow.

The lambskin rug right in front of the couch was nice, though. Maybe that's why Tierney went barefoot in his house. It probably felt great to rub against.

"Here we are," the man himself announced, flopping onto the couch, grinning up at Dalton and patting the cushion next to him. Last time they met he'd been sincere and serious, but he'd had this same intensity. A way of making Dalton feel like he was the only person in the room.

I am *the only person in the room.* He sat next to Tierney and focused on the big screen across from them—it had to be huge to see it from that far away—and his butt instinctively knew Tierney had picked out this couch and that TV. And the sound system that became evident the second Tierney hit the Play button. It was the old *Star Trek*, with Kirk in full Lothario mode talking passionately to a green-haired woman in a tinfoil bikini.

Then Tierney poured himself another drink from a bottle on the coffee table in front of them, and Dalton couldn't keep his mouth shut. "Do you really want that?" God, so much for nonjudgment. But he'd said it now, so he met Tierney's startled look, trying to appear supportive in fact if not in word.

"Do *you* want it? I can get another glass." Tierney lifted the drink, holding it out toward Dalton.

Oh, that was a horrible idea, and not what he'd meant at all. Dalton leaned closer though, until he could smell the whiskey and the man. He'd already thrown caution to the wind by coming over here . . . "I shouldn't." Wouldn't that be enabling Tierney?

Enabling him to what, exactly? As far as he knew, Tierney could stop anytime.

"Why not?" Tierney blinked at him. "Oh yeah, you said you don't drink."

"Much. I don't drink much." He looked at Tierney's hand, feeling like the star of an after-school special. Did he take the drug the evil pusher was offering him? *It's just one drink.* "I'll have some." He stood up. "I can get my own glass."

Tierney stood next to him, nearly bumping shoulders. Maybe his personal boundaries changed when he drank. *Maybe he just wants to be closer to me.*

"No, really, take this one. I should prolly slow down anyway." Tierney bent over to grab the remote and muted Kirk, then stood even closer, turned toward him fully, holding the whiskey right in front of Dalton's chest. Close enough for Dalton to feel the heat radiating off his fingers.

Temptation made his lungs tighten and his lips tingle. So few people had truly green eyes, but Tierney's were close to the genuine article, the color broken only by occasional flecks of brown arrowing through the irises. And God, he hadn't shaved recently. Dalton wanted to feel the scruff along Tierney's jaw, let it prickle his fingertips.

Instead he took the glass, gripping it just under Tierney's hand, emphasizing the friction of skin against skin. Tierney's pupils widened, and he took a deep breath. They stood there like that, barely touching but totally absorbed in each other for a few seconds. Then Tierney relaxed his hand and let it fall away, but he didn't back off.

"Thank you," Dalton whispered before he lifted the drink to his lips, touching the glass with them, wondering if that's where Tierney's lips had been, watching Tierney's jaw go slack and his eyelids get heavier.

"Drink it," Tierney murmured.

Dalton tilted it back, holding Tierney's gaze, opening his mouth more, letting the liquid slide over his tongue—

Then he spewed whiskey everywhere as his survival instincts forced out the stuff burning through his esophagus.

Tierney laughed, thank God.

"I'm sorry I blew whiskey all over you," Dalton croaked when he could speak again.

"This is *bourbon*," Tierney said, holding the bottle up and grinning. He still had tracks on his cheeks from where little amber rivulets had run down his face. He turned and headed toward the kitchen. "Be right back."

Dalton watched him walk into the darker end of the loft, passing a huge table with scrollwork legs and fret-backed chairs. Totally not the right style for this place or that man.

Had he actually been trying to *seduce* Tierney?

Didn't matter. Even if he had been, it was an obvious fail. Spewing all over your object of interest tended to have negative consequences. Slouching on Tierney's couch, resting his head on the back and closing his eyes, he listened to Tierney run water in the kitchen. Okay, yes, that had been embarrassing, but a potential save, right? Because anything happening between them would be a nightmare.

The water shut off, and Tierney's footsteps—soft, bare ones—started back toward him, but Dalton didn't move. He was trying to figure out what to do from here. The couch bounced under his butt when Tierney flopped down next to him, and it jogged his brain into providing the answer: *get to know Tierney better.* Because, as douchey as he could be around other people, Tierney still intrigued Dalton.

He opened his eyes and rolled his head to see Tierney studying him, face serious, brows pulled together. "I thought you were sleeping."

Dalton smiled. "I can't fall asleep that fast. I was just thinking." He straightened out of his slouch. "Did you bring back a rag so I can clean up?"

Tierney inspected his own shirt. "You pretty much only got it on me, and I cleaned me up." He reached out, grabbing one of two glasses on the coffee table. He'd also brought a different bottle back from the kitchen. It was shaped like a wine bottle—that's what Dalton had thought it was at first—but then the small bowl of ice and pitcher of water next to it wouldn't be necessary.

"Gonna teach you how to drink bourbon." Tierney seemed so pleased with the idea, lines around his eyes crinkling up with his smile.

"You might start by teaching me how to drink. I'm sorry about that."

Tierney waved him off, dropped some ice cubes in the glass, then poured a small amount of the alcohol in.

"Eagle Rare," Dalton read aloud.

"The bourbon before wasn't aged as long as this. This stuff's better, you'll be able to get it down." Tierney smiled as he added water until the glass was half-full. He lifted it, turning to Dalton and letting it hover just under his chin. This time when Dalton took the drink, he didn't try any more suggestive finger porn, barely touching Tierney's skin.

It still made him tingle a little. But maybe that was the alcohol tickling his nose. *Uh-huh.*

"Sip it carefully," Tierney said.

Dalton raised his brows. "I thought that's what I tried before."

"That was straight alcohol. This is smoother, has water cutting it, and you know what to expect now."

"I've *had* bourbon." Just not for years, and he'd hacked until he was hoarse that time. And for all he knew, that had been whiskey.

Tierney grinned. "Yeah, I could tell."

Sigh. It *was* much lighter in color. He sipped, glancing at Tierney from under his lashes, like maybe that would give him a clue whether he did it right.

He didn't cough, but he had to fight the urge. His throat still burned, though, and he'd be hard-pressed to tell someone how the bourbon actually tasted.

"See?" Tierney turned back to the coffee table and dropped some ice cubes into the other glass. "It's pretty good."

"Eh."

The expression of horror on Tierney's face was priceless. Dalton laughed. "Sorry. It's all right, but I really don't think I'm the ideal consumer of alcohol. I've just never been that into it." He settled back into the cushions, sipping once more—yeah, still not great—and watched Tierney fill his glass half-full of bourbon and splash a teaspoon of water in on top. Why bother with the water at all?

Tierney took a drink and sighed, making a weird sort of pleasure-grimace. "Wanna watch more *Star Trek*?"

Dalton shrugged. "Not really." He wanted to talk. See if there really was anything more to this man.

"You don't like *Star Trek*?"

"I do, but I'm a fan of *The Next Generation* and the other series after that. Kirk's so . . ." He curled his lip, hoping that would explain it.

"'M starting to think that too." Tierney looked absently at the television. Whatever episode had been on before was over, and the screen saver program was starting, landscape photos drifting across the black. "Sulu's hot though. I used to watch it as a kid all the time; I was really into it. I even tried to get my dad to take me to a convention."

"So you were a geek?" Dalton teased, feeling better now. He'd embarrassed himself, sure, but it had turned out all right, and now he had a solid mission of friendship to undertake. It made things seem brighter. Or maybe it was the mellow glow spreading out from his stomach that was affecting his outlook.

Tierney snorted. "Yeah, pretty much. I was the dorky kid and my brother was the future business tycoon. That dude formed a golf team in our grade school. Freak."

"You just have one brother, right? I have three—two cops and an accountant."

"Andrea, Ian's assistant, is your sister, right? Why does she hate me so much? Never mind, I think I know."

Thank God, because he'd have a hard time answering that. He didn't want to tell Tierney it was because he was a general asshat even if they both knew it was true. "Yeah, she's my *only* sister. She's almost seven years older than me, and two of our brothers are older than her. My brother Luke was five when I was born. I was a surprise. It's a very Catholic thing." Okay, maybe the bourbon was kind of nice tasting. Or at least not repulsive.

"You're the baby? So'm I, but there are only the two of us, and Chase is just a couple years older than me. We don't really like each other."

"Chase Terrebonne . . ." Dalton wrinkled his nose up. "I know that name; it's on your company letterhead." *Duh.*

Tierney nodded. "He's the operations VP, and Father is the president." He leaned closer and whispered, "Really, he's the CEO, but Father likes the way 'president' sounds better."

"And you're the vice president of PR and government affairs."

"Yup." Tierney turned, tucking one foot up on the couch, rubbing it with his fingers.

"Why don't you and Chase get along?" *Why am I so nosy?* Did he really have a right to be asking this man such personal things? Although Tierney had opened up to him before, so maybe.

Tierney sighed and ran a hand down his face, letting it fall into his lap. "It's weird growing up the way we did," he said finally. "I don't know, maybe it's not, but everything was so fucking *competitive*. He was better at sports and talking to people, plus he was older. I just never . . ." He met Dalton's eyes. "I was jealous."

"And he's not gay," Dalton said softly.

Tierney's face changed, mouth pulling down at the corners and lines growing on his forehead. "Yeah, that." He slumped into the couch, picked up the remote next to him, and turned off the television.

"So, you're still staying in the closet because of your family?" It had to be the whiskey affecting him; he normally wouldn't pry like this.

Tierney shifted again, tracing the rim of his glass with his finger. "Yeah. Now that Grandfather's gone . . ." He swallowed. "I've been lying about it too long. They wouldn't handle it well."

Who exactly is it that wouldn't handle it well? Dalton couldn't ask it, because it was so obviously Tierney himself who was terrified of facing the world as an out man, and he'd pushed enough already. He didn't want to inadvertently find Tierney's breaking point. Guilt flooded him because he'd led them into this conversation. He emptied his glass down his throat, barely noticing the taste, and set it down on the floor. Then, leaning back again, he turned toward Tierney, settling his arm on the back of the couch, thumb inches from Tierney's neck. "We don't have to talk about it."

"This's embarrassing," Tierney whispered. "I keep spilling my guts to you, and I ambushed you in the parking garage, and I drunk-texted you, and now you're here and—" He ran his hand through his hair.

"I embarrassed myself by doing a spit take on you." Dalton brushed his fingers across Tierney's shoulder, warm under the soft fabric, trying to tell him it was fine. "And I've been prying. I'm sorry, I shouldn't."

"It's okay." Tierney snorted. "But my life's not really interesting."

"It is, kind of." He couldn't suppress his smile.

"You're weird." Tierney sighed and let his head fall back on the couch, grazing Dalton's hand. "So what's your story?"

"My story?" He thought he knew what Tierney meant, but he was stalling. Giving himself a few seconds to shore up his defenses before telling the tale. Because he felt a connection with this man that went beyond the way his hair tickled and slid along Dalton's fingers. If—when—he told Tierney about his coming out, it would be a far more intimate conversation than the one he'd had with Sam.

"Yeah." When Tierney nodded, Dalton could feel it in the suddenly-very-sensitive palm of his hand. "You gotta have some trauma in your past, otherwise you'd blow me off."

"I guess my past does make me more empathetic to your situation," he began slowly. Tierney gazed at him, waiting for him to go on.

How much do I tell? How much do I trust him? "I'm kind of trying to pay it forward, I suppose," he said, stalling a little longer.

"Pay what forward?"

"After my parents found out I was gay and kicked me out, my brothers and sister were supportive . . . but I was so hurt. And I guess I was mad at them for not being able to make it better." He still couldn't quite understand why he'd been so angry with them.

"You were living with your parents?" Tierney shifted again. "You were just a kid, huh? Where'd you go?"

"My brother's place. And then I found a boyfriend who wanted me to live with him." He let his bangs hide him from Tierney's squinty-eyed expression.

"So . . ." Tierney began. "He was older than you. Had his own place."

Dalton shrugged. "He was thirty. I was eighteen."

Tierney let out a low whistle. "How long did that last?"

"Less than a year." Dalton felt his lips twist into something mirroring the derision he felt inside. "Then I found another one to move in with."

"Oh." Tierney said almost soundlessly. "So, you, um—" He cleared his throat. "You faced it."

Dalton blinked, staring at him. This was the point of the conversation where he obliquely admitted he used a string of older guys for security, while they used him as a boy toy. Yet somehow Tierney had missed the obvious. "Faced what?"

"You didn't hide in the closet." Tierney's mouth thinned into a straight, hard line. "Like me." He jerked upright, back hovering near the cushion but not resting on it. "*I'm* a coward."

"I don't believe that," Dalton objected, but that was all he had to offer. Because on the surface, Tierney did appear to be a coward, and Dalton couldn't explain why he didn't believe it. Long seconds of silence stretched out between them, during which Dalton wanted to touch Tierney, comfort him somehow, but the man was frozen, one hand gripping the opposite elbow while he stared into space, focused away from Dalton.

All at once, Tierney slumped, dropping his head on the back of the couch, hair trailing on Dalton's fingers again as he shifted to look into Dalton's eyes. "Thank you for not believing that," he whispered. "You're always so nice to me, and I don't deserve it."

Oh God, these were the things that made Dalton *so* susceptible to this attraction. When Tierney got vulnerable, it made Dalton's chest ache. He could see so much inside the man wanted out, and the more he saw the more he wanted it to come out and play too. Before he could stop himself, he ran his fingers through Tierney's hair.

Tierney turned into his hand, letting Dalton stroke his scalp, his eyes going half-closed. "Are you tired?" Dalton asked.

"I'm sorry."

"For what? There's nothing to be—"

"Made you come over here. 'Cause I felt lonely."

"You didn't make me. You asked me and I came."

"If I hadn't had anything to drink . . ." Tierney leaned further into Dalton's touch. "I needed to not be alone," he whispered.

"Everyone has moments like that." Dalton ran his thumb quickly across Tierney's cheek, wanting to cup his face, but he settled for these smaller caresses. He was already pushing the boundaries he'd set. *But these touches are just comfort, not seduction*. Just friends. Intimate friends.

"More than a moment." Tierney's lip curled up on one side. "It's sorta . . . I still feel like that."

Somehow they'd gotten closer. So near that Dalton could breathe in Tierney's heat. He tried to take small sips of air, keep a clear head. "You still don't want to be alone?" *Oh God,* Dalton's heart pounded out in Morse code.

"No. I'll . . ." Tierney began, so softly that Dalton wouldn't have heard a thing if he weren't in so personal a space with him. "I'll wake up in the middle of the night, and that's when it's the worst."

"I'll hold you." Oh God, he'd said that *out loud*. "I mean." He cleared his throat. "I'll stay here with you awhile longer, if you want me to."

OhmyGod, ohmyGod. This way lies danger.

Tierney licked his lip. "You'd do that for me?"

Ungh. It made his heart ache even more, but Dalton pulled away, just slightly. "You could lie down if you want to, and I'd stay here. On the couch."

Tierney's eyes widened. Or wait, maybe he was leaning toward Dalton? He *was* getting closer, lips parting, lids lowering. *Oh no, he's going to kiss me!*

Dalton braced himself, if swaying toward Tierney could be called "bracing." His heart inched up his throat, wanting to be nearer to the action. *One kiss*. He'd let Tierney kiss him this one time, and that would be it. One brief moment of benefits, then back to only friends.

Or two's good.

Show some self-control. One, he told himself firmly, and just in time, because Tierney was almost there, in that visual zone where most people closed their eyes since seeing someone's pores in microscopic detail was disconcerting, but Dalton kept his open, focusing on Tierney's lips and his whiskers. *I could touch them*. It was totally acceptable to caress someone's face when you kissed them right? Even if it was just a friend kiss. More of an instructional kiss, because how many guys could Tierney have kissed? Maybe *none*.

Why is this taking so long? Dalton's heart demanded, nearly to his epiglottis.

"Thank you," Tierney whispered, and then lurched forward in a sudden and semicontrolled fall, settling his head in Dalton's lap, squirming as if making a nest for it there.

Wait . . . What?

False alarm. And thank God, right? Dalton eased out a breath, his heart slowly slinking back down his throat, ashamed of its eagerness. He rested a hand in Tierney's hair. Apparently they'd had a misunderstanding about who was sleeping on the couch.

"Do you think other people would be as nice as you are if they knew the real me?" Tierney asked, blinking heavily up at Dalton.

"Yes, I do." He smoothed Tierney's bangs back. Tierney smiled at him and rolled onto his side, tucking his hand under his cheek.

So sweet.

"You're good to me," Tierney murmured, then his eyes closed. "Such a good friend." He went lax everywhere all at once.

Dalton watched the man sleeping in his lap and gave up trying to figure out the situation. He'd wait and see what happened. Let possibilities arise. Meanwhile, he could give Tierney the comfort of human touch in his sleep. The atmosphere was perfect: low lights, warmth blowing in from Tierney's heating system, the low gurgle of something liquid—maybe Tierney had one of those tabletop fountains somewhere—and a sense of security wrapped around them. Dalton could feel it against his skin, and he could see it in the relaxed lines of Tierney's face.

Strange how hair could always feel the same, just like hair, but each time it was also a new tactile experience. Or maybe Tierney's hair was special. *Silky*. It didn't look like it would be soft. He'd expected it to be more wiry, especially with that slight curl and the hints of red in it.

Letting his fingertip slide along Tierney's nose, he traced the trajectory of its slope, then did what he'd been wanting to all night. He felt up the man's scruff. It was silky too, at least for facial hair, and long enough that Dalton's thumb could smooth it one direction, then the other. It always sprang back to short, upright little nubs, but it was more than a five-o'clock shadow.

Staring at a guy should become boring after a half hour, but somehow Dalton didn't get there. It might have been the slight euphoria from the bourbon. Did all high-quality alcohol give one this sense of lassitude and well-being? No wonder Tierney drank it when he was stressed. Unfortunately, though, Dalton's thigh muscles cramped up after a while. Carefully, he stretched one leg out straight, then the other.

Tierney hauled in a breath and moved, letting Dalton ease his legs more, work his jeans down his thighs so he didn't cut off circulation to anything important. Tierney rolled over and tucked his hand under his chin, resettling to face Dalton's body. Mouth inches from Dalton's dick. Breathing on it—hot, moist air passing right through denim and briefs.

Oh no. Don't enjoy it.

If he held very, very still and didn't look at Tierney's slack jaw or how his lips were parted so invitingly close to Dalton's groin, maybe his penis wouldn't notice. But genitals had a knack for knowing when they had attention focused on them, even unintentionally, and once they noticed, they tended to get demanding. Dalton's started growing, bulging toward Tierney. Reaching out, eager to initiate contact.

Groan. He let his head flop back on the couch, concentrating on directing his blood flow. *Away from the pelvis, away!* But it kept pulsing toward his cock.

Tierney's head nestled closer, but when Dalton jerked up to look, the man was still asleep. He had to do something to stop this *now*, because as ridiculous as the situation was—sleeping man in his lap, nuzzling around his dick—he totally wanted Tierney to wake up and touch him for real. Mean it when—*if* he took Dalton's cock in his mouth and buried his nose in Dalton's pubic hair.

Tierney's head shifted again with the clenching of Dalton's thigh muscles. If they stayed like this, something would happen. It could be the bourbon—he was such a lightweight—or that damn book he'd been reading, but something between them seemed so *possible.* Tierney was cute and vulnerable and needy with Dalton.

He's not that way in public. This wasn't part of the friend plan. He should take himself in hand, leave (then take himself in hand), and let things progress naturally. If they were even going to. If he even wanted them to.

Okay, so leave. He moved slowly, sliding one leg sideways. Tierney's head lolled closer to Dalton's dick, forehead brushing against the straining fabric—*ungh*—before Tierney readjusted his position. His brow wrinkled for a split second, and Dalton froze.

Tierney didn't wake up.

This is ridiculous. If he wakes up, he wakes up. Just get out of this situation. He nudged Tierney's shoulder gently, trying to ease himself to the side and slip out from under him.

Then Tierney's eyelids flickered open, inches from Dalton's hard-on, and everything changed. Instead of Dalton doing what he'd meant to—pushing Tierney away gently, or just standing up and dumping the man on the floor—he froze. Forgot all about plans to escape as his heart sped up and all the heat in his body surged to his cock.

Tierney was staring at it—*it must look huge from that angle.* He swallowed, meeting Dalton's gaze for a second that felt like forever. One of those moments where, in spite of what had been said before and what they would pretend afterward, they both knew the truth right now.

Dalton wanted Tierney to touch him, and Tierney wanted to.

Dalton's ability to ignore future consequences was threatened when Tierney hesitated. Before he could come to his senses fully, he found his hand on the back of Tierney's head. Not pushing, just encouraging. When Tierney licked his lips, Dalton fell back into the moment, unbuttoning his fly with his other hand, moving things along, working his fingers into his shorts and pushing them down, baring skin and hair.

Tierney's breathing sped up, pupils widened and totally engrossed. He lifted his head, and Dalton tightened his grip reflexively before loosening it. But Tierney wasn't pulling away. He was too captivated by Dalton's dick. Under its spell.

Easing himself out slowly, he tracked the motion of Tierney's eyes and the way his Adam's apple bobbed. The elastic band dragged across the head, making Dalton's hips jerk and Tierney's breath catch. The cooler air of the room brushed his naked skin, alternating with warmer gusts from Tierney's open mouth.

"I want to—" Tierney gulped the rest of his words, reaching up with a shaking hand and stroking his fingertip down Dalton's shaft. Dalton groaned, barely audible, and Tierney met his eyes again. "I've never done this," he said, right before he slid off the couch and knelt on the floor between Dalton's legs.

Muscles clenched involuntarily, tightening everything in Dalton's groin. He groaned louder, widening his knees and slouching to be closer to Tierney's mouth.

Tierney hesitated again, so Dalton showed him the way. Smoothed his owns palms up the insides of his thighs until his fingers circled his package, then worked his thumbs into the waistband of his briefs and pulled it down, under his balls, which were so tight and sensitive he swore he could feel Tierney's eyes.

Tierney moved all at once, grasping Dalton's dick in his fist, forcing Dalton to take a shuddering breath. Then Tierney's tongue was sliding around and searching under the rim of his head and in the slit on top. Finally, he sealed his lips over Dalton's cock and sank down his shaft.

"Fuck," Dalton gasped, but his palms were over Tierney's ears so he probably didn't hear. Dalton could hear—and feel—Tierney's small noises just fine, though. Sucking and tiny moans that never made it past the back of his throat before shivering their way down Dalton's dick. Then Tierney's fingers worked under Dalton's shirt, tracing his abs and searching up his torso. Dalton nearly bit through his tongue when Tierney found his nipple and grasped it, squeezing.

Tierney took too much and gagged, but didn't pull off. Dalton yanked his hands back, fighting his urge to force Tierney's head farther. Not just to take more of him, but to *make* Tierney choke on it. *Why?* He pushed the thought away—he could figure that out after he came.

After he shot into Tierney's mouth and felt him swallow Dalton's cum down.

OhmyGod. He raised his hips off the couch, nearly there, and Tierney gagged again, which felt crazy good. So good Dalton felt the echo from behind his balls to the tip of his cock, nearly in Tierney's throat. He didn't even warn him, he just started emptying himself into the man, his hand back on Tierney's head and doing far more than encouraging.

It was the ultimate reward for letting himself have this moment—slipping into the orgasm dimension, where everything was pure pleasure for as long as he stayed there.

But orgasms never lasted, and reality always reasserted itself.

Reality was Tierney pulling away from him, falling back against the coffee table and staring up at Dalton with wide eyes and spittle running down his face, coating puffy lips.

In his last few moments in the orgasm zone, that was sexy.

Then he felt supremely guilty. *I wanted to make him choke on it.* Had made him, at the end. He'd never been a guy who got off on power before, so why this time? As Tierney's expression grew more troubled—with a hint of fear—Dalton's guilt turned into shame. He slid off the couch, joining Tierney on the floor and pushing the coffee table back with one hand, taking Tierney's shoulder in his other hand and urging him to lie down.

Tierney's eyes went wide, darting around the room, and he resisted.

"Let me do it for you," Dalton whispered.

Tierney didn't move.

"Do you want to sit on the couch? I could kneel on the floor." He owed Tierney that.

Tierney stared for another second, then shook his head, lying back. Trust overcame fear.

He'd gone soft, maybe from fear. But as Dalton ran his fingers all over Tierney's body, pushing under his shirt to feel his trail of hair, then started to open his fly, he could see Tierney's erection growing.

"Do you want a condom?" Tierney rasped.

He should, but, "No." He passed his hand over the front of Tierney's briefs, tracing the length of him, cupping the shaft in his palm as it grew hotter and harder. Then he worked Tierney's jeans and shorts below his hips, exposing him slowly. Tierney's cock was trying to rise off his stomach, bowing up toward Dalton, and his hairy nuts were wrinkled and pulled up snug against the base of his dick. Dalton took a few seconds to look at him before touching, not analyzing or comparing, but enjoying the way Tierney's shaft widened in the middle, and stretched up into a bullet-shaped head.

Tierney's gulping breaths filled the room, and the smell of his excitement drifted off of him. *Not scared now.* Dalton leaned over and buried his nose in Tierney's pubes, in the joint between his groin and his hip, inhaling him. Breathing in lust.

Just the taste of him in the air made Dalton start hardening again, and when he ran his tongue up the big vein on Tierney's dick to lick his head, they both groaned. Using his lips, he coaxed Tierney's cock upright, then he started the serious business of going down on the man.

Dalton made more effort with that blowjob than he ever had in his life. Maybe it *was* guilt, but he thought there was something more. It excited him to swallow around Tierney as much as it had excited him to make Tierney choke on his dick. The way Tierney squirmed under him and arched up when Dalton wormed his thumb under Tierney's balls and massaged his taint was as powerful as holding Tierney's head between his hands had been.

When Tierney clutched Dalton's hair and thrust into his mouth, crying out as he came, Dalton was rubbing his own cock into the lamb's wool rug, reaching for himself with his hand.

I want him to fuck me.

That thought killed his desire. As he swallowed the last of Tierney's cum, the magic of the moment drained away.

He flopped onto his back, panting, listening to Tierney breathe in counterpoint. Out of sync with him. Dalton closed his eyes and scrubbed his hands up and down his face, trying to avoid reality for a few minutes more. But it reasserted itself, of course. Reality was such a pushy bitch.

He needed a high level of trust to let someone top him. And Tierney couldn't meet that bar. Oh, he might be sincere and even reliable in his way, but the second something threatened his closet, he'd throw Dalton and whoever else was in the road under the bus.

Dalton groaned.

Then Tierney made it all worse. "I'm sorry," he said quietly.

Oh God, so am I.

Chapter 7

For the first minute after he came, Tierney was euphoric. But then Dalton pushed away from him and moaned. Tierney peeked, and the dude's dick was out but pretty much soft, so that wasn't the problem. He averted his eyes, inspecting his ceiling. He wanted to shift, because the edge of the rug was digging into his back, but for some reason he was afraid to move. Afraid to draw attention to himself.

Dalton was so quiet. Christ, he *had* done something wrong, hadn't he? "I'm sorry."

"What do you have to be sorry for?" Dalton asked, but Tierney could hear the edge in the dude's voice that told him he definitely needed to apologize.

He just didn't have a clue why. "I don't know," he said. "There's usually something I did."

Dalton sighed heavily. "So, how was it?"

"Good." *Amazing. Enlightening.* So much better than an anonymous blowjob, forget *giving* one . . .

"Yeah, it was good," Dalton agreed, which meant Tierney could breathe again. And he didn't have to suffer the embarrassment of asking if he'd done all right.

"Really?" he squeaked. *Seriously? Way to humiliate yourself, dude.*

"Really," Dalton said. "I can't believe that was your first time." He sat up, back to Tierney, moving around like he was tucking his dick away behind his fly.

"I, um, I paid attention in class, I guess." Tierney started on his jeans, pulling them up his hips, trying not to make any noise. *Why?*

Dalton froze. "What?"

God, he was an unmitigated dork, wasn't he? Tierney squeezed his eyes shut and tried to explain. "When guys would blow me, I, like, noted what felt good. In case I ever got a chance to use—"

"You've been blown before, but you never blew anyone? How'd you get away with that?"

"Well, I mean, that's the way it works at glory holes, right?"

Dalton moved all at once, scrambling on the floor. Tierney swallowed and opened his eyes to find the guy gape mouthed, staring at him.

"*Glory holes*?"

Tierney's chest tightened up, restricting his lungs. "I mean, either you're on your knees on one side, or you're standing with your dick out on the other. No one ever asked me to blow them after . . ."

Dalton had covered his face with his hands, shaking his head. "I cannot *believe* we didn't use a condom."

Tierney jackknifed up. "I've always used one, I swear. I mean, at least since college. Even with women. And I get tested yearly as part of my physical and I'm disease-free."

Dalton groaned, then half laughed, lifting his head to pin Tierney with a look. "Any other risky behaviors you want to tell me about now that I blew you?"

"I'm sorry." It was Tierney's turn to scramble and tuck himself in. He stood up as soon as he could without flopping around. "I asked you if you wanted a condom."

"You didn't tell me I *needed* it," Dalton snapped, tossing his bangs back before getting on his feet too. "You said you'd never done that before."

"I meant I've never suc—"

"I get it." Dalton held up his palm. "But since they don't cover blowjob etiquette at glory holes—in the future? You need to tell your partners they *have* to use a condom." He planted his hands on his hips, glaring.

Tierney swallowed, trying to keep a clear head. Trying not to freak. But his stomach felt like a toilet bowl, swirly and gross, and the inmates were clanging on the bars of their cells. As a "first" sexual experience—his first time with a guy he actually knew—this blew chunks.

I want to be held, one of the inmates whined. Tierney threw that fucker into solitary confinement. "Hey man, I figured since you were willing to let a guy you barely like touch your dick, you were okay with some risk."

Dalton dropped his hands. "What do you mean, 'barely like'? If I didn't like you, I wouldn't be here."

Bullshit. "It *is* a game for you, isn't it, dude? You get off on fucking with guys' heads? Tell them you don't want sex, you just want to 'help,' then wait until they're drunk and, I don't know, bestow pity fucks on them? You got kind of rough there, at the end. Did you like shoving your dick down my throat?"

Dalton blanched, but Tierney barely noticed. His head was throbbing, and the whole room was pulsing in his vision. Anger. Anger was such a pure emotion. If he was angry, he couldn't feel humiliated.

"You know what? I'm not going to be your pet project. I fucked up." He threw his hands in the air. "I shouldn't have trusted you." He turned away and paced the two steps to the coffee table. His bourbon was right there, waiting for him. May as well drown his sorrows because his life just got a whole lot shittier. He sneered at the cap when it wouldn't come off right away. Fucking thing was resisting him. Dalton's footsteps came up behind him just as the lid fell, bouncing on the floor. Then Dalton laid his fingers on his shoulder.

Tierney spun around, knocking the dude's hand off of him, backing away. "I can't believe I was such a fucking dumbass. I convinced myself you might actually *want* to be with a guy like me. But there's no way—I'm a fucking *prick*. In the closet *and* a homophobe. You know what I did to Ian when he told me he was gay? I kicked his ass!"

"Tierney," Dalton said, shaking his head. "That's not—"

"You saw his black eye. I'm no better than those fuckers who beat up Sam and Mil—"

"That's not *true*!" Dalton got right in his face again, like he had that night outside Ian's house. "You aren't like those guys at all. I hate hearing you talk about yourself that way."

Great way to goad him, then, wasn't it? "I'm a loser," Tierney said, leaning in and enunciating. "I'm a *douche bag*, and you sucked me off. Without a condom. What does that say about you, huh?" He snorted, turning away from Dalton's wide eyes and perfect face. Stunning. He'd had those stunning lips on his dick, and he'd better remember it for the rest of his life because that was as good as it would ever get. "Well, since I got everything I'm gonna out of you, I guess I'll take my bottle and go to bed. You can let yourself out. Don't worry about locking it."

Tierney had about half the bottle of bourbon left. He considered going back out into the kitchen to get more, not sure if that would be enough, but he hadn't heard Dalton leave. The dude could have been quiet, or he could have slammed out when Tierney was in the bathroom, head between his legs, trying not to puke. He wouldn't have noticed an earthquake then.

Didn't matter—he wasn't leaving his bedroom to find out. Better to hide in here. If he chugged what was left of the bottle, it would do the job. Too bad he didn't have any sleeping pills— With the way he'd been drinking lately, it was better not to have them around. Six swallows and he'd emptied the bottle of Eagle Rare, the alcohol burning its way down and then spreading out from his stomach. A slow-acting sleep potion.

It took longer than he'd like. He sat on the bed in his briefs and T-shirt, staring at the floor, then at his gut. When had he stopped working out? The memory of tracing Dalton's perfect abdominal muscles with his fingers wormed its way into his mind, making him more nauseous before he forced the image away. Finally, when he couldn't follow much of a thought at all, he lay down, the room spinning around him. The drunken carnival ride swooped around his head, up until he faded out.

He woke later than normal for self-recrimination hour—after four—to find Dalton in his bed, asleep. Tierney blinked, trying to remember how that had happened. Had he blacked out, and they'd somehow . . . What? Not had more sex, because Dalton was fully clothed and on top of Tierney's bedding, covered with a throw that looked kind of familiar. He squinted at it, which set off a pounding in his brain. *Going to be a hell of a hangover*.

But then he remembered—that was the blanket his interior designer had put on that stupid frilly ottoman she'd bought and he hadn't touched since. As far as he knew, this was its first use in three years.

Which explained nothing about why Dalton was here. Half-drunk and all fuzzy-headed was no time to figure it out. There would be answers later, and possibly accusations. Best to put all that off (since he could) and deal with the torture of now. Tierney drifted, fighting the bad memories and the barbs of the inmates. Arguing with them.

Tons of people stay in the closet their whole lives.

This is only a temporary period of intense stress.

Who needs love?

He said *it was good.*

They overran him, though, looking for blood, and eventually Tierney gave in. Surrendered and let them kick him while he was down, just like those guys had done to Miller. He curled up and tried to protect his internal organs while they hit him with the same thing, over and over. And he couldn't disagree.

Yeah. Totally unlovable.

Eventually he wandered into half sleep, dreaming about being that giant dude in the land of those teeny tiny people. They tied him up and poked him with their spears until the sheets under him were damp with his blood. Would they let him bleed out? What did they care? He was just a big, ugly monster to them.

But another monster came along, taking his wrist and untying it, then stroking fingers through his hair. This other monster scared away all the tiny savages that had been torturing Tierney. An angel-monster, one with bangs that glowed like a halo and obscured one of his eyes, and a soft voice that said Tierney's name. It felt so good every time he murmured "Tierney." Healing. Like medicine, or maybe a balm that flowed through him and sealed all the miniature wounds.

Then the angel-monster kissed Tierney on the cheek, high up by his temple, soothing the pounding in Tierney's skull. "Can you wake up?" he whispered in Tierney's ear.

He nodded carefully, and when his headache didn't grow stronger again, he opened his eyes.

Dalton. "What are you doing here?" he rasped.

"I was worried about you." His gaze flickered behind Tierney for a second, then refocused on him. "I'm sorry."

"For what?"

"For what happened last night."

Oh. Oh fuck. Tierney groaned and rolled onto his back, Dalton's fingers trailing out of his hair. He laid his arm over his eyes. "The blowjob?" he mumbled into his armpit. The longer he lay there, more and more of what happened came back to him. *Jesus. I'm such a dick.* He was the one who should be apologizing. He didn't believe any of what he'd said about Dalton. The dude was a good guy, but Tierney obviously wasn't worth his effort. He'd proved that. The inmates were pissed, but he was relieved. Meeting expectations was something he only failed at.

"What I said to you after," Dalton whispered. "I overreacted. It's . . . complicated."

Tierney snorted, even though it hurt his sinuses. Why did they always burn after he drank too much? "It's okay." He didn't need this pity-laced brush-off, he just needed Dalton to leave so he could do what he did. Repair his facade and carry on. Live the life he'd carved out for himself. "Don't worry, though. I don't have anything."

Dalton was silent for a few seconds. "That's not what I'm worried about."

His fingernails dug into his palm, but Tierney didn't move otherwise. "Look, you don't have to do this, I'm not that fucking fragile. Just leave."

"I'm going soon or I won't have time to get back to my place and get ready for work, but I want to talk to you later. It's important. Are you listening to me?"

Tierney nodded.

"Will you meet me this evening? After work? We can go to Klunhausen's again."

"Okay." If he just agreed, this would end sooner. The torture of the little people—Lilliputians? Was that right?—was looking pretty mild right now. He bet the inmates would make those spear-wielding freaks look like Smurfs with butter knives by the end of the day.

"What time do you want to meet?"

"Uh, I don't have my schedule. How about I let you know?"

"Okay." But Dalton didn't move. Tierney could feel his breath on the back of his arm. "Will you be all right if I go?"

"No worries, man. I've been taking care of myself for a long time."

Dalton took a deep breath and sighed it out. "Text me," he said, then the bed rocked as he moved off of it. It made Tierney a little seasick, and it would help if he uncovered his eyes, but he didn't want to see Dalton again. Ever. "Or call," Dalton added.

Yeah, he didn't want to do that either.

"Bye," the dude said from the doorway. But he didn't walk away. Tierney could feel him just standing there, waiting.

Christ. "Bye."

Finally Dalton left. Now Tierney could enjoy his misery alone.

It's best that way. He never failed at meeting his own expectations, as long as he kept them low enough.

Dalton wasn't surprised when Tierney never called, texted, or dropped by the office, but he had a large stake in being annoyed. Mostly with himself, as the memory of what had gone down Thursday insisted on replaying in his head over and over.

I shouldn't have stayed.

Except he'd felt too guilty not to stay. Besides, he'd said he would. A half hour after Tierney had told him to go, Dalton had tiptoed down the hall to peek into the man's bedroom, wondering if maybe he really *should* leave. Then he'd seen the empty bottle of bourbon on the nightstand. Earlier, when Tierney had left the living room, it had been half-full.

Dalton didn't know what Tierney's tolerance was, but if *he* drank that much bourbon at once, he'd be worried about alcohol poisoning. Sleeping next to the man had seemed like the safest thing to do at the time.

By Sunday afternoon, on his way to meet Sam for lunch, it seemed like the stupidest thing to do. Sleeping next to someone always created intimacy. Dalton shook his head, disrupting that mental train and turning onto Simpson Avenue, slowing enough to look for a parking spot. Why had he thought driving would distract him from overanalyzing the situation?

If he could, he'd go back and not drink the bourbon at Tierney's place. Do everything right up until that point, but after that, he'd change things. Because he'd taken advantage of a guy he knew had issues, led him on, when he had no intention of following through beyond that blowjob.

Did he?

Did it matter? *Tierney's in love with Ian.*

Plus Dalton had sworn off needy, closeted men. Not just for his own benefit, but theirs too. Someone like him wasn't good for guys like that. His attraction to those types of men *could* be blamed on his parents' rejection, but Dalton had a suspicion there was more to it, something more basic in his makeup that made damaged men seem desirable. Something that made *him* a little bit damaged. And how could two damaged men equal one healthy relationship?

Finding a spot, he turned on his blinker and started backing in, which was the opportunity his punitive self had been waiting for. *I wanted him to choke on it.* How nice of that thought to come along and torment him again. As if he hadn't beaten himself up enough over making Tierney gag on his dick?

Maybe it would be easier if he didn't know why he'd had that urge, but Dalton totally knew where it had come from. It was the part of him that was frustrated with Tierney but that instinctively liked him in spite of all the drawbacks. That part of him wanted the man to live the way he truly could. That part of him wanted things to be different, so he could see what might unfold between them.

But he couldn't make Tierney show his real self to the world, and he couldn't be with Tierney the way he was. Friendship was the most he could hope for at the moment.

Sigh. He had to have this worked out before he saw Tierney again, at Ian's meeting on Tuesday. By then, maybe he could convince himself to let the man live his life as he saw fit, rather than trying to shove his own standards down the guy's throat.

While his thoughts were consumed by Tierney, he'd resolved not to discuss what had happened with Sam. Instead, after meeting his friend, sitting down at their table, and ordering, he outdid himself dredging up other topics.

"You're moving into your own place?" Sam asked after Dalton had offered up his first conversational gambit. He seemed surprised, but he only pointed his fry at Dalton for a second before turning it toward his mouth and taking a bite. So only mild surprise. Dalton was becoming fluent in Sam's use of food as a sort of body language enhancer. French fries were the most common aid, probably because he could just pick up a new one when he finished off its predecessor.

Dalton swallowed his mouthful of chicken Caesar salad. "I found a great place last week near work, and they let me know yesterday that I could have it."

"I have a place to myself," Sam said. "I was in a huge house with a bunch of roommates and I was so sick of them. They didn't really miss me when I left, I don't think." He shrugged and smiled. "But I pretty much live alone in name only now."

Dalton had to be imagining that Sam was drawing hearts in his pool of ketchup. "Same situation for me. Huge house and my roommates won't miss me either." All four of them were guys he was social with, but he wouldn't say they were close friends, except Vance. Really, their only unifying factor was that they were all gay.

"So why's this place you found so perfect?" Sam asked, waving a french fry in the air.

"It's got huge windows," Dalton began. "On an upper story, the fourth, so the view is good. I mean, it's just of the street and some of the skyline, but it's not a parking lot or a cinderblock wall. The neighborhood isn't *great*, but it's becoming gentrified."

"Revitalized," Sam corrected with the blessing of his burger.

Dalton nodded. "The owners just restored the building and put in wood floors—straight-grain fir, so it hints at being Danish modern. Plus the walls are smooth finish and white. Do you know how hard it is to get a contractor to do that? The orange-peel texture is so much quicker to apply, but flat-out fugly."

Sam's brow was a bunch of wrinkles. "Orange-peel? Like, the plaster?"

Okay, he'd totally let himself get carried away. "Yes, that." He focused on his salad, chasing down a piece of chicken that tried to hide under a lettuce leaf.

"So, when do you move? Oh!" Sam leaned forward, face lit up. "Let's borrow my boyfriend's truck."

"At the beginning of the month. You're helping me move?"

"Is that all right?"

"Well, *yeah*." He didn't want to move on his own if he didn't have to. He'd figured Vance would help if asked, but otherwise he'd be calling his brothers, which he'd rather avoid. His siblings were so overprotective, and he didn't want to hear the crime statistics in his new neighborhood as casual conversation, or Andrea telling him what to put where. The problem with family was that they had an unshakable belief that their opinions were not only welcome, but correct.

So he and Sam made moving plans, and ate, and then out of the blue Sam said, "Two of the bashers made bail."

Dalton's fork halted halfway to his mouth. He stared at it a half second before turning his gaze on his friend. He'd been hoping *none* of the assailants would make bail. It had been set very high due to mandatory sentencing laws, but apparently not high enough.

"I can't believe they came up with that kind of cash," Sam said. "Two hundred fifty thousand?"

"Whoever bailed them out only has to come up with ten percent." He set his salad-laden fork down on his plate, suddenly uninterested in eating.

"Oh, yeah." Sam looked at his food, playing with french fries and ketchup, throwing on some salt. "Nik—my Indian friend?—he said those two are grass-seed farmers' sons, so they have a lot of money. Anyway, I guess one of the guys that got out is the one that had the baseball bat."

Well, just knock the wind out of him. Dalton stared across the table, nails biting into his palm.

Sam heaved a sigh. "And I testified at the grand jury the week before last."

Not *worse* news, at least. "Really?" He hadn't had to testify, since Sam's account would be more or less the same and could easily sway the grand jury into sending the case to trial. But why hadn't Sam mentioned testifying last weekend? *Probably still traumatized.* He shifted, realigning suddenly itchy shoulders.

Sam nodded and took a huge bite of his burger, killing all follow-up conversation for a minute. Did that mean he didn't want Dalton to ask? But he'd brought it up . . . "How was it?"

Sam chewed faster, head tilting back and forth with the motions of his jaws, before gulping down his food. "It was horrible."

Definitely why he hadn't mentioned it before. "You didn't see any of *them*, right?" Dalton's knowledge of pretrial processes was a little hazy, but he was sure his brother Luke said they wouldn't have to see any of those guys before trial. If there *was* a trial—if all the bashers plea-bargained, there wouldn't be.

Sam shook his head, hair swinging with the motion. "The judge said they can't go near me or Miller or the witnesses as, like, a condition of their bail. Ian couldn't come in with me, but he waited outside. He's being *really* protective."

Totally understandable. Dalton nodded.

"One of those guys?" Sam continued, leaning forward intently. "Is the son of a *county sheriff*. Some guy Ian knows—so do Jurgen and Nik—and he's pissed about that."

"Oh my God." Dalton knew there were "bad" cops out there, but still. "Who?"

Sam scrunched up his face into a worried frown. "Honestly? I didn't ask. I just couldn't. All Ian said was that the guy's father, the sheriff, refuses to bail his son out of jail." Slowly, he eased back, until he was slouching into his chair, hunched toward his food and playing idly with fries in ketchup again. "I don't like to, you know, dwell too much on it."

Dalton didn't ask any more, because if the defendants *did* go to trial, he'd have his own experiences to dwell on. Not to mention witnessing the crime in the first place. He pretended to eat while trying to think of something to say that wasn't either awkward or just *ugly*.

The conversation got back on track when he dredged up one of his planned diversions: stories about his cat, a seriously grumpy orange tabby named Blue. People could garner thousands of hits a second on the internet from showing pictures of their cats, so he should be able to distract one guy with the tale of how his cat had gotten his name.

"After getting him from the kid at the grocery store," he said, feeding Sam's avid interest, "I took him to a vet, and when the receptionist asked what his name was I just . . ." Smiling, he shook his head, still a little appalled at how—and what—he'd named Blue.

"What?" Sam was nearly leaning into Dalton's food.

"I don't know *why*, but I told her, 'His name is Blue Balls.'"

The distraction was successful, even if it meant seeing a few mouthfuls of chewed-up potato as Sam laughed himself into tears.

Chapter 8

In the weeks following the old guy's death, hangover had become its own entity, but unlike the inmates, Tierney didn't detest and try to hide—or hide *from*—it. Sure, it made it physically harder to get through the day, but it also reprioritized feelings and actions and rendered other people's opinions as inconsequential. It focused Tierney on the immediate necessities of staying awake, successfully following conversations, and not puking. A state of emotional subsistence. Hangover muffled all of life's sharp edges in bubble wrap and cushioned him from the real world. That place where he longed for someone to lean on.

Like Dalton. He'd nearly texted the guy about ten thousand times in the last four days, but why? To rehash that colossal fucking disaster they'd shared?

He didn't have time to figure it out, and he'd be damned if he let the uncertainty stop him from doing his job.

So, on Tuesday morning when the snooze alarm went off for a third time, instead of slapping it into silence again, Tierney gave in to the necessity of getting out of bed. Seven was a brutal start time for a meeting, but that's what happened when all the big chiefs decided they needed to attend. He turned on the lamp, which set off the headache he'd been expecting.

Sweet. There was the hangover, right on time. *This is going to suck.*

He felt better after brushing his teeth and showering. Still insulated from life but totally capable of doing his job; glad-handing and cutting deals and manipulating people. He could do this, and he'd be well fucking dressed too.

He hadn't looked at his new Tom Ford suits since he picked up the two—uh, three—he'd bought a few weeks ago, but one of them had to be the right thing for this meeting. After dropping what these babies cost, they'd better all but read "power suit" on the breast.

Checking them out, he found the perfect one: Subtly outrageous, in a muted gray-and-brown plaid. It made a total "don't fuck with me, I'm a wild card" statement, but only when the enemy got close. He definitely wasn't dressing for Dalton, no matter how the cut of the jacket hid his growing gut—man, he needed to find time to go to the gym again.

Some eye drops for the redness, some ginger ale for the nausea, some ibuprofen and coffee for his head, and he was good. A drink would be nice, but Tierney hung on to that last bit of control over alcohol by his proverbial fingernails. He wasn't going to be the kind of guy who took a drink when he got up, no matter how much the hair of the dog would help.

He wasn't greeting Dalton with alcohol on his breath first thing in the morning.

Maybe he could pretend he didn't remember Dalton's name? *Nah, that's seriously pushing it.*

When he got to the Interagency Disaster Blah-blah-blah office, he took a few seconds outside the frosted-glass door, closed his eyes, and tried to wipe all expression from his face. Prepare himself. "Gotta do it, man," he murmured. *Deep breath in, deep breath out, turn the knob, walk in—*

Dalton's chair was empty.

"Oh hey, dude, you're here already?"

Tierney turned toward Ian's voice to see the man himself poking his head out of an open doorway. "Uh, hey. It's—" he checked his watch "—6:50. I'm early." Christ, how had he managed that?

"Hang on a minute, I gotta start the coffee." Ian disappeared. "I think Dalton got us set up with donuts or something. Can you look in the conference room? Should be open."

He was physically weak with relief, but disappointment still staged a sit-in in his chest, weighing him down. Of course Dalton wasn't here. He didn't start work until later. *Maybe I'll get to see him then.* Not speak to him, just look at him. He might appreciate this suit.

Get a grip, dude. Yeah, right. Okay, donuts. Where were they?

"You can't *do* that," Tierney said to the Marlyle County sheriff. This meeting had spiraled way out of control, but they often did when the top brass were involved.

Sheriff Fowler smiled, but Tierney could see a muscle in his jaw ticking and spite in his eye. "Now, I thought this meeting was to determine just what it is that's *needed* to comply with the new federal requirements."

"It is," Ian said firmly, slicing through some of the tension. "And no one is saying that Marlyle County will get an unfair percentage of the funds—"

Tierney bared his teeth at Sheriff Good Ol' Boy.

"—Today's agenda is simply for you all to give me *realistic* estimates of what you need to meet the new federal standards."

"And new countywide radio equipment isn't realistic, it's *greedy*," Tierney snapped.

"This is what we'd like in a perfect world," the Marlyle County fire chief interjected. He pointed at Tierney. "Didn't you say you needed Cyanokits for every one of your employees? You know damn well that's gonna be a fortune, and you'd have yearly replacement costs."

"I think it's time to take a break," Ian said. He sounded like he was talking through gritted teeth. Or to toddlers. Tierney's nieces were only a couple of years out of that stage, so he was familiar with the tone. He shoved his chair back and stood up, hearing it hit the wall behind him. Ian caught his eye, glowering, but Tierney stalked out of the room and right through the empty reception area into the hall. He didn't know where he was going, but he ended up in a deserted bathroom a floor above the conference, pissing for lack of anything else to do. Turned out he had to anyway.

It shouldn't have surprised him this meeting had gone to shit. Too many big egos in the room, too much money at stake. He'd known it would be tense, but he'd expected a little more help from Ian. The dude was being all moderate and neutral, though.

Someone walked into the men's room behind him, and Tierney put his head down farther, like he needed to inspect his urine for blood or foreign objects. The last thing he wanted was conversation. With his luck it would be Sheriff Fowler.

He'd done a lot of things in men's rooms, but he'd never punched someone. He was up to the job, though.

"What the fuck is *wrong* with you?" Ian asked, unzipping at the urinal next to him.

Christ. Still, his friend was better than Sheriff Redneck. "What?" That dumb act wouldn't fly, but it might buy him time.

"You fucking know what," Ian said. "You know damn well Marlyle County won't get that much money, so why get all worked up about it? Let's just get through this meeting."

Why was everyone picking on him lately? Tierney was done, so he closed up and headed for the sink. Best thing he could do was ignore Ian's question and the way that blood vessel in his neck had started fluttering. His own private high-pressure gauge.

His refusing to argue didn't stop the dude. "It's bad enough I have to deal with Fowler's homophobic digs and just fucking *knowing* who the man is and who he's related to," Ian continued, following Tierney. "But then I have to keep you from careening around the room like a loose cannon? C'mon man, help me out." He yanked on the faucet handle, turning the water on full blast and frowning down at his hands.

Tierney shut his water off and rounded on him, pulse starting to beat in his ears. "By what? Keeping my mouth shut? Are you saying I shouldn't do my job? Not represent my company and their interests?"

Ian snorted. "No." He didn't look at Tierney, reaching for paper towels instead. "I'm saying you *used* to think your job was to be reasonable and ignore how these fuckers posture and piss on stuff. You know none of that shit will do them any good in the end, not in this case."

Tierney walked over to Ian and ripped out his own paper towels, bunching them and twisting them in his hands, then slamming the ball into the garbage. What the hell was this douche bag doing, telling him how to do his job? "Sometimes my job is to piss on stuff too." Anger banged away under his ribs, knocking to get out.

Ian huffed at him, narrowed his eyes, and met Tierney's stare. "You know I'm not going to recommend their stupid radio system."

Tierney's hands clenched, but he forced his fists to stay at his sides, even though his heartbeat urged him to defend. Get physical. "So I can count on you to make sure Metropolitan will get everything it needs?"

Ian's nostrils flared, and his voice got lower and rougher. "You can count on me to recommend you get what's fair, and the best deal for *everyone*."

"Yeah?" The pounding filled his skull now, goading Tierney to get right up in Ian's face. "Not good enough. I'm here to get everything we can, fuck what's fair for everyone else."

Ian stepped away, shaking his head and leaving Tierney suddenly confused. Wait, weren't they about to throw down?

"T, what the fuck, dude? You know how this shit works, why are you acting like this? I'm not your enemy, and you know goddamn well I'm not going to pass you deals under the table because we're friends."

"Well, I guess I need a better class of friend."

Ian's eyes widened, then his face went blank. Emotionless. "What you need is some class," he said before walking out of the restroom.

Tierney stayed put another minute, heart slowing down. His muscles were shaky, and he felt dizzy. *Man up*. He needed to get back in there, fight the good fight, since he couldn't count on Ian.

Why is everyone always abandoning me?

Tierney bitch-slapped insecurity. Whiny, teenage emotion. One he didn't need right now, as it slowly dawned on him that he might have just done the unthinkable—let himself step over that line he barely maintained with Ian. The point of no return, where he'd pushed the guy too far, and would lose him forever.

Slamming out the door into the hall, he left that thought behind. It was the only way he'd survive this fucking day, to keep going and not think about consequences or ramifications. Thank fuck the pounding in his eardrums was so distracting.

He made his way back to the meeting, taking the stairs to the right floor—the elevator arrived, but it was too closed in. Everything seemed too small. The hall to the office was too narrow, but also too long, and the door into the reception area was too tight. He'd never fit through. *Gotta do it, man.* Just like earlier.

He turned the knob, took a deep breath, walked in—and there was Dalton, front and center. Piercingly blond head bent over something on his desk. He glanced up when Tierney choked on air, and the meeting of their eyes pinned them in place, both of them still, like they could make everything stop if they just didn't move. Then Tierney wouldn't have to find out what happened next, would he? He could just freeze here and this would be the end. No more of this bizarre life he'd chosen to live.

I want that.

But Dalton stood up, and time started moving again. He didn't let Tierney look away as he walked around his desk and came over, keeping their gazes locked until he was right in front of him, close enough to ask quietly, "Are you all right?"

Tierney swallowed. "Of course I'm all right."

"You look . . . pale. And sweaty." He leaned even nearer. "And Ian's angry."

The heart drum started up again in his ears. "Christ, just stop," Tierney whispered around gritted teeth.

Dalton frowned.

"I have this very important meeting to get through, and you're going to do it again, aren't you? Try to *help* me. Is it the same kind of help you gave me last time? Because I think it would pretty much out me if you sucked my dick right here."

Dalton flipped back his bangs, mouth settling into a hard line. "I can promise you, I won't offer you help anymore." He turned and stalked off.

Tierney wanted to puke, because he'd fucking done it *again*. "I'm sorry," he blurted. "I didn't mean—"

"Tierney." Andrea, Ian's assistant director, poked her head out of the meeting room, face carefully neutral. She knew Ian was pissed, didn't she? She was probably gloating inside. "Recess is over and we're all waiting for you."

That man had a lot of nerve.

Dalton sat at his desk after Tierney walked by—whispering "I didn't mean it" as he passed—peering intently at (but not seeing) the report he'd been working on. A little shaky, a little disoriented, and very annoyed.

When Tierney had appeared in the doorway disheveled and pale, that insidious ache had started in Dalton's heart. Then the man had opened his mouth and twisted Dalton all up inside.

Seriously, you need to give up on him. For both their sakes.

Ian had. Dalton could tell when his boss came back in to the meeting. Ian's jaw had been set, and he'd nodded stiffly as he stopped at Dalton's desk to say, "If T isn't here in two minutes, we're starting without him." Totally unnecessary to say that, but Dalton got the message.

So. That's that. He mentally dusted Tierney from his hands and focused on the report under his nose.

What was he doing again? Reading it or writing it?

And where was that yelling coming from?

The conference room. Dalton didn't need to tiptoe up and put his ear to the door to know it was Tierney's voice. He did, of course, because he couldn't make out what was being said otherwise.

"—trying to suck money out of the grant to benefit your county in ways that have nothing to do with these requirements, and I'm not going to stand for any more of your unethical *bullshit*!"

Slam! Something hit a surface. A chair? A fist?

"What did you call me, boy?" That *had* to be one of the rural chiefs. His voice was strong, but not quite yelling. "I think you better take that back before you regret it. We all know the Marlyle County contract is up for bid next y—"

"That's what I'm talkin' about!" Tierney was nearly screaming "Bring it on, you overfed, undereducated motherfucker—"

Cringe. Okay, seriously, that was way over the top.

"—Keep threatening me! Prove to everyone how *im*moral your fiber is."

Tierney was *losing* it. Dalton grasped the door handle, uncertain, fingers twitching. Waiting for Ian to save the day.

"*Listen* you half-baked, fancy-pants dog turd—" Dalton could picture the other poking at Tierney's chest. "You better shut the fuck up now, or it's not just you that's gonna regret it."

Oh God, Tierney *laughed*. "I hear you loud and clear, Fowler"—*Marlyle County sheriff* Dalton's office specialist brain supplied—"you're saying if I don't back down you'll run to that pretty little county commissioner you're doing and tell her not to give Metropolitan the area service agreement, aren't you? That's all kinds of unethical, *dude*, and everyone in the room knows it. How about I make it easy on you? Tell your girlfriend that we don't need her lame-assed county contract."

Dalton didn't think any more, he opened the door and stepped into the frozen silence. Everyone in the room was gaping, or blanching, or trying to hide horrified amusement, but they were all focusing on the two men in the center, both out of their seats, hands planted on the table, staring each other down. The sheriff was mottled with rage and breathing heavily, but Tierney? The idiot was *smiling*.

"I don't know what you're talking about," the sheriff snarled.

Tierney laughed shortly, right in the man's face. "What, Fowler, you didn't think anyone knew you had a thing going with her? The only person in the state who *doesn't* know is your wife."

Someone gasped. Someone else choked off laughter. Out of the corner of his eye, Dalton caught the person closest to him surreptitiously lifting their smartphone—that evil hospital administrator.

He stepped forward, bumping into the back of Aspell's chair hard enough to jar him and his infernal upload-directly-to-the-internet device, announcing loudly, "Mr. Terrebonne, you have an urgent phone call."

No one commented on the fact that Tierney carried a cell phone, or that Dalton could have used the intercom. No one commented on *anything*. The only sound in the room was the sheriff's enraged mouth breathing.

Neither of the opponents moved. If they got any closer, their noses would touch. Tierney's vicious smirk grew, and before Dalton could interrupt again, he said softly, right in the sheriff's face,

"Thinking about hitting me, Fowler? 'Cause you're a bully aren't you, just like your son—"

"Tierney," Dalton snapped. He put everything into his tone. All his concern and that part of him that liked the hidden man, and the piece of his heart that ached for Tierney's pain, even if it *was* his own fault, and even the shock over realizing right then that *this* was the sheriff whose son had taken part in the bashing.

Later. Deal with this *now.*

After a few tense seconds, Tierney exhaled heavily through his nose, shoved his chair back, and stalked out. Dalton smiled professionally to the room in general, catching Ian's stunned eye for a second, then left, shutting the door behind him.

Tierney stood next to Dalton's desk, hands on hips, head hanging down, lungs working overtime. Like he was trying to regain control.

"Right this way," Dalton said. He led Tierney to the vacant office in the back that they used as a storage room. When he opened the door, Tierney marched past him, into the middle of the stacks of boxes, halting next to a forlorn, empty desk. There was no phone on it, but Tierney didn't seem to notice. He stood rigid, back to Dalton.

"Which line is it?"

"There's no call," Dalton said.

Tierney spun around, snarling, and stormed Dalton, grabbing the door from his grasp and then slamming it in Dalton's face.

He should have expected that. He'd committed the ultimate sin *again*, hadn't he? Helped Tierney. Dalton closed his eyes and leaned his forehead against the wood. Gathering strength to walk back to his desk and sit down, hide the shaking of his fingers, and prepare himself: for the people about to leave that meeting, especially Fowler, and for more of Tierney's irrational anger, followed by Tierney's regret.

How much more of this are you going to take from him?

Not much, I swear. That was the last time I'll offer him a hand.

Dalton was a good little office worker, so he returned to his station, woke up his computer, and opened a document. Something random he could fake being engrossed in if anyone came by.

"Thank you."

He jerked his head up to see Tierney in front of him. His hair stood up on end in places, and his face was gray and slack. He'd been messing with his suit, pulling on the tie and generally disheveling himself. All the physical manifestations of massive internal conflict.

It made that thing in Dalton's chest ache like crazy, beating against his breastbone, wanting to get out and touch Tierney. Soothe him. Fuck, that was annoying. Did Tierney feel *anything* like that for him? Probably not.

"I owe you so much," Tierney rasped. "I don't know why . . ." He shook his head helplessly.

Dalton couldn't speak. He hadn't prepared himself for this sweet, grateful guy who couldn't understand why anyone would go out on a limb for him.

Tierney's voice dropped so low Dalton didn't know which one of them he was talking to. "I'm such an asshole."

Before Dalton could respond, the conference room door opened, and Tierney flinched. Andrea and Chief Brown walked out, chatting with each other until they noticed who stood there. They both shut up and gawked, while Tierney changed right before Dalton's eyes. Shoved his hands into his pockets and slouched, showing his normal sullen expression.

Dalton braced himself for Tierney's inevitable slam or deliberately careless insult. His grand "fuck you all" exit. But when Tierney finally opened his mouth, he only said, "I'll see you around." Then he turned and walked quickly out of the office, head down and shouldering the door open.

Dalton spent the rest of the day with a leaden lump of "Will he recover from this?" sitting in his stomach. He couldn't eat, and he couldn't concentrate on much, but it didn't really matter, because no one expected anything from him, work-wise. At lunchtime, Ian—whose shock over the meeting had manifested as a foul mood—walked out of his office and said, "I'm going home and I'm not coming back until tomorrow."

"Ian," he blurted. The other thing that had been eating at him since the meeting forced him to ask, "Sheriff Fowler, his son is the one who . . .?"

"Yeah." Ian nodded, a muscle in his jaw tensing up and nostrils flaring. He gripped the handle of his briefcase tighter.

"How can you even be in the same *room* with him?" Dalton couldn't force his voice much above a whisper. A tight ball of fear in his chest choked him.

"It helps that Fowler is letting his son rot in jail until the trial." Ian ran his hand through his hair. "He called me up, just after it happened. Apologized and said he'd make sure 'his boy' got what was coming to him, but . . ."

"You don't believe him?"

Ian snorted. "He's a known homophobe. But I gotta give him the benefit of the doubt and do my job."

What was there to say? Dalton just nodded.

Ian sighed. "I'm outta here."

"Have a goo—" Seriously? *No one* was going to have a good day after this morning.

Ian gave him a tight grin, a shared moment of gallows humor. Pushing out the door, he waved over his shoulder.

After Ian left, Dalton didn't even *try* to work. If he were the boss, he'd go home too.

He came back to reality a while later when a giant basket full of fruit walked into the office, spikes of crowning pineapple glory barely clearing the door. As far as distractions went, Carmen Miranda's headdress on legs was an excellent one.

A voice reached him from behind the arrangement. "I'm looking for Dalton Leonard."

"Well, you've found Dalton *Lehnart*." People were always mispronouncing his last name.

The basket jogged up and down in a shrug. "Close enough for me, dude." The legs zigzagged toward Dalton's desk and set the basket down with a soft grunt. Then a dark-haired, bearded man straightened up from behind it. "Delivery," he added.

Smiling as much as he could manage, Dalton tried to come up with something polite to say. "I'd sort of figured that out."

The delivery man grinned at him. "Yeah, my wife says I have a real knack for stating the obvious."

Whatever. He'd already depleted his casual chitchat reserves. "Do I need to sign for this?"

But the man had already turned and headed for the door. "Nah," he called. He was hidden from sight by the giant arrangement before he'd left the entryway.

Dalton stared at it. *For me?* Who'd send him fruit? Or anything? He hadn't had a love interest in ages.

Tier—

Oh, please. If nothing else, could the man have moved this fast? And didn't he have more important things to think about?

But still . . .

He stood, his chair flying back on its wheels, and snatched the card out of the center. *Dalton Lehnart*—spelled correctly—was scrawled on the front, but he didn't recognize the handwriting. Even so, his heart floated upward a little while his fingers opened the card to reveal two words: *I'm sorry.*

No signature.

Tierney. Could it really be? It just seemed so unlike him, and so *soon.*

But who else had done him wrong recently? And as for his more distant past . . . His next breath tangled in his throat, but he forced his body to behave. Function properly. *Never.* His parents simply wouldn't apologize, and for his own sanity, Dalton had to remember that. He'd spent years in therapy learning to accept it.

His heart settled back into reality. So, he knew as much as he had before he opened the card.

Which left him with one option. He called the fruit basket company—the number was printed on the back of the envelope. "I received an arrangement today, but the card wasn't signed. I just wanted to make sure it wasn't a mistake." Although how many Dalton Lehnarts could there be in the city?

"Can you give me your name?" asked the woman who'd answered. After telling it to her, the sound of a clacking keyboard drifted over the line, then she continued, "At the Interagency Disaster Relief Coordination Department?"

"That's me." He tapped the card against his lip. "Um, can you tell me who it's from?"

"Just a moment, please." She put him on hold, but only for a few seconds. "No, I'm sorry, the purchaser specified he wished to remain anonymous."

He. So it could have been Tierney?

"Can I help you with anything else, sir?"

"Oh, no. Thank you," Dalton assured her, but immediately contradicted himself. "Wait, can you tell me what time the order was placed?"

"Just around 9 a.m.," she responded.

Probably not Tierney then. He'd been in the meeting, and Dalton was nearly certain they hadn't taken a recess that early. They'd all come back from a break just after he had, a little after ten.

He thanked her again and hung up. Preoccupied with trying to puzzle things out, he nearly dropped onto the floor when his chair wasn't quite where his butt expected it to be. He got it all sorted, though—arranged himself at his workstation, staring at his computer, hands gripped tightly on his desk.

For a second he thought about calling Peter or Luke and asking them to investigate, but that couldn't be ethical. Or necessary. He'd have to figure it out on his own.

What if it was Tierney apologizing for the blowjob and not for today? Dalton dismissed that idea, more because he didn't like it than for any other reason. As a matter of fact, as he studied the fruit basket, he didn't like it much, either. It looked somehow wrong. Ostentatious. Insincere.

He tossed the card back into the pile of fruit, where it landed on top of an orange before sliding down the peel to rest precariously between a kiwi and a banana. *It's just a basket of fruit.* That he didn't want to eat. Or even look at anymore. Who knew *who* it could be from? Maybe one of his exes was currently between boys and hoping Dalton would be his stopgap. *Forget this*. He'd put it in the break room. The others would eat it, but he wouldn't touch it again. Wouldn't sully his hands.

It was much heavier than he'd expected, and huge, so as he carried it in, he didn't take the time to make sure the room was vacant. "What's that?" Andy's voice asked from the direction of the table.

Lovely. Dalton heaved the monstrosity onto the counter and turned to her. She sat there with yogurt in one hand and a spoon in the other, perky and wide-eyed. "It's a fruit basket." He might have sounded a bit too much like her little brother.

She tilted her head. "I can see that, but where did it come from?"

He tried to lift a single brow. "If you wanted to know where it came from, why didn't you ask me that first?"

"I will *never* be too old to sit on you and pull your hair." She licked her spoon clean, pretending to ignore him.

"Someone sent it to me." *And I don't want to talk about it.*

"Who?"

"Are you certain that's the question you want to ask?"

She got up and walked over to stand in front of him, eyeing him unblinkingly.

Sigh. "I don't know."

"There wasn't a card?"

He gave up his attitude. "There is, but it's not signed and it just says, 'I'm sorry.'" Maybe she'd have some idea who it could be from.

But she only wrinkled her nose, probably just the way he was doing right now. They shared the same confused expression. DNA was so random.

"I called the company that delivered it, and it wasn't a mistake. Someone bought it for me, but insisted on being anonymous."

"Huh." She shrugged and headed back to sit down again. "Maybe you have a secret admirer."

"For a second—" *more than a second* "—I thought maybe Tierney had sent it." Judging from the way Andy whipped her head around and stared at him—mouth and eyes wide open—he probably shouldn't have volunteered that. *Duh.*

"Why would Tierney send *you* an apology basket?" she demanded.

Dalton shrugged and turned away, pretending to straighten the arrangement. Fluff the fruit. "Well, he was kind of rude to me this morning."

"Yeah, but it's Tierney. Does he even know who you *are*?"

Now it was his turn to whip his head around. "That's insulting."

"It's no reflection on you," she said, flapping her hand as if dispelling a bad smell. "It's a reflection on that douche bag."

"He's not a douche bag," he shot back before he thought better of it. "Not all the time."

"*What*?" She gaped at him. "He's a freaking homophobe."

He really needed to shut up, so he pretended his jaw was wired shut and made a face instead. The whole conversation had made her suspicious—he could see it in the way her eyes narrowed and she lowered her chin.

Time for his exit. Past experience told him just knowing Andy was stewing for the rest of the day, uncertain about whether she'd truly won an argument or not, would give him the most satisfaction. So Dalton smiled pleasantly and left the room.

Chapter 9

Tierney went home instead of to work after his meeting disaster. He cracked open a bottle of booze, then called Gina to tell her she'd have to handle everything for the rest of the week.

"At least that long," he added after thinking a second.

"What?" she half shrieked. "You have, like, five appointments *tomorrow*, and th—"

"Yeah, I need a mental health break." He felt strangely uninterested in how she interpreted that. It could be the three shots he'd had already, or it could be the fact that the inmates had pretty much taken control. Another thing he was uninterested in figuring out.

"*What*?" Wow, the girl could really pierce an eardrum, couldn't she? He'd never noticed that before.

"The meeting this morning didn't go well," Tierney said in lieu of explanation.

Gina groaned. "Tierney, what did you *do*?"

"Oh, honey, I—"

"I've asked you not to call me that."

"—totally screwed the pooch on this one. Fucked it right up the ass."

"Seriously, *boss*, some people would sue you for harassment for language like that."

Whatever. He knew she didn't really care, otherwise she wouldn't still be working with him after almost two years. "Check Edward Asshole's Facebook page. I'm pretty sure he filmed it. If it's not there, I bet he has a YouTube account." Tierney scooted his butt forward on the couch, reaching for the bottle of bourbon and his remote. Time for a little Captain Kirk and some more Jim Beam. The two Jameses.

Gina made a noise like she was drowning. "What am I going to tell your brother?" she whispered frantically. He could hear the clicking of her keyboard. Then she gasped. Aspell must have posted it.

Faintly, Tierney could hear his voice yelling, "—pretty little county commissioner you're doing—" then just noise.

"Oh noooo," Gina wailed. "Oh my *gawd*!"

"Just send Chase a link to the video." Tierney waved his hand in the air grandly, flicking an imaginary bombshell email off to his brother. "He'll figure it out on his own."

Gina moaned, and something thunked in his ear. Her forehead on the desk?

Whatever. "I gotta go. Mental health time doesn't start itself, you know."

"Tierney, do *not* hang up, we need to—"

He hit End, then the power button. Good thing he didn't have a landline, or he'd have to find it and unplug it or take the batteries out or something. He turned around to see the intercom next to his front door. Could he disconnect that? Maybe he'd just cover it up with duct tape. Did he have any duct tape?

If not, could he pay the hardware store to deliver it? And some stuff to board up the windows too. Maybe he could pay Gina to deliver it. *He* couldn't go shopping. Tierney had so utterly fucked himself over it was like declaring war, and the public might just shoot on sight. It was safer here. He needed to barricade himself in, hunker down, and . . . What?

Drink, James said. Kirk or Beam, he didn't know, but it didn't matter. It was an excellent idea.

Shit. He'd need to bribe Gina to bring over more booze too.

It turned out he *did* have a landline. Even worse, someone had the number. After the fifth consecutive phone call—each one lasting seven *looong* rings—he answered it.

"Wha'?"

"What?" Chase yelled. "*What*? I will *tell* you what, you fuckwad!" A long string of semiarticulate cursing followed, but Tierney didn't feel it necessary to pay attention. Besides, the force of Chase's voice made him dizzy. He turned and stumbled back to his couch, holding the phone to his ear.

"If you're jus' calling to be rude, I'll return to my reg'larly scheduled program," he said when Chase paused to gulp some air. Then he hiccuped.

Chase switched to moaning. "Oh my God."

Huh. "Tha's what Gina said."

"You're *drunk*."

Tierney snorted. "Uh, *yeah*. Wouldn' *you* be drunk?"

"If I'd single-handedly destroyed the family business? Probably," Chase muttered. "Thank God Grandfather isn't alive to see this. Jesus. Now you need to fucking sober up and get your ass in here."

Tierney scrunched up his face at the ceiling. "Why woul' I wanna come there?"

"We have to do damage control, you dumbass!"

Tierney waggled his finger in the air while singsonging, "If I wan'ed you to do something for me, I wouldn't call *you* names."

"You aren't just doing this for *me*. Your salary is paid by the ambulance company too."

Tierney smiled. He had an answer for this one. "Yeah, bu' I can live on the trust fund Grandfather left me." The one that couldn't be taken away from him now. "*I* don't have a wife and daughters." And he never would, would he? Which was a little sad, but in this instance he was okay with it.

Chase made a sound like a moose in a noose. *Moose, noose. Hah!*

"Are you *laughing*?" Chase yelled. "I will *give* you something to laugh about when you show up here—"

"Now I'm *def'nitely* not coming." Tierney sniffed for emphasis. Or it might have been more of a snort.

"You know what? Forget it. Don't come in. You'll just make it worse—"

"Prob'ly." Tierney nodded.

"Gina and I will come up with a plan. But dammit, I expect you to be at the wake Saturday, not hiding—that's just admitting wrongdoing. How the fuck do you think that makes the rest of the family look? Or the company? Not everything is about you, you fucker."

Nothing is about me. But more importantly: "Wake? Wha' wake?"

Chase laughed, not like it was funny but as if he was about to enjoy himself very much. "You're a real piece of work, aren't you? It's the grand send-off Mother planned for Grandfather's ashes, if you'll recall. And you're giving the official farewell."

"*OhGodno.*" He'd totally forgotten, in an attempt to forget the bastard all together. Chase was saying something about a Terrebonne family toast, but Tierney was too wrapped up in his own misery to catch it. "Do I *hafta* go to that?"

"Oh yes," the evil bastard agreed. "We have to play close-knit grieving family for a few hundred of the Terrebonne's most valued friends and business associates." Chase dropped his voice, as if imparting a secret. "You might want to shower first."

"I *can't* go, I jus' publicly humiliated myself."

"Which is exactly why you're going, and why you're going to pretend everything's normal, or as close to it as you can manage. You're showing up at the damn thing, and that's final."

"Oh God," Tierney groaned. "I need to stock up on booze."

The Saturday afternoon of Grandfather's big send-off, Tierney was reaching for the bottle of Jim Beam on his coffee table when the doorbell rang. He'd reconnected the thing this morning, in anticipation of the cab driver, but he hadn't called for one yet, had he? He'd been planning on having one more drink, *then* calling for a taxi.

Huh. He shrugged it off and reached for the bottle again, but again the chimes of his doorbell stopped him. Was it the movement of his arm that was somehow making the thing go off? But it sounded again a half minute later, and he hadn't moved a muscle.

Shoving himself off the couch and making his way to the foyer, he turned on the security camera monitor to find Gina about to ring again.

"What are you doing here?" he asked her through the intercom.

"Chase is doubling my Christmas bonus if I make sure you get to the wake." Even if the sound quality had been perfect, there probably wouldn't be a trace of shame in her voice.

"Are you giving me a ride home too?"

She sighed, loud enough to be heard over the static. "I suppose."

He narrowed his eyes at the speaker, not sure he trusted his assistant. She appeared to be working with his hostile allies, and that wasn't part of their treaty as he understood it. "I wanna get out of there as soon as possible."

"Doesn't everyone?" she responded. "Just after the toast, we'll make our excuses, okay?"

Toast. Doom tapped him on shoulder, trying to get his attention, but he couldn't figure out why. *Whatever.* He buzzed Gina into his building, then waited in his doorway until she stepped out of the elevator. "Are you going to give me some kind of list of acceptable behaviors?" Like he cared. Chase was in charge of the rules, so they'd be bullshit, anyway.

Gina shrugged. "Your brother and I felt it was better to impose fewer restrictions on you." She stood in the hallway, expectantly, even after Tierney stepped aside to let her in. "Are you drunk?" she asked matter-of-factly.

Tierney nodded. "'S'only way I'll get through the wake. 'S'how I got through the last four days."

Gina sighed, fisting her hands on her hips. "I'd assumed as much."

He slouched against the jamb. "Yeah, I'm pretty much all about living down to your expectations."

"It's one of your finer talents." She tilted her head, eyeing him critically. She couldn't have any complaints—this was another of his new Tom Ford suits. "Can we go now? Are you ready?"

Tierney spread his arms wide, looking down at himself. "As I'll ever be."

When they arrived at his parents' manse, it became clear Tierney's mother had been pregaming with the booze as well. She met them as they entered the foyer, eyes overly bright and cheeks flushed, wearing a stylishly understated black dress and holding a nearly empty glass of champagne. They'd showed up before any of the guests, of course, because Father insisted on it. He wanted a Terrebonne receiving line in the entryway. This whole shindig was a carefully orchestrated show of familial unity in the face of sorrow, after all.

Mother rose up on her toes to kiss his cheek. "Darling. Your father was worried you wouldn't make it, but I *told* him you'd never miss your favorite grandparent's wake."

Deep down inside him, derision snorted up a storm. "Of course I wouldn't. I don't want to disappoint the family." He couldn't totally squelch the sarcasm in his tone, but she was too drunk to notice.

Mother patted his cheek and smiled over at Gina, clasping Tierney's hand between her own. "And who is this you've brought with you?"

By Tierney's count, this would be the fifth time his mother had met his assistant. He turned to his chaperone and smiled lovingly. "Mother, I'm very excited to introduce you to Gina."

"So wonderful to make your acquaintance." Tierney's mother swamped her, yanking her forward for a hug—probably one of gratitude. Gina shot visual daggers at Tierney until Mother pulled away from her.

"Mrs. Terrebonne," Gina said, somehow making her voice less sharp than normal. Almost polite. "I'm your son's *personal assistant*. I'm only here to—"

"Babysit me," Tierney said, hiking his thumb into his chest like a proud two-year-old.

"Darling!" Mother slapped him playfully on the shoulder. "What have you done *now* that requires you to have a babysitter?"

Father, entering the hall just then, heard her and interrupted before Tierney could think up a good answer. "Ah, here you two are. We're just waiting for Chase and Emily, then we'll have a relaxing drink—"

"Mother and I have already had a few."

"—before the guests begin to arrive." He took his wife's arm and began to lead her away after tipping his chin at them. "Glad to see you've made it, Gina."

Gina smiled and leaned toward Tierney to whisper, "What he means is he's glad to see I made *you* make it."

"Yep. Is it any surprise that I am the way I am?" Tierney asked her. "I'm a product of my environment."

"So's your brother," Gina said, arching her brows. "And he seems to be doing all right."

Tierney stuck out his tongue at her, then hightailed it out of the room and toward the study and his father's well-stocked bar.

Being part of the welcoming committee was excruciating, but it wasn't as bad as it could have been. Everyone who could possibly know about his meeting freak-out—plus the few who'd witnessed it in person—pretended to be ignorant. Still, Tierney had a drink in his hand the whole time as a prophylaxis against any snide looks, and he made a point of standing next to his favorite family member—his sister-in-law, Emily. By the time the torture of the receiving line was over, he was too blotto to notice if anyone was gossiping about him.

Total bonus: Ian didn't show up, at least not before Father declared they'd done enough receiving, and the family moved on to the ballroom—the only room big enough to hold all the mourners his mother had invited. It also had a few nooks and crannies where Tierney could hide.

In spite of any unrequited feelings he'd had for Ian, he hadn't been thinking about the dude the last few days. He hadn't been able to think much at all, and the times he was sober enough to follow the workings of his brain, he'd mostly been concerned about his own survival. Which in turn encouraged him to stay as drunk as possible.

Dalton had floated across his mind many times since the disastrous meeting, though. Stunning Dalton who didn't seem to hate him, even though he should.

But Ian hates me. He had to after the shit Tierney had said in that restroom. If he put all the people he'd pissed off or offended on a balance sheet against all the people who liked him . . . the page would bleed red. He was a social pauper. *Wouldn't Grandfather be so proud?*

He was still grinning evilly over that when Chase's hand landed on his shoulder. Possibly it appeared to be a friendly gesture to people around them, one brother comforting another, but to Tierney's pressure points, it felt more about control. Chase was gripping him tightly enough to cause pinches of pain, sending Tierney a familiar message through some kind of nervous system Morse code: *Don't embarrass the family name.* Terrebonnes *certainly* did not grin at wakes for beloved family members.

Tierney turned to smile brightly into his brother's face.

"Just try and hold it together for another half hour, until after the big toast, then I'll have Gina get your drunk butt out of here," Chase said, smiling at him. Well, it might appear as a smile to anyone watching. To Tierney it looked like a grimace.

That toast thing again. He straightened up, trying to clear his mind enough to remember what it was that he should be worried about.

"I'm ready to go whenever you give me the sign," Gina said, suddenly at his other elbow. How long had she been there? Tierney nearly lost his balance turning to look, but his brother's hand steadied him. He tried to give her some side eye, but he couldn't be sure it hit its mark—she was mostly a blob in a navy suit in his peripheral vision.

"Good," Chase said, nodding at the blob. "I hate this fucking pretense," he added in a mutter.

God, did he ever agree. "Dunno why they can't send out a three-page holiday newsletter like ever'one else and say he kicked it."

Chase squinted at him for a few seconds. "You drink too much," he said, sounding dissatisfied. Not concerned or upset or even angry, just dissatisfied. One more family member who wasn't up to par.

Or at least that was Tierney's read on it. "You golf too much."

"It's not the same thing."

*Whatever, asswip*e. His answer must have been all over his face, because Chase curled his lip and walked off.

"Tierney," Gina sighed. "What are you planning to say?"

"Huh?" He spun around, and she grabbed his forearm to keep him from falling over. "Planning to say for what?"

"For the—"

"May I please have your attention?" Mother's amplified voice boomed out over the room, hushing people up. "As you all know, we're here to mourn the passing of Grandfather Terrebonne, who was felled by a massive heart attack just two weeks ago." She turned her head slightly, as if overcome, and dabbed at her face with a cocktail napkin.

"However, we're also here to celebrate the way Milton Terrebonne lived his life: honestly and courageously."

Courageously? The word hit Tierney like a ton of bricks, and again Gina had to keep him from falling on his ass. Was that really how the old guy lived? Was hiding every aspect of yourself that might be lowbrow or open to criticism courageous? Well, shit, if it was, that made *him* the definition of courageous, didn't it?

But I'm a coward. Tierney blinked, as Mother said something that filtered into his brain. Something about sharing memories. "... like to invite everyone who has a memory or sentiment about Grandfather Terrebonne to come forward and share it."

As Mother kept talking, something inside him insisted he listen. *It's important.* Necessary-to-his-survival kind of important. Something about Grandfather and cowardice. No, courage.

"Afterward, our youngest son, Tierney—" Mother paused to smile at him "—who spent much time with his grandfather during his formative years, will make the official Terrebonne family toast to Milton's passing." She beamed, then leaned forward to whisper—sharing an aside with the whole room. "Tierney's taken his death quite hard."

He couldn't object to the lie, because he was still reeling from the sudden recollection: he was supposed to prepare some kind of speech. *Motherfucker.* A toast to send the old bastard off in the style he was accustomed to or some shit. *Probably shouldn't call him that when I'm talking.*

His mind raced, but everything he dredged up about the old guy was hateful, or mean or just fugly. He couldn't tell everyone that the reason he'd spent so much time with the dick was because Grandfather wanted to suppress any deviant behavior that might rear up. Couldn't share how controlling the old guy was, or how Tierney himself had become the drunk, friendless, abhorrent, disgusting fuckwad he was today under that bastard's guidance.

Could he? "Christ," he muttered.

"I knew it," Gina whispered in his ear, reminding him she was there. "You didn't prepare a toast, did you?"

He glared at her.

She nodded once, compressing her lips. "Just listen to what other people have to say, and rephrase the good shit."

Oh, yeah. That'd work, wouldn't it? "You totally deserve that Christmas bonus," he told her. She smiled but nudged him toward the front of the room.

Listening to people talk about Grandfather didn't help. Brain whirling, he kept hoping they'd throw out something to trigger his own gilded memories of the prick, but all the things the guests said about Grandfather were useless. Maybe he should make up some gilded memories? That might be best, because the pronouncements about what an upstanding citizen the dude was, and how he'd lived by a strict code of ethics made him want to puke. Same with the stories from Tierney's great-aunts about the old guy saving puppies from gunnysacks thrown in rivers as a boy or some shit. *Had to have made* that *up*. Tinkling laughter followed a few of the stories, but Tierney wasn't getting the jokes. He was too full of other emotions to experience humor: anger and head-pounding hatred and confusion.

Gonna be hard to put a good spin on thinking he was a controlling, manipulative bastard. But Tierney could, couldn't he? That was what he *did*—he'd told Dalton that the first time they really spoke. Told him *he* was the manipulator, the glad-hander.

The one who concealed his true self to meet the world's expectations. Courageously, just like the old guy, right?

Suddenly a whole future unfolded in front of Tierney's vision, superimposed on top of this ballroom full of well-dressed and superficial mourners. Some kind of alcohol-fueled nightmare mirage, where he forced himself to marry, have kids, keep up the facade in an effort to enforce a dead man's "strict code of ethics." A world where he became the same kind of douche bag as the old guy, and passed on the pain to future generations.

". . . one of the bravest men I knew," someone said. Was the dude talking about him or Grandfather? Which one of them had died? "Stalwart in his beliefs. He didn't brook cowardice in anyone, and was never shy about calling others out over their own craven behavior."

Mother. Fucker.

Tierney's imagined future popped like a bubble as something came unmoored inside him. Some part of him that knew how to stop that hell from happening and he *had* to. He couldn't live like that. He'd kill himself first.

I don't wanna die.

Things began shifting all around him. The colors went dark, then bright, and shapes changed. A conglomeration of triangles and circles turned out to be a guy standing nearby. Smells got loud and the expressions on people's faces tasted different. All his senses seemed to be realigning themselves.

It was kaleidoscopic. And fucking disorienting. He blinked and then found himself moving toward the front of the ballroom. *Gotta do it. Gotta do it. Gotta do it . . .*

Do what?

He stumbled, catching himself with a hand on a large potted plant.

"Is everything okay, sir?" a passing waitress asked.

"Fine." Tierney took one of the glasses of champagne off her tray. It was necessary . . . but why, again? *'Cause I gotta make a toast.* A semihysterical giggle escaped him, and he slapped a hand over his mouth. *Keep it together. Be coherent.* Just a little while longer, then he could lose it, and no one would give a shit.

And he'd be free. Of that future, and this shell and all the stuff that made his life shit.

Another blink of time and he was nearly there, bumping into people but carefully protecting his champagne. Couldn't let it spill. *Can't lose a drop. Very important.* Not that he could say why.

Because I have to give a toast.

"Here he is, right on time." His mother's voice. She smiled at him, face flushed, beckoning him forward and leaning over to kiss his cheek. "Give your grandfather the farewell he deserves," she whispered in his ear before stepping back to make room for him at the microphone.

"Oh, I will," he promised. Tierney faced the room and the crowd went wonky, like a fish-eye lens. A little claustrophobic. *Have to fix that.* "'Scuse me, can you hold this a sec?" he asked a lady near him, handing her his champagne. Then he took the mic off the stand, shoved it into his suit pocket, and climbed on the table, foot only slipping once before he managed to stand up.

Turning quickly made his world tilt (it had been doing that a lot lately) but it was all right, he caught himself with a step back and a minor pinwheeling of the arms. Over the building murmur of voices someone hissed, "Tierney, what are you *doing*?"

Gina. He ignored her, holding up his hands for silence as he faced the mourners. "Hello there," he said, smiling easily. He felt lighter.

Like he could float on up out of here at any second. As soon as he was done speaking. "My champagne?" He held his hand down and the woman gave him his flute, smiling back at him. Maybe his own was infectious? It *felt* infectious.

Then he caught the hardening of his father's features, and it hit him that some people might be immune to the infection. He fished the microphone out of his pocket with his free hand. "Um, I'll make this short 'n' sweet, how 'bout?"

A rustle from the audience was the only answer. *Am I really doing this?* His throat felt suddenly tight, as if his tie were strangling him. Tierney yanked at it, pulling it down, and as air flowed easier into his chest, so did a sense of *knowing*. Knowing what to do. *Only way.*

"I'd like to share somethin' deeply private with you all," he said, lips grazing the mic like a lover. Sharing intimacies. A few eyebrows quirked and heads tilted. "Show'a hands," he said, gesturing with his glass. "How many people in this room know me person'ly?"

Confused murmurs answered him, but so did a large number of raised hands. Including Ian's arm from where he stood at the back of the room.

He did *show up.*

Wish Dalton could see this. "I wan' you all to know I'm the man I am today because of my grandfather. He knew something about me, a secret—th'one I'm about to tell—and he worked his whole life to squelch it. Keep. Me. *Down.*" His index finger stabbed the air in time with his words.

Shit, Chase and Father were heading toward his impromptu podium, and his mother had clasped her hand over her mouth in horror as the noise of the crowd began to swell. People talking about him. Tierney raised his voice. "Grandfather would've died to keep me from telling y'all this, but he's dead already, so . . ." *Almost there, spit it out.* "I'm gay!"

Something burst in his chest, flooding him. Fear and nerves and joy, making his pulse boom. *Not done yet.* The toast. Mother wanted him to.

He lifted his glass high, as if that could make everyone hear him more clearly, and shouted, "Here's to you, Grandfather. I hope you get the afterlife you deserve, you controlling, manipulative motherfucker!"

The boom the microphone made when he dropped it on the floor wasn't even noticeable over the excited babble in the room. He tilted his head back, ready to pour the whole glass of bubbly down his throat—

And fell off the buffet table, champagne showering him. When he slammed into the floor, the wind was knocked out of him, leaving him gasping. As he flapped his lips, trying to get some air, a drop of the alcohol slithered down the corner of his mouth, the taste hitting his tongue and exploding into flavor, like a revelation of . . . something.

"Are you all right?" someone shouted into his face. Tierney closed one eye to focus on whoever it was. *Gina.* With Father and Chase standing behind her, expressions a mixture of shocked and glowering. He nodded, swallowing the essence of the champagne down. Savoring it as if it was the last he'd ever taste.

"Can you speak?"

He tried, coughing, then breath shuddered into his lungs. "Sorta," he croaked.

"Tierney, are you okay?" a different voice asked. On the opposite side from Gina. He had to stretch his neck around to bring the person into view—*Ian.*

Tierney grabbed his arm, holding it tightly. "'M sorry. For everything." More than he knew.

"It's all right," Ian said, gripping Tierney's hand in something between a handshake and the precursor to a bro-hug.

"I dunno." Tierney shook his head. "I don't know if that was the right thing to do."

"I think it's for the best, man." Ian's eyes flickered up toward Gina, then back to Tierney. "Uh, in the long run."

Tierney nodded at him, but he couldn't really see him anymore. The dude's face was a blur. The room seemed to be spinning. "Now seems like a good time to pass out," he said.

"I agree," Gina piped up.

"If you think so," Ian concurred.

"Yeah, thin' so." At least, he thought he said it aloud.

Chapter 10

Dalton kept expecting to hear from Tierney after that disastrous meeting, but didn't in the week that followed. A few times he wondered if he should check on him, but he couldn't decide. Tierney could be so touchy . . . but on the other hand, Dalton was fairly sure he was the man's only friend.

Ian had been in a horrible mood since the meeting, and because that was due to Tierney, Dalton couldn't ask *him* how Tierney was. Instead, he planned on pumping Sam for information on Sunday, when they met for lunch.

On Saturday, Sam called to confirm, but Dalton got the feeling he wanted to impart some other info. He was right.

"Ian has to go to Milton Terrebonne's wake tonight," Sam said sotto voce. "He's in a really bad mood."

Milton Terrebonne. The grandfather. "Um, has he said anything about Tierney?" For some reason, he kept his voice just as low as his friend's.

"No. Shhhh," Sam whispered. "I'll tell you whatever I find out Sunday at lunch, okay? Same time, same place?"

In the end, Andrea beat Sam to the punch. Sunday morning, while Dalton was still in bed, Andy called to tell him about the wake. Not that she'd seen it—apparently, news of what happened had been making the rounds.

"Jerry Brown said Tierney stood up on the buffet table and announced he was gay to the whole room," she said in a rush.

A high pressure system formed in Dalton's head, sending wind whistling through his ears. "He *outed* himself," he said, like maybe he needed to hear it in his own voice to make sure this wasn't a dream.

"I know," his sister crowed. "I can't believe it either."

Dalton sat up, shoving his covers off his legs and dislodging the cat. Blue yowled at him and leaped to the floor, tail switching as he walked away. "I don't understand why he'd do it."

"Be gay?" Andrea joked. She still thought this was juicy news.

"No, just tell everyone like that. And after the meeting last week . . ." He sat on the edge of the bed. "The man's falling apart." God, should he check on him? It might be worth Tierney's caustic tongue just to make sure he was all right.

"You knew he was gay, didn't you?" his sister asked in a suspicious drawl.

He snorted and chose to walk into the kitchen and turn on the coffee pot instead of answering.

"Why didn't you tell me? You *knew* I'd want to know that. Does Ian know?" Her voice peaked, reaching its fully annoyed wail. "Does *everyone* but me know?"

"And why would you need to know?" Dalton snapped.

"Because—" She sucked in a breath. "Because it's great dirt to have on someone like him," she finished after a second. "Okay, I can understand why you didn't tell me, but seriously, little brother, where do your loyalties lie? I mean, I get that there's some kind of code of honor that prevents you from outing someone in the closet, but every time Tierney's name comes up you all but defend him, and whenever he's around—"

"I like him." Somehow his fist landed on his hip.

Her silence was blissful. For a brief second. "When you say 'like,' how exactly do you mean that?"

"I'm not sure." Part of the truth. She'd consider it a lie of omission that he didn't mention his feelings might lean toward more than friendship.

"Me-*owww*," Blue reminded him, cry echoing down the hall. He'd unsheathe the claws and scratch up Dalton's shoes if he didn't move fast enough. He'd dumped dry food in the cat dish and was spooning out some wet when it hit him that his sister had been silent far too long. The silence continued while he threw the dirty spoon in the sink and began carrying Blue's breakfast toward his room. Had the shock been too much for her system?

"Andy?"

"How could you *possibly* like him?" she choked out.

"When I've spent time alone with him, he's not a dick, that's how."

"You've been spending time *alone* with him?" she shrieked.

Blue patted his leg when he walked into the room, like it was a toy, and Dalton set down the food, then had to put his hand back on his hip. It helped him confront. "Listen, I know he can be a total jerk."

Andrea snorted in agreement.

"But, he's . . ." Dalton rubbed his forehead, thinking. How much could he say? "He's damaged, somehow."

"Oh no," she moaned. "You and damaged men."

"I know, I know." He threw up his palm, as if it would keep her from going on. "But it's not like that."

"It's not like you're repeating your past mistakes?" she snarked.

Dalton flinched, but couldn't back down. "Just because he seems similar to some of my past boyfriends doesn't make him the same kind of person. There's *substance* there, under that facade he shows the world."

"Some men are too fucked up to fix. Remember your last damaged man?" Her voice had gone sympathetic. He hated that from her. It was too close to pity.

"I remember him very well. I'm keeping that in mind, I swear. But, Andy?"

She sighed. "What?"

"Coming out like Tierney did last night? What if that's a sort of cry for help? Or his way of tearing everything down before rebuilding?"

"Dalton," she warned. "Do *not* start reading into it. Jerry said he was so drunk he could barely stand—he probably doesn't even remember doing anything, and when he wakes up this morning, he'll find out what he did and, I don't know, suck on his gun."

"*Andy*!" She may as well have punched him. "Oh my God, I have to go."

"Don't! Shit, I never should have said that. You *cannot* save him, D—"

He hung up on her while yanking on the jeans and shirt he'd worn last night. It took mere seconds to get dressed, but that was too long.

He grabbed his phone from where he'd tossed it onto his bed and ran for the door, snagging his coat at the last second.

Are you all right? He didn't want to mention specifics in his text, because what if Tierney really didn't remember or even know yet what he'd done?

Tierney hadn't responded by the time Dalton was in his car, shoving his key into the ignition. He checked quickly—two minutes since he'd sent the message. That wasn't long, but . . . He started the car.

Consciousness seeped in slowly. Tierney didn't know what he'd been dreaming, but he knew when he began to wake.

He was pretty sure something unpleasant awaited him. Not just a pounding head or the certainty that a big dog (named Hangover) had taken a dump in his mouth while he slept. Something even worse than usual.

When he reached the conscious equivalent of the gray light of dawn, the shock of the memory—of what he'd done last night—knocked the wind out of him as surely as falling off the table at the wake had. *What do people think of me* now? If they thought he was a dick before . . .

The question made him puke. Literally.

After stumbling into the bathroom and throwing up everything he'd eaten in the last month, he pressed his clammy forehead against the seat and rested his pounding head and heart.

Wow, had he burned some bridges or what? But he could never put on that slick persona again, could he? It would be like putting on wet, muddy clothes after taking a shower.

Except . . . He hadn't liked himself, sure, but he *knew* that version of Tierney Terrebonne, sleazeball extraordinaire. Others knew it too, that smarmy, sexhound, blowhard role he'd developed. That's who he *was* to them. Even worse, he didn't have a clue how to not be that guy.

And he was afraid. Terrified. Of what people would say, and of being excluded from the tribe of humanity.

Yet last night . . . *No one can call me a coward now.*

The flare of pride didn't last more than a few seconds. What he'd done was awesome, great, but now he couldn't go back, and he didn't know how the fuck to go forward. Maybe he should have made a fucking plan for what to do next. What kind of man was he supposed to be?

Time. He just needed time to adjust. A few days. Or weeks. He could hole up here. People rarely stopped by without warning. He could tell them he had Ebola and the health division had him quarantined in his home.

Ding-dong.

Oh fuck. Okay, no. No way would he answer that.

Ding-dong.

No matter how persistent the bell ringer might be.

Ding-dong ding-dong ding-dong.

Even if the sound made his head split open. He'd just let it happen, regardless of how painful it was. His head would probably disintegrate from the noise reverberating in his ears, and in a month or two when his family finally came looking for him . . . They would eventually, right? Well, when *someone* came looking for him, they'd find his body here, desiccated brain peeping through his cracked skull, dried blood all over the floor. It wouldn't *technically* be suicide, since he hadn't done it to himself.

He'd just let the sound of the doorbell do the job.

Too bad it had stopped.

Wait, what was *that* sound? *Footsteps*?

"I should have known I'd find you here."

Father. Tierney groaned into the toilet bowl, and it echoed back at him, buffeting his eardrums enough to make him think about puking again. He lifted his head to avoid a repeat. "How did you get in here? And do you really want to be speaking to me?"

"Emily still has the key you gave her so she could look after your fish the last time you went on vacation."

Tierney meant to groan again but he opened his mouth and belched instead, making them both flinch. "So Emily's here too? And Chase, I suppose."

"And your mother," Father added.

Tierney scrunched his eyes even tighter and tried to remember if his mother had ever been to his place before.

Until Father barked at him. "Get off of the damned ground and put something more on. I'll be waiting in the living room for you with the rest of the family."

That made him open his eyes. He swung his head around to look at his father. The man's normally distinguished white hair stood up in places, and the lines bracketing his mouth seemed more obvious than usual.

"What's going on? Why're you all here?"

Father tilted his head and peered (further) down his nose at Tierney. "We're here to perform an intervention."

Tierney should have expected this, shouldn't he? He'd known they'd have to come up with *some* response to him being gay. It was yet another thing he hadn't thought about before he'd opened his mouth.

Like you thought at all, douche bag.

Well, fuck them if they thought they were going to send him to some bullshit ex-gay program. *They can't make me go.*

Staring into his mirror in the bedroom, fists clenched at his sides and chin firmed, he believed in himself. *I did that last night.*

Hopefully he could keep up the self-determination. He nodded to his reflection. Time to go face the family. Just maybe not in nothing but tighty-whities.

He didn't have any pajamas, and when he picked his bathrobe up off the floor, the worn, threadbare thing made him pause for a second. His mother had given it to him when he went off to college, and it showed some serious use. Since no one ever saw him in it, getting a new one had never occurred to him. Unless someone else would see and be impressed by his clothes, he didn't much worry about them, did he?

Weird.

I don't care about appearances. The way his insides flinched made him wonder if that was true. Another thing he didn't know for sure about the new Tierney.

Whatever. His family could face him in this fucking holey robe. He threw the thing on over his briefs and belted it on his way to the living room. It'd have to do for battle armor.

Mother recoiled when he appeared, probably frightened by the state of his undress. Chase and his father nodded curtly. Emily smiled faintly. Everyone seemed full of adverbs this morning. He, for example, was slovenly.

"Morning," he muttered to Mother and Emily, refusing to look at his other family members, standing in front of his floor-to-ceiling windows. He sat down in a chair across from the couch where the women were. As he did, he could've sworn an invisible elephant wearing a *Just Ignore Me* T-shirt tiptoed into the room and settled on that stupid frilly ottoman. "Well, let's get this bullshit underway."

"Tierney!" Mother gasped, as if she'd never heard the word before.

He could feel his lower lip poke out. "It's my intervention, I can curse if I want to."

Emily stood up, smoothing her skirt. "I think I'll find the coffee and open the donuts we brought." She glanced at Tierney.

"It's in the cupboard above the dishwasher, and the coffeemaker is right there on the counter."

She gave him another weak smile before heading toward the kitchen area, leaving awkward silence behind her. At least, it felt awkward to Tierney, but his head still pounded and he couldn't come up with much to say after everything he'd already blabbed at the wake. Didn't matter—they'd started this, they could continue it. He listened to the water gurgle in his fish tank. How come it sounded louder when a room full of people were completely silent than it did when he was here alone?

Father fixed on his gravest expression and began to pace. Back and forth in front of Tierney's stellar view, forcing Chase to step out of his way. Thirty-some laps later, he said, "It's come to our attention that you've been behaving erratically lately."

"Really." Tierney put his feet up on his coffee table and watched his mother open her mouth, then shut it and look away.

"There is, of course, last night's—" Father cleared his throat "—*incident*, and that other debacle—" He broke off to breathe heavily out his nose, lips compressed.

"There was *another* debacle?" Mother whispered, clutching her pearls.

Father ignored her. "Further, Chase has told me about a few other irregularities you've exhibited in the past few months."

Tierney thought he caught a fleeting glance of something other than superiority from his brother, but it didn't last long enough for him to make a guess about it. "Like what?" he asked Chase.

Father answered. "Well, you've indulged in daily liquid lunches, so to speak, and a lot of extravagant spending."

Tierney hunched down further in his seat and crossed his arms over his chest. None of that was unheard of for any of them. Although he couldn't deny that he'd done too much of both recently. Silence seemed like a good idea.

"In short, you aren't behaving normally."

Normal behavior was how he got here, and he cared fuck-all about being normal. Or did he? He let his head flop back on the chair and closed his eyes, trying to shut out the world. The headache he'd been successfully ignoring renewed its attack, hammering in his temples. Waiting for them to get to it. Tell him what nice facility they thought they were sending him to so someone could pray his gay away.

"Darling," Mother said. He'd forgotten she sat there across from him. "What your father is trying to say is that we've arranged for you to get some *help*."

Tierney lifted his head up and stared at her. "Help, huh?" *Here it comes.*

She nodded. "It's called the Dunthorpe Centre for Rehabilitation and Wellness, and I'm assured it's up to our standards." She reached over to pat his knee.

Huh. Shoving his feet against the coffee table, he sat up. "So, like, an ex-gay thing?" he clarified.

"No," Chase bit out. "A mental health facility."

Riiiight. "You're asking me to check myself into a loony bin?" One that thought homosexuality was a mental illness.

"No!" Mother said.

"Certainly not," Father said at the same time.

"Pretty much," said Chase.

Emily walked in just then with a tray. "Here we are."

His family fell on the coffee like it was a gift from heaven. He'd thought only he and Mother—well, and Emily—were nervous, but it turned out Father and Chase weren't so calm themselves. They gladly took the diversion, swarming around the pot and cups, not to mention the box of donuts.

Who brought donuts to an intervention? For that matter, who in his family ever bought donuts, period? It had to be Emily. She hadn't grown up the way Tierney and Chase or even their parents had. Her family didn't have money or social standing or influence. She was, to put it bluntly, not their kind.

Marrying her had to be the smartest thing Chase had ever done. When Tierney's eyes met hers, she smiled at him again. A small, sad smile. Then, to Tierney's surprise, she came over while everyone else was busy with the refreshments. She sat on the arm of his chair and looked down at him, but didn't say anything.

"Um, hi."

"Are you doing all right?"

Tierney blinked. In what way did she mean? All right with being gay, or all right with the family wanting to send him off to the funny farm, or something else entirely? And who the fuck was she to offer him sympathy? Had he asked for it?

"I'm *fine*," he spat out, quietly but viciously enough that it knocked her off the arm of his chair. Right into his fucking brother's sheltering embrace.

"Don't be an asshole to my wife," he snapped, bending to set down his coffee, and then pulled Emily closer.

"Sweetheart, give him a break," she said loud enough for Tierney to hear. Chase turned to her, as if inspecting her for damage. Like Tierney would have fucking hurt her. *Please.* He stared at them sullenly, but that was a mistake. Watching them meant he saw *it*—the moment of silent communication that happened between two people who were intimately connected. Not in the physical way only, but the emotional too. Emily telling Chase somehow that it was okay, *she* was okay. And Chase, that motherfucker, understood her because why? Because he cared about her so much he'd bothered to learn that language of the eyes or whatever the fuck it was.

It made him think of Dalton.

Tierney vaulted out of his chair, startling his mother so much she fumbled her coffee. "I'm not going to your fucking ex-gay camp, so you guys can all go home. Your work here is done." He clapped his hands at them, trying to herd them out like ducks. "Intervention's over. Thanks for coming," he sang. His robe was gaping open, but he didn't care.

His father stood. "It's not an 'ex-gay' program. It's a place for you to relax, goddammit!"

"By separating me from the people who stress me out? Brilliant idea." Tiny droplets of spittle flew into his father's face as he shouted, but the guy didn't back down.

Then Chase got in on the act, letting go of his wife and seriously violating Tierney's personal boundaries. "We're sending you there so you can dry out, you lush."

"The pictures of the grounds are lovely." Mother reached from her seat on the couch to take his hand, patting it. "It's in the California wine country. You'll have a wonderful time."

Tierney stared at her a second, then yanked away, stepping back out of the familial triangle of aggression. "I'm. Not. Going. None of you can make me, and so far no one has given me a valid reason for checking myself into this place. What's my diagnosis? Don't I have to be nuts?"

"You just need to be fucked up enough to an—"

"Chase!" Father thundered. "Stop that now! You aren't helping in the least." He glared at him until Chase went skulking back to Emily. Tierney smirked. He was on the verge of sticking out his tongue when Father continued. "Son, it's a chance for you to get your head back in the game. We all know you haven't been yourself for . . ."

Ever. At least since his teen years.

"A while now, I suppose."

Tierney looked away, taking a moment to belt his robe. "What about what I said last night? About being—" *swallow* "—gay." Everyone seemed to suddenly have clothing to adjust, or a frog in their throat.

Except Emily. "Well, it's certainly not something that can be hidden now. If you even wanted to try."

Tierney met her cool gray eyes and was swamped with guilt for snapping at her earlier. He tried to tell her in that silent way—they were friends, maybe it was possible—but she turned back toward Mother and Father.

Dalton would have gotten the message. He squelched the thought.

"My understanding of this place, the Dunthorpe Centre, is that it's not prepared to handle any 'reprogramming.' It really is for professionals on the verge of a nervous breakdown to restore their equilibrium," his sister-in-law added.

Father nodded and turned toward Tierney, straightening his shoulders. "We're hoping that, after sufficient time there, you'll find that your, well, *penchant* for men will . . ."

"Fade?" Tierney shook his head. "It's not going anywhere. It's had twenty years to fade away and it hasn't yet."

His father's eyes widened. "That wasn't just something you said? Some sort of rebellion?"

Tierney heard Chase snort as he said, "No."

Father looked over at Mother, eyes wide, and she sat forward, folding her hands in her lap just so. "Let's simply deal with your, well, nervous breakdown first. We're more concerned about your state of mind in general right now. I think it would be the best thing for you. Take a little vacation from your stresses, and you'll come back good as new." She smiled brightly. "And then we'll discuss that other thing." She whispered the last three words.

"Vacation," Chase repeated, scowling. "More like a chance for you to hide after thoroughly disgracing yourself—and all of us, I might add."

Hide. His mind seized on that word, not because he really wanted to hide, but maybe he could take some time to find himself, like he'd been supposed to do in college but never had. Learn to deal with being "out" before he actually went *out*. Then when he came back, he'd have an idea how to act, right? He could make a plan while he was at this rehab place, so he'd at least know how to fake his way through it. Fake his way through life.

Wasn't that how I got to this point?

He turned away from his inner voice and met Chase's gaze. He was sneering, daring Tierney to take it on the chin "like a man" instead of hiding. Walk in to work tomorrow and face the rest of his life in this state of unknowing and vulnerability.

An image popped into his head, glowing just like the grail-shaped beacon in that Monty Python movie—a bottle of bourbon. His own personal talisman for vulnerability. *If I stay here, I'll just end up doing the same shit.* Even now that everyone knew he was gay. He totally had the mad skills to be a gay douche as well as a straight one.

And fuck his brother's smirk. When they were kids, Chase used to dare him to do a lot of things that, as Tierney later figured out, the dude wasn't willing to do himself. Jump off the roof of their three-story house for instance. By his count, he'd broken five bones thanks to that prick brother of his.

Following Chase's advice had never done shit for him before. Following the path Grandfather'd laid out for him had gotten him here. *Pick my own path.*

He turned back to Father. "Okay, I'll go hide."

Twenty minutes. That's how long it took for Dalton to drive to Tierney's place, and he didn't receive a single text during the entire journey.

There were so many solid, nonemergent reasons why Tierney might not have responded yet. He could be avoiding him, or passed out with a dead cell phone. He could be in the shower. He could be in the hospital with alcohol poisoning, or injured from a drunk-driving accident.

Or he could have eaten a bullet.

Ker-thunk ker-thunk ker-thunk ker-thunk ker-thunk. How could a heart beat so fast and yet so strongly at the same time?

Finally, coming up to Tierney's building, Dalton could confirm for himself that there weren't any ambulances, cop cars, or fire trucks ringing it. Just a woman a few years older than him walking out the main entrance, carrying a navy-blue overnight bag. He couldn't swear his tires didn't squeal when he stopped at a conveniently free parking spot next to her—judging by the woman's sidelong look, they might have. Dalton ignored it, and in return she walked down the street shaking her head but otherwise ignoring him.

Out of the car and standing at the entry, he watched his fingers shake, hovering over the buzzer for Tierney's apartment. What did he do if no one answered?

The door opening beside him made him leap away as the man himself came through it, wheeling a large suitcase behind him. A navy-blue one that matched the overnight bag that woman had been carrying. Dalton blinked at the luggage, trying to make it fit the story he'd created. The story that told how Tierney'd be, at best, lying on his floor, moaning and possibly in shock.

Not fully dressed at ten in the morning, leaving with bags packed and in the company of a woman.

Talk about repeating past mistakes.

"Dalton?" Tierney asked faintly, staring at him a lot like Dalton stared back.

"Who's that woman carrying the other suitcase?" *Cringe.* But he had to know, because right now his brain was pinging around, thinking new things and jumping to conclusions he didn't want to entertain that didn't even make *sense* and—

"What? What woman? What are you doing here? I thought—"

"The woman I just saw walking out this door with a bag that matches yours." Dalton pointed at the suitcase, shocked at how strident his voice had become. *I sound like Andrea.*

Tierney's brows inched in toward his nose, but he didn't seem annoyed yet. That was all Dalton. "She's my sister-in-law. Emily. *Chase's wife.*" There was the annoyance. It arrived at the same moment Dalton's blood pressure plummeted and his legs grew shaky.

Thank God. He leaned a hand against the wall, propping himself up. "You're all right."

"What are you *doing* here?" Tierney's voice rose. "You heard already, didn't you? That didn't take very fucking long. Come to see how badly I fucked myself? Gawk at me and report to your sister?"

He was forever messing up with this man. "No, I—"

"Shut up." Tierney's eyes had gone wild, whites flashing. "I don't know what your game is, but I'm *fine*, okay? Tell everyone that—"

Dalton reached for him, took Tierney's wrist, and pulled him into a hug. Tried to be an emotional lightning rod, safely diffusing his anger and fear. Just like in the coffee shop that time, he felt the emotions shudder through Tierney, but now much more intimately. He could track their progress through his body where they touched. "I'm sorry," he whispered once the man was still again. "You just— You push all my buttons."

Tierney took a shaky breath, then moved. Not away, but closer, free arm clinging around Dalton's waist, digging his fingers in and gripping so hard he pinched Dalton's skin. "I didn't mean any of that, I was just . . . freaking. I can't believe you came over here."

Dalton responded by tightening the embrace, because he didn't know what to say. He wanted to make promises about things getting better, and offer things he shouldn't even be considering. Say something incredibly profound that would make everything easy. But he bit his tongue and pressed his forehead under Tierney's ear, into his neck, listening to Tierney's uneven breathing and smelling the day-old alcohol and his fear, both underlaid with that smell that was all him.

"Are you going somewhere?" he asked after another minute of standing there like that. In some weird indefinable clinch that made no sense logically but they both seemed to understand they needed.

Tierney swallowed, then his voice rose up from his chest. "California. To a place called the, uh, Dunthorpe Centre. Um, my family felt that I might, you know, need a little break from stress, and I kinda . . . I guess I don't know what else to do for now. How else to, you know. Fit into my life. After last night."

"I'm so proud of you." It just slipped out, leaving Dalton's breath hitching in its wake. He still didn't even know if Tierney had intended to do it.

Tierney choked, but managed to say, "I'm not a coward."

"I never thought you were," Dalton whispered, stretching up on his toes so he could stand cheek to cheek with him. Feel the rasp of Tierney's whiskers. His lips pressed what they hoped was an unobtrusive kiss near his ear.

Tierney sucked in a breath and his grip tightened. "Dalton?"

"Yeah?" He closed his eyes, because the sound of Tierney's voice was all he wanted to focus on. That and the slide and press of his body.

Tierney turned his head, and for a split second his lips returned the caress. Then Tierney's mouth moved against his skin. Words. "Sometimes I think that you're, you know, attracted to me."

Dalton waited for more, suspended in the moment until Tierney finished.

"I'm totally attracted to you," he continued in a rush. "So, like, maybe I'm imagining it. Wishful thinking or something . . ."

Sliding fingers up into Tierney's hair, Dalton found his lips with his own, pressing until Tierney parted them, tilting his head. Kissing him back feverishly, sucking on his tongue. Something thudded to the ground, and then Tierney's other arm was around him, fingers splayed across Dalton's back, pulling him in so tightly that Tierney's shirt buttons pressed into his skin.

Then a horn blared right behind them, and they leapt away from each other. Only a few inches—they were still touching, but not holding on so tightly. Tierney scowled over Dalton's shoulder at whoever had honked, then refocused on Dalton.

"I don't understand *why*," he rasped. "I've been horrible to you."

Dalton had to be honest. "Sometimes."

Tierney flinched, backing away a little.

"But sometimes you've been sincere and funny, and I get to see the guy you hide behind this personality that, to me, doesn't seem like yours. As if you borrowed it. It's that real part of you that I want to—that I'm attracted to."

Tierney cleared his throat, staring into Dalton's eyes. Then he removed himself, taking his fingers from Dalton's waist to run them through his hair and shifting until Dalton's hands dropped from his shoulders. "I'm sorry," he said, biting his lip. "I have a plane to catch." But he stood there still.

Dalton took a long slow breath in through his nose, holding Tierney's gaze another second. "I know," he whispered. Oh God, the ache of unshed tears in his throat was killing him. Soon it would spread into the bones of his face, making his cheeks and skull throb. It was a special kind of pain, reserved for those times when something was too heart wrenching to even cry over. He nodded. "Go."

Tierney swallowed, bent to pick up his fallen suitcase, then turned and walked away.

Chapter 11

This wasn't how Tierney had imagined adulthood to be when he was a child. He'd naively thought he'd have no one to answer to anymore, but instead it turned out he had to answer to a much higher authority than his grandfather—himself.

Or rather, the self he'd like to be.

It wasn't *fair*. Wasn't as if adolescence had been a picnic. Puberty in particular had been such a cunt. Swooping in and taking over his body, hormones swimming around until he could barely think, and then came the "nocturnal emissions." The damned dreams, when he'd wake up sweaty and already getting hard again, his body thrumming from the simple idea of Ignacio the lawn boy.

If only Iggy hadn't mowed the grass shirtless in the summer, Tierney might have lived in denial longer. A few more blissful months, at least, if not another year, until the advent of the next lawn-mowing season.

Would a few more months have made any difference?

Chances were it wouldn't change where he was now—having just finished his intake interview at Dunthorpe, discussing his course of treatment.

"I think you should go directly into our LGBT holistic treatment program," Pam, the woman who'd spent hours asking him questions, said. "You show many signs of alcohol dependency, although I wouldn't go so far as to definitively call it addiction."

"Damn, and I tried so hard," Tierney muttered. Pam tilted her head, squinting slightly, but otherwise ignored his lame attempt at humor.

"The program is aimed at our LGBT clients who've used drugs or alcohol to cope with the issues of bigotry, repression, and denial. You'd have group therapy, an educational track, and individual counseling sessions."

"What, there's, like, a bunch of us here?" *Thunk.* Every time he admitted to being gay aloud, regardless of the words he used, his heart punctuated the moment by banging on his rib cage. He hadn't decided if it was a celebration or a protest.

"You aren't the only one who found coming out difficult," she said. She was very no-nonsense, although Tierney would have appreciated some nonsense right then. "And yes, one of our features is an LGBT-specific program. There's quite a bit about it on our website."

At her inquiring look, he mumbled, "Uh, yeah, I think my sister-in-law did all the research on this place." Had she told his parents? Did Chase know? Whatever, he had a lot to thank her for. Well, if this worked out he did. Maybe he should thank her anyway, though. "Um, what kind of education?" Would it cover the ins and outs of dating guys? Guys like Dalton?

"About the physical and psychological effects of drugs and alcohol, and your relationship with them. Your therapist will be working on the issue with you as well, I imagine—addiction treatment here is a scientifically based, disease model. It's not a twelve-step program," she added when he just stared at her. "It's a cognitive behavioral therapy approach to dealing with substance abuse."

He maybe shouldn't have been so honest about his drinking during his intake screening. But honesty was something he was clinging to like a rock in a river—it was all he had now. Honesty began with complaining. "I thought I didn't have to partake in any sessions I'm not comfortable with."

She nodded. "You don't, but since you're here voluntarily, I'm assuming you're asking for help, and I'm attempting to guide you along the path to the recovery you're looking for."

That made an annoying amount of sense. "All right."

He spent the next few minutes listening to Pam's proposed itinerary for him, interspersed with wondering why the "L" came before the "G." Maybe lesbians were more politically connected. Once he returned home and took his place in the LGBT community, he'd see what he could do about that.

Home. His heart found that word as alarming as any mention of his new, out status. It also found following Pam through the Dunthorpe Centre—regardless of how posh and serene it was—to his assigned room pulse-racing, not to mention the idea that he was about to commit to a rehab program. Did he really want to? Need to?

Wait. He stopped, suitcase in his hand, watching Pam march down a long, semi-institutional hallway. A very nice, well-monied institutional hallway, but still, it was a *hospital.* One that treated guys like him with stress-related issues and addictions. *What if I just went home?*

I'd probably end up in a place like this someday. Except it'd be years down the road, and he'd have the opportunity to do a lot more harm to himself first. There'd be no ambiguity about whether he was a committed drunk.

Slowly he started walking again, his shoes scuffing on the utility carpet. Ahead of him, Pam disappeared around the corner, and Tierney's heart *ker-thunked* once more. What if she never noticed he was missing, and he wandered around Dunthorpe forever? Alone and without the help he needed—whatever that was—as lost in this place as he'd been the last few years of his life.

His feet started moving faster, pushing him forward, because his head may not know whether this was a good idea, but his emotional self understood the plan: he was here to get his shit together. *Just check it out for a few days,* one of the inmates urged in a soothing voice. *You can always bail later. Can't hurt, right?*

His brain might have thrown up another objection, but just then Pam poked half her body back around the corner. "Mr. Terrebonne? There you are. I was afraid I'd lost you for a second." She smiled at him, a real smile.

Tierney bobbed his head. "Yeah, just got caught up in my thoughts for a second."

He expected her to lead on, but she stood there, waiting until he came nearer. Close enough that she could clasp his forearm for a brief squeeze and say, "The next two or three weeks will be trying, but you'll reap rewards you can't imagine now in the long run."

Tierney blinked at her, running that through his mental processes a couple of times before he cleared his throat and responded. "Thanks."

She smiled again, then turned and took him to his room. He dumped his bags on the bed—it looked like a regular double bed, if a little on the frilly side, but somehow it made the place feel like a nursing home. It could be the striped and flowered wallpaper, or the extra-wide, fake-wood-grain doors to his private bathroom and the hallway. He nodded and occasionally murmured a reply as Pam told him to, "Settle in, look around the center, but don't interrupt any sessions. If you have questions, Sandoval is at the information desk. Just turn right out your door and walk to the end of the hallway."

Then she left, and Tierney began the depressing business of accepting that this place was his reality for a while. This room and endless therapy. He couldn't be sure yet, but this "recovery" thing was shaping up to be the most harrowing thing he'd done in his life.

"It was my grandfather," Tierney explained to his LGBT cohorts a week later, when it was his turn in the hot seat. The therapy group had Tierney pinned down, with little hope of escape from Drag Betty and all her fucking questions. He looked around the circle—it didn't matter how fancy Dunthorpe was, they still had institutional rooms with office chairs for situations like this. At least the chairs were padded and the windows were plentiful and had good views of the very perfect lawns and gardens. "I stayed in the closet because of the old guy."

"You said you hated him," Betty poked at him verbally. "You spent twenty years hiding because he told you to?"

"He threatened to take away my family! And cut me off without a dime," Tierney added, certain these people would understand—they all had to come from money to be able to afford this place, didn't they? "I mean, the money is one thing, but my *family* . . ."

"Why'd you stay in the closet for them?" Gary, one of the senior members of the group, asked. "They don't give a shit about you."

"I never said *that*." Not in so many words. He'd only used a couple of them. "They made me come here; they must give a shit."

Drag Betty sniffed. "According to you, sweetheart, they sent you here to turn you back into their picture-perfect son. The one you were before."

"And what about this guy you were in love with?" Gary chimed in again. "You said you were pretty sure he was into guys for a while before he came out. Didn't you say months before? But you never approached him, in spite of waiting years for him." Gary leaned forward, pointing at him when Tierney opened his mouth to object. "Those were your words, T. You waited *years*."

He gave up facing them down and dropped his head into his hands, scrubbing at it. Thinking. "Okay, so . . ." he began, not that he knew where to go after this. *Why* did *I do that?* Wait years.

"You *let* your grandfather stop you," Gary said, softly.

"I was fourteen!"

"What about later?" some voice he didn't recognize asked. The newest member, Alicia. Only eighteen, but she had deep scar tissue marching up her arms in neat, parallel lines. Tierney hadn't realized "cutting" was a thing until he met her last week. "When you were older. Aren't you, like, in your thirties, now?"

"Okay, yes, but—"

"But you were scared," Betty said.

"I thought this was a fucking support group." Tierney stood, shoving shaking hands into the pockets of the new robe his mother had sent him. "Why're you all attacking me?"

No one answered, not even Curt, the "facilitator." *He* apparently facilitated emotional abuse. Tierney kicked his chair back with his foot and stepped outside the circle, heading for the door, anger boiling up inside him. He had to leave or he'd say shit and he was fucking tired of ruining his life by letting his mouth have control.

"Tierney," Curt said.

Tierney stopped, waiting even though his blood was urging him to move. Hit someone or run away. Gallop through the halls in silk pajamas with his robe billowing out behind him, screaming insanely and generally living up to the assumption that he was crazy.

"Sometimes the best way to support someone is to make them face hard truths." Curt's words snuck up behind him, soft but hitting him with the force of a body slam. He swayed.

"I don't wanna," some small voice said. A kid voice.

"You've been here a week," Betty said, and even her tone sounded almost supportive. "Maybe it's time to try."

He closed his eyes, fighting a battle inside himself. Some of the inmates were resisting, but others wanted to do it. Figure this shit out.

"It's why you're here," Gary said. "Not even your family can *make* you stay, not without a court order. You're going to have to face it sooner or later. Doing it now will be easier. We *understand*."

Truth. He could deal now, or have a few more years of denial, then another big meltdown like . . . He turned back to them, going to his chair. Arranging his robe carefully as he sat, pulling it around his pajamas as if he'd suddenly developed modesty.

Shuddering breath into his lungs, he said it: "I was scared." He had to swallow down the lump that floated up into his throat with those words. "I'm *still* scared. People will judge me. I don't—you don't *know* . . . this is how my life is." Something tickled his cheek, and he wiped it off. A tear. Staring at it, he found himself with more to say. "*Everything* is about appearances. My family, my upbringing, my social life, my career. It's all about presenting the proper image of—*fuck*. I always felt, like, different. Like I had a fucking birth defect, and if this secret got exposed, I'd be cast out from, I dunno, the tribe of humanity." He had to swallow again, and wipe more stuff off his face. He had to finish. "On my own. I don't know if he did it on purpose or not, but that bastard used my fear against me." He gulped another breath. "But *I* did it. I let him. D-didn't I?" God, his voice broke, and then he was sobbing and he should be ashamed to break like that in front of anyone, but as he cried, and hands patted his back and rubbed his shoulders while people murmured things to him, he didn't feel ashamed at all.

It was all relief now. No shame. And, for the first time in recent memory, the inmates weren't torturing him anymore.

Chapter 12

Dalton didn't know much about how rehab or mental health inpatient programs worked, so he'd resolved not to worry if he didn't hear from Tierney while he was gone.

Which was why he was definitely not preoccupied the next Saturday afternoon, as he was coaxing Blue into his cat carrier for the ride over to their new apartment. "You'll be much happier there, I swear."

Blue meowed at him nonchalantly and flopped gracefully onto his side. Up against the wall, under the bed. The bed Dalton wasn't taking with him, so he and Sam hadn't dismantled it, making it a convenient place for Blue to be aloof and recalcitrant.

"Please, baby cat, don't make me come after you."

Blue blinked and turned away from him.

"Want me to slide in under there?" Sam offered. "I'm ganglier than you."

Dalton sighed, pushing onto his hands and knees, then to standing. "He'd slice you up like toilet paper."

Sam scrunched his brow.

"He likes to unroll and shred bathroom tissue. And claw people other than me."

Sam nodded, but the look on his face was uncomprehending. "Oh." Clearly, he'd never owned a cat.

"Don't worry, I know how to get him out." He'd bought a special treat for just this instance.

In the kitchen, his preoccupation waylaid him, though. He couldn't claim to be surprised Tierney hadn't contacted him, and Dalton knew he couldn't reach out himself. The man had stuff to work on, and who even knew if he had his phone? Would they have taken it away?

"Is it still bothering you?" Sam asked from right behind him, and Dalton jumped. "What's going on with Tierney."

He evaded the question, not that he'd be able to for long. "I was just staring into the fridge, wasn't I?" He had one arm holding the door open and the other braced on the counter. How long had he been standing here before Sam came looking for him?

"Yeah."

He rolled his eyes at his emo self and grabbed the little deli container of organ meat. *Blech.*

Sam made a face. "What's that?"

"Bribery. Two cooked chicken livers. I'll open the container and put it into the crate, and by the time we have the rest of the boxes in Ian's truck, Blue will be in there."

Sam's face brightened, probably at the mention of Ian's pickup rather than the imminent capture of the cat. Dalton was starting to get the feeling Ian didn't often let Sam drive it, based on the way Sam bounced up on tiptoes every time the vehicle was even mentioned.

After their next trip to load more of Dalton's stuff, they came back into the room to find Blue mostly in the cat carrier, long orange tail trailing out and switching back and forth. Dalton moved fast, putting the rest of Blue in with one hand and shutting the wire door with the other. The cat growled at him, then went back to his container of liver.

"That can't be good for him," Sam said, grimacing.

Dalton shrugged. "If he cooperated more often, he wouldn't have to worry about overeating."

Sam dropped onto Dalton's former bed. "So, are we going to talk about what's bugging you?" He had that inquiring tilt to his head, and was watching Dalton avidly.

"I guess." Dalton had confessed most of what had happened last weekend when he and Sam met for lunch. It had been less than an hour after he'd said good-bye to Tierney, and he hadn't had time to cobble his insides back together. Telling his friend about it had been cathartic, at least. Maybe talking about it now would help too. He leaned his weight against the wall opposite the bed. "I just don't know what . . ."

"Is going to happen?" The excitement in Sam's expression told Dalton what was coming next. "In a romance novel—"

"This isn't a romance novel." He really needed to have that printed on a T-shirt he could wear whenever they hung out.

Sam shrugged one shoulder. "Romance novels have an often uncanny ability to predict reality." He smiled dreamily, eyes glossing over. "The wounded billionaire. *Such* a cracky trope."

"Cracky?"

"Uh, like crack. Love-crack. You know, if you're into, you know. Romance."

"Tierney's hardly a billionaire. Millionaire, probably."

Sam waved that off. "Yeah, but 'millionaire' just doesn't have the cachet it used to. You *have* to say 'billionaire,' even if he's not, to fulfill the parameters of the trope."

"Do we *need* to fulfill the parameters of this trope?"

Sam blinked a few times, then squinted at him.

That was probably answer enough. Taking a deep breath, Dalton brought up the one thing he most didn't want to. "Do you think it's possible he could get over Ian?"

"Uh, *yeah*," Sam said, nodding vigorously. "He only *thinks* he's in love with my boyfriend."

"How do you know he's not?"

"Because it doesn't work that way. Only one soul mate per person, it's like a law." *Duh*, his expression read.

Dalton sighed and crossed his arms over his middle. "I don't even know if I *want* to be with him." Not exactly the truth—it was more that he didn't know which version of Tierney would come back from Dunthorpe. "Isn't it against romance novel law or something to pin your hopes on someone changing into the right person for you?"

"But that's not what you're doing," Sam insisted. "He's not changing, he's transforming into what he's meant to be. Like a butterfly," he finished, gazing dreamily into thin air.

Dalton's head drooped under the weight of doubts, and he found himself inspecting the floor. "Oh God, I hope so. Otherwise I'm crushing on a self-involved coward who thinks cover-your-ass is a blood sport and he's *just* like my exes."

Springs creaked, and then Sam's footsteps came closer to him. "You were attracted to those guys for a reason, right? Like, it wasn't just, you know, their ability to take care of you financially?"

Dalton flinched. "Not totally. I kind of . . . I like being in a supportive role. Knowing the man I'm with, um—"

"That's what I'm thinking," Sam said, saving Dalton from the embarrassment of finishing his thought. "See, he's your *type*. Just because you had bad experiences with your type in the past doesn't mean this one will be. You made *changes* in your life." Sam's hand landed on Dalton's arm, squeezing a second before letting go. "You're a different man, so it follows that your man should be different too." He was beaming when Dalton looked up from under his brow.

But still. "Is this more romance novel logic?"

"Oh, honey." Sam waved his hand carelessly in the air. "That's the only kind I know."

A knock on the front door interrupted Dalton's reply. He had to answer it since, for once, none of his roommates were home. Four college-aged guys who all had to be somewhere at ten on Saturday morning? Not likely. They'd all heard "help move" and had come up with excuses.

"I'm coming," he called when the knock came again, firmer and more rapid this time.

It's him.

No, it's not.

A week wouldn't be enough, would it? *Of course not.* Tierney needed to deal with things. Come to terms.

Except it was possible coming to terms took less time than Dalton thought.

He doesn't even know where I live.

He has my number. He could look it up online or something.

He reached the entryway, turned the knob, drawing breath to say something welcoming and comforting, that would put the man at ease—

Ian.

"Oh. Hi." The slumping of his spine *had* to be obvious to his boss.

"Um, hey," Ian responded, smiling tightly.

Dalton remembered his manners, straightening. "Would you like to come in?" *Even if you aren't who I wanted you to be.*

"Yeah . . ." Ian ran his hand through his hair, looking off to the side, as if something fascinating might be in the front yard. "I guess I just wanted to make sure, you know, Sam didn't have any problems with the pickup. He's not really used to driving something that big, and . . ." He frowned.

Dalton leaned forward and whispered, "You're very transparent. You're going to have to come up with something better than that if you want to convince him you're here for some reason *other* than not trusting him to drive your truck."

"Hell," Ian muttered, then, when Dalton stepped out of his path, he walked into the house. Halfway in he halted, expression clearing as he turned to Dalton. "Maybe you could tell him *you* called me be—"

"No." He shook his head. "Sorry, but no. Besides, I would have told him first." He patted Ian's shoulder. "Sam managed to get it over here, and I haven't noticed a single scratch or dent. I'm sure he can handle it. If you leave now, he never has to know—"

"Ian? What are you doing here?" Sam stood in the middle of the hallway, fists planted on his hips.

"Hi, Squirrel."

Squirrel? Really, Dalton should leave them alone to hash this out in private, but they were blocking his escape. He had no choice but to stay and listen.

Ian walked toward Sam, who didn't look very welcoming.

"Well?" Sam raised his brows. "What are you doing here?"

Ian rubbed the back of his neck. "Um, I was in the neighborhood?"

"Okaaaaay," Sam said. "And how did you say you got here again?"

Ian cleared his throat, then mumbled something Dalton didn't catch.

"You *hate* taking the bus." Sam scowled, crossing his arms over his chest. "But today you just *happened* to get on the bus and you just *happened* to end up here?"

"I couldn't help it," Ian said, reaching out toward his boyfriend. "I'm not used to being home by myself on Saturdays. I *missed* you."

Oh, Sam would see right through *that.*

Except, "Really?" he asked, eyes widening. "You wanted to be with me so much you took public transit for me?" He took Ian's hand, stepping closer.

"Yeah, kiddo." Ian nodded earnestly.

"What did you do on weekends before we got together?" At least Sam hadn't completely lost *all* skepticism.

"I don't know. I guess I was just marking time until I met you."

Oh gag. But Sam totally fell for it, resting his hands on Ian's shoulders and smiling into his face. Ian brought him closer and kissed him. Dalton had to look away, not for their privacy but for the sake of his stomach. When he glanced back to see if they were done, Sam was rolling his eyes at him over Ian's shoulder.

So he *hadn't* bought it? *Whatever*. It was official—Dalton had had enough of their little relationship drama. "Excuse me," he said, working his way around them. "I'll get back to moving while you two discuss this."

"Oh." Sam pulled away from his boyfriend. "Since Ian's here, he can help us too." He beamed.

Ian smiled weakly. "Sure."

Heh. The guy totally deserved that. Dalton tried to remember if he had anything particularly heavy or awkward to load still. Too bad he wasn't bringing his bed, but he'd promised it to Vance so the guy could stop sleeping on a mattress on the floor.

"I'll just go check, you know." Ian nodded toward the front of the house. "Make sure the load is balanced in the back of the pickup."

It's not a mule. But Dalton kept that to himself and returned to his room to assess what was left. He really didn't need Ian—he barely needed Sam's help—to move so little stuff. There were only three boxes in there still, plus Blue, who he'd carry out last and who would ride in his lap. When he checked the crate, the cat was washing himself, and there wasn't a shred of chicken liver left. Blue had even licked the container clean. He blinked at Dalton, meowed, and then went back to tonguing his paw and swiping at his ears with it.

"You're going to like our new place, baby cat," Dalton told him. Blue started cleaning his stomach.

"He's probably going out to make sure I didn't put any marks on his truck," Sam said, walking into the room behind Dalton.

"Why did you let him get away with that?" Dalton got up off the floor and turned to his friend.

Sam shrugged. "He's so cute when he lies to spare my feelings. Besides, he'll be racked with guilt for days and try to make it up to me over and over."

"Got it." Dalton picked up a box, heading toward the door with it. He didn't want to spend any more time pondering the inner workings of someone else's happy relationship. *We're in a mood today, aren't we?*

He passed Ian in the hall. "Just a couple more boxes, then we can go."

Ian nodded.

At the truck, Dalton found Sam right behind him once again. "Do you feel any better?" Sam frowned and hefted his box onto the tailgate next to Dalton's.

Sigh. "Not really. I think the stress of moving is getting to me."

Sam tilted his head, studying Dalton. "You've been looking forward to this."

"But there's still a lot to do."

"We're almost done with this part." Sam eyed him a few seconds, then opened his mouth—

"Shit!" Ian yelled, just as Dalton heard Blue's enraged yowl.

Oh no. He started running for the open front door, but he didn't make it before an orange streak of fur, claws, and fangs ran through it. "Blue!"

The cat hurtled around the side of the house, out of sight for the few seconds it took Dalton to skid around the corner. He just barely caught a flash of Blue's tail disappearing behind the overgrown hydrangea.

"Will he come back?" Sam called.

Dalton didn't answer, saving his energy for catching his pet. It could take everything he had, he knew that from experience. Blue would come back, eventually, but Dalton didn't want to wait around all day for him to wander home. He wanted to move into his new apartment with his cat and get domestic *now*. Nest. Just the two of them.

Hours later, finally alone in his own place, Dalton watched Blue exploring. Sniffing boxes and then rubbing against them, occasionally taking a galloping trip around the kitchen, skidding to a halt on the linoleum with wild eyes and hair standing up. Just playing at being scared, though. Not really scared, as he'd been this morning when Ian had decided to carry the last box out to the pickup with Blue's carrier on top of it. *Of course* it fell off, and *of course* the door sprang open when Ian tried to pick it up. But his fatal mistake had been trying to stop the cat from running away.

After the drama of the escape, catching Blue had been almost anticlimactic. Dalton had found him next to the garage, growling but amenable to being picked up.

Ian, however, would have a scratch down his cheek for days, and his hands were a mass of scabbed-over claw marks. "He doesn't really like to be touched," Dalton had tried to explain when he got back to the driveway.

"Thanks for the heads-up," Ian snarked. Dalton let it go.

God, what an exhausting day. Not just the move, but losing Blue had worn on him, even if it had only been for a few minutes.

"Want some dinner?" he asked the cat, getting up from his new chair. He should be unpacking, but he'd set up his new bed and did it really matter if all he had for a few days were a place to sit and a place to sleep? He'd managed to find the dishes, and he'd gone shopping. They were set. Just the two of them. Ready to begin life as mature, self-reliant adults.

Well, Dalton was. He couldn't swear Blue gave a damn.

"It's so fucking *obvious*, now," Tierney whined to Marty, the counselor he had his one-on-one sessions with. The revelations that had followed his watershed group session gave them lots of material to pick over. Therapy was weird—sort of like wandering through the woods and trying to follow a trail of bread crumbs to enlightenment or whatever. Damn things were hard to find, and he kept losing his way. Fortunately, he had a shrink trail guide.

Marty pursed his lips and nodded thoughtfully, epitomizing "psychologist" for a moment. Most of the time, the only thing that made him seem like a mental health professional was the notepad he occasionally scribbled in. His hair was long and scraggly on the sides and nonexistent on top. It matched his bug eyes well, and his extreme thinness. He looked like a crazy medieval monk who'd traded his robes for khakis, a plaid button-down, and a doctorate in psychology. "Why don't you say more about that?" Marty *sounded* like a therapist all the time, though.

"About Ian?" Did he *have* to? *Yes.* "Just..." Shrugging, he slouched further into the couch cushions, studying the hand he'd rested on his thigh. Palm up, fingers curled inward, like a creature that had starved to death. "I was fooling myself. I don't think I was ever in love with him. If I was, how come I waited all that time for him to come to me? If it was so fucking painful, why didn't I blurt it out and end the anguish? I don't *like* pain. I think years of anesthetizing myself with alcohol proves that."

Marty leaped right in and pointed out the next trail marker in Tierney's path. "So, you think you used your friend as a crutch?" He always did it that way, asking questions so it could almost seem like Tierney was finding the bread crumbs and figuring shit out on his own, if he wanted to believe it.

"Yeah, I used him." Tierney sighed, closing his eyes for a few seconds. "I used him as an excuse not to face myself."

"But you've done that, now," Marty said, prodding him. *Bread crumbs don't find themselves, boy.* "Faced yourself."

Jerking upright, he asked the only question that mattered. The one with the answer he couldn't find on his own. "But how the fuck do I *keep* doing that?"

"That's what we're going to work on." Marty's eyes bulged convincingly and his voice was soaked in confidence. "Before you leave Dunthorpe, you'll have a plan for sticking to the path you've chosen."

"I want to be *authentic.*" Tierney swallowed. "The real Tierney." Forget the Terrebonne part of the equation.

It took most of his hour-and-a-half-long session, but by the end, Tierney had his first concrete step toward authenticity figured out: he had to apologize. Sincerely. As soon as he got home. Not just to Ian, but lots of people.

Still, the dude was foremost in his mind. Pretty much all the other times he'd apologized, it was just him trying to make sure he didn't lose the friendship. The relationship he'd totally abused. He'd wallowed in the progressive destruction of his heart that seeing Ian caused, but never pursued what he thought he wanted. On top of that, he'd made Ian pay for all the times he felt neglected or shorted. Especially when Ian fell in love with someone else, and Tierney had freaked.

So, yeah. He had an apology to make to the guy.

That night he lay in bed, thinking about the shit he hadn't revealed to Marty.

I'm so proud of you.

When Dalton had said it, Tierney'd felt nearly numbed by those words, but with an edge of scorn—for himself, not Dalton. He still didn't quite know how to take them, but . . . he wasn't sure he recognized the feeling, but he'd almost label it "worthwhile." Not a complete waste of space.

He had a hard time trusting it, though. And he had an even harder time trusting the little whisper in his mind that insisted Dalton might truly be attracted to him. Why would he be? Everything that had happened between them so far had gone wrong. He'd been a strung-out freak when they first met, then that shit at Ian's house, and the blowjob. And fuck, that *meeting*.

He pushed himself off the bed and out of his room, trying to outmaneuver his memories. Wandering down the hall, past the info desk and into the common area, he found the poker-playing faction of the ladies who formerly liquid lunched. They were a constant fixture.

Tierney peered over Rita's shoulder. "Wanna sit in a couple hands?" she asked in her pack-a-day voice.

"Sure." Nothing else to do.

"New bathrobe?" Angela eyed the pale-aqua grandeur of it. Of the four ladies at the table, she had the most beauty, and he'd bet it was largely unaided by surgery. Her boobs defied gravity, though.

"Uh . . ." He looked down and plucked at the fluffy collar. "Mother sent me this."

"Damn, that thing's horrifying." Sabrina lifted her brow—no mean feat for someone whose face had been so precisely sculpted and Botoxed. "What's a gay boy like you wearing something that ugly for?"

Tierney snorted. "It's my defense against cougar attacks."

The ladies all laughed, even Sabrina, then Rita settled a baseball cap on her head, and arranged a carrot stick so it dangled out of her mouth like a cigarette. "All right, enough chitchat. Five-card stud, fours are wild."

The first time he'd played cards with the former liquid lunchers, he'd blurted out, "I'm g-gay," in answer to some stupid question he couldn't even remember now, totally terrified about how they'd take it.

But their interest had faded into resigned acceptance quickly, although Sabrina had piped up with, "It's always the young ones with the firm ass muscles, isn't it?"

At the time he'd been shocked into silence, but he was used to her suggestive comments now. Tonight, he gave her as much crap as she gave him. It was a great distraction.

Later, fed by the good feelings, the laughter, and the ladies' scornful amusement over how they'd gotten themselves landed in rehab (not to mention their guffaws at his cougar jokes), Tierney went back to his room and let himself think that maybe Dalton could really want to be his friend.

The ladies who formerly liquid lunched seemed to like the real him—or whatever he had left without the facade.

Still, he was too much of a mess for anyone to *want* him. Wasn't he?

Christ. He *did* need to bring this up with Marty.

On a Monday, just over two weeks after arriving at Dunthorpe, Tierney turned down the in-flight cocktail service on the plane ride home for the first time ever. He didn't even have to force himself to do it. He didn't want a drink, or the snack mix packet. As soon as he'd walked out of rehab—the very second he'd stepped foot back into the real world—a tiny fissure had torn open in his gut, and acid had started spilling out of it, causing his insides to burn in various spots at various times in various intensities.

Everyone probably thinks I'm a dumb-fuck for getting shitfaced and announcing my deepest, darkest secret to a roomful of people. But the longer he put off facing the world, the more his anxiety increased. Since he'd committed himself to being the most authentic Tierney possible, with all his scars and defects hanging out, the sooner he got on with it the better.

As he got closer to home, he expected to get even more agitated, but it didn't happen. If anything, he felt calmer. It took hours of staring out the little oval window into the passing clouds, but he finally figured out why: he'd started remaking himself into a man he *liked*.

Authentic Tierney had some rough edges, but he was a happier, better guy than Tierney Terrebonne, sleazeball extraordinaire.

Gastrointestinal distress or not, he had hope for himself for the first time in . . . ever.

Chapter 13

"I'm going to make Ian take me to lunch." Sam's stream of words followed in his wake as he loped past Dalton's desk.

"Have fun." Dalton didn't bother to look up when Sam opened Ian's door, but he *did* check to make sure Sam had actually shut the thing. He may be able to pretend he had no idea what they were doing in there, but he'd discovered he couldn't will himself deaf.

As he refocused on his computer, he caught someone coming into the office out of the corner of his eye. "Can I—" he began, turning his head. *Gasp*. "Tierney."

His heart performed a somersault, but Dalton played it cool, standing up, smiling warmly and *not* asking why the other man hadn't called or texted or even sent a postcard. *He had other things on his mind.* "Welcome back."

"Thanks." Tierney shoved his hands in his pockets, coming forward but not meeting Dalton's eyes. He looked completely different than when Dalton had first seen him a little over a month ago, now wearing jeans and a pinstriped button-down. The whisker scruff and artfully disarranged hair had a more intentional look today. He was so humanly insecure right then, he seemed, well, semiedible. "I'm, um, I'm here."

"I see that," Dalton said softly. Should he go around for a hug or lean over the reception desk and give Tierney a quick peck on the cheek? Or possibly just a handshake, because now the man was shifting his weight. "I'm glad."

"Here to see Ian," Tierney blurted.

Ian? Dalton's heart stuttered, but his work persona kicked in, saving him from doing anything ridiculous like asking, "You aren't here to see *me*?" Instead he pasted on that professional smile he was so adept at and said, "I hope you had a pleasant vacation."

Now Tierney's eyes locked on his, the corner of his mouth turning down. But he pretended along with Dalton. "Very relaxing. Hardly made it out of my bathrobe. I know Ian's busy." His gaze flickered away again. "I followed Sam in."

Dalton had reached for his phone before the man had finished. "I'll tell him you're here, I'm sure he'll want to see you right a—"

"Don't worry, I'll wait." Tierney turned to the chairs available for guests, sitting and picking up a golf magazine. *He hates golf.*

Dazed and confused, Dalton dropped into his own seat, recovering quickly when it tried to roll away from his butt. Forcing it into behaving, even as he forced his emotions to get with the program. It didn't matter that Tierney came in here and acted as if they were mere acquaintances, rather than people who'd shared intimacies, with promises of more. Here and now, he had a job to do, and damned if he'd ever again let a man turn him into an emotional, ranting shrew. *Been there, done that.* And he hadn't wasted any money on the fucking T-shirt.

God, what if Andy was right and Tierney *was* too damaged to fix? Looking at him, though, he seemed okay. Nervous, yes, but calm enough to sit there, leafing through his reading material with focus. Not trying to talk his way into Ian's office or having a meltdown. Or sharing anything personal with his friend. The guy he claimed to be attracted to.

Maybe he *was* fixed and that meant he was no longer interested in Dalton?

Or he was more attracted to Ian.

Andy came out of her office on the other side of the reception area, saving Dalton from having to think about it any further at the moment. She couldn't help but pass in front of Tierney, and God forbid she should simply keep going, maybe with a nod or a "hello." No, she had to stop, inspect Tierney like a germ under a microscope, and say, "I see you're back."

Tierney glanced up. "Yeah, sorry about that." He lowered his gaze, but he wasn't reading about golf any more now than he had been before.

Andy stood there a second, probably teetering in indecision—did she harass him, or let things lie?—but finally she moved on toward Dalton's desk, catching his eye when he didn't look away fast enough. She made all kinds of weird movements with her facial muscles which possibly meant "What's going on?" or "Did you notice that? He's *different*."

Dalton shrugged and began typing nonsense on his computer. Fortunately she stopped in front of his station, where she couldn't see the screen. "Is Ian free? I need to talk to him about something with the eastern counties' rural protection districts. Actually, is his calendar clear for lunch?"

"Sorry. He's got a meeting." *Ker-thunk?* his heart asked. But it suddenly seemed like the perfect solution.

Andy squinted at him, and Dalton imagined his spinal column turning into steel before she could interrogate him more.

"And who's this meeting with?"

"Mr. Terrebonne." Sam would *kill* him, but it had to be done. The sooner Ian saw him, the sooner Tierney would be out of here. Dalton's peace of mind required it.

He flicked a glance at Tierney, and yes, the man had frozen in place, fingers holding one half-translucent page of the magazine. Then he shook his head, as if trying to knock something loose. "Um, please call me Tierney." He looked up and met Dalton's gaze. "Thanks."

Dalton tilted his chin, then turned away and hit the intercom button just as Andrea lost her dumbstruck expression and opened her mouth. He beat her to the punch. "Ian? Your lunch meeting is waiting." *Please don't let them be in the middle of something.*

"What?" *Lovely.* The sound of *both* of them gasping for breath came over the speaker loud and clear. "What meeting? I have a meeting? I was going to ta—"

"I'm sorry, I must have forgotten to tell you I scheduled it. It won't happen again." As if he ever forgot. *Please.*

"Oh. Uh, no problem. I just need a minute to, um . . . who's this meeting with?"

Dalton leaned closer to his phone. "Tierney Terrebonne."

His first morning back, Tierney'd gotten up bright and early and headed for the Interagency Disaster Relief Coordination Department to pop his homecoming cherry. When he'd walked into the Bureau of Health building and seen Sam already there in front of him, he'd almost turned around. He didn't have an issue with Sam, exactly. It was more like he had an issue with having to face anyone who'd known him before. Especially anyone he'd been a dick to.

Which meant pretty much everyone.

Go me.

He dropped the dumb golf magazine on the table and gave up trying to appear calm, resting his forehead in his hands before peeking through his fingers at Dalton. Should he thank him for making up that meeting, and for chasing Andrea off? What should he say at all?

Should he apologize for asking if Dalton was into him? The dude was watching him. At least, Tierney thought so. He caught flashes of blue eyes under very long, dark lashes, and then Dalton lifted his head and looked directly at him.

Tierney flinched and dropped his hand, accidentally meeting Dalton's gaze.

They both jerked their heads away.

"It should only be another minute or two." Dalton's voice almost sounded jittery, but that had to be Tierney's imagination. He glanced back toward the reception desk, using his own lashes to hide his eyes. The dude wasn't watching him anymore, he was staring straight ahead at his computer, but not typing or anything. His mouth had turned down, and his face had gone pink.

"Um, thanks. For setting up that meeting for me."

Dalton nodded, still looking straight ahead. "I thought he'd want to see you. Since you've been gone."

"Yeah." Tierney snorted. "I'm sure he wants to know where I disappeared to."

Dalton turned to him, and Tierney met his gaze on purpose this time. He tried to smile.

He didn't get an answering smile. "I told him." Dalton swallowed. "About Dunthorpe."

"Thank you," Tierney said again, a little bit of tension easing out of his muscles. "That makes one thing easier."

Dalton opened his mouth, and Tierney leaned forward. But before Dalton could do more than draw in a breath, Ian's door opened, and Sam came out.

Tierney grabbed the golf magazine and sat back in his seat, flipping through it for all he was worth, listening to Dalton and Sam mumble something about lunch. Was Sam mad? Why did that make him feel a little damp under the arms?

"Hi Tierney," Sam said, suddenly right in front of him, and Tierney almost dropped the magazine. He managed to fumble it shut and stood up. Seriously, did the dude *have* to be taller?

"Hey. How've you been? I just came by to see your, uh, Ian."

Sam's huge mouth broke out in a huge grin. "I figured. I'm on my way back to campus, but I was just telling Ian he should invite you over sometime."

Tierney blinked. Like, for bridge or tea or something? He inspected Sam for signs of pity, but instead he found some sort of shiny emotion in his eyes. Excitement? Why would inviting him over make Sam excited? Christ, he didn't, like, want a threesome, did he?

With me? Not.

"That'd be cool, I guess." *Way to sound friendly.* "I'd like to hang out with you guys." Jesus, he needed to work on this social thing.

"Awesome." Sam literally bounced up on his toes. Hopefully he didn't see Tierney flinch away. But his attention had switched to Dalton, for that second at least. Then he turned to Tierney again, stepping closer. Like, about to touch him? Why would he want to touch—

Oh my God, he's hugging me! What do I do?

Hug back, douche bag.

He attempted it. One arm around Sam, patting him between his shoulder blades, the shock of full-body contact with another man making him dizzy, then Sam let him go and Tierney fell back into his seat. Next thing he knew, Sam was over in front of Dalton's desk again, both of them standing and talking in those low tones.

So weird that they could both have blond hair, blue eyes, and such suggestive lips but be total opposites. Sam was dorky-cute in a gangly baby animal way, while Dalton should have been modeling some very pricey androgynous cologne in a black-and-white print ad. God, if he could see those lips on him again—

Shut up.

Tierney closed his eyes and shook his head, trying to will the image away.

"Bye!" Sam sang. Tierney jerked up to see the kid waving to both him and Dalton as he went out the door.

"Hey, man, wanna come in?" Ian's voice startled him. When Tierney swung around, his friend was standing in his office doorway, smiling.

"Uh, yeah." He stood, wiping his palms on his jeans even though he tried to tell himself not to. Walking over to Ian, he kept Dalton's bright hair in his peripheral vision, then caught the guy's eye one more time when he glanced up and mouthed "thank you" again.

"You look pretty good," Ian said, shutting the door after Tierney had come through it. "Dalton said your family sent you away after what happened at your grandfather's wake, but he didn't tell me why. It wasn't some kind of thing to make you straight, was it?"

Tierney snorted. "You seriously think I'd announce I like dick to all those people and then agree to get all ex-gayed?"

"No." Ian headed back toward his desk, sitting as Tierney reached a visitor's chair. "So, was it alcohol?"

"Sorta." Tierney waved a hand around. "I wasn't in alcohol rehab so much as, like, life rehab. Alcohol was part of it, though. I'm, um, a nondrinker now."

Ian's brows pulled together, and he planted his elbows on the desk. "Just tell me what's going on, T." His voice was soft. *Trying to be gentle with someone fragile.* "I want to know. I'm trying to figure out what's changed and how to, I don't know . . . help you, I guess."

"I came to apologize." Tierney gripped the arms of his chair, digging his fingernails into the industrial upholstery. "For real."

Ian nodded, but his jaw had gone hard. "Yeah, dude. Here's the thing." He sat back and steepled his fingers under his chin. "Do it with actions, not words. Because you've cried wolf too many times. I hear you say, 'I'm sorry,' and I think, 'Here we go again.' I have a hard time believing it anymore. Show me, because the words mean fuck-all."

Tierney swallowed. "I'm gonna. Show you." He *so* deserved that from Ian. Squeezing his eyes shut, he blurted the thing that had been running around in his mind the last few weeks, "I've always been kind of an asshole, haven't I?"

"Pretty much." Ian's chair creaked.

"But we're friends, right?" Carefully, he met the guy's gaze again. "I mean, we used to be. Real ones."

Ian smiled slightly. "Yeah. We are."

Tierney took a deep breath. "If I change everything about me, do you think we'll still be friends?"

"Like, if you stopped trying to be the biggest dick around? Yeah. I think we'll still be friends."

All his muscles went slack. He'd been hoping for Ian to be sure, but he'd take that answer. "Jesus, I'm pathetic."

Ian curled his lip. "What makes you say that?"

"This whole fucking situation. I fucked my life up good."

"Because you were honest for once?"

"That's one way of looking at it, huh?" he said, smiling. Relaxing all over again, but in a more controlled way. Settling his nerves. He'd done it, gotten the hard stuff out.

Ian laughed. "I guess. Listen, man, you should come play rugby again. McDaniel set up a bunch of off-season scrimmages, and it'd probably help you to do something normal, you know? Plus we could just hang out, like old times."

Tears prickled his eyes. It had happened all the time at Dunthorpe, but he wasn't expecting it here. Probably because he hadn't been expecting this much support from Ian. Didn't believe he deserved it. He forced out a response past the constriction in his throat. "Thanks. I'd like that."

How dare he? It took Dalton long minutes of staring at his desk to form a coherent reaction, but really . . . *how* dare *he*? Tierney had behaved as if they barely *knew* each other. What the *fuck* was with that?

Tierney'd *kissed* him, not in a drunk-and-met-in-a-club way, but in a very this-could-become-a-relationship way. An *intimate* way. Emotional.

Except . . . did Tierney *understand*? Maybe it was like one of those hookups that seemed as if they had potential for more, but ended up going wrong once both parties had come.

Tierney may not have been drunk that morning he left, but he was the next thing to it—emotionally strung out and hungover.

He'd thought there was more to them. Convinced himself it could work in the future. Even the fact that Tierney had feelings for Ian hadn't seemed insurmountable. Even Dalton's misgivings about repeating his past mistakes hadn't kept him from hoping Sam's romance novel logic would hold true.

But he'd led himself astray before. It was possible he couldn't be trusted to fall in love with anyone suitable.

I sound like one of Sam's gothic heroines. And this isn't falling in love.

I want a pizza. He'd brought a couple of Vietnamese salad rolls from home for lunch, but now he was sick at heart and feeling immature and craving a double-cheese pizza. *Eating for solace.* Ian's office door opened while Dalton contemplated the merits of having bacon *and* chicken on his pizza.

"Hey," Tierney said, coming to stand in front of Dalton. "That went better than it could've." He smiled, lips curling up on one side, hands resting on Dalton's desk. He'd lost that intent, face-tightening focus he'd had before he met with Ian—now he seemed tired but relieved. As if he'd dealt with the important shit, and now he could deal with the inconsequential things.

Dalton's anger rushed back, like a wave, drowning out whatever the man was saying. How *dare* he? Anyone with half a brain would know Dalton's expectations were realistic, regardless of whether they were gay or straight, and Tierney had fucking *ignored* him.

Well, that's just not acceptable. I'll show him how ignorable I am.

"—was thinking, later, we could like . . ."

Whatever. "Your shirt is kind of—" Dalton waved his finger in circles near his own neck, pretending to explain without actually explaining.

Tierney's brows drew together. "Huh?" He stared at Dalton, then patted at his throat ineffectively.

"I'll do it," Dalton said, standing up and coming around the desk. The closer he got to Tierney, the wider Tierney's eyes got, and the more frantically he fiddled with his collar. Dalton smiled, but it felt more like baring his teeth. Tierney started backing away.

"Just tell me; I can fix it," he babbled.

"It's okay," Dalton said, holding his palms out nonthreateningly. He feinted to Tierney's right side, then when Tierney moved to block him, he stepped around the man's left, inches from Tierney's back, breathing his scent in—which, yes, smelled like man, and something rich but not quite spicy that was totally unique to Tierney, something other than cologne. And maybe a hint of toothpaste.

This is such a bad idea. What am I trying to prove?

"No, really," Tierney said. "I don't need you to—"

Dalton didn't listen. Instead he touched the man. Faux-accidentally brushing the side of his hand across the skin of Tierney's neck, and the connection zipped through his fingers, lighting up that old, familiar ache in his chest, feeding it like a drug. Dalton began falling under his own spell.

The touch acted on Tierney too, like an off switch. He froze. Letting Dalton admire him. His skin was darker here, and small hairs bristled at his nape where they'd been clipped off in a neat trim. Well-groomed, unlike the Tierney from before. Kempt rather than unkempt. Masculine. Dalton ignored his urge to finger-comb Tierney's hair, and started adjusting the shirt collar that didn't really need it, reaching over Tierney's shoulder, following it with his fingers as if checking that it was buttoned correctly, pressing against Tierney's back to do it.

Tierney's breath sped up.

Dalton smoothed his hand down the front of Tierney's chest, dangerously close to Tierney's rapid heartbeat, and where his pectoral muscle swelled out from his sternum. He pulled his hands back slowly, trailing his fingers along Tierney's lats as he passed over them. They tensed up even further, then relaxed before Dalton continued, having to step away, sliding palms across Tierney's shoulder blades, as if straightening the fall of fabric down Tierney's back. Pretending to neaten Tierney.

But it was total shirt porn. Proving to himself he could affect this man. *You did it, now stop.* Dalton swallowed, bowing his head for a second, still touching him. "You look good. Relaxed."

Tierney inhaled shakily. "Thanks."

A door opened down the hallway, and Tierney jerked away from him. Kendra walked out, looking toward Dalton. He smiled automatically, tilting his chin in that welcoming way that people who fixed other's shit were so adept at.

"Hey . . ." she began.

Tierney shifted next to him, and when Dalton turned, he was already fleeing. "I'll see you around." And then he was simply gone, and Dalton was dealing with his coworker, helping her find some random EMS training instructor in Diablo County. All the while thinking the only thing he'd proved by doing that to Tierney was that—like everyone else—he had his petty, childish moments too.

It certainly hadn't proved that Dalton had any special place in Tierney's heart, or that Tierney ached for Dalton the way Dalton did for him.

For once Dalton skipped out of work early, but Ian had told him to, so he didn't feel guilty. Much. He hadn't been doing his job, anyway; he couldn't concentrate on work after what he'd done to Tierney. It kept replaying in his head, shaming him. He'd wanted to punish Tierney so he'd used the only tool he had—lust.

It was going to be a long night. He had a heavy load of self-castigation ahead of him.

Now that he lived so close, Dalton tried to walk to and from work, but this morning he'd taken his car because he'd gone to the gym first, which meant that after work, instead of clearing his head with a walk, he had to drive.

The parking structure was still full of cars, but deserted of people when he got to it. Except for one. As soon as he looked up from digging his keys out of his bag, he saw Tierney's dark-auburn hair and the line of his jaw. Waiting for Dalton—he had to be, why else would he be next to his parking space? Dalton's heart lifted and bounced gently along, like a carefree balloon at a birthday party.

He popped the heart balloon. Or rather held it down with his foot. The man could be here to yell at him for that scene in the office.

"Hey." He stopped about five feet away, behind the bumper of the neighboring vehicle.

Tierney smiled briefly, not taking his hands out of the pockets of his overcoat. "Hi. Um." He cleared his throat. "I wanted to talk to you." His face was half-shadowed, exaggerating some features and making others disappear.

"Okay." Dalton nodded, totally uncertain about what was happening. This wasn't angry Tierney or drunk Tierney. It was the new man, and maybe he'd give Dalton a chance to explain about earlier.

"There's something I'd like to ask you," Tierney said, gesturing with his hands still in his pockets, making his coat tug around his frame.

Oh God, this was just painful. Both the ache in Dalton's chest and the way Tierney struggled with whatever it was. "Please, just ask."

"Why did you touch me like that?" Tierney rushed out. "This morning."

Dalton closed his eyes a long second. "I'm sorry."

Tierney frowned. "Why?"

"I shouldn't have done it," Dalton fumbled. He took a calming breath. "Just, I was surprised because I had no idea you were back." *Since you never contacted me.*

"Do I have something to apologize for?" Tierney asked, then swallowed.

"No, no," Dalton assured him. "It's . . . Okay, listen, I'm just going to tell you." He studied his key, trying to order his thoughts.

"Tell me what?" Tierney's voice had a sharp edge of alarm.

Dalton met his eyes. "Nothing, really, just that I was, um, mildly hurt when you barely said hi to me earlier."

"Shit," Tierney muttered, dropping his head and yanking a hand out of his pocket to run it through his hair. While it didn't look completely unkempt anymore, it did look like he'd been finger-combing through it all day. "I didn't mean to, like, ignore you. I was focused on what I needed to tell Ian." Another pass through his hair. "See, I came back from Dunthorpe with a list of people I have to apologize to—"

"They said you had to?"

"*I'm* making me."

Dalton nodded, biting his lip and waiting for him to go on.

"I wanted to get it done so badly I had tunnel vision, I guess. I knew you were there, but you weren't who I *needed* to see."

In spite of himself, Dalton's pulse picked up. Did that mean Tierney *wanted* to see him, instead? "So . . . have you said you're sorry to everyone you should?"

"Except my parents, but the jury's still out on whether I'll apologize to them. Have to go to dinner at their place tomorrow. But, yeah, now I'm on to thanking the people who helped me."

"Oh." His heart drooped a little. "How many of those are there?"

"Just you."

"Oh." A totally different "oh" than before. Dalton cleared his throat. "Um, should we go somewhere and talk?"

"There's . . . shit." Yet again with the hair, but this time Tierney stepped forward, facing Dalton. He took a deep breath. "I need to tell you something. I don't know what you thought . . ." His gaze dropped. "But when I left, *I* thought I might come back and you and I could, um, you know."

He knew. He played dumb anyway. "Know what?"

Tierney shifted, jaw tightening. "Never mind, I'm being a freak. It was just me thinking stupid shit."

Ouch. "No, it wasn't." Dalton stepped closer, brushing Tierney's arm with his fingers. "I thought the same thing."

Tierney's face went slack in surprise. "So you are, like—" he coughed "—you really *are* into me?"

"I am," Dalton whispered, staring at him for long seconds. "And I thought, when you got back . . ."

"That we'd, like." Tierney drew in a shaky breath. "Start something?"

"It seemed possible."

"Maybe it is," Tierney said, but he was shaking his head "Sometime in the future, but right now I can't really do that. I mean, my therapist thought—and, you know, I can see his point, and I kinda agree—that I need some time before I, um, make any major decisions, or enter into a romantic relationship." He licked his lip quickly before adding, "Even if I want to."

Dalton got it, really, he did—wasn't that common for people coming out of rehab? "Um, so you don't start drinking?"

Tierney nodded, but he was still focused on his feet. "Yeah. I used alcohol to deal with stress, and even good stuff can cause stress, so . . ." He shrugged, glancing up at Dalton from under his brow.

"I understand. But we can still be friends." And friends was fine, wasn't it? It didn't matter—it was what Tierney needed from him. He just had to make sure all of his various parts were kept on board with that.

"Thank God." Tierney's whole body relaxed, making Dalton realize how rigid he'd been. "I wasn't sure . . . I mean, I don't know if *I'd* want to be my friend if I were in your shoes."

"Tierney," Dalton said, not to get the man's attention, but as a sort of comfort. Verbal encouragement.

He cleared his throat, straightening up but not meeting Dalton's eyes, looking off to the side instead. "Someone's coming," he muttered, frowning.

"They won't be here long." He glanced at his watch. Yeah, the flood of government employees would start up any second. Or already had. He should suggest they go someplace more private, but to be honest he was afraid to. He didn't want to be alone with Tierney, because he felt *too* pulled toward him at the moment, even here in semipublic, with simple friendship between them. He wanted to lie down with him and let Tierney rest his head on Dalton's chest and listen to him spill his guts about the last two weeks.

But in a totally platonic way.

"Um," Tierney began. "We could go—"

Someplace private. No! Bad idea.

"—sit in my car." He tilted his head to the left, nodding toward something. "Talk awhile there."

Oh. "Okay." Perfect.

Chapter 14

Tierney hated this car. It wasn't that he didn't want to have a nice ride, it was the memory of the way he'd walked into the dealership and custom-ordered a "fully loaded" BMW, throwing money around to impress people.

Not to mention the number of times he'd said, "Chicks dig it," when talking about the beemer.

Does Dalton dig it? He was half-curious and half-repulsed by the thought. He hadn't dragged the guy in here to, like, put the moves on him.

Even if he wanted to.

The rustle of Dalton shifting on the passenger's side brought to Tierney's attention just how long this silence had lasted—since they'd both settled into the bucket seats a few minutes ago. Turning just enough to catch Dalton's profile in his peripheral vision, Tierney saw the dude swallowing. Or something like that—some uncomfortable jerk of his upper body. No matter how expensive the leather on the seat was, it couldn't make a high school move like asking the guy to sit in his car with him in a mostly deserted parking garage any less sleazy, could it?

Just as Tierney was about to blurt out, *Don't worry, I totally know this is just a friend thing, I wasn't thinking anything would happen,* Dalton asked, "You didn't send me a fruit basket, did you?"

Or they could make small talk. "Fruit basket?"

Dalton shrugged, "It came with a card that only said, 'I'm sorry,' but there was no signature. I thought maybe, since you're apologizing . . ."

"Christ," Tierney groaned, pressing his palm to his forehead. "I should've done *that*." Was it too late to order one for his parents in lieu of coming to dinner?

"So you didn't? Send me one?"

"Uh, no." Scooting around in his seat, he half faced Dalton. "I would've signed my name. I mean, it's not like you don't know I owed you, but . . ." *Fuck*. Why *hadn't* he felt like he needed to beg Dalton's forgiveness, also? "Um, I guess I sorta meant it when I apologized to you in the past."

"Huh?" Dalton's nose wrinkled up.

Tierney took a deep breath and held it in his cheeks a second before letting it whoosh out. "The people I'm apologizing to now that I'm back?" He waited for Dalton's nod before finishing. "Anytime in the past I said sorry to them, it was just to cover my ass, but, like, with *you*, I guess it sorta, you know, felt sincere. To me." His cheeks were hot enough to spontaneously combust.

Dork.

But Dalton was smiling, and biting his lip like he was trying to hold it in. A half-mischievous, half-pleased expression that reminded Tierney of an elf—the ethereal Tolkien kind, not the more cutesy pop culture ones. Tolkien elves were so much hotter. If he met one in real life, he'd totally want to fuck.

I am such *a horndog*. But really, he hadn't expected that to go away once he came out and had his personality-adjustment procedure. He was probably destined to spend most of his life horny, at least until his sixties, when stress and high blood pressure caught up with him and he couldn't get it up without medical help anymore.

Yeah. Totally time to knock his thought train off track. "Uh, so your anonymous fruit." *Total* porn movie title. *Shut up*. "No one else needs to apologize to you?"

"More like the people I think should apologize to me don't agree, and I can't think of anyone who would and needs to."

"Guess it wouldn't have been the bashers," Tierney thought out loud.

"No." Dalton pressed back into his seat, eyeing him. "Of course not."

Tierney suppressed a shudder. "That night scared the hell out of me," he admitted. "I drank more in the two weeks after it happened than I had in the two months before. I think it maybe even was part of why I came out."

"Usually stuff like that *stops* people from coming out." For a brief second Dalton's fingers brushed across Tierney's thigh.

"Yeah. I've always been a backward freak. When Sam and Miller were—" he had to take a breath "—attacked . . ." He shook his head, trying to knock loose the words he needed. "How different was I than those guys?"

"Very." Dalton leaned closer, over the console. "You're nothing like them."

"I kicked Ian's ass when he came out to me." He snorted, but not in amusement.

"The way I heard it, he won that fight." Dalton winked at him.

Tierney grimaced. "It was probably about even. Anyway, what if I'd eventually gotten to that point? Where I hated myself so much I'd do what those guys did?"

"Enough to assault someone in a dark alley for threatening your closet?"

Tierney swallowed in lieu of nodding.

"I don't think so," Dalton finally answered. "You didn't do it, did you? You came out instead."

"If I hadn't— I only did it because I was afraid of becoming like Grandfather." The words spilled out of him like pus out of a pimple.

"But you *did*. That's the important thing." Dalton moved even closer, scrunching down and putting himself squarely in Tierney's line of sight. "I think you would've come out no matter what, sooner or later."

Tierney shook his head. "I don't know . . . If I hadn't just sort of sprung it on myself like that, I'm not sure I ever would have."

"It doesn't matter; the point is you did, and now you're trying to fix things by apologizing to Ian and the other people. You're dealing with your life instead of running from it."

Tierney groaned. "Can we not talk about it? I mean, I'm sorry, but—"

Dalton smiled sympathetically. "We can not talk about it."

Ignoring his own request, Tierney went on. "Having to face all those people, it's, I don't know, *humiliating*." He whacked the steering wheel, but more as punctuation than in anger. "Everyone knows I'm gay, right? They're talking about it. About me."

Dalton nodded. "I'm sure." Fortunately, he didn't make that big-eyed pitying face other people did or anything.

"So now? I'm the idiot who stayed in a closet for twenty years, who has to go around telling people I'm sorry for the shit I did because I was terrified of exposing my queerness." He covered his face with his palm.

Dalton laughed. Softly and only briefly, but he chuckled. Tierney dropped his hand, because he had to see that. He'd never heard Dalton laugh before. Dalton's voice wasn't high, but it wasn't low, either—very middle of the road, but his laugh sounded heavier, like the earthy counterpart to his ethereal attractiveness.

For the five or so seconds it lasted, Tierney could only stare at the shape of Dalton's lips, which led to his jawline, and that curved up to Dalton's cheek and then his temple, where his bangs obscured the arch of his brow because he was looking at Tierney in a way that, on anyone else, he'd think was coy, but on this guy was just cute.

"Doesn't your hair get tangled in your eyelashes?"

Dalton's nose wrinkled up. "Um, every once in a while."

"Did I really ask you that?"

"You did." Dalton smiled at him.

"See? Told you I'm a freak."

Dalton had found Tierney's car to be just as swank inside as outside. Leather everywhere, heated seats, the fanciest stereo, and lots of switches and dials and knobs that did God knew what. His urge to climb over to the driver's side, straddle Tierney's lap and then push a few of the man's buttons was so, so wrong.

He'd managed to avoid the temptation, but when their talk was over, he nearly turned and kissed Tierney before climbing out. Not simply a friend kiss, either. One of those kisses that people shared after having an intimate, emotional conversation. He froze a moment, long enough for Tierney to leave the car, then come around to Dalton's side and pull his door open.

"I'll walk you back," he said as Dalton finally stood. Oh, *that* didn't feel like a more-than-platonic gesture or anything. While they made their way across the garage, Dalton resolved to stop this—stop overthinking the casual touches and reading into every little thing.

"Thank you," he said when they stood next to his parking spot. He didn't squelch his urge to lean forward and kiss Tierney on the cheek. *It's just a friend thing.* See? They could totally do that. Too bad he couldn't look at Tierney after it, instead focusing on getting his keys out of his coat pocket.

"Welcome," Tierney croaked, then cleared his throat. "Be careful."

Dalton jerked his head up, trying to figure out what he needed to be concerned about. Oh, he could see a lot of the green of Tierney's eyes under these lights.

"Just in case that fruit basket isn't totally innocent. Promise me you'll be careful."

"Of course." He nodded to add weight to the words. His pulse thumped a couple times in agreement.

Tierney pressed his lips into a straight line while glancing around the garage. "And call or text me if anything else weird happens."

"I will, I promise. And anytime you need a friend, use my number." Hitting the button to unlock his car, he got in with more haste than grace.

"I will, I promise." Tierney smiled.

"Good."

"Go," Tierney said, another repeat of Dalton's own words, but from much further back. From the morning he left for Dunthorpe. Dalton could only nod and close his door, very aware of Tierney watching while he put on his seat belt and started the car. At the garage exit, in his rearview mirror, he could still see Tierney standing there.

Tierney's worst hangover ever began to look like a picnic in the park compared to dinner at his parents' place post-Dunthorpe, post–coming out. He'd really been hoping for a one-course meal in the breakfast nook.

Hoping, but not expecting.

They sat down to potato soup in the formal dining room, at the table that could seat twenty if necessary. Agatha brought in each course from the kitchen.

Through with the basic pleasantries, now they were eating in almost comfortable silence. But he could feel The Conversation looming over them. He poked at a piece of celery floating in his bowl, watching his mother pour herself another glass of wine out of the corner of his eye.

God, I want a drink.

He picked up his goblet of ice water and pretended. *May as well get the ball rolling.* Tierney opened his mouth to say something—he didn't know what, maybe ask if they wanted to know about his "vacation." Before he could work it out, the housekeeper shuffled in through the swinging door, carrying a giant mountain of roast on a plate.

"Agatha!" Mother shouted.

The woman kept inching toward them, like a very slow steam engine. She couldn't see Mother waving at her because her head was nearly in the meat. In her old age, she'd become more and more hunched, as if always standing over the stove peering at her white sauce. Still a good fifteen feet from the table, she heaved a sigh and paused a second. Winded?

"*A-ga-tha*!" Mother bellowed when the old lady started moving again.

The housekeeper stopped so fast she teetered and the roast slid forward on the plate, pushing a few carrot medallions right up to the rim of the platter, where they peeked over like tiny lemmings. "Eh, ma'am?" she shouted at Mother.

Mother leaned toward her. "No one rang for the main course!"

Agatha drew herself up to her full height. "I've never done your laundry, and I'm too damned old to start now."

Tierney didn't bother trying to speak to Agatha until he reached her and took her arm to lead her to the table. "Mother just said we aren't quite ready for the roast yet, but since you're here we'll be happy to take it," he said directly into her ear.

She pulled away from him slightly to gawk in his face. "Then why did she ring for it?"

He had to lean to the side to counterbalance her and keep them moving.

"I didn't ring!" Mother screeched.

"She was confused," Tierney told Agatha.

"*I'm not confused.*"

"There's no need to shout, ma'am. I can hear you just fine," Agatha snapped. They reached the table and she half dropped the meat on it, making the water goblets tremble and slosh. "Here you go, young man." She beamed at Tierney and pinched his cheek. "I made your favorite, beef roast and green beans."

"Jesus Christ," muttered Father.

"Thank you," Tierney said, as soon as his face was free from her fingers. He loved the way she made beans, with garlic and that squeeze of lemon juice. She beamed and turned around—taking ten feet or so to do it—hobbling back out of the room.

"It might be time to think about forcing her to retire," he said to his parents as he sat down again.

Mother scowled. Father rolled his eyes. "You try talking her into it. She listens to you more than either of us."

Ha. Agatha didn't listen to anyone.

"Darling, are you sure you wouldn't like some chardonnay?" his mother asked, startling him into fumbling his water.

Tierney laid his fingers on the stem of his goblet. "No, thank you. If you'll remember, I just spent two weeks in rehab learning how to deal with myself sober, and it's kind of soon for me to start drinking again." He bared his teeth at her.

She smiled back at him and reached over to pat his hand. "Of course, I keep forgetting."

Un. Believable.

But she had more to say on the subject. "I don't quite understand this part about you not drinking. You didn't go there for alcohol treatment, dear."

"Mother," he began, but he had to interrupt himself, trying to rein in some of his exasperation. "Before I left, I'd been drinking a *lot*, and I was doing it to avoid dealing with—" he circled his hand in the air "—some *things* in my life. The point of me going there was to start learning a healthier approach to managing my issues." Good lord, he sounded like a self-help text for children. "Dealing with problems by drinking isn't *okay*." Judging by her furrowed brow, she was at least trying to understand.

It wasn't that his mother was stupid, after all, but she really loved her wine.

"You mean the problem about your being . . ." She leaned forward and whispered, "Homosexual?"

He leaned toward her and whispered back, "Yes." He had to nearly bite his tongue off to not add, "Shhh, don't tell Father," but then he'd laugh hysterically, probably until he fell off his chair and rolled on the floor, and they'd send him right back to Dunthorpe.

Now that the subject of the past month had been broached, his father pursued it. "Tell us how it went, son." He pointed a fork at Tierney, then speared a piece of meat with the tines, waving it at him when Tierney didn't respond soon enough. "You have yet to say if your trip was successful."

And there went his acid reflux. He busied himself with wiping his hands. "How would you define 'successful'?"

The long pause was answer enough, but Father cleared his throat and asked anyway, "Are you still attracted to men?"

He ignored the little run of nerves that raced up his spine. "Very."

Father paused in the middle of cutting another bite of roast. "I suppose that's the next step to getting your life back on track: figuring out how to rid you of this predilection."

Tierney's backbone straightened. "I think I'd like to keep this predilection."

Father's fork stabbed into the plate. *Clink*! "What? But why would you do that? I've been looking into it in case this happened—"

"Arthur, you never told me that. I thought we ag—"

"Hyacinth, I felt it necessary."

Mother subsided, nodding. God forbid the woman expressed her own opinions to his father. Not that she had any problems telling Tierney about them.

"Son." Father placed his fork down carefully, resting it mostly on his plate, just the last inch or so cantilevering over the side, as etiquette required. "I've discovered there are some excellent therapies for helping one become, as they say, 'straight' again. I've identified the ones with the higher success rates and—"

"I'm not." More nerves made themselves felt, muscles in his legs beginning to get antsy. *Might need to finish that sentence.* "I'm not going to be undergoing any of those therapies. I won't. You can't make me." He straightened his shoulders the instant he caught himself trying to hunch them.

Elbows on the table, Father gave Tierney "the look." It didn't seem to have the same effect on him that it used to. Father's hadn't ever been as powerful as Grandfather's stern face anyway. Instead of opening his mouth and babbling out whatever he thought the dude wanted to hear, Tierney gazed back at him.

"Have you thought about this carefully?" Father eventually asked.

Tierney leaned toward the head of the table, harnessing some of his nervous energy and using it to power his voice. "I've spent years thinking about nothing else."

Father's Adam's apple bobbed. "Have you given any thought to how this will affect the rest of the family? Or the company?"

Tierney's adrenaline really started to flow, making him feel like a live wire. "*Of course* I have. What do you think shut me up all those years? Grandfather's harping on behaving like a *Terrebonne*. But here's the thing no one seems to get: this is *my* life. I spent years living it the way you expected me to and—"

"Darling, we *never* told you not to be gay." Mother's hand flew to her sternum in affront.

It was grit his teeth or laugh in her face. "You didn't get the memo I sent out at the wake? Grandfather *did* tell me that. And right now?" He shoved a finger in his father's direction. "*He*'s trying to tell me the same thing. Either way, it's. My. Life." He pushed back from the table, standing up. "I don't know a whole lot about anything right now, but I know one thing. If I'm desperate enough and stupid enough to announce my sexual orientation to a crowd, then I'm going to stand by what I said, what I *am*. I'm thirty-four, so it's about damn time I did." His parents sat frozen, wide-eyed and fixated on him. He could hear his own breath echoing off the walls, so he forced himself to sit back down, trying to slow his heart by will alone.

Father unfroze, looking at Mother, then toward Tierney again. "As vice president of PR and government affairs, will you be able to adequately represent the company as a gay man?"

That did it—Tierney laughed. He killed it quickly, but he lost it for a brief second there. "I knew it!" He pointed at Father again. "I *knew* it. This is why I never wanted to be out in the first place. You'd actually do it, wouldn't you?" This time when he stood up, his chair nearly went over. "You'd force me to leave the company because I like to—"

"Tierney!" Father stood up also. "That's *not* what I meant." They stared at each other a second, while a small but compelling thought tickled Tierney's mind. *Let's listen to him.*

He sat back down once more and arranged his face into exaggerated interest.

Father took a deep breath, dropped into his chair, and took a fortifying sip of wine. "I do understand that my father could be very . . . rigid. It's possible we relied too much on his guidance, but I do feel it necessary to say that, no matter how much things have changed, people see homosexual men *differently*. Next time you go to Washington for the company—"

"Next time I go to DC, I won't spend half my time having meetings with Republicans through glory holes!"

Mother shrieked, hitting herself in the cheek with the hand that flew up to cover her mouth. Then she dropped it and asked Father, "What's a glory hole?"

"I'm very certain we don't want to know." Father turned to Tierney. "What are you saying?"

"I'm saying, if you think there aren't any queers running this country, you're dead wrong." Tierney waited for his mother's shriek, but it appeared she'd hit her shock limit. Or didn't know what "queer" meant, either.

"But they aren't *out*, Tierney. If they were, you wouldn't be meeting them at holy places would you?"

"Father, here's the deal: If they aren't out, it's not my problem. All I can worry about is me. As for my job, I think you need to let me show you whether or not I can still do it before you make assumptions."

"I suppose you have a point," Father said after a moment. "We'll revisit this topic in the future if necessary." With that, he picked up his fork to resume eating. Mother grabbed her wine glass and chugged it.

Apparently, the discussion was over.

Tierney sat there, staring at his food, drained. He'd done it. Nothing had been decided, it hadn't gone as horribly as he'd expected, but he'd won his first showdown with his parents.

He felt kind of let down by the whole thing.

The fun wasn't over, however. At the end of the evening, Tierney stood at the front door, hand on the knob, presenting his parents with his fakest smile after saying his good-byes. Father stepped forward, picking up something from behind a ridiculous vase that stood on the table in the entryway.

"Until this is, um, resolved, I want you to take precautions against any lasting ill effects." In his outstretched hand, he held . . . a box of condoms.

Tierney blinked. "I can buy my own— I mean, I really don't—"

"Just take them," his father barked, shoving it into Tierney's chest.

"It will make Arthur feel better," Mother whispered, as if they could have a private conversation. Tierney jerked around to look at her, and she *winked.*

He opened his mouth to say . . . something, but just then Agatha tottered in, carrying his jacket. "Here you go, young man," she said.

Jesus Christ. Tierney took the box, grabbed his coat, and then fled into the night.

Chapter 15

When Dalton's phone rang late that evening, it was Tierney, calling from his car, sounding as dried out as a crusty sponge and so relieved to talk to someone "normal." Already in bed and reading, Dalton set down his book and curled up with his blankets and pillows, content to let Tierney talk it all out. Tell Dalton how his parents didn't think he could do his job, and how he hadn't even begun to think about apologizing to them, and how generally bizarre his family was.

Dalton said, "Mm-hmm" and soothing things like that a lot.

After about ten minutes, Tierney finally began to run out of steam. "Father's hoping I'll, like, grow out of this or something. He wants to send me to an ex-gay thing now. As if two weeks at Dunthorpe wasn't enough? Christ." Something thumped over the line, as if he'd hit his steering wheel or dashboard.

A pang of alarm made Dalton ask, "But you aren't going, right?"

"Fuck no." Tierney snorted. "He can't make me." A rhythmic clicking that sounded like a blinker started up as he said, "This fitting back into my life thing, it's stressful."

"That's not surprising." It was a pretty sad attempt at comfort. Dalton swallowed, because what he was about to offer would be the ultimate test of *just* friendship. "Would it help if I came over?"

Tierney hesitated. *He wants me to come over.*

"You don't have to," he finally responded. "It's late."

"Did you ever have sleepovers as a kid?" Dalton asked quickly, pushing out of bed—he was doing this. Tierney needed him. "When your friends would come over and you'd hang out and talk all night?"

Tierney huffed. "I never had any slumber parties when I was a kid because Grandfather thought they were unseemly. Except they were only unseemly for me. Chase gotta have 'em."

The man's grandfather was an A number one dickhead. "You can have them now." Dalton reached for his backpack on the upper shelf of his closet. "All the sleepovers you want."

"With you?"

"Yeah," Dalton responded softly, matching Tierney's tone. "A friendly sleepover," he added, in case Tierney was worried about that.

"When?"

"It starts in twenty minutes," Dalton said, searching for a shirt to wear to work in the morning. "As soon as I get there."

"Oh thank God," Tierney said in a rush.

Tierney was standing at his door waiting when Dalton got off the elevator. His hair was standing up in spots again—he must have been finger-combing it—and his cheeks seemed hollow. But his eyes were still that mixture of brown and green, and he still had that jaw and the scruff and he was looking at Dalton like he was the last lifeboat on the *Titanic*.

Scrumptious.

I'm in. So. Much. Trouble.

Forget any fears Dalton had about repeating his past mistakes, there were a million other reasons why Dalton shouldn't want the man—he was just coming out of the closet, he'd had a personality transformation, he'd gotten most of his sexual experience through a hole in the wall, he was (as Tierney put it himself) a serious fixer-upper, and to top it all off, beginning a relationship could actually jeopardize all the remodeling work he'd begun.

But the bones are good. The structural elements of this man were as solid as midcentury wood-frame construction. Solid enough for Dalton to ignore all those warning signs, and simply trust his gut.

Not that it mattered, because this was just platonic, right?

"Hi," he said, after standing in front of Tierney for what had to have been five seconds of silence.

"Hi." Tierney sighed, reaching to place a hand on the ball of Dalton's shoulder. He squeezed once and let it drop. "Thank you."

Dalton let the warm glow in his chest infuse his smile. "Let's get this party started."

It wasn't much of a party, but it seemed to be what Tierney needed. Once they were in his living room, he fell onto the couch, lounging in his old, nearly threadbare T-shirt and pajama pants.

"I'm so exhausted," he mumbled.

"We don't have to do anything," Dalton said from his corner of the sofa. "Do you want to just go to bed?"

Tierney blinked at him heavily. "Last time you were here, you came and slept with me."

Dalton sat up, straightening his spine. "I was worried about you."

Tierney fidgeted, but wearily, like he couldn't work up to the full expression of his nerves, simply tapping his fingers on the arm of the couch. "You don't have to tonight."

"You don't want me to?" Dalton asked before he could stop himself.

Tierney squinted at him, like he thought maybe Dalton was crazy. "Of *course* I want you to."

"But?"

"But." Tierney ran a hand over his head, messing his hair up even more, a few brown strands shining reddish in the lamplight. "I don't want you to think . . . you know."

"I won't," Dalton whispered. Wondered if he'd put up with this neediness from anyone else. Probably not, given his past and his attempts to guard against his personal weaknesses, but unlike most people who exhibited the trait, Tierney didn't *want* to be needy.

Unless I'm fooling myself.

No. He stood. "Lie down," he ordered.

Tierney stared at him blankly, until Dalton started making "get horizontal" hand motions. The confused expression didn't change, but Tierney stretched out on the cushions. Dalton reached across to turn off the lamp next to the couch, leaving the one near the television on. The rest of the condo was dark, so they had a little cave of low-lit tranquility in the room. At least, that was the effect Dalton was going for.

Now the difficult-ish part. He lay down next to Tierney, not too close. Not touching everywhere, although there was no place for Tierney to put his hand other than Dalton's waist, and their sock-clad feet got tangled together.

It was all in the name of stress relief, though. Perfectly acceptable. Nudging a throw pillow under their heads, Dalton sighed and let his body settle, chest centimeters from Tierney's and his forehead level with Tierney's mouth, bangs shifting with the man's breath.

"What are we doing?" Tierney whispered after a few seconds.

"We're cuddling," Dalton whispered back.

Tierney's fingers dug into Dalton's side. "Isn't that, like, a romantic thing?"

"This is friend cuddling." If there wasn't such a thing already, they were pioneering it tonight. "For stress relief."

Tierney didn't say any more, and slowly Dalton felt the tension drain out of him. The fish tank gurgle provided the perfect white noise, and body heat and proximity were enough to keep them warm.

Once Tierney's breathing had evened out, Dalton rested his lax fingers on Tierney's cheek. He tensed.

"Human touch is good for you," Dalton said, and Tierney's muscles loosened again. "When my skin touches yours, your body releases a hormone that encourages feelings of well-being."

"I think it releases a couple other hormones too," Tierney said, but it was barely a murmur.

"When it's just friend cuddling, we don't listen to those hormones, 'kay?"

"'Kay," Tierney whispered, then his lips grazed Dalton's hair. "I like this," he said so softly Dalton almost couldn't hear him over his own heartbeat.

"Me too."

Tierney fell asleep quickly after that. Dalton had thought he would, since most people underestimated how exhausting emotional stress could be.

Underestimating was going around because, in spite of thinking *he* wasn't tired, next thing Dalton knew, Tierney jerking awake roused him too, nearly knocking him on the floor.

"Sorry," Tierney said. "Fell asleep. God, I keep doing that to you."

"Only the second time," Dalton said, trying to blink himself more conscious.

"It's only the second time you've been here." Tierney sat up, maneuvering over him to sit at Dalton's feet and rest his face in his hands. "Such a dork, falling asleep in your lap like that," he said quietly. "Last time."

"It was kind of sweet."

They stared at each other, and Dalton *knew* they were both thinking about what happened afterward.

"We should go to my bedroom." Tierney stood. "We'll both sleep better there."

"Okay." He took Tierney's hand when it was offered, grabbed his pack from off the floor, and followed the man down the hall.

The alarm on Dalton's phone went off at six. He'd set it to the "crickets" tone, because that should be less jarring than "car alarm" or whatever, but it never was. Crickets woke him up just as abruptly. He cracked one eyelid and aimed for the glowing red circle, poking at it until the insects shut up.

Even only half-awake, he wasn't disoriented. He knew immediately that the faint warmth at his back was Tierney, and the door he could just make out in the wall across from him led into Tierney's bathroom, where he'd brushed his teeth and given himself a stern "just friends" talking to last night.

He closed his eyes again, tucking his hands under his head, and imagined this was real. That Tierney slept so close to him in such a huge bed because he wanted to be near Dalton, not because that was his habitual spot. That Dalton could turn over and kiss Tierney awake, maybe get them naked and they could rock against each other until they both gave it up.

Groan. Why had he let his mind go there? They'd successfully negotiated sleeping together all night without introducing sex, and he couldn't ruin that now. He rolled over carefully, trying not to jostle the bed too much. Tierney looked rough. Dark circles under his eyes, hair sticking up like crazy, mouth slack, whiskers growing in.

Yummers.

"Are you leaving?" Tierney asked, blinking. His voice was low and raspy and had a way of worming into Dalton's ear.

He nodded. "I have to get ready for work."

"Yeah." Tierney reached for Dalton, taking his hand and holding it loosely. "Sorry about last night."

"Nothing to be sorry for." He tried to imagine lying in bed with Sam or one of his other friends—even one of the friends with benefits he'd had in college—talking like this in the predawn light, inches apart. Holding hands. It wouldn't happen. One of them—if not both—would read it as an invitation for sex, but with Tierney it was simply intimate in some undefined way. Unformed. Things could become anything between them. "I offered to come over."

"My first full day as the new man in the old life," Tierney said. "Guess I survived."

"It'll probably be the first of many firsts."

"Yeah," Tierney agreed, locking gazes with him, the air around them suddenly charged with tension. "You're the first guy I've ever kissed, or been with who I knew. Like, your name."

Dalton lifted his head off the pillow. "So, you're saying . . ."

"I'm a thirty-four-year-old virgin."

Dalton could see why admitting that might be uncomfortable for Tierney, but something in his expression radiated acceptance of the situation. Dalton settled his head back down. "You've been with women, right?"

One side of Tierney's mouth curved up. "Well, yeah, but that doesn't really seem like it counts anymore."

"I've never been with a woman," he offered.

Tierney took a breath, holding it for a second. "Your first time, it wasn't that guy was it? The one you moved in with after getting kicked out."

"No, it was my high school boyfriend, thank God." Dalton rolled onto his back, because it was easier to face the ceiling than his bed partner.

"Thank God?"

"Well, just, if he'd been my first . . ." He ran a hand through his bangs, letting them fall back on the pillow while he inspected the paint job for answers. If Hugh had been his first, it would be as if he'd sold his virginity to the highest bidder.

"I get it," Tierney said after a few moments.

He probably did. Dalton shifted until he faced him again.

"Maybe I'll have a first boyfriend, some day," Tierney said in a low voice.

"I'm sure you will." The thought made his heart pound harder, but he forced his mind away from danger, and simply hoped Tierney had a better first boyfriend than he'd had. "My first relationship was how my parents found out I'm gay. My mom walked into my room while we were making out."

Tierney scooted closer to him. "Sorry I brought it up. We don't have to talk about—"

"I want to." For the first time, he thought someone might truly understand. Not be sickened and angry like Andrea, or titillated like Sam. "My family *coddled* me. I was the youngest and everyone gave me everything I wanted, but when my parents found out I was gay, I went from being this pampered kid who wasn't ready for the real world to a kid who was completely on his own. I didn't know what to do." He shrugged one shoulder. "And I was mad. I wanted to hurt them back, so I sort of . . . whored around awhile." He took a deep breath. "I needed to be *needed*, so I went from guy to guy for almost four years, and eventually, I went into each relationship knowing it was actually an *arrangement*." He smiled, totally inappropriately, but it was one of those uncontrollable, nervous reactions. "There's a whole group of guys who do that, you know. Stay in the closet but have boys stashed away on the side."

Tierney huffed softly. "I guess I could have been a guy like that instead of coming out." He locked gazes with Dalton. "Except I don't think I could have done it."

"It's a lot of deceit." So much so that his stomach roiled remembering it. "Some guys are okay with that, and I can see why they'd need to, or feel they need to, but I just couldn't do it. Not after a while."

"Yeah, the most sneaking around I could handle were glory holes."

Dalton's laugh felt appropriate this time, thank God.

Tierney chuckled along with him but then went serious again. "It's weird, you know? I was totally the type of guy you'd expect that out of, stashing some secret piece on the side, but I just *couldn't*—like, I didn't even consider it. I don't know why."

"I know why," Dalton said. "You were horrible at pretending to be straight because you're horrible at lying to yourself. Having a whole hidden relationship doesn't seem like something you could stomach."

"I guess." Tierney sighed. "Doesn't explain how I do my job, but . . ." He gazed at Dalton a long moment. "I kind of think you're right about me."

Moments like this, silent communication running between them, intensified Dalton's attraction to Tierney so much. He'd never had this with anyone, and he liked it.

Tierney scraped his teeth across his lip a couple times before asking, "Why did you stop? I mean, stop finding sugar daddies."

This part. He'd never told anyone about it, but maybe he should. If he spit it out, it would be like lancing a boil. Not as gross, but as painful. "I found out my last *keeper* had a girlfriend."

Tierney's eyebrows flew up.

"I thought she was his beard. The woman he took to functions when he had to have a date, but she thought she was his fiancée." He squeezed his temples with his thumb and finger. "She—Vanessa—found out about me and came to the door screaming one day. It was like she'd thrown ice water all over my life, and I could see what I'd become clearly for the first time. It all seemed so *tawdry*." It still did. "I didn't want to be that guy."

Tierney shifted. "So you just left?"

"Yeah." He sat up in bed, feeling a little nauseous now. "I say they needed me, and they did need *someone*, but none of them wanted *me*. I was interchangeable. Any reliable piece of ass would do."

"Jesus." Tierney sat next to him, gripping Dalton's shoulder. "Don't beat yourself up about this. You realized you needed to change things a long time before I did. What were you? Less than twenty-five, right?"

"Twenty-two." He nodded. "I was twenty-two before I started to grow up and stopped trying to find someone to take care of me."

"That's young. I mean really," he said when Dalton just looked at him. "Most people don't figure their shit out for years, and I'm not talking about only me; lots of people don't deal with their reality. It's *impressive* that you did so young."

"Maybe," Dalton said. God, his muscles felt weak. "So much for my revenge on my parents." He turned away, sitting on the edge of the mattress, not sure what to say now. The bed shook under his butt, and suddenly he felt warmth on his back, then Tierney's arms came around him, trapping Dalton's own against his torso in a tight squeeze before loosening. But not letting go.

"Thank you," Tierney said against Dalton's neck, whiskers scraping his skin. "For telling me."

Dalton had to swallow to speak. "That's the first time I've ever told anyone that much." He reached up and touched Tierney's jaw, letting the beginnings of the man's beard prick his fingertips.

"You don't laugh enough." Tierney had come into the living room, where Dalton had gone to put on his shoes, and found him sitting on the couch, frowning into midair, and holding a black oxford in his hand. Had talking about his past upset him?

Someone like Dalton should be happy more often.

The dude shook off whatever was occupying his thoughts, and lifted his foot. "We haven't had a lot of things to laugh about. I haven't seen you laugh much, either." He looked over his shoulder, tying his laces.

Tierney came around and sat next to him. "Yeah, but I know *I* laugh. Right now we're talking about you."

A smile was flirting with the corners of Dalton's mouth. "I was talking about you."

"Uh-uh. My house, my conversation. We're talking about *you*."

Dalton was grinning now, all done with his laces. He turned to Tierney. "Maybe you just aren't funny."

"Ooooh," Tierney said softly, shaking his head. "Now you've done it. I'll *give* you something to laugh about."

He jumped, digging his fingers into Dalton's sides, because everyone was ticklish there, right? Dalton definitely was—that earthy laugh spilled out of him, and he scooted back, trying to escape. Tierney pursued him until they were both half-lying on the cushions, in danger of falling off if he didn't stop making Dalton squirm. The laugh was addictive, though. He needed to hear more of it. Just a little, to help get him through the day.

"Stop," Dalton begged between gasping, giggling breaths. "T-Tierney, please s-s-stop."

He did, because Dalton's face was totally flushed and both their chests were heaving, working to get more air in. Grinning down at him, Tierney mentally patted himself on the back. "See? Made ya laugh."

Dalton laughed again, which effectively hog-tied Tierney, making it impossible for him to move away. Such a sexy sound. Tierney wanted to lay his palm on Dalton's chest and feel it vibrate through him.

So he did.

It just seemed so *possible*, touching Dalton like this. Maybe it was the blue of his eyes or how happy he seemed right now, or just the way he looked at Tierney, as if Tierney had given him a gift. The *perfect* gift.

Some tangible connection pulled him toward Dalton, like an elastic band, to the point of no return, where Tierney *had* to kiss him.

Just the press of Dalton's lips made him hard; he didn't need tongue. Dalton gave it to him, though, opening up and offering Tierney free rein inside his mouth. At first it was wild and desperate, but Dalton's hand in his hair focused Tierney. Dalton arching up into him made it a full-body experience that left them both gasping when it was over, staring at each other.

Dalton licked his lip. "Was that just a friend thing?"

Tierney's heart thumped extra hard in his chest. "If you want it to be."

For a second, he really thought Dalton would kiss him back. His eyes searched Tierney's like he could read a message there.

But then, Dalton slid his hand out of Tierney's hair, until his fingers rested along Tierney's cheekbone. "Then I guess that's what it was."

Chapter 16

Pretending was a useful skill—at his first few days back to work, Tierney had pretended to be a normal guy (who'd completely humiliated himself, then disappeared for a couple weeks to have a minor personality reconstruction procedure) coming in for a normal day at the office. When he walked through the front doors of Metropolitan Ambulance the first morning, the receptionist had actually gasped and slapped her hand over her mouth. That's something he bet Dalton would never do. Raise an eyebrow or maybe blank his expression, but not gasp loudly.

Tierney had walked past her with a wave and smile. Well, hopefully it'd looked like a smile.

Gina, though, deserved whatever future raises Chase wanted to give her, because she was fantastic about the whole thing. Sympathetic, but not cloyingly so, and that first day, when he'd asked her how she felt about him being gay, she'd only snorted and said, "It explains a lot of things."

The rest of that week—only three days, thank all that was unholy—was complete pretense as well. He played deaf whenever he walked into a room and overheard the last few words of a conversation that was clearly about him. He faked stupid when people asked him how his vacation had gone, and if he'd "straightened everything out." He spent every fucking day affecting the demeanor of a guy who didn't care what anyone thought.

Total lie. He'd died inside a few thousand times, worrying what people thought.

All those years of playing Tierney Terrebonne, Sleazeball Extraordinaire should have made it easier to fake it now, but it didn't.

Then he'd been acting out of self-preservation. *This* felt like he was forcing himself to walk into traffic every second of the day.

By the time Friday rolled around, he was exhausted. He wanted to stay home in bed—no more pretending to be oblivious, no *Star Trek*, no porn. Nothing. Just sleep.

Except he couldn't rest, because the worst was yet to come.

That afternoon, he had a meeting.

When he walked in and Gina reminded him, "Don't forget, you have that tri-county emergency services thingy at the hospital today," he froze for a second, waiting for the "dun-dun-*duuuuun*" tone that signaled impending doom on sitcoms.

"Tierney?" Gina prodded. "Hellooooo." She stood and leaned over her desk to wave a palm in Tierney's face.

He started. "I remember."

She furrowed her brow. "Are you sure you don't want me to go instead?"

"No." He shook his head. "I gotta get the first one over with." He had to deal with those guys who'd been in that meeting at Ian's office. Well, not all of them, because Ian and a few others wouldn't be there, but a majority of them. Like Aspell and Chief Fowler . . . "I'll just be sitting at my desk until it's time to go, puking my guts out into my trash can."

She handed him a plastic garbage pail as he passed by. "Yours is made of wire mesh. Too many holes."

Christ, this was going to *suck*.

And it did. Oh, it started out all right, everyone greeted him like always, and no one made any obvious jokes at his expense, but halfway through, he realized they weren't texting him.

They were texting *each other*, he could see by the way people surreptitiously stared at their laps, hands under the table. There were only two explanations for that behavior, and no one would masturbate in a meeting. Well, not as a group.

Normally everyone but the chair messaged everyone else, making jokes about the agenda, or how bored they were, or sniping about someone's car or golf game or whatever. The chair knew it was happening—in every other meeting he or she was in and *not* chairing, they did the same thing.

This time, Tierney was not the chairperson. Yet he was being texted *around*, not texted *to*.

Which could only mean one thing. *People are texting* about *me*.

He swallowed the knowledge down, past his increasingly rapid heartbeat and indulged in a little creative visualization, imagining his butt glued to the chair. He absolutely would not get up and flee no matter how much of him wanted to. The old Tierney would've done that. Actually, the old Tierney would be texting about the new Tierney, saying vicious things. More vicious than anyone else's jabs.

Homophobic things.

I'm not a homophobe, I'm a homo.

He and Marty had planned some sort of coping strategy for these situations, hadn't they? For the life of him, he couldn't remember what it was. His spine was so rigid, he trembled from the waist up, and he couldn't relax no matter what he did—even meditative breathing didn't help because he couldn't settle into a rhythm. Mostly he kept his stare fixed on the wall behind Chief Brown's head, enduring.

Jesus, this was the thing he'd been afraid of his whole life—ostracism. Being the lone wolf. His butt glue came close to failing, but then movement in his peripheral vision caught his attention. It was Jerry—Chief Brown—peeking at him, eyes skittering off when Tierney caught him.

Oh, did he know *that* look: guilt. Jerry felt badly for texting about him. Probably Aspell, that fucking hospital administrator, was leading the pack, and Jerry was too big a weenie not to follow along. *Conformist.* Tierney's face muscles loosened up enough for him to scowl across the table, but the chief wouldn't look at him again.

Well fuck that. He wasn't leaving until Jerry had the balls to meet his eyes. *Pansy ass.*

Tierney's anger kept him present. In the room with all the dickheads texting about him, staring people down—the few who weren't avoiding his gaze.

Only Jerry showed any guilt, but eventually there was a lessening of busy hands under the table.

When the meeting was over, he walked out. Didn't say anything to anyone, even ignored it when Jerry called his name. Instead he took the elevator to the fifth floor of the parking garage, found his car, and sat in it, forehead resting on the steering wheel for a half hour before calling Gina and telling her he wouldn't be back until Monday.

He'd lived through that meeting, kept his butt in the seat, but there was no rush of accomplishment. Wasn't he supposed to feel vindication or soul-deep truth or self-righteousness or *something*? Something good and positive, pushing him forward into this new life he'd begun to carve out for himself.

Instead he felt beat down. Not completely hopeless, but . . . dull. Scarred. That swirling in the pit of his stomach, he knew it well. His old enemy fear had come creeping back, saying "I told you so."

Fuck, he didn't want to deal with that asshole tonight.

On the way back to his condo, he bought a fifth of bourbon.

Hours later, sitting alone in his living room, mesmerized by the nearly full bottle and the untouched glass he'd poured a drink into, he wondered what the fuck he thought he was doing. Thinking about having a drink, but not because he craved *it* so much as the insulation it bought him from the pain of day-to-day life. The cutting slights and insults.

Until the effects of the booze wore off, and the sting of those little cuts became worse than they would have been if he'd never had the drink in the first place. He really only had two choices—take it on the chin now, or drink up and pay a steeper price later.

In spite of knowing what was best, he was having a hard time forgoing the booze.

He knew what he was supposed to do when tempted like this—call Marty, or the therapist he should have contacted now that he was back home. Even calling someone in the support network he should have set up would work, or finding an AA meeting.

But he wasn't a *real* alcoholic, so why did he need to do all that shit?

So you don't end up like this, dumbass.

Alone and friendless, desperate to be numb and dumb. Why had he decided to go down this road, if he was going to give up this easily? Wasn't the point to face life rather than hide from it, even the painful shit?

How did people *do* this, though?

Friends.

I have a friend.

Carefully, like it might bite him if he startled it, Tierney leaned forward and set the glass down on the coffee table, next to the bottle. Then he picked up his phone, turned it back on, and reached out for help.

Slumped in his favorite (and only) stuffed chair, Dalton watched the lights of downtown through his windows. Well, what he could see of them. He should turn on a lamp, but darkness felt more contemplative.

It was one of the best things about having his own place—every space was his, and if he wanted to just sit a couple of hours and not do much of anything, no one would interrupt him.

Although he needed to wash some clothes. And it wouldn't hurt to unpack the rest of his books. Since he'd started reading some of Sam's suggestions on a new e-reader, the print copies seemed both more precious and more likely to be left stored in a box.

"What should we do tonight?" he asked his cat.

Blue blinked at him sleepily from the top of the empty bookshelf before he stretched, bowing his back and extending one paw and then the other in front of him, claws unsheathed as far as possible, yawning the entire time.

"Okay, what should *I* do tonight?" Dalton's phone beeped before Blue could not answer and instead curl up for his tenth nap of the day.

Clearly, he could still be interrupted, even in his own place. He should ignore it, but his overdeveloped sense of obligation couldn't stomach that, so he got up to find it and read the message.

Thank God he did. It was Tierney, wanting him to come over for an "intervention."

Dalton's pulse thumped a few times in his ears, because that particular word implied one thing—Tierney'd fallen off the wagon.

I'll be there as soon as I can, he responded.

The ten-minute trip wasn't as anxious a drive over as it had been the morning after Tierney came out, but Dalton's adrenaline raced through his blood stream, revving to go at every stoplight.

Tierney buzzed him into the building without a word, and he was waiting in the doorway when Dalton got off the elevator.

"Hey, I'm here," he said, feeling suddenly nervous and shy for no reason he could pinpoint, except that things felt *different*. As he walked toward Tierney, he realized most of what was different was the man himself—resting against the jamb, hands in the pockets of his suit pants, dress shirt untucked, and tie gone. In seconds, Dalton stood in front of him, combing Tierney's hair back and cupping his face. "Are you all right?"

Then Tierney was hugging him, fingertips digging into his shoulders. Dalton wrapped his arms around the man's waist and let him squeeze as much as he needed to, until he shuddered with one big release of tension and his muscles began to relax. Dalton could feel them loosen as he smoothed his palms up and down Tierney's back.

"Better?" he asked when Tierney eased his hold, not quite pulling away, but letting some air between them.

"Yeah," Tierney croaked, lifting his head to show red-rimmed eyes.

Dalton kissed him. A chaste kiss. A short clinging of lips and no tongue, but still it sent a jolt through his body, lighting up that spot in his heart reserved just for this man. He smiled, trying to cover up how not platonic he felt right then, sliding a hand down Tierney's cheek before letting it drop and backing up slightly. He forced a short laugh. "I'm sorry. That was just a friend thing."

"Sure." Tierney swallowed. "Come inside?"

"Yeah."

But Tierney didn't move right away; he stared at Dalton a few more seconds. "Thanks for coming over," he finally whispered, then turned, leading Dalton toward his sectional, and the nearly full bottle of golden liquid on the coffee table. As he flopped onto the cushion, he picked up a glass with more booze in it, resting it on his thigh.

"Are you sure you want that?" Dalton asked. He sat down right on the edge of the couch.

Tierney took a huge breath, then hesitantly set his glass on the coffee table. "I don't. I've been trying not to drink it for hours."

"You were successful." He'd not had any on his breath when Dalton kissed him. *Totally a good excuse for kissing him*. He just needed to watch the touching. Keep it friendly. "Do you want me to get rid of it?"

Tierney hung his head, elbows on his knees.

"I could put it in the kitchen?" One of his hands got away from him, fingers landing on Tierney's forearm. His skin was damp, but it hadn't been earlier. "Tierney?"

"Why don't you call me T? People always get tired of saying my name and shorten it."

"I like your name." He made the executive decision and stood, picking up the alcohol. Tierney said nothing as Dalton stepped around the coffee table and walked through the shadowed dining area. In the kitchen island, he found one of those little bar sinks, so he dumped out the drink, ice cubes clinking against the stainless steel, and set the bottle next to it. Emptying that seemed like too much distrust. Too presumptuous.

Until Tierney called out, "Get rid of the rest of it." So he did, listening to the bourbon *glug-glug* and rush down the drain.

When he got back to the living room, Tierney was still staring at the wet ring his drink had left on the coffee table. Dalton sat, angled toward him but leaving Tierney his space, trying not to disturb the cushions. As if he were afraid to wake someone walking in their sleep.

Except disturbing him might help him work through this sooner. "What happened? Do you want to talk about it?"

Tierney groaned and covered his face with his hands.

"You don't have to tell me anything." He *had* to put his arm around him. "We can just watch *Star Trek* and grunt monosyllables at each other."

Tierney's shoulders shuddered under his hand, and Dalton gripped him, feeling the strength of his muscles. God, he wasn't going to cry, was he?

But Tierney dropped his hands and straightened up, blinking. "I thought I was ready for it . . ." He blew out a heavy breath and leaned toward Dalton, listing into his side.

"For what?"

"For facing all those people."

He may not know exactly which people, but Dalton could imagine. The people he worked with. His peers and colleagues. "Yeah, being out isn't always easy." He trailed fingers through Tierney's hair, the same way he might caress his cat. Like Blue, Tierney turned into it, pulling his leg up on the couch so they mirrored each other, knees touching. "But you faced them, right?"

Tierney grimaced. "Yeah, then came home and nearly drank."

"But texted me when you decided not to." Dalton dropped his arm off the back of the couch to take Tierney's hand.

"Texted you because I didn't know if I could stop myself. I should've been able to deal," Tierney whispered. "I had a plan. But I didn't follow it."

"What's the plan?" Dalton asked cautiously. Again, totally not his territory.

Tierney pulled in a breath, lifting his head. "I'm supposed to call my therapist. Or someone in my support network, if I can't get him."

"So did you try your therapist?"

Tierney swallowed. "No."

"Um, am I in your support network?"

"Well," Tierney said with a quick, tortured grimace. "You're pretty much the whole thing. Probably should've talked to you about that, huh? Sorry." For a second, his eyes flickered to Dalton's, but then he looked away again.

"It's fine." He twined their fingers together, trying to physically express his willingness to be Tierney's man. *Support* man. "So, if I'm your support person, does that mean I'm supposed to give you guidance?"

"I think you're supposed to make sure I don't drink."

"'Kay, so we've done that . . . Now what?"

"I dunno." He flashed a weak smile. "I was kind of hoping you'd have some idea."

"So that means I'm in charge?"

Tierney shrugged.

God, don't let me fuck this up. "Maybe you should call your therapist and refresh your memory?"

"You think?" Tierney ran his teeth across his lower lip a couple of times.

"Yeah." Dalton smiled, trying to reassure even more with a squeeze of his fingers. "As your official support network, I'm saying you have to."

"Um, okay . . ." Tierney took another of those heavy breaths. Like an inverse sigh. "I'll do it."

"Go." Dalton released his hand. "Do it someplace private. I'll be here when you're done."

Tierney stared at him, eyes big and bottomless, nearly pure green. "I kinda need you to be," he whispered.

"I promise." He couldn't stop himself from leaning forward and hugging him, just a quick one. A friendly, supportive, encouraging embrace, before Tierney inhaled deeply one more time, took his phone off the coffee table, and walked down the hallway.

Tierney spent a half hour on the phone with Marty before coming back to the living room to find Dalton still there. *Thank God.* The dude had the television figured out, even though it took three remotes to get anything to stream with sound. But Dalton had it ready to watch, the menu for *Star Trek: The Next Generation* displayed on the screen.

He looked up from the magazine he was flipping through and smiled, tilting his head back to see Tierney, his bright hair falling away, brushing the back of a cushion. Tierney'd never felt so welcomed to his own couch. "What're you reading?" Not that he cared, but he had to say something.

"Um . . ." Dalton bent the cover over his hand so they could both see it. "*National Geographic.*"

"I get that?"

"It's addressed to you."

Tierney came around the front of the sofa, and for a second he was pretty sure Dalton was checking him out. Then it hit him that the jeans he'd changed into while talking to Marty were the same ones he'd been wearing the first time Dalton came over. *Shit.* Would the dude notice? *Of course not.* But if he *did*, would he think it was on purpose? *Was* it on purpose, but, like subconsciously?

And if it *was* subconsciously on purpose, what did that mean?

"What are you thinking about?" Dalton asked. Tierney'd stopped right next to him, standing there like a dork. He spent a lot of time being a dork around this guy.

"Uh, what Marty said," he blurted. *Not.*

"Mmm." Dalton patted the cushion next to him. "Want to sit and watch some television? You don't have to think about this anymore tonight, do you?"

Tierney collapsed onto the sofa. "I don't," he sighed.

Dalton nodded, then picked up the relevant remote. "You wanna pick an episode or you want me to?"

"You. I don't watch this series."

"Cool." He grinned, pointing the thing at the screen as if it were a phaser. "I'll make you watch all my favorites."

He hoped Dalton had a lot of them and he'd want to stay for, like, a month, making Tierney view them all. That's all they'd do, except order pizza. Well, he'd probably stare at Dalton a lot, and maybe figure out what he had to do to get the guy to hug him again. Or just hold his hand.

"You'll like this one." Dalton's murmur brought Tierney's attention back to the present from potential futures. "It's sort of a remake of an episode from the original series." As the title flashed on the screen—"The Naked Now," which sounded promising—Dalton slouched into the couch, settling himself, smiling at Tierney when he did the same.

Tierney recognized the episode's main issue as something that Kirk had dealt with in his day—a virus that caused the crew to go nuts and start offing themselves—but he couldn't say whether he liked the show or not. He mostly thought about other shit, like Marty's sigh when he'd said he hadn't contacted the local counselor and Marty's reaction when Tierney'd confessed to calling Dalton for support.

"Dalton," Marty had repeated. Then Tierney heard the dude typing on a keyboard. After a few seconds of that, Marty said, "We discussed him in some of your sessions."

Uh-oh. "Yeah . . ."

"Having a lover as your main support person isn't usually a good idea."

"He's not my lover, really. I mean, yeah, I totally *want* him to be, but, you know . . ." He'd taken a deep breath. "You warned me about not entering into any new relationships. He's fine with that. We're just friends."

"Okay," Marty had said in that tone Tierney knew meant it really *wasn't* okay. "I'd still urge you to find someone else as your primary backup."

"You're thinking so hard I can hear it." Dalton's hand landed on Tierney's thigh and squeezed, reminding him he wasn't on the phone anymore. The guy had paused the show, but Tierney hadn't noticed.

He tried to smile in response.

"You need to give yourself a break," Dalton continued.

"I'm pretty much all about the self-recrimination. Giving myself a break isn't in my repertoire."

Dalton didn't laugh at the joke, which made sense because it was lame. "It isn't, huh?" He tilted his head, then said, "As your official support network, I'm going to make you."

"You are?"

"Yes," Dalton said firmly, standing up. "Friend cuddling. Now. Lie down."

Oh thank God.

Friend cuddling was very successful, from Tierney's perspective. Other perspectives might not agree.

This time, Dalton lay behind him, arm wrapped around his waist while they continued watching whatever the hell—Tierney squinted at the screen, trying to remember, but a haze of non-friend hormones was swarming, fogging up the higher reasoning centers of his brain and gathering in his groin.

Oh yeah. *Star Trek: TNG.*

That was the last bit of attention Tierney paid to the television, preoccupied by the proximity of Dalton's groin to his ass. Because Dalton was shorter than him, in order to see over Tierney's shoulder he had to be propped up a little higher, which meant his thighs made the perfect haven for Tierney's butt. They were just the right shape to cup the curve of his cheeks, aligned so that Dalton's hard leg muscles pressed against the underside of Tierney's ass, and every time the dude shifted even a centimeter, the sensation rolled through Tierney, resonating in the sensitive spot right behind his balls.

Was it his imagination, or had Dalton's breathing gotten choppy?

"This might have been a bad idea," Dalton whispered after a few minutes, providing the context Tierney needed: that he wasn't the only one trying not to squirm or—*fuck*—rock his hips rhythmically.

Unless he was reading this wrong? "What's a bad idea?"

"This." Dalton shifted behind him, muscles tensing and releasing, rolling his hips until his hard prick was snug against Tierney's ass.

Tierney gasped before croaking, "I dunno, I kinda like it."

Dalton didn't answer. He just lay there, plastered along Tierney's body, arm tensed around Tierney's ribs, with his palm flat against Tierney's chest. Breathing unevenly against Tierney's neck.

Rendering Tierney not much more than a human-shaped, throbbing mass of desire.

The smart thing would be to move. Roll off the couch and stand up, apologize to Dalton, and then tell the guy where the extra bed was. But his horny self guarded that info like a missile silo was concealed under the guest room's nightstand.

Dalton moved, though, starting to push himself up, like he was going to climb over Tierney. "I'm sorry, I shouldn't have done—"

"Huh-uh." Turning, Tierney cursed his impatience. He just couldn't wait to see how things panned out, could he? *No.* "This is going to keep happening. Every time we get together . . ."

"We end up like this." Dalton swallowed, eyes searching Tierney's. "What do we do about it, then?"

"I don't know. This is the first time I've ever had this happen."

Dalton smiled, a quick rush of amused relief, as if Tierney had somehow normalized the situation. "Another one of your firsts?"

His firsts? Oh yeah. Like Dalton being the first guy he'd kissed, or the first guy he'd blown or whose name he knew before being blown. The first guy who'd slept in his bed. "All my firsts are with you," he said absently, caught up in the heat and atmosphere swirling between them.

"You have a lot more firsts coming," Dalton whispered. "Not all of them have to—*will* be with me."

The way Dalton's glance flickered away from and then returned to his flooded Tierney with hope and possibility. All the things he'd been craving last time, when he'd kissed Dalton, lying on this couch, seemed so attainable. Like two parallel worlds had collided, but the wormhole between them would only be open for a brief time, so he had to *act*. Ask for what he desired or lose the opportunity. "What if I want another first time with you?" He brushed back Dalton's bangs, so he could see those blue eyes clearly.

"What kind of—" Dalton's breath hitched. "What kind of first?"

"Uhhh . . ." Christ, he didn't even know how to say it. Well, he knew *how*, but his mouth wouldn't form the words.

"And what would we be?"

"Huh?"

"To each other," Dalton said. "I mean, we're friends, now, right? So, if we, um, have sex, are we still simple friends? Or is there more?"

"What do you want?" Tierney asked over the thump of his heart in his ears.

"I want what's best for you." Dalton looked at him a moment longer, then stretched forward for a kiss. A simple kiss, just his lips brushing Tierney's. "I don't want to jeopardize your recov—"

"Benefits," Tierney blurted, sensing the moment slipping away. The divergence of their two worlds.

Dalton stared.

"We're friends now, but we already have kissing benefits, right?"

Dalton licked his lip, then pulled it into his mouth with his teeth before letting it pop back out, wet and reddened. "Yeah."

"So we can have *other* benefits, if we agree to some, I don't know, boundaries."

The long silence made Tierney nervous, but the way Dalton's fingers kept combing through the hair at his nape seemed hopeful.

"Boundaries like, 'This is just helping out a friend'?"

Sure, what the hell. Tierney nodded quickly.

Dalton sucked in a breath and held it a second before, "I can agree to that," burst out of him.

Tierney lunged, his chest surging upward against Dalton's, adjusting until they could get that perfect angle. He kissed with so much more intent than that accidental, hormone-driven one the last time Dalton had been here. Consciously pulling and pushing until they could touch everywhere, his hard dick grinding into Dalton's hip, rocking them together.

Then Dalton drew away, gripping Tierney's shoulders as if he had to forcibly hold him off—which he probably did.

"What first?" Dalton sucked in a huge breath of air, like he'd been running a marathon. "What first do you want?"

He froze, because here he was again. He had to say the words, or he might wimp out and never do it, and then what kind of guy would he be? The dude who could stand on a table and announce he was queer in public but could never fully *be* it in private. "Um . . ." *Say it, you pansy.* "I want you to fuck me."

And, oh Christ, Dalton seemed dumbstruck, eyes wide. Like he couldn't believe what Tierney was asking for, or he didn't do that, or maybe he was grossed out—totally repulsed by the idea of sticking his dick inside him. Just when Tierney was at the point where he was about to start spewing out all kinds of shit, probably about not meaning it, or not being good enough, Dalton asked, "Do you have any condoms?"

"Yeah." He nodded vigorously, putting all his relief into it. "My father gave me some." *I can't believe you said that.*

"Do you have lube?"

"Uh, Father prolly didn't know I'd need it." *You fucking* dork, *shut up with the father thing.*

"It's okay," Dalton said, swallowing. "I, um, I threw some in my pack before I came over. Just, you know"—he shrugged one shoulder—"in case."

All the noise in Tierney's head died. The crackling surge of hormones and the thump of his pulse and the desperate whispering, hoping—it all froze up, letting the words sink in. *Dalton brought lube "in case."*

In case something happened, and Tierney didn't have lube.

"So you actually *want* to do this?" he asked under his breath, afraid to say it louder.

Dalton's smile broke out all over his face. "I do."

Everything unfroze inside him. A tidal wave of sound and hormones and surging blood propelled Tierney off the couch, all of it urging him to make this happen. He stood and held out his hand to Dalton. "Let's go, then."

Chapter 17

The full weight of doubt hit Tierney while he was in the shower. If they'd just been able to fall into bed and start going at it, things might have been easier, but they couldn't, could they? Cleaning up had seemed necessary, not only for hygienic reasons, but also because he had this weird, unshakeable sense that he was about to partake in some kind of sacred ritual. Ablutions were, like, mandatory before all rites of passage or whatever.

Only he would be dorky enough to believe he couldn't be totally gay unless he took it up the ass. But he *did* believe that—no matter what arguments he made to himself—and he'd never feel authentic unless he did. "Maybe I'll be into it," he muttered to himself as he stood under the hot spray of water.

Ten minutes later, he came out of the bathroom wearing the freakish aqua robe his mother had sent him at rehab, because as ugly as it was, he was pretty sure it was hotter than his naked self. While he'd been soaping up his body, he'd realized that while he may be thin, he sure the fuck wasn't in shape.

Dalton was in shape. Perfect shape.

Now, back in the bedroom, he could verify that. See all the perfectly defined slimness of Dalton, his smooth chest showing textbook-ideal muscles. He lay on the bed mostly naked, except for a pair of briefs. They were the kind of underwear Tierney had always suspected gay men wore in real life, patterned with something he couldn't identify in the low light. Probably cheeky and very of-the-moment, but abstract. Only straight men wore boxers patterned with objects like airplanes or monkeys.

I have utterly lost my mind.

He grabbed the belt of his robe, hanging tightly to the ends. "This isn't just a pity fuck is it?" *Get a clue*. He whacked himself in the forehead with his palm. "Shit, *of course* it's a pity fuck. I asked you to have sex with me because I've never been with a guy before, and you're taking pity on me. That's, like, the *definition* of a pity fuck."

Dalton had lifted his head from the pillow, and was now wrinkling his nose at Tierney. "What are you *talking* about?"

"You're so . . . stunning. Like, everything about you. You even have *abs*. I mean, I don't even know if I *own* those, let alone could make them show."

"Tierney." A smiled flitted across his face.

"What?"

"Come here."

Climbing on the mattress and knee-walking across to him was awkward swaddled in a bathrobe, but Tierney did it, lying down on his side next to Dalton when he patted the bed. He ended up with his head on the same pillow as Dalton's, staring into his eyes.

Then Dalton took Tierney's face in his hands. "How many times do I have to say I'm attracted to you before you believe me?"

"Um." Tierney swallowed. "Probably more times than you're going to." *In my life*.

"Can you at least believe that this isn't a pity fuck?"

"I think so." *He brought lube, just in case*. "Yeah."

"Are you certain about doing this?" Dalton smoothed his warm palm over Tierney's shoulder, under his robe and down his arm, baring it to the air. Squeezing his biceps.

Tierney's skin prickled where Dalton's hand had been, and a wave of something shivered through him. "I think so. I mean yes."

"That doesn't sound very certain."

He took a huge breath and let it out slowly, but he still had to swallow before he could say anything. "I'm a thirty-four-year-old virgin. I don't think *not* being nervous is an option."

Dalton didn't respond, not verbally. He kissed Tierney instead. Soft lips, like a question. Tierney answered by stretching toward him, pushing his mouth against Dalton's. Unsure what to do, because they'd kissed before, but this time it was intended to lead to something else, and maybe—

Dalton engulfed him. Nudging with his tongue until Tierney opened for him. He didn't ravage his mouth—instead he caressed Tierney, convincing him this would all be all right and he could do it. Convincing him he actually wanted it so thoroughly that when Dalton drew away from him, Tierney found his thigh wrapped around Dalton's legs, holding them together. Dalton laid a hand on Tierney's hip and brought his hard cock against Tierney's through the layers of fabric.

Dalton smiled and kissed him quickly once more. "It's good to know you're excited about it." He ground them together, sending another wave of sensation through Tierney. One strong enough to make him suck in a breath and grab Dalton's arm and hold on.

Dalton coaxed him the rest of the way out of his fluffy aqua armor while Tierney soaked in the feeling of being touched like this by someone he *wanted*, no barriers between them. Dalton worked down Tierney's body, feeling him everywhere with his fingers, then his tongue. As if he didn't find Tierney's muscles weak or his skin too pale at all. Like maybe he actually *was* attracted to him.

Then Dalton lay between his spread legs, gripping Tierney's dick in his fist while looking up at him, lips moving.

Tierney blinked, straining to hear over the blood rushing in his ears, trying to figure out what he was supposed to do. Give the dude permission? Ask for it again? Was there some ritual saying he should know, but didn't because he hadn't been watching the right porn? Shouldn't someone make an instructional video for dorks like him?

"Tierney." Dalton's lips moved again, this time with soundtrack. "Hand me the lube."

His lungs seized up, just for a second, but then he managed to reach across the bed and grab the bottle Dalton had left on the nightstand. After handing it off, he closed his eyes and lay back, searching through the catalog of meditative breathing exercises he'd learned for the one most likely to get him through this.

"Relax," Dalton whispered, the word brushing against the head of Tierney's dick. *Best breathing exercise ever*. He shivered, gasping when Dalton's lips glided over the same skin. Then his tongue, swirling across the top of Tierney's cock, tracing contours.

"That's—*fuck*—totally relaxing."

Dalton's quick laugh vibrated down Tierney's shaft as the guy sucked it into his mouth. It was better than the first blowjob Dalton had given him, mostly because of how Tierney felt about Dalton. He didn't trust anyone else enough to ask them to fuck him, only this guy. Dalton wouldn't sneer at him, he'd take care with him.

Like now, he was taking care to make sure Tierney was suitably distracted before pressing a fingertip against his asshole. Oh, Tierney *noticed*, but it wasn't alarming so much as surprisingly pleasurable, even when Dalton had to use slight force to get past Tierney's ring of muscle. But Dalton made it in, slowly working his finger back and forth, until it was moving in the same rhythm his mouth was on Tierney's cock.

Then came another finger, in tandem with the *slurp* of a long pull up Tierney's cock. And he kept introducing more that way—distracting, exciting suction on Tierney's dick, another digit in—until Tierney didn't know how many were in there and didn't care. Seven maybe. Having his dick in Dalton's hot, wet mouth, tongue pressing against the bottom of Tierney's shaft, while something filled his ass, felt so much better than he ever thought it could. When Dalton pushed inside him, it was a weird kind of desirable discomfort. His nerves sent alarm signals at the same time as they were beguiled by the feeling, encouraging Tierney to rock with the rhythm. His sphincter stopped trying to force the intruders out and started gripping them, wanting them to stay and play awhile. When Dalton rubbed against his prostate, it felt even better, although it wasn't the jolt of bliss Tierney had expected. The best sensations came from the stroking in his hole, coordinated with the bobbing of Dalton's head, engulfing his dick.

Such amazing sensations that Tierney had to twine fingers in Dalton's hair and gasp, "'M really close."

Dalton pulled off of him and pulled out, and Tierney reached for him, dug his fingers into Dalton's shoulders, and dragged him along his body, grabbing his head and holding it while stretching up to kiss him. He shoved his tongue into Dalton's mouth to taste where his cock had been only seconds before, shuddering when Dalton sucked on it. Tierney's dick was sliding against Dalton's belly, bumping into Dalton's hardness, and Tierney surged against him, nearly there, wanting to come all over Dalton's skin so badly. He could feel the orgasm starting, a swirling in his nuts, like sea currents flowing and getting stronger.

Dalton jerked away from him, lifting his hips, slick lips sliding from Tierney's. He held himself up on one arm, gulping for air, swiped his hair back, and locked onto Tierney's gaze. "Just a sec, I gotta . . ." He swallowed and moved to kneel between Tierney's legs, still watching his face.

Oh yeah. Tierney nodded quickly, trying not to tense up, then let his head drop back on the pillow and bent his legs, lifting his butt when Dalton started to shove a pillow under him.

He thought there'd be more of a buildup, but before he knew it, Dalton had put on a condom and was there, holding his dick against Tierney's hole. The first touch of Dalton's head sent a thrill through him, and Tierney grabbed his cock in some sort of need to hold on. To hold on for the rest of this, because it would be amazing. Life altering. Dalton would make certain of it.

Dalton pressed into him steadily, pushing through what was left of Tierney's resistance. His resistance to the idea of living this life, and his resistance to bottoming, and his resistance to fully accepting what he was. The pressure inside him increased, until Tierney had to give way and let down his last barriers. Stop defending the fortress gates. Let Dalton in and receive all the good things that came along with being gay and the incredible sensation of having someone inside him. Dalton's cock surged into him, until Tierney arched up from the bed and moaned—his final protest for what he couldn't be.

Then Dalton was filling him up, and Tierney no longer regretted a single thing. "Oh God, that's so—"

"Does it hurt?" Dalton gasped out, pausing.

"Yeah," he panted, because it did, but somehow that didn't really matter. It *should* hurt, at least some—life-changing events always hurt. It was just like every other one so far: too big for Tierney to contain, stretching him too thin.

Dalton started to ease out, but Tierney grabbed him, digging his fingertips into Dalton's ass. "Don't stop. I want this." Even though it burned and ached more now that he'd bothered to acknowledge the pain.

"Tell me what will make it better," Dalton said, looking down at him, elbows locked and starting to shake.

Tierney gritted his teeth. "I think . . ."

"What?"

"I think I need you to move." Then this knife-edged tension in his ass would ease, and the nerve endings that had liked Dalton's fingers so much before would recognize that sliding, rubbing caress again, and maybe forget about the warnings his body was sending out about foreign invaders and imminent tearing.

Dalton thrust slowly, working another centimeter into Tierney with each forward push. Like a battering ram trying to coax open a door with gentle yet clumsy persuasion.

"Maybe this hurts more."

Dalton froze.

Oh, yeah, no. "Definitely holding still hurts more." He nodded, gripping Dalton's ribs. "Move."

He didn't. "Are you sure you don't want me to stop? I could finish the blow—"

"No." Tierney shook his head, rubbing his hair into the pillow. "I think I want . . ."

"What?"

"I want you to kiss me."

Pressing Tierney's legs up, into his chest, Dalton did, thrusting farther inside at the same time, too far, until it hurt worse. The pressure increased and pushed Tierney's nerves to that point where he really did want to quit. He pulled out of the kiss, about to say it, but the look on Dalton's face kept him quiet. It held so much worry and effort, the muscles below his eyes tensed up into an expression of concern, but his jaw hard and clamped tight, as if he had to hold on to control by his teeth. *He's doing all this for me.*

More than anything, Tierney wanted to do something for Dalton in return. "Can I be on top?"

After that it was easier. Yeah, he had to work himself down on Dalton's cock again, but it was more uncomfortable than painful, and Tierney had control. He could stop the very second some part of him got alarmed, or shift a millimeter left if he needed. Dalton tightened his fingers on Tierney's thighs and let him experiment with movement, sometimes whispering questions about how it felt, and if it was getting better.

"Don't worry about it," Tierney finally said. He had Dalton in pretty much as far as possible, but still he managed to lean forward and kiss him quickly, brushing his hair back. "Just let me do this."

Swallowing, Dalton nodded.

All of the stuff going on in Tierney's head and his heart overwhelmed the physical sensations, made them totally secondary. This wasn't like any other sex he'd ever had, solo or otherwise—it wasn't about reaching that end goal; it was about the experience. Straddling Dalton's hips, rocking on him, was the most real thing he'd ever done in his life. His most authentic action ever. One that required him to reach out and fully connect to another person.

When he shifted forward slowly, Dalton's lips parted. When Tierney moved back, taking all of Dalton's length into him, twisting his hips a little, Dalton arched his neck and gritted his teeth.

I'm *doing that to him*.

Discomfort lessened to something more like unfamiliarity as he focused on Dalton's small physical tells. The way he bit his lip, upper teeth pressing deep, and the way he gasped when Tierney rose up on his knees. When Tierney shifted a certain way, the wrinkles in Dalton's forehead grew extra-pronounced. He couldn't stop working for those responses. He planted his hands on Dalton's chest, anchoring himself for leverage, slowly putting together a rhythm made up of all the things that got the biggest reaction. A rhythm that made Dalton actually groan and dig his fingers deeper into Tierney's leg muscles, then finally arch up, eyes flying open and breath hitching, like he was trying to choke out words.

Coming. *I made him come*. He could feel it, not only in the way Dalton jerked, but in the way Dalton's cock surged inside him. Tierney bent forward and kissed him, holding Dalton's face between his hands while his body shook under Tierney's.

As soon as it was over, though, Tierney eased himself off. Sore and throbbing (in a not-totally-good way) and uninterested in his own orgasm. He lay next to Dalton, petting his smooth chest and listening to his breathing slow from gulping air to barely faster than regular.

"You didn't come," Dalton said, then shifted. Taking off the condom, Tierney realized.

He took it from the guy's hand and dropped it over the edge of the bed, before rolling onto his side and working one arm under Dalton's neck. "It's okay. I made *you* come."

Dalton turned toward him, smiling. "Yeah you did. Did you enjoy it at all?"

"Ummm . . ."

He sighed. "I don't know anyone who had a good first time. Not *really* good."

Tierney pulled him closer, suddenly aware of not having shaved recently and of how his jaw rasped against Dalton's temple. Weird how he could feel that touch everywhere, even in his chest and toes. "Not surprising. I mean, our whole lives we're pushing things out of our ass, and then one day someone suggests we put something *in* it? That takes some getting used to, dude."

Dalton was laughing before Tierney finished speaking, and it gave him the same sort of happy jolt making him come had. Like maybe he really *was* the man.

"Some people like it, though. Maybe not the first time, but later," Dalton said, fitting his head under Tierney's chin and kissing his chest, right in the very center of his sternum.

Some guys. "Do you?" The question came out half-strangled by a surge of excitement that arrowed up from his nuts. Now that he had bottoming out of the way, maybe . . .?

"I do," Dalton whispered, then slid down Tierney's body, dropping kisses and words on his skin as he went. "If it's the right guy, I really like it." He gripped Tierney's hip, pushing until Tierney turned onto his back. His cock was starting to show serious interest in the proximity of Dalton's lips, slowly plumping up again. Dalton kissed it, right on the end, then sucked Tierney into his mouth, making any further conversation impossible.

He came within minutes, like his orgasm had been waiting, half-built, gathered into a small ball of tension on hold. And yes, he was sore, but the throbbing in his ass added to his excitement—all the fantastic things Dalton could do and make him feel were even better with that thump of accomplishment backing it up and fueling the inevitable explosion.

Exhaustion hit him almost immediately, as soon as Dalton slid back up and fit his head under Tierney's chin again, sighing and settling in. "Postcoital friend cuddling," Tierney mumbled, letting his hand fall onto Dalton's back, exerting himself just enough to pull the guy a little closer.

Dalton kissed him on the chest, exactly where he had before sucking him off. "Was it worth it?"

He got what Dalton was asking, but he was too exhausted to talk about the serious shit right now. "The blowjob or the whole thing?"

"The whole thing." Dalton lifted his head, which meant Tierney sort of had to open his eyes. "Did you get what you needed out of it?"

"Yeah." He trailed his fingers up Dalton's spine until he could stroke the hair at the nape of his neck. "Thank you."

Dalton's smile was warm enough to light up Tierney's insides. "Anytime."

In the morning, Dalton woke first, then he kissed Tierney awake.

"I should brush my teeth." Tierney tried to push up from the bed.

"I don't care about that," Dalton said, locking his arms around Tierney's shoulders so he couldn't escape. None of his former boyfriends would *ever* have kissed him with morning breath, and it was of the utmost importance that Tierney be nothing like them at that moment, not while Dalton was rubbing their bodies together, jockeying the man into just the right position over him, until Tierney's thighs were sliding along his and Tierney's hard cock was bumping up against Dalton's.

"This is," Tierney panted while he worked his hips into the perfect tempo. "It's hotter than I woulda . . ."

"Yeah." Dalton smiled, cupping the back of his head and pulling him down for more kisses, not letting him go until they'd both come all over each other's stomach.

"Our last sleepover, I wanted to do that so badly when I woke up in the morning," he admitted, saying the words into Tierney's hair while the man recovered, lying on top of him.

He could feel Tierney's mouth stretch into a smile against his shoulder. "I think I figured out why Grandfather didn't want me to have sleepovers with boys."

"Yeah?"

"'Cause they're messy," Tierney said, rolling off of him and making a face at his cum-coated abdomen. The trail of hair that led from his pecs all the way down to his dick was gummed up with it. Just as Dalton reached out to run his fingers through the reddish-brown curls, Tierney turned, searching over the side of the bed for something. He yanked up that horrendous robe and wiped himself off with it, then offered it to Dalton, whose hand was still reaching out to touch him. Caress him lovingly. Like a boyfriend would.

He took the robe instead, ducking his head and paying more attention to cleaning himself off than he needed to.

This whole thing—waking Tierney up for sex, and cuddling, and kissing and touching him—it was so much more than friendship. *I can't do this.* Even if falling in love—*gulp*—didn't seem like a problem, or a cruelty, it could be for Tierney, couldn't it? Even good stress could derail him.

And it wasn't just about Tierney, was it? Dalton had to be very careful, because last night and this morning, he'd been *really* into the sex. Not just because it was sex, but because it was Tierney. Tierney, the guy who was, on the surface at least, like Dalton's exes. *Am I repeating myself?*

Tierney sighed and let his head flop onto the pillow, smiling. Totally unaware of Dalton's distress. "I had a meeting yesterday, and that's what threw me," he said, voice smoothing out from the roughness of sleep and sex. "I thought I could handle it, but I was fooling myself."

"That's what it was?" Dalton couldn't help himself. "You and meetings." He lay down next to Tierney, but not too close.

Fortunately, Tierney smiled again. "Yeah, well I kept my cool in this one, sorta. It was afterward that I freaked. It was with most of those same guys."

The same guys as in that meeting with Ian. "No wonder it was so rough."

"Yeah. I had a lame-ass plan . . ." He shook his head. "I should've had the counselor and the rest of my support network all set up. But really, it wasn't that bad. I mean, it's over, right?"

Dalton nodded. "Still, you should do that today. Find some more people to support you."

"Yeah," Tierney agreed. "Marty doesn't think you're the best person to be my main backup."

Dalton almost missed the alarm that flashed across Tierney's expression, because he was too surprised and hurt. Not that he should be hurt—he didn't even know Marty. But by that token, how did this therapist know Dalton wasn't the best person?

"I'd told him about you," Tierney said quickly. "He said a lover isn't the best support."

"I'm not your lover." There went his fluttery pulse again. "I mean, not really. Am I?" He couldn't be, right?

"Fuck, I'm a dork," Tierney moaned, rubbing his eyes with his fingers. "I told him you weren't. He was saying that because you came up in my sessions. I, you know, told him I *wanted* you to be my lover, before—"

"We can't," Dalton said. His lungs hitched, nearly strangling his words. "Last night was just . . . benefits, right? We can't do that again . . ."

Tierney swallowed and pushed up on his elbow. "Unless I get a better support network."

"But . . ." He shook his head, trying to readjust what he'd thought with reality. "I thought we couldn't get romantically involved because you're working through—"

"Oh, yeah, totally." Tierney waved his hand airily, cheeks darkening. "Not what I meant at all. Just, you know, I need some other help and maybe, um . . ."

"So get some other help," Dalton said in a calm voice, all out of proportion to how hard his heart had started to beat.

"I will," Tierney said, sitting up and scooting to the edge of the bed. "Right away."

After Dalton left, Tierney found himself highly motivated to call the drug and alcohol counselor he was supposed to have made an appointment with as soon as he got home. He had to leave a message since it was Saturday. Then he called his sister-in-law and arranged to meet her for lunch. Emily was one of the few people he'd been able to rely on over the years, even if her husband was a douche.

"What's this about?" she asked. "You already apologized."

"It's about other shit I should have done when I came home. Like, found some backup for if I slip and start drinking again." He tried to sound all casual, but they knew each other well enough that she probably wasn't fooled.

"Tierney, did you—"

"No. I didn't, someone helped me out and I didn't drink. But, like, I was supposed to have a whole support network and I never really set it up." He cleared his throat. "Just him."

"Him who? Oh my God, is this the guy you were kissing that day you left for—"

"Em, please, don't," he whined. "Not now."

She cackled. "Oh, dearest brother-in-law, this lunch is going to be a *lot* of fun."

"Yeah," he muttered. "I'm totally looking forward to it."

She was still laughing when he hung up.

He managed to think himself in circles before he had to go meet her. About Dalton, and what he'd meant when he'd said "so get some other help." Tierney didn't *think* the sense of urgency to do it was only his. There'd been too much intensity in Dalton's voice and his eyes. Like, it was important to their friendship—whatever that might turn out to be—for Tierney to have other options for support.

Except the dude had just left after they got out of bed. He'd kissed Tierney good-bye, and said he'd see him "soon," but turned down a cup of coffee and simply said he had to go.

No freaking brilliant conclusions slapped him smart before he showed up at the restaurant to find Emily waiting for him, grinning smugly. Like that cat in that book he couldn't remember the title of. Some children's classic that she probably read to his nieces.

The teasing about Dalton began immediately. Every time he repeated, "We're just friends," she laughed and pointed at his blush.

The worst part was when she got semiserious and said, "You were never like this when talking about women. You hardly mentioned them, period."

Tierney shrugged and rearranged the lamb chop on his plate, because that needed doing.

"Nope," she said, pointing at it with a fork. "I don't buy that sort of avoidance tactic with my daughters or husband so it's really not going to work for you."

He shrugged again.

"You're different, you know that?"

"Uh, *yeah*. State the obvious much?"

"Ah, and there's the former Tierney we all knew and loved." But she smiled at him, apparently not offended.

"Jesus." He planted his elbows on the table and watched her a moment from behind his clasped hands. Like they offered some sort of protection. "Sorry."

"You worked so hard to appear straight," she mused.

Hands didn't make much of a defense bunker, turned out. "Not with you. You're my brother's wife, I couldn't, like, hump *your* leg as well."

Em shook her head. "I used to watch you and wonder what the fuck you were up to. You were so obvious, and so over-the-top lecherous. At least I thought so."

His stomach churned up some indigestion. That lamb chop would be coming home with him, completely unmolested by teeth. "I put on that act to hide behind, and I hated doing it, but it was like I couldn't stop. Like I was addicted, even though I hated it." And people he respected had watched him do it and hated it too.

"You know what, T? I may be one of the few women in the world that's seen the real you, and I don't think you're a loser. Maybe a bit of a dick, though. Before."

"I was that." Still was, sometimes. *Work in progress.*

"At any rate." She began twisting strands of linguine around the tines of her fork. "Now the rest of the world gets to know the guy I already saw." She smiled like she'd given him a present.

"Great," he muttered. "I can't wait to meet him."

"Most importantly," she went on, "the *boys* of the world get to see the man I had a feeling was in there."

Tierney jerked away, slamming his spine into the booth cushion behind him. "You thought I was gay? Before?"

She shook her head "no" and waved her hand in the air, still chewing her bite of food. Finally she swallowed, wiped her mouth, and leaned across the table, her eyes twinkling. "I thought you were *nice*."

He shuddered, and she laughed at him. "Don't worry, sometimes the nice guy gets the boy."

Changing the subject to whether she'd be part of his support system was a relief. Compared to fielding her comments on his love life, it was easy. Actually, he kind of wondered why he wanted her in his support system after that, but she dropped all the playfulness and took it very seriously, urging him to call her anytime and she'd do what she could to help.

"What about AA meetings?" she asked him.

"Well, I kinda wanted to wait and see . . ." If he really needed them.

Emily tilted her chin and lifted her eyebrows at him.

"Yeah, I'm looking into them." He planned on making a list of all the places and times of meetings near him. It couldn't hurt to have a schedule just in case, right?

After Tierney'd paid the bill—which Em let him do because, as she pointed out, "Our money comes from the same place"—and they were pulling on their coats, she said casually, "Chase would be there for you too, you know."

Tierney snorted.

"He doesn't hate you like you think he does."

"The reverse isn't true."

"He knows that," she snapped. "Why do you think he's such a dick when you're around?"

"C'mon, Em," he said, trying to smooth things over, or explain. "How am I supposed to believe you when the dude is always a jerk? I mean, he doesn't go out of his way to, like, *show* me he cares."

She glared at him, but then it melted into a more thoughtful expression. "I'm going to tell you something he made me promise not to."

"I wish you wouldn't." He had a bad feeling about this. "Seriously."

"When you came over after you got back from Dunthorpe and thanked me for finding a center with an LGBT treatment program? That wasn't me. It was Chase who found it, and then he convinced your parents that was the best place for you to go."

"See?" he half whined. "I really didn't need to know that, 'cause the next time he's a dick to me I won't be able to be a dick back. I'll be all grateful and shit."

She ignored him to dig her keys out of her purse, and then started for the door. Tierney trailed along behind her like a chastised child. Out front she let him off the hook, though. "I'm sorry, I shouldn't have told you that—"

"Oh God, don't apologize, that makes it worse."

"—you and your brother have too long a history of hostility."

Relief over her change of heart became alarm as she went on.

"Neither of you will ever be able to forgive the other, will you? Not unless one of you has some kind of drastic life change, and begins to accept reality." Rising up to her tiptoes, she kissed Tierney's cheek and turned to walk off.

It took him a couple of seconds to recover from her parting shot. "I see what you did there," he called after her. "It's not going to work, you know. Try it on *him*, why don't you?"

She just waved over her shoulder.

Chapter 18

Tierney nearly called Dalton on Saturday after his lunch with Emily to see if he wanted to hang out, possibly with a sleepover, but he didn't.

The memory of him asking, "Did you get what you needed?" after he'd fucked Tierney stopped him.

That word: need. Everything that had happened between them so far, from the first day they met, had been about what Tierney needed. His need for a friend or reassurance, or his need to figure out how to be gay, or his need for help to not drink. He fucking hated that dynamic. He didn't want to be anybody's charity case, especially not Dalton's. Dalton was beautiful and cool and totally out of Tierney's league, and the last thing Tierney wanted from him was pity.

Emily may think that nice guys sometimes got the boy, but pathetic whiners didn't *deserve* the boy.

His mood increasingly spiraled out of control, and by the time he went to bed Saturday night, he was pissed. Angry with Dalton for enabling his dependency but mostly mad at himself for being weak. As he slept, his anger didn't fade, either. Tierney woke up Sunday morning livid. Thank God he had rugby to look forward to. Maybe he could work out some of his aggressions on the pitch.

He shoved himself out of bed, stalked into the bathroom, ripped his toothbrush out of its holder and took his aggressions out on his teeth. Except that wasn't enough to cool his jets, so he got in the shower, scrubbing himself too briskly under water that was too hot. Then he attacked his hair with a brush.

Breakfast was brutal. That poor oatmeal never stood a chance. And the grapefruit . . . tragic.

None of it appeased his anger. In fact, his mood got worse. An hour later, standing on Ian's porch waiting for the dude to answer his knock, he was seething. His breath grated in his ears, and a current of rage vibrated through him.

Sam opened the door.

"Huh." Sam wasn't the kind of guy he could just pop off on, or be a dick to as a way to relieve some of his foul mood. He wouldn't *understand*.

"Hey T." Sam smiled at him, stepping out of the way to let Tierney in.

"Um, is Ian ready?" He shifted his weight, but stayed on the porch. "We're gonna be late."

Sam leaned against the doorjamb. "He's in the shower."

"He's showering before rugby?" Forget that he'd done that himself.

"Um." Sam turned slightly pink, pressing his lips together like he was trying not to smile. "He kinda needed to." The dude had beard burn in spots, especially his neck. His skin was so pale—although less pasty than it used to be—Ian probably roughed it up just by breathing nearby.

Dalton has skin. Lots of it.

"Christ, you two," he muttered. "You're like horny teenagers."

"Ooooo-kay," Sam said, eyes going wide. "So, you coming in to wait or what?"

He'd just be a dick, sitting there trying to chat with Sam about whatever Sam chatted to people about. "You know? I think I'm going to take a lap around the neighborhood as a warm-up. Tell him I'll be back in ten and he'd better fucking be ready or I'll leave without him." He turned, not waiting for an answer, and bounded down the porch steps, hitting the sidewalk at a fast jog. Three blocks later, his madometer was still redlining. Made no sense—exercise usually calmed him. But he didn't investigate why, because it made him feel alive in a way he hadn't for months. Maybe years.

Well, except for a couple of times, like when he and Dalton had . . . Shit, now he was *really* pissed.

When he got back to Sam and Ian's, the dude was just walking out the door, frowning. As soon as he saw Tierney on the front walk, he stopped, pointing at him. "Were you being a dick to my boyfriend?"

Did I upset the little woman? Tierney bit his tongue on the words—Sam didn't deserve his anger—and took ten seconds to slow his breathing, hands on his hips, squaring off against his friend. "I just wasn't in the mood to come inside." He ignored Ian's narrow-eyed look and bent over, as if stretching his legs. In reality he was searching for a rock. Just the thought of beaning Ian in the face with it made Tierney shudder with desire. Not *that* kind of desire.

No projectiles presented themselves—*prolly for the best*—but within seconds Ian's shoes halted directly under Tierney's nose. He took his time straightening up.

"What?" He could see it in Ian's eyes—dude was about to throw down, and Tierney wanted it so bad he could smell blood. He urged him on with the curl of his lip, the precursor to a growl.

The fucker backed away, dropping his hand. His chest was still all puffed up, but he broke their staring match, turning his head to reveal a ticking jaw muscle. "I'm giving you the benefit of the doubt, man."

"Don't do me any favors."

Ian snorted. "Sam made me promise not to get into it with you." He headed toward his truck. "C'mon, let's go. We're late."

"I'll drive," Tierney announced, walking the opposite way. He didn't look to see if Ian followed him.

They *were* late, not that it was a surprise. They also weren't talking to each other, as proven by the tense, silent ride to the field. In Tierney's car. Which Ian hated. Which Tierney totally knew.

He kinda hated it also. *Need to trade this thing in.* It was too flashy—made him look like he was overcompensating for something, which, *duh*, he had been when he'd bought the fucking thing. Mad at the beemer now, he parked it in a screech of brakes and slammed the door shut too hard after getting out.

Ignoring Ian, he headed toward the bench to drop his pack and change his shoes. He didn't even have to warm up before whipping off his sweatshirt and track pants—his anger kept him warm, even sitting in the chilly November air while he laced up his cleats.

Today was just a scrimmage. The Beaters had come to their turf, and next week they'd go to the other team's pitch, but it wasn't a league game. Thank fuck it wasn't just the normal practice routine or else Tierney wouldn't get a chance to beat the shit out of some anonymous rugger or three in the name of sportsmanship.

McDaniel, their captain, jogged up while Tierney was still tying his shoes and announced, "The Beaters only have twelve guys."

"What? So no scrimmage?" Completely fucked with his plans to work out his aggressions through the letting of blood.

McDaniel shrugged, not quite meeting his eye. "Not unless we loan them one."

"I'll sub for them." He could rough up guys on his own team as easily as the other.

He ended up playing flanker. Usually he was a winger or one of the other backs, but the Beaters didn't feel it necessary to take Tierney's own skills and preferences into account, despite him doing them a favor. He let that feed into his mad too, stoking up the bonfire until, by the time they formed up and Tierney found himself opposing Ian, he was past caring.

In a way, it was perfect. The dude *should* pay for enabling Tierney's lifetime of poor decision making. Tricking him into thinking he was in love with his so-called best friend and fucking saving himself for the dude or something.

Motherfucker.

In the first scrum, as soon as he could get away with it, Tierney wrapped a fist in the back of Ian's jersey.

"What the *hell*, dude?" Ian yelled in his face, spittle flying.

Tierney yanked hard, making it impossible for Ian to do his job. Ian stomped his cleat on Tierney's boot, twisting away and wrenching Tierney's shoulder at the same time. In spite of the holes in his toes and the throbbing shoulder, he didn't lose his grip, digging in and dragging Ian closer, until the guy had to let go of the lock next to him, and they were nose to nose. He shoved Tierney back, and just when it was about to happen, when Ian was about to lose it, the Stallions' hooker got the ball to the scrum half and the rest of the players were gone, leaving Ian and Tierney facing each other, gasping for breath and glaring.

"Prick," Ian spit, then turned and chased the game down the field.

What the fuck did he have to do to get a fight out of the guy?

He never got one, even after using every dirty trick in the book, and convincing his temporary teammates he was sabotaging them. Ian got the ball a couple of times, and Tierney made sure he sacked the fucker hard, even raking him with his cleats when Ian was down—an unusually legal move—but other than Ian doing the same in turn, no fists flew. Maybe if he'd done some shit-talking, but all the anger inside him had made him inarticulate, so he had to rely on physical communication.

But as he chased Ian up and down that field—fuck playing the game—something miraculous happened. The bonfire of rage reached critical combustion temperature, and started consuming stuff. Things Tierney had been carrying around for *years*. Like soul plasma, it burned away all that rot and depression. Murdered it. Pure, white rage killed the emotional fungus loving and losing Ian had left in Tierney's heart.

It was a beautiful thing.

Until the second half, when he was grappling with Ian again, just about to let his fist fly. About to smash in that face he'd thought he loved.

"What the *fuck* is your damage?" If this were a cartoon, Tierney's hair would have flown back with the force of his friend's voice.

For a split second, everything froze—the noise and the game and all the twisting bodies and flying mud.

I'm doing it again. What Marty had warned him about—falling into the same patterns. "Sorry," he croaked. His arms lost their strength, slipping from Ian, letting him get away.

An apology. He'd made a real apology to Ian before, in the dude's office, and now he'd started on the same shit. Victimizing his friend, using the guy as his personal whipping boy instead of facing the truth.

Tierney barely remembered playing the rest of the game. The Beaters would never ask him to fill in again, but he couldn't care less. Afterward, he made it back to the car and sat in the driver's seat, waiting to see if Ian would even come looking for him. Tierney'd take his ass kicking without protest. He totally deserved it.

The passenger side door flew open, and Ian wasn't even fully inside before he started talking. "You have issues, man." His voice was so sharp it stung Tierney's skin. "Big, *huge* motherfucking issues. Issue number one is that I would *kick your ass* if Sam hadn't made me promise not to."

"Dude, I— *Fuck.*" Tierney hunched over until his forehead rested on the steering wheel, bearing the weight of his whole upper body. "I was feeling like a loser because of some stuff and I took it out on you, which is totally how I used to deal, but when I realized—"

"I *know.*"

Swallowing, Tierney nodded.

"When I left California? I worked through my shit in therapy, but I *get* it. I'm still fucking pissed at you, but I get it."

Slowly turning, he looked at Ian to find the dude not stony-faced or full of rage, but only annoyed as hell. "I really am sorry."

Ian pointed at him. "I'm giving you one more chance, T. Considering all the changes in your life lately? You get a 'get out of jail free' card, for, I don't know, emotional distress." He scowled and dropped his hand, flopping back into the passenger seat.

It took Tierney half a minute of blinking at Ian for it to settle in. He was being forgiven. Again. "I don't deserve it," he objected. "I wouldn't—"

"Dude." Ian sighed. "You stopped yourself when you realized what you were doing. Before? You'd never admit guilt. And like I said, *I get it.* I've used rugby as an outlet too. It's way more therapeutic than talking to Janet for an hour and paying her a hundred fifty for the privilege."

Tierney came close to arguing against it more, but he didn't. Truth was, he needed this friendship. He needed the support. "Thanks for sticking by me. I don't deserve a friend like you." Fumbling, he finally got the key thing worked out and started the car.

"You're a work in progress," Ian said. "I just try not to expect much."

He managed a smile for the joke—dude was probably half-serious, anyway. Leaving the car idling, he turned in his seat to look Ian square in the eye. "Um, you wanna be in my support network?" He ignored how high his voice went. Fuck it if he sounded nervous, he *was*. Ian deserved some emotional honesty from him. "Like, talk me down if I call you because I want a drink, or I just had a shitty day." He swallowed when his friend raised his eyebrows.

"Sure." Ian clapped his palm on Tierney's shoulder, a total good-buddy kind of moment. Or it would have been if Ian wasn't still half-scowling.

The weight of being a pathetic loser burdened him the rest of the day. It wasn't just falling into old patterns with Ian, it was also what had happened with Dalton. Maybe it hadn't been a pity fuck, but it was still charity, wasn't it? It was still a sign that Tierney couldn't function normally without someone holding his hand.

The whole situation ate at him, making him feel worthless. A familiar feeling, and one he used to be able to take care of with a drink.

But that wasn't an option now, was it? *Can't do that*. It'd be more of the pattern repeating, wouldn't it?

At 8:13, standing in front of his fish tank and watching the nearly brainless creatures swim back and forth, he dialed Emily's cell.

"Tierney?" she answered. "Is everything all right?"

"Not so much," he said.

"Will talking on the phone be enough or do you want me to come over there?"

He swallowed. "Can we just talk awhile? What about the girls?" His nieces went to bed late for their age.

"Chase can handle them," she said, a door closing in the background. "So, you want to talk about what set you off, or how you're dealing with it?"

Thank God. "Let's talk about how I'm dealing."

Tierney didn't call Saturday evening. Dalton hadn't known he was expecting it until it didn't happen, but the way he stayed totally attuned to the weight of the cell in his pocket—even while out at a club with Vance—was impossible for him to ignore.

Maybe he shouldn't have left so quickly that morning after their conversation about support networks, but he'd been hyperaware of everything after that. Of knowing he wanted more, and wondering if Tierney might be suggesting more—at least more benefits, if nothing else. Except all the issues around Tierney's recovery made everything foreign. Dalton hadn't known how to act, and kept reading significance into stupid things. Like the way Tierney had walked into the bathroom while Dalton was brushing his teeth and smiled at him. It had read as a "I like seeing you in my house, doing mundane things" kind of expression at first, but it could easily have been a "you look funny foaming at the mouth" smirk. He was too agitated to tell, so he'd left before the situation got even more awkward, assuming they'd talk as soon as Tierney had worked on his support network.

One thing he'd forgotten to determine was how long that might take. Dalton had no idea whether it was unreasonable for him to be worried about it yet or not. Vance noticed his preoccupation early Saturday evening, and eventually they ended up in a quieter bar, just chatting.

But Dalton didn't explain why he was so distracted, and Vance didn't ask. In the end, he was home before midnight.

He definitely didn't have the right to be anxious over Tierney not calling him for any *other* reason. Yes, they'd had sex, but with the explicit understanding that it was a friends-only arrangement. Obliquely aiming at a future relationship together didn't give him any rights now.

So, was he being dissed or not?

He was totally wrapped up in worrying about it, and that scared the hell out of him. Being friends, and only friends, with Tierney wasn't just good for Tierney, it worked for him too. Because he didn't have to face the possibility that he was revisiting his past mistakes if there was nothing beyond friendship there.

And now benefits.

His emotional limbo continued through Sunday, until his regular lunch with Sam, which Dalton went into firmly promising himself he'd not say a word about what happened with Tierney.

A promise he kept right up until Sam's conversation turned machinating.

"Did you know one of the clubs stays open on Thanksgiving?" he asked, eyes excited. "They do it for the people whose families cut them off after finding out they're gay."

"Like me? It's fine, I have plans for Thanksgiving." Dalton was spending Thanksgiving with Luke and Andrea this year, and they'd do the same thing they always did, regardless of holiday—go to the Kok Won Dim Sum Restaurant.

Sam stopped himself just before taking a bite of fry. "Um, how late do your plans go?"

"Probably not after three."

Sam grinned. "Good. You can meet us at the club around nine."

Uh-oh. "Us who?"

Sam shrugged, wearing an expression of forced innocence. He chewed and swallowed before saying airily, "Just, you know, the whole group."

"We have a group?"

"Well, this is sort of the group I'd *like* us to have."

Oh no. *Definitely machinating.* "Is Tierney part of this group?"

"Well, *Ian* thinks we should include him."

"Ian." Dalton nodded exaggeratedly. "I'm sure he suggested it."

Sam shoved his burger in his mouth and took a huge bite.

"Um, I'm not sure if I'll be able to make it." Dalton used the tines of his fork to arrange his pasta in a snaking pattern on his plate. "I'll have to see." *If Tierney calls me.* Because he couldn't go if the man was avoiding him, could he? Having Dalton there and alcohol in easy reach wouldn't be good. Which made him think. "Are you sure it's a good idea to invite Tierney out to a club? He hasn't even been sober a month."

"Oh." Sam swallowed, smiling. "I was thinking that you'd talk with him about that, make sure it's all right. Maybe your being there would be help . . ." he narrowed his eyes at Dalton ". . . ful. Something happened, didn't it? I should've known when you ordered the pasta. Are you eating carbohydrates for comfort?"

Sigh. "Sort of." That stood as an answer to both questions. The rush of relief from admitting it encouraged him to go on. "We kind of, well, broke through the 'friends with benefits' barrier."

"I *knew* it!" Sam couldn't contain himself, bouncing and clapping, splattering drops of ketchup from the fry in his hand onto the table. "I *knew* you guys would get together."

Dalton wiped up the mess with a paper napkin while Sam had his little fit of joy. Time to rain on his friend's parade. "I'm not sure it was a good idea."

"Um, *I* think it's a good idea."

"I'm not sure it's going to happen again, either."

"But it *has* to." Sam gaped, paling, all excitement gone.

Dalton sighed and dropped the crumpled napkin next to his plate. "No, it doesn't. This isn't a romance novel." He could swear he was repeating himself.

"Pfffft." Sam waved that off. "It has to happen again because you *like* him. A lot."

Now the napkin in his lap needed some attention. Dalton straightened it, then wadded it up, which meant he had to flatten it out with his palm once more. "Friday night was just . . ." He heaved out a breath. "He needed to talk to someone, and things just got out of hand."

Sam studied him so long Dalton couldn't avoid meeting his eyes. "You know," he began, tilting his head and assuming his *lecture* pose. "This is a typical device in a romance novel, to have one of the protagonist's friends act as a sounding board for the protag's feelings. There's this point where the friend has some wise observation to make that changes how he sees the budding romance with the hero."

"I take it we've reached that point." Dalton gestured "gimme," then went back to pretending to eat.

Air swirled around Dalton's face as Sam took a huge breath, then spit out, "Are you at all concerned that you might only be into him because you're susceptible to needy men and he's loaded just like the kinds of guys you used to, you know, 'date'?"

"Yes." When Dalton's dropped fork clattered onto his plate, he didn't even flinch. Leave it to Sam to get to the root of the matter. "I'm totally worried about that."

Pushing his food away, Sam folded his hands on the table, expression grave. "Okay, then as the protagonist's friend, it's my duty to say that maybe you need to think about this seriously and make a logical decision. Like, one unaffected by your emotions."

Well, yeah. He did. "So, if I'm going to do that, does that mean you won't be machinating Thanksgiving night?"

"Of *course* I will." Sam rolled his eyes and pulled his plate back toward him, picking up a fry to make his point with. "I'm totally sure you'll make the logical, unemotional decision and show up with Tierney."

"But what if nothing's changed, and we're just friends?"

"Please." Sam snorted. "You and I are 'just friends.' He's something else to you altogether."

Lying in bed Monday morning, Tierney did what he'd been doing all weekend: he obsessed about Dalton, trying to line up what he thought with what he felt.

He *thought* the dude felt sorry for him. That's the nicest thing the old Tierney would've done in Dalton's shoes. It was wondering what the new Tierney would do that gave him some hope.

New Tierney *felt* like there was so *much* there between them. Like an ocean of possibility waiting for him to get his shit together and dive in. New Tierney believed Dalton liked him, and, in brief glimmering flashes, even thought Dalton might have *feelings* for him.

But what the fuck did he know? He was probably emotionally stunted. It sucked that gay relationships weren't any easier to navigate than male-female ones had been. The ones between guys were worse because he had a vested interest in the outcome.

Staring at his ceiling for an hour after his alarm went off didn't give him any more answers than he'd had last night, after he got off the phone with Emily. Though it *did* help him avoid dealing with the aftermath of Friday's meeting.

Okay, this was it. He needed to get dressed and go into the office, and fuck any feelings of humiliation left over from what had happened last week. He had shit to do, and he wasn't going to let a bunch of juvenile douche bags or his dumbass self-esteem issues stop him.

I'm a work in progress.

He pulled his last unworn Tom Ford suit out from the back of his closet. Because he needed that kind of protection today, plus the boost it gave him knowing he looked as good as he could. At least wardrobe-wise. *Dalton would li—*

Shut up.

Studying himself in the mirror after he shaved, it hit him how good he looked, period. Not, like, attractive exactly, but healthy. His skin didn't have that dull tinge of gray anymore, and his eyes were so clear. The whites really were white. *Well whaddaya know?*

So maybe he was a successful work in progress?

At the office, Gina smiled when he walked in, and didn't comment on him being a half hour late.

"How was the meeting Friday?" she asked instead.

"Ugh."

She frowned sympathetically. "That bad?"

"Yeah. But I survived it." Shrugging as he passed her, he got settled in and had even turned on his desktop before someone else bugged him.

"How did the meeting go?"

Christ, again? It was Chase, standing in the doorway of his office, half-scowling at him.

He leaned back in his chair, propping his hands behind his head, and considered throwing his feet up on the desk before answering. "Fine." Looked like knowing Chase had done him a solid didn't change their relationship dynamic at all. *Sweet.* Tierney's smile grew in proportion to his brother's glare.

"'Fine'? That's it?"

"Yup." What the hell. He propped his heels on the edge of his computer cart.

Chase was grinding his teeth now. "You don't have any information for me?"

Uh-oh. Tierney pulled up his shit-eating grin. "And what information would that be?"

Hopefully Chase would tell him instead of stomping off, because Tierney didn't want to spend half his day trying to remember why he'd gone to that fucking torture fest. He had other stuff to tackle today. Like trying to figure out what to do about Dalton.

"Do we need to start prepping a bid for Diablo's service area or not?" Chase nearly yelled.

Oh, *that.* Tierney dropped his attitude and feet, resting his elbows on his desk. "I don't know yet. I can't tell if they're open to other bidders or if they'll just hand it to American again and it's not worth the effort."

"Fuck." Chase whacked the doorjamb with his palm. "We've got to know soon and start investigating other options if they're out. Since Marlyle is a no-go, thanks to you."

For a second there, Tierney had been willing to play nice with his brother, since the future of the family business was at stake, but the douche bag just had to bring up Marlyle County, didn't he?

"Don't worry," Tierney snapped, picking up the handset for his office phone. "I'll find out today. Someone owes me." He spun around in his chair, glaring out his window at the wondrous view of the parking lot. And his stupid, pretentious car.

Chase left without taking any parting shots. He'd won that round, after all. In a way, it had helped—now Tierney could call Jerry in the proper, pissed-off frame of mind instead of mooning over Dalton.

"Who may I say is calling?" the Diablo County Fire secretary asked after he requested Chief Brown's extension.

"Chase Terrebonne."

A click and a few seconds of hold music later, Jerry answered. "Hey, Chase."

"I lied. It's Tierney."

"Shit," Jerry said under his breath.

"Yeah. I'm calling so you can tell me what I missed in that meeting Friday. I was a little distracted, not really paying attention. You know that meeting, Jerry? The one where that asshole from the hospital was texting trash about me to everyone?"

"How'd you know what he was saying?"

"C'mon, dude. I've been doing the same shit for years. I *know* douche bags."

Jerry grumbled, then sighed. "Sorry."

"Oh, that was heartfelt. Thanks."

"T, you know how it goes. We were just messing around."

"Sniping about me being gay?"

Jerry had what sounded like a coughing fit, a nice long one. "Jesus," he croaked, then gulped some water or something. "I've never heard you just say it like that, I mean, other than at the wake."

"Gay gay gay gay gay gay gay ga—"

"I get it already. I've just never known anyone like . . . that."

"Hello! You've known me a dozen years, dumbass. *And* you know Ian Cully."

"Yeah but he's— Fuck, this is confusing."

"No, it's not, Jerry." But the dude was going to have to work out his acceptance level on his own. Tierney'd done his part. "So tell me what that dick said about me."

"I thought you called to get the lowdown on that meeting. And don't you want to find out if Diablo would look at a bid from another ambulance company?" Jerry sounded like a frantic mouse.

"You can tell me that after you tell me what was flying around that room."

Jerry groaned. "Man, don't make me do it. Some of it was kinda over the line."

Mother. Fucker. "Changed my mind," Tierney snapped. "Now cough up what you've heard about the ambulance contract."

He barely caught Jerry's sigh of relief. "Well, I'll tell you one thing: none of the cooperating agencies are happy with American."

"What about the county commissioners?"

It took a while, but using the fine scalpel of guilt, Tierney got Jerry to give up a whole lot of insider information on the situation in Diablo, with the bonus of hearing Jerry's (more) sincerely awkward apology at the end of the call. Tierney accepted it with a hint of condescension. Hey, he was a work in progress. By the time he hung up, his mood was buoyed by remembering what made him good at his job. He had people skills. Manipulating people skills.

In retrospect, sitting in front of his office window, studying his car out in the company lot, it didn't sound like such a laudable talent. Since he'd managed to make one major alteration in his life, he could do some more remodeling if necessary, right? Sure, the way he'd gone about the first change had caused the most possible humiliation, but he'd managed something douche bags like Dalton's exes were too terrified to do. Not that Tierney hadn't been terrified, but he'd lived through it, hadn't he?

Between Jerry's apology and the small, glowing hope flickering in his chest, he managed to write a polite email to his brother, informing him that they should start putting together a bid for the Diablo County area service agreement.

Then he went to trade in that stupid phallic car he had.

Chapter 19

On Tuesday after work, Dalton walked into the employee parking garage, as distracted as usual, juggling his messenger and gym bags, searching for his keys. The structure was deserted, since he left a few minutes late—state workers tended to leave at five on the nose, if not earlier. The coral glow of the lights inside the lot matched the last bits of sunset on the horizon outside. His heels made a lot of noise on the concrete, a small drumbeat celebrating his freedom from work. He'd worn his new motorcycle boots as a little bit of a pick-me-up after a couple of days of thinking almost constantly about Tierney—about whether he really liked the man, or simply liked being needed. Nearly driving himself insane but coming to no conclusions. At least, not any he was certain were driven by his higher brain.

The only thing he knew for sure was he'd take almost any excuse to talk to Tierney. Make sure he was all right. Make sure that actual penetrative sex hadn't turned him straight.

Stop it. Now.

Finding the keys and his car, Dalton got in, started it up, and then saw the manila envelope trapped under his windshield wiper. The front was facing him, his name spelled out neatly in capital letters.

Tierney? His heart bobbled. Except, he'd always suspected Tierney's writing would be messier. But who else would leave him a note here?

The person who'd sent the fruit basket?

He turned off the car and stared at his name another few seconds, various options presenting themselves. But the only way he'd figure out what was in the envelope or who it came from was to open it, right? So . . .

Undoing his seat belt and unlatching the door came automatically, but he hesitated at pushing it open and climbing out. The car dinged over and over, reminding him he'd left his key in the ignition, while he wondered what it meant if this envelope had been left by the same person who'd sent the fruit.

Would that be *stalking* behavior?

Don't be ridiculous, he told the fear that sluiced through him.

Maybe it *was* from Tierney. What if his secretary had addressed the envelope? Did Tierney even have a secretary?

Why wouldn't he just come up to the office and give it to me? Maybe because it was a note confessing his undying love, and he'd been too shy to give it to Dalton in person.

I sound like one of Sam's romance heroines. That got him right out of the car to yank the envelope free. His name was lettered in felt-tip marker, and faint pencil lines were just visible, as if a kid had drafted it out as painstakingly as any science fair poster.

Well, *that* didn't seem like Tierney at all. He flipped it over and fumbled the clasp open, nearly tearing it, shaking out the contents on the hood of his car. Two pieces of stiff, multicolored paper fell out, about the size of . . . tickets? He bent to see them better, his brain scrambling the visual, until it suddenly resolved like a digital image. The City West Opera Company logo was splayed across the top, with *Rigoletto* printed in that dot-matrix font underneath.

Ummm . . . He turned back to the envelope, peering inside. One more piece of paper was stuck in a crease. He freed it, then pulled it out to read: *A little something to make up for what happened that night.*

Only Tierney would think he had something to apologize for after their sleepover Friday. It was just three nights ago, but Tierney made it sound as if it had been weeks or longer and that kind of overexaggeration was so *him.*

But *ugh*, the opera. Dalton hated opera. One of his exes used to drag him along, when socializing with his other closeted gay friends and their boys. Somehow, though, getting tickets to *Rigoletto* from Tierney wasn't annoying, not after a few seconds of reflection. In fact, it had him squirming like a happy puppy on the inside.

Two tickets . . . *Clearly, I'm meant to invite someone to go with me.*

Relief rushed through his chest. *I can talk to him*. Thank God he had a good excuse for ignoring Sam's advice. He didn't have to be careful and thoughtful and make logical, nonemotional, adult decisions. In fact, he *had* to call Tierney, because it would be rude to not respond to this gesture.

His fingers only shook a little as he dialed.

"Dalton. Hi." Tierney sounded surprised. Good surprised or bad surprised?

Well, he'd instigated this, so . . . "Would you like to go to the opera with me? I happen to have these two tickets." He smiled, waiting for Tierney's response. Would he play along awhile or admit he'd left them right away?

But when Tierney answered seconds later, his tone was more flummoxed than playful. "Um, opera?" Flummoxed, and a bit put off.

"Opera," Dalton confirmed, disoriented, trying to figure out what he'd misread. Did Tierney expect him to find a *different* date?

"I gotta be honest with you, I'm not a huge fan of opera."

"You're not?"

"No."

Dalton's breath caught in his throat, but he forced out a question. "Did you think *I* was?"

"Why would I think that?" Tierney asked.

A tingling numbness invaded Dalton's fingertips, right where they touched the envelope. "So . . . you didn't leave two opera tickets on my car with a note that says 'A little something to make up for what happened that night'?"

"Yes, I'm saying that."

"Then who left them?" Dalton half whispered. The numbness began creeping up into his hand. Because there was only one other incident in recent memory that could reasonably be referred to as "that night."

"Okaaaay . . ." Tierney said. "Are you thinking what I'm thinking?"

Dalton swallowed. "I don't know. Probably."

"I'm thinking of the bashing."

He nodded, but couldn't actually voice agreement, as if the numbness had invaded his vocal chords.

"Dalton." Tierney's voice became very focused, as if each word were of supreme importance. "Call one of your brothers. One of the cops, not the accountant."

He coughed out whatever was keeping him from speaking. "You really think I should?"

"Yes! You're a major witness in a high-profile hate crime."

"It's not high profile, not rea—"

"Just call. Please."

"Okay," Dalton whispered.

"Are you parked in your usual spot?"

"Uh-huh."

"I'll be there as soon as I can." Then he ended the call.

Knowing Tierney was on his way warmed Dalton up, reversing the numbness, chasing it back down his arm to his fingers. He carefully tucked the opera tickets into the envelope, and stuck that under the windshield wiper, as close to its original position as he could remember.

Then he called Luke.

"Are you sure you aren't overreacting?" Luke asked for the fifth or eighth or hundredth time. Within minutes of Dalton calling, he'd arrived, and he'd even informed dispatch. Dalton totally appreciated it, since the garage was now completely deserted and the sky outside was dark. Luke wasn't actually on shift, but he could still do police-type things.

Too bad he ruined the rescue with his typical big brother act.

"No, I'm not sure," Dalton told him again, in the singsongy speech of the truly annoyed. "I think it's entirely possible I'm overreacting."

"And you called me anyway?"

"Yes." He drew out the word, because Luke clearly had some kind of hearing deficiency. "I could swear they had a minimum intelligence requirement for police officers."

Luke lifted an eyebrow. "Dude, there's no need to be a dick. You're the one who called me for help."

"Sorry. I'm just—I'm a little freaked out."

"By opera tickets? Are you sure you don't have a secret admirer?"

Dalton nearly stamped his foot. "It said 'something to make up for that night.'"

"Yeah," Luke smirked. "What'd you do to him?"

"I think I'd remember it if I'd been with anyone recently and they'd done something they needed to apologize for." Dalton folded his arms across his chest, glaring along his nose at his taller brother. "Is this how you treat all your crime victim customers? Because I can see why the police sometimes get a reputation for being uncaring. I don't think I need to remind you that I'm a key witness in a felony hate crime case, and the phrase 'that night' *could* refer to said hate crime."

Luke snapped to attention, like Dalton had called forth the ghost of drill sergeants past. Oh, they were really about to get into it, weren't they?

But his brother surprised him. "Sorry, you're right." He nodded once and turned toward the car, then started doing his cop thing, officious and investigative without actually touching much, squatting and leaning and bending.

Dalton hadn't touched anything else either, other than to take his keys out of the ignition to stop the maddening dinging. He hadn't even noticed it in the first few minutes after calling Tierney, but by the time Luke was on his way, he'd calmed down enough to hear it over the drumming in his ears.

"Do you have any clean sandwich bags or something?" Luke asked.

Dalton blinked. "What? Why would you—"

"Evidence."

"*Sandwich* bags?"

Luke shrugged, poking at the tickets with a pen he'd produced from somewhere. "I don't carry them around with me. If you wanted someone always prepared to investigate a crime, you should've called Peter."

"He keeps plastic baggies in his trunk in case he randomly has to do some evidence collection?"

Luke snorted. "Or clean up after that mini horse they call a dog."

"Let me see." Dalton headed toward the rear of his car. He didn't think he had any, but maybe a box had fallen under the seat the last time he went grocery shopping. *Not likely.*

The sound of a vehicle squealing into the garage stopped him a few feet short, his heart slamming into high speed again. He didn't recognize it—shiny new, black, built like a sports car, with a maniac behind the wheel. Moving toward them so fast that Dalton didn't have time to jump out of the way before it screeched to a halt ten feet from him. He'd barely recovered from that when Luke was standing in his way, blocking whoever was getting out of the vehicle.

Tierney.

Dalton tried to step around his brother, but Luke's arm across his rib cage stopped him. "Do you know this guy?"

"Who's this dude?" Tierney asked at the same moment, advancing on them, fists balled but held next to his thighs.

He chose to answer Tierney. "He's my brother."

"He is?" Tierney halted midstep, brow clearing.

One man may have stopped charging, but the other one's voice got harder. "Who's *he*?" It wasn't a cop voice, Dalton knew that tone, but he knew this one better: big brother. And looking at Tierney, he got it right away. New car, designer suit, and he was here almost as soon as Luke, so obviously Dalton had called him.

He thinks I have a new sugar daddy. Forget that it had been years since Dalton had been with anyone who qualified as such.

"It's okay, he's just a friend." He gripped Luke's arm, pulling it back, as if he could get his brother to not be so protective. Or think stupid things.

Luke didn't stand down. "Does *he* know that?"

Tierney's brow started to get mulish again, lowering over his eyes. He took another step toward them.

Dalton shoved at Luke's arm until it moved, hurrying to Tierney and grabbing his wrist. Tierney stopped immediately and finally met Dalton's gaze.

"You got a new car."

Tierney blinked. "Um, yeah. It's a hybrid."

"Looks like a sports car to me," Luke said, just a bit of the annoyed singsong tone in his voice.

"You should've seen what I had before."

"It's still a BMW," Dalton pointed out.

"Yeah, well, they're good at brand loyalty." Tierney's cheeks had darkened. Was he really blushing?

"I like it." He would have said it even if he didn't like it, because Tierney was getting agitated.

"Why are we talking about my car?" Tierney asked too loudly. Dalton slid his hand down and laced their fingers together, hoping it would calm him a little. His voice was back to normal when he leaned closer to Dalton to search his face like he was inspecting him for damage. "Are you all right?"

"I'm fine. A little . . ." A one-shoulder shrug would have to do because he couldn't come up with any appropriate words.

"Did you tell your brother about the other thing?" Tierney spoke loud enough for Luke to overhear.

"Um." Dalton squeezed his eyes shut a second. "Not yet." He really had intended to tell him, but Luke had started acting overbearing right away.

"What other thing?" Luke jerked his head toward them.

"Why not?" Tierney asked at the same moment.

Sigh. He turned his brother. "Someone anonymously sent me a fruit basket with a note that said, 'I'm sorry.'"

"Huh." Luke scrunched his nose up. "Did you tell anyone?"

"I told Tierney." *Weak.*

Luke tilted his head and raised his brows, eyeing first Dalton, then Tierney, then their intertwined fingers. "This is him?"

"Hi, you must be Luke," Tierney said, holding out his right hand, but still hanging onto Dalton's with his left.

Luke rolled his eyes but stepped forward to shake. "I meant," he said afterward, "did you tell Detective Johnson about it?"

"Would *you* have?"

He shrugged his eyebrows, but admitted, "No."

In the end, Luke was far more serious than he had been earlier, calling in to dispatch, "for the record." Then he did more poking around, and even found a baggie to put the envelope in.

As soon as Luke was on the other side of the car, out of earshot, Tierney asked, "Why doesn't anyone believe we're just friends?"

"Um, I guess we don't act like just friends?"

Tierney glanced down to where he held Dalton's hand. "Yeah. I guess they aren't used to friends being as, uh, close as we are."

"Guess not," Dalton said, biting his lip in an effort not to smile.

Tierney's cheeks darkened. "I can't take you to the opera—"

"Thank God, I hate opera."

"—but they're having Star Trek night at the X Theater. Wanna go?" Change jingled as Tierney's other hand fidgeted in his pants pocket.

"X Theater?" Wasn't that one of those movie house pubs?

"I'm not going to drink," Tierney said immediately.

How sad that that was his first thought. "Of course you won't." Dalton gave him a reassuring squeeze of the fingers. "I'd like to go."

"Cool. Um, *Wrath of Khan* starts at seven. I know the schedule 'cause I was gonna call and ask if you wanted to see it."

He was? Dalton's heart fluttered, distracting him before he could object to that stupid movie.

"Or we could watch the newest one, *Into Darkness*."

"Oh, I haven't seen that yet. Wasn't it released a while ago?"

"Yeah, year or two. It starts at 9:40. We'd be out kinda late."

"I don't mind."

"Um, cool." Tierney nodded. "It's a good movie; there're all kinds of sexual undertones between Spock and Kirk."

Yeah, that seemed to be going around.

Joining them again, Luke said, "If any other weird things happen, you call 911." He pointed at Dalton, but also glanced Tierney's way. After they'd both nodded, he said to Dalton, "Walk over to my car with me."

Of course. As protective as his family was, the typical thing now would be for Luke to see him home, instruct him to lock everything, test said locks, and give him a lecture on taking another self-defense class.

Trailing behind his brother, Dalton began to formulate his plan for making Luke leave. He didn't get the opportunity, though. After locking the evidence baggie in his trunk, Luke turned to him and said, "Okay, I'm taking this to the station. See you on Thanksgiving."

"You're *leaving*?"

"Yeah." Luke smirked. "I think you'll be fine all alone here with your *friend*."

Dalton narrowed his eyes at his stupid brother. "You just made me come over here with you because you wanted to see me squirm, didn't you?"

"Yup." He was all-out grinning now. "It's been a long time since you've had a *friend*. I have a lot of teasing to catch up on."

"Lovely." Well, at least Tierney was worth it.

Tierney *had* been trying to think of ways to contact Dalton without putting himself in the position of needy, whiny loser, but before he could work it out, Dalton solved the problem by calling him instead.

The dude was even in need at the time.

Amazing how such a little thing could make three days of twisted guts and angsty, teenaged pacing around the condo vanish like fingerprints after quality glass cleaner. Standing in the parking garage, watching Dalton say good-bye to his brother, he tried to figure out if he should confess to all that anxiety. Did the authentic Tierney *always* have to put it all out there?

Before he'd made any decisions, Dalton came back toward him, boot heels clicking on the concrete rhythmically, confident gait bringing him closer. Blue eyes smiling at Tierney, their expression infusing his whole face, brightening his skin and making him nearly glow.

Stunning.

Fingers twitching, Tierney nearly reached for him again, almost taking Dalton's hand as if it was the most obvious, natural thing in the world for them to be skin to skin whenever near enough.

"I've been avoiding you," he blurted. Good to know he was as smooth now as he'd been before rehab. *You're the man.*

Dalton stopped cold, right in front of him, happiness leaking from his face, bleeding out of his eyes to make room for hurt feelings to move in. "Why? Should we not have—"

"No. No, it was my own shit, not that." Swallowing, he pushed the rest out. "I thought I was, like, your charity case."

It took a few seconds of staring before Dalton responded. "Because you needed my help. And because of the sex."

Tierney nodded. He didn't have words.

"I've told you I don't see you that way. I *like* being with you." Dalton shook his head, reaching to stroke his palm down Tierney's arm. "What do I have to do to make sure you don't feel like that again?" God, that earnest, concerned expression was adorable. Like it actually hurt him to hurt Tierney.

"Well, you kinda already took care of it by calling me when *you* needed help." Scratching his temple with his fingernail gave him an excuse to avoid Dalton's gaze a few seconds. "But, I was tied up in knots after we did that. Had sex. I had to, um, rely on my support network to keep from drinking one night."

Tierney worked up to meeting his eyes again, but Dalton was glancing around the garage, chest lifting in a quick breath. "Would it be better if we just stopped hanging out?"

No. "Is that what you want?"

Dalton dipped his chin, voice dropping with it. "Honestly, no, but if that's better for you of *course*—"

"I don't want to either. I mean, I have some people set up to help me out, you know, a support network, and my first appointment with the therapist is tomorrow. As long as I can keep things in *perspective*, we can continue this." Tierney gestured back and forth between them, illustrating the connection like a dork, in case it wasn't fucking obvious enough. "Our, um, friendship."

Now Dalton was smiling again, just a little. That and looking at Tierney through his lashes. "All of it? Even the benefits?"

Tierney had to swallow before repeating his earlier question. "Is that what you want?"

"Yeah."

Thank fuck. "Me too," he said in a rush.

"But we have to be careful. If at any time you begin to feel like—"

Grabbing Dalton's hand shut him up pretty fast. "I'll talk to you, I promise."

Apparently, that was enough discussion about it. Dalton simply nodded, smiling.

Tierney very nearly leaned in for a quick kiss, to seal the deal, but then he remembered they were just friends. Who held hands. And kissed on occasion. But now that he'd reminded himself, he couldn't go ahead and do it. Too awkward.

They really needed to agree on an official list of benefits, just not right now.

After following Dalton home so he'd know where to pick the dude up later, Tierney raced back to the condo and dressed in something casual, brushed his teeth, reapplied deodorant, finger-combed his hair—totally went all-out, ready to go at 7:15.

He'd said he'd pick up Dalton at eight.

But he couldn't just wait around his place. Too antsy. So he drove around awhile, feeling like a high school kid about to go out on his first date. Except he'd never been nervous like this before any previous date. Of course, those had all been with girls, and this would be his first date with a guy.

Not that it was a real date. Just a friend date.

Felt like a real date, though.

Should he bring flowers?

Somehow, he found himself standing in the entryway of a grocery store, staring at the floral display, totally dissatisfied with it. The blossoms were all too perfect, and the prearranged bouquets all had little signs perched in them, with things like "I love you" embossed on plastic hearts.

Even if they'd had one that read "I love you, good buddy," or "Platonic relationships rule," he wouldn't have bought a bouquet. They were too impersonal.

Fuck flowers. He was getting Dalton something else, something personal that showed he valued their friendship. That showed he'd been paying attention, and knew what the guy might like. He was going to buy a thoughtful, considerate gift in the next—

7:48 claimed his watch.

Fuck.

—next five minutes.

Turning around in a panic, he saw a book display rack near the check stands.

Dalton likes to read. A memory surfaced, of the book he'd seen in Dalton's backpack last time he'd come over to Tierney's. The cover'd had a couple in a clinch on it. This place ought to have something similar, right? Romance novels were popular.

Turned out grocery stores weren't great places to find reading material. He finally settled on the least offensive cover—an uptight, business-suit-wearing woman with a prim mouth stood in the foreground, glancing back over her shoulder at a guy wearing coveralls, grease stains, and a knowing smirk.

It's the thought that counts.

Minutes later, standing in front of apartment 4C waiting for Dalton to answer his knock, he realized he was nervously—and repeatedly—slapping the gift bag containing the book against his thigh. He forced himself to stop just before the door swung open.

"Hey." Dalton was pulling on his coat, blond hair damp. A faint, woodsy-soap scent surrounded him. "I'd invite you in, but we should probably go or we won't have time to eat first."

"I got you something." Holding out the stupid present, he noticed the bow was smushed from his fidgeting. "Uh, it's just . . . It's sort of a thank-you thing. For being there."

"Oh." Dalton's eyes went shiny, just like at the garage when he'd been walking toward Tierney. He came toward him again now, stepping out into the hallway to take the gift from only a few inches away, bringing his scent and warmth closer, looking at the bag a second before reaching into it and pulling out the paperback.

Tierney winced when he saw the cover again. On its own, *not* next to books featuring bare-chested pirates and windblown hussies, it seemed really . . . sordid.

"*The Billionaire's Baby Daddy.*"

Fuck, *that* was the title? "Well, um, I know you like to read, and they didn't have . . . uhhhh . . ."

"Thank you," Dalton said, meeting Tierney's gaze and hugging the book against his chest, smile softer but somehow better. Fuller.

Tierney followed his impulse, leaned forward, and kissed Dalton, taking his lips between his own, like a hug. Which was dorky, because it was supposed to be a "thank you for the gift" kind of kiss, but that would have been Dalton's job. He was always fucking up this friendship shit, wasn't he? He straightened after a second, clearing his throat. "You're welcome."

Fingers—Dalton's fingers—sliding up the back of his neck made him shiver, then the scratch of fingernails through the hair at his nape gave him a full-out attack of goose bumps. Dalton used his free arm to pull Tierney closer, bringing them chest to chest, with the book trapped between them, mouths only centimeters apart.

Tierney's heart knocked against the paperback, trying to break through the barrier. "I had to buy it at the grocery store," he whispered. "It's a lame gift."

"It's not." Dalton shook his head, lips brushing back and forth against Tierney's, piling goose bumps on top of his goose bumps. "Are you hungry?"

All the blood in his body raced toward his groin—the liter or so that wasn't already there—then it occurred to Tierney that Dalton might be talking about actual food. "Uh . . ."

"We could skip dinner and you could come inside. See my place." Dalton stretched closer, giving him a soft, clingy kiss. "I have a new bed."

"Yes. Absolutely. Yes. I very much wanna look at your new bed."

Dalton had no excuse for seducing Tierney like this, except gratitude. For the gift, or rather the thought behind the gift. For making him feel special, and acknowledged. For taking Dalton's own preferences—even a simple, mundane one like reading—into account.

Had anyone, ever, done that? As the youngest of five, he'd been spoiled, but with the things others thought he'd want, and as the boy toy of wealthy men, he'd been indulged, but only when it was convenient. No one had ever thought about what *he* would like.

At least, right now, it seemed as if Tierney was the only person to ever really care enough. Or the only person that mattered. Why *would* anyone else matter when he had this man pressed up against him, kissing Dalton like oxygen was optional, arm cinching around his waist and hand creeping down his back to his ass? His right leg wrapped around Tierney's thighs all of its own volition, pulling them groin to groin, within grinding distance.

Tierney groaned explosively, which Dalton hadn't known was possible until the man yanked out of their kiss and did it in his ear, pushing Dalton nearly through the sheetrock. *We're still in the hallway.*

"Come inside." Taking Tierney's wrist, he slid along the wall until the jamb scraped against his shoulder blade. He walked back through his open doorway, towing Tierney along with him. Leaving the gift on the table next to the entry, he yanked Tierney within intimate distance again.

Their journey to his bedroom was passionate in that way Sam's books always described, but Dalton had never experienced. Over the hissing and growling of his cat—"Ignore Blue," he gasped between kisses—they stumbled down his hall, not able to stop touching each other, leaving a trail of clothes along the way, beginning with Tierney's button-down in the entry. Dalton struggled out of his jacket and left it in front of the bathroom, whipping his shirt off just as they stopped in his room, between his wardrobe and his bed. Inviting Tierney to rub his hands all over the naked skin, and encouraging him to map out all his sensitive spots by moaning whenever Tierney found one with his fingertips. Even groaning, "Please," when Tierney hesitantly toyed with the top button of his fly.

He flicked it open immediately, shoved inside, and grasped Dalton's dick through his briefs, squeezing.

God. All this time the man was worried about being too needy, but as far as Dalton was concerned, this, right now, was about what *he* needed. He needed Tierney's pants off, and he needed to feel Tierney's cock sliding across his palm.

"Let me make you come," he whispered as he worked his fingers down the front of Tierney's still-buttoned jeans. Under the waistband and into the short curly hairs. Reading the man's excitement through the intensity of heat and sweat.

"No," Tierney gasped, yanking his hand out of Dalton's underwear, stopping all motion except the working of their lungs, until he said, "I wanna— I mean, can I fuck you?"

Dalton's rational brain tried to remind him that he couldn't do this lightly. Let someone inside him. And this was just friends with benefits, even if it felt like so much more. But he'd already prepared for it. *Needed* it, regardless of how much that sounded like a line from one of Sam's romance novels. "Please. I want you to."

Just for the next hour or so, he'll be my boyfriend, then we'll go back to just friends. One night of lavishing Tierney with all the attentions he'd give a man he loved, as if they were a real and actual couple, with full benefits.

Chapter 20

Tierney couldn't say how, but they made it to the bed, shedding the last of their clothes. Dalton pulled out condoms and a bottle from his nightstand, tossing them onto the covers, then lay down, arranging himself so he was next to Tierney.

He propped himself up on his elbow, facing Dalton. "Tell me what needs to happen"—he slid his palm down perfect abdominal muscles—"so I can fuck you." Just the word made him shudder and his vision go blurry for a split second.

"It's been a while for me," Dalton said, meeting his eyes, circling a thumb around Tierney's nipple. "So I have to be prepared. I can do it for myself, or—"

"Me." He was already pulling Dalton's leg up into the air, moving to kneel between the guy's thighs. Fuck yeah, he was greedy. But he'd waited years for this, and more importantly, Dalton *wanted* him to do it. Wanted *Tierney* to fuck him.

At what point did excessive shuddering become convulsions? Dalton gripped his forearm, stopping Tierney from reaching for him. "Put the condom on now, so you don't have to think about it later."

It boosted his confidence that Dalton wanted him to do it himself. Like he was really in charge here. Truly capable of taking the lead, in spite of having almost no experience. *Dalton* believed he could do it.

So Tierney believed too, and did it. Dalton had to guide him through the rest, though.

Eyes trained on the sight of Dalton's hard dick bowing up over his stomach, just inches from Tierney's fumbling hands, his muscles could barely follow commands. He couldn't get the lube open, so Dalton did it. The sight of his own shaking finger reaching for Dalton's hole nearly made him giggle when, for a split second, it looked like E.T.'s reaching to point out his home planet. He half expected to hear "phoooone hoooome."

Be smooth, for once. Be the man, you unmitigated dork. Soon he was lost in how tight and hot Dalton felt around his fingers, and then, when Dalton wrapped his hand around Tierney's shaft to guide him, the friction against the head of his cock.

When the resistance of Dalton's hole began to give, grudgingly swallowing Tierney's dick, they sounded off in unison, like cheering on an athlete, except more gasping and less shouting.

"Feels good?" Dalton asked breathily.

Tierney groaned, looking down just in time to see Dalton grasp his own dick and stroke it, his thumb making some special move that could only come from years of practice and familiarity with what really did it for him. "Oh fuck, that's hot."

"Watching yourself?"

"No. You." He gulped in some air. "So sexy. Do it again."

Dalton grinned at him, damp bangs clinging to his forehead and eyes shining. "I *am*."

"The thing with your thumb."

"Like this?" He stroked up on his shaft, and Tierney followed his lead, pushing further inside all that tight heat, and then Dalton did that move again, flicking his thumb and stroking sideways just under his cockhead, right in the center, and Tierney could *feel* it. As if he were inside Dalton's body but also getting that handjob.

So of course his orgasm ambushed him right away. That didn't make it any less intense—it was all the muscle spasming wave of sensation he was used to, and even better because he had Dalton's body clenched around him. But still humiliating. He tried to apologize for coming so soon by groaning and shoving into Dalton's ass farther, but he had a feeling something got lost in translation.

Propped up on his hands, eyes scrunched shut, still inside Dalton, he tried again once he was done. "Sorry."

Over the sound of Tierney's panting, Dalton said, "It's okay."

Nope. "Not okay."

"You'll last longer next time." Dalton sounded nearly as out of breath as he was, and there was another sound, a familiar one. Tierney opened his eyes and his suspicions were confirmed—he was still jacking himself.

It'd be even hotter if that was my hand. "I wanna do that." He slipped out, took off the condom, and dropped it over the side of the bed, then put his hand over Dalton's, learning the strokes he liked, and feeling the excitement pulse through him. Dalton came within a minute, cum rushing out all over Tierney's fingers, and even *that* was hot.

Then Dalton pulled him down on top of his body and wrapped his arms around Tierney, holding him against his damp skin and panting in his ear.

"Was that okay? Like, the sex?" Tierney pushed up to see Dalton's face, because he really wanted to know, truthfully.

"Yeah." Dalton was smiling, then he lifted a hand and ran his fingers through Tierney's hair. "It felt good."

"So I did it right?"

"As long as you're not doing it wrong, you're doing it right."

"Um, then did I do it wrong?"

"No, you very much *didn't* do it wrong."

"So, you'd, like, do it again?" He traced the curve of Dalton's cheekbone with a fingertip. He'd always wanted to do that, but he hadn't realized it until now. And the guy's eyebrow, he wanted to stroke that too.

"With you?" Dalton blinked sleepily. "Yes."

He wants to do it with me. Tierney kissed him, just a small one to test the texture of his lips against Dalton's. "When?" Between this being his first time fucking a guy and the sneak-attack orgasm, he probably wouldn't be down for long. Plus, this was Dalton, and Tierney was beginning to think he'd never get enough of the benefits they had with each other.

Dalton laughed. "When we're both ready, I guess."

Tierney was right, it didn't take long.

The second time was even better than the first. They tried a new—to him—position, with Dalton on his stomach. At some point, watching the guy underneath him, Tierney forgot about his dick being an instrument of his own pleasure, and began to see it as a way to make Dalton feel good. When Tierney moved inside him in certain ways, Dalton's breath would hitch, or he'd even moan quietly. One angle in particular made him tense up everywhere and gasp out a soft "uh" every time Tierney thrust into him. Tierney tried a different stroke, adjusting his pelvis a little lower, and he could actually see the sexual tension easing out of Dalton's spine, so he changed back to the previous angle, fine-tuning the rhythm by reading Dalton's back muscles and his increasing noises.

And then the most amazing thing happened. Dalton came while Tierney was inside him. Buried almost all the way, so focused on hitting that one spot that made his partner jerk and groan, he was taken completely by surprise when Dalton whispered, "Oh God Tierney," and then clamped down on his dick, muscles contracting around him while Dalton moaned and reached under himself for his own cock.

He'd been so intent on making Dalton happy, he forgot coming was the end goal right up until his body shuddered with the release of all that sensation coiled inside of him. *Another sneak attack.* Squeezing his eyes shut, he let it shoot through him, out the top of his head and through his toes and fingertips. He might have even been streaming light for all he knew—so hot inside that some chemical reaction must have been occurring, making him glow.

Afterward, laying with his chest on Dalton's back, their heartbeats created another rhythm altogether. Dalton's tapped rapidly under his ear, and his own pulse answered, booming inside his rib cage nearly as fast.

"I had no idea sex could be that good," he mumbled against the skin of Dalton's neck.

"Me neither," Dalton sighed.

It was a nice thing to say, even if it wasn't true.

Then the dude's cat sank his claws into Tierney's ass and afterglow was *so* over.

"I'm so sorry about this," Dalton said for the umpteenth time. They were in his bathroom and he'd just finished cleaning the scratches that Blue had given Tierney. The wounds were shallow, except at the end of one long line of red, ripped skin, where there was more of a puncture. He pressed a quick kiss on it, then picked up the tube of antibiotic cream from the counter where he'd left the first aid supplies.

Tierney sighed and shifted. "It's okay."

"Would you rather lie down while I do this?" Dalton was using the toilet as a seat with Tierney standing in front of him. It put him at the right eye level for doctoring buttocks.

"You're almost done, right? This is fine."

"I'd say Blue isn't normally like that, but I'd be lying."

"If I didn't know better," Tierney muttered, "I'd think Grandfather's ghost possessed the fucking thing."

"No, Blue's just mean." Although he hadn't had a guy in his bed since he got his pet, so maybe Tierney was special? Or it was karma, for Dalton trying to pretend Tierney was his boyfriend, and not honoring their "friends only" agreement. Except then shouldn't the cat have sliced *him* up?

"Wouldn't be so bad if *you'd* clawed me."

If he was making jokes, he couldn't be *too* angry, right? The second after Tierney had yowled—sounding a lot like Blue—and leaped off the bed, Dalton had steeled himself. Even before he knew what had happened, he'd braced for the asshole side of the man to appear and spout shit he'd regret later.

Annoyance made an appearance, but Tierney's temper didn't flare up.

If Blue had scratched any of my exes, they'd have put me out.

Dalton ripped open a bandage and carefully applied it to his lover's butt over the deepest part of the wound. He'd so much rather still be lying in bed, with Tierney's body weighing him down and the man's whiskers scratching the back of his neck.

"Never done this after sex before." He smoothed the edges with his thumb, taking more passes than necessary.

Tierney's laugh was further assurance he wasn't seriously pissed off, thank God. Dalton gave him a little pat on the cheek, and Tierney stepped away, heading toward the door. He looked so cute with a bandage on his ass.

"Cat scratches are notorious for getting infected." He winced inside when Tierney stopped and turned to blink at him. He didn't *think* things would go sideways now, but the man had always been unpredictable.

"What?" His eyes went wide and questioning, rather than narrowing to mean slits. "That's why you put that stuff on it, right?"

"Well, yeah, but he *really* scratched you. They're deep." Dalton finally stood, coming closer. Letting it finally sink in that the old Tierney wasn't going to appear and freak out.

"Feels like it," Tierney muttered, shaking his head. "Are you saying I'm going to have to go to my doctor, show him the claw marks on my ass and ask him if they're infected?"

"Or you could wait a couple of days to see if it gets inflamed." Close enough now to touch, he slid his arms around Tierney's waist and kissed the ball of his shoulder. "Sorry," he whispered again.

Tierney returned the hug immediately. "Seriously, stop apologizing. And thank you for playing doctor."

Back in the bedroom a minute later, the next awkward moment attacked—did they get dressed and go about their individual lives now, or go to the movie, or get back in bed, or . . .? Dalton stood in front of his closet, trying to look nonchalant while naked, waiting to see what Tierney would do. Knowing full well that if this were truly a simple friends-with-benefits relationship, he'd be getting dressed without a thought. He'd never had a moment like this with the guys he had arrangements with in college.

Tierney found his briefs and stepped into them. "I guess your cat doesn't want me here."

"Probably a safe bet." Hopefully he'd managed to put humor into his tone, but it was difficult with a sinking heart.

Glancing at his watch, Tierney bent to pick up his jeans. "We missed the movie. If you come back to my place we could just dial it up on pay-per-view."

Dalton shrugged, as if thinking it over, but *duh*. "Sure, sounds good."

Tierney smiled. "Cool. Bring clothes for tomorrow and we can have a sleepover."

"Okay."

Dalton couldn't claim to be well rested when he stayed at Tierney's, but he totally owned well sated.

"It's not like this is your only shot at getting some," Dalton teased Tierney in the middle of the night, lying next to him in the very center of the huge bed.

"What if this is my only chance with *you*?" Tierney loomed over him, holding himself up on his elbows.

"It's not." Dalton smoothed away the wrinkle on Tierney's brow with his thumb. "If you want more time with me, you can have it."

"What if I want a lot more time?" Tierney was so still, as if holding his breath until Dalton answered.

You can have as much of me you want. "I'm here for the foreseeable future." Lifting his head, he pressed a kiss on Tierney's lips. "I like being with you. I like *sex* with you."

"You don't feel like, um . . ."

"What?"

Tierney played with Dalton's hair for a second. He must have a fascination with it, because he moaned whenever Dalton's bangs brushed his naked skin. Especially when Dalton was blowing him.

"You said those guys you used to be with all needed something from you—"

"This is totally different." He covered Tierney's lips with his hand. "You aren't offering to pay my bills or telling me I can't have a job so I can be at your beck and call 24-7."

Tierney bobbed his head side to side, as if thinking about asking just that. When Dalton dropped his hand, he went on seriously though. "I just don't want to be the only guy getting something out of this."

"I'm getting laid." Dalton grinned.

Tierney smiled, but only briefly.

Time to own up. "I like knowing that if I call you when someone leaves a threatening pair of opera tickets on my car, you'll come check on me." He swallowed, because this was the thing he never admitted, but Tierney needed to know. Still, all the blood in Dalton's body rushed toward his center, calling in the troops, as he said, "I like that I can tell you about those guys I was with before without you being disgusted by it or making me feel like I was a . . . prostitute." Oh God, somehow this had gone from joking to uncharted territory. *Here be monsters.* He might be seasick.

Tierney's whole forehead wrinkled up. "I was in the closet for most of my life because my grandfather threatened to take my trust fund away, and you think I'm going to care that you let some of your past boyfriends support you? Next to me you're a fucking saint."

Dalton stared at him. "You did it so you wouldn't lose your family."

"My family?" He half smiled, then kissed Dalton's nose. "I was just scared of being alone. You were *already* alone when you hooked up with those dudes."

"I always pretend it doesn't matter," Dalton whispered. "Like, I pretend it was a different person, or I'm above the question of whether I was, um, selling my ass, but . . ." He shook his head, muscles trembly, as if he'd just run a few miles. "But I was. Those guys all needed a discreet, reliable booty call, and I needed to feel like someone cared about me. But none of them really did." Tierney didn't say anything, just combed Dalton's bangs back and kissed his forehead. Maybe if he'd responded verbally, Dalton wouldn't have continued confessing. "You know the worst part?" He swallowed. "I was *into* it. The sex. Not being with an older man so much, but being with a man who had power and influence. I liked—" His throat seized up for a second, but he struggled to get the rest out because right now that secret was poison. "I *liked* being someone's boy toy."

"Oh, baby," Tierney said softly, almost crooning it while stroking his fingertips down Dalton's cheek, then across his lips. He leaned close to kiss Dalton's temple, then murmured in his ear, "That's a pretty lame deepest secret."

Dalton laughed so hard he stopped caring that he'd just revealed his most humiliating hidden desire.

"Being into it is nothing to be ashamed of," Tierney said when Dalton had quieted down. He was still hanging over him, bodily maintaining the cocoon of security and trust they'd created. "It doesn't mean you won't someday be able to find someone who wants *you*, but can also, like, feed your kink." He grinned quickly, then got serious again. "And stop with the beating yourself up about it. The trophy boy statute of limitations expired a long time ago. It's been five years, and you changed things when you realized you weren't being true to yourself."

Lifting his head, Dalton pressed a kiss on Tierney's lips. "Thank you." He wasn't ready to claim he felt all clean inside, but knowing someone else thought his kink wasn't that horrible helped more than he would have guessed. None of *those* men would have worked this hard to comfort him—Tierney really was nothing like them, was he?

"Welcome." Tierney's mischievous smile flirted with his mouth. "And just so you know, if you ever want to *play* boy toy, I can totally help you out with that."

Dalton's pulse suddenly made itself felt everywhere in his body, but especially his dick. "Ohhhh."

He bit his lip a second, trying to decide. While Tierney may be caring and thoughtful in a way none of those exes had been, he still shared some of the very qualities Dalton had found to be a turn-on. Was it really so shameful that he was into the important-businessman schtick? Especially if it was just a game they both knew they were playing?

He gave in to the pull of desire in his gut. "Yeah, we could do that."

"Sweet." Tierney smiled, but his eyes were intent as he shifted, bringing his body further on top of Dalton's and sliding his hard dick up the inside of Dalton's thigh. "How about now?"

In answer, he wrapped his legs around Tierney's and kissed him.

The next morning, standing in Tierney's kitchen, Dalton caught himself mesmerized by the coffee he was stirring, reliving that boy toy conversation, not to mention what happened afterward. Trying not to wonder what it meant that he trusted Tierney this much. "Want some coffee?" he called toward the living room.

"Eh." Tierney was sitting on the couch in his very nice, *trés* sexy designer suit, staring pensively into midair.

As Dalton walked through the dining area and got closer, he revised "pensive" to "pouting." Tierney was in classic sullen mode, lip out, brows pulled together in a V, and hands fisted on his legs.

"What's wrong?" Dalton patted him on the thigh as he sat next to him.

"I don't wanna have to see a therapist."

"It's not abnormal or anything." He nudged Tierney's shoulder with his own, but got no response, verbal or otherwise. "I used to see one." No change in the man's expression whatsoever. Dalton stifled a sigh. Tierney may *like* him, but he didn't think of them as being similar. Setting his mug on the coffee table, he straddled Tierney's lap so he had to pay attention. And Tierney did, looking up questioningly, hands automatically unclenching and cupping Dalton's ass. "You had lots of therapy in rehab, right?"

"But I'm done with rehab," Tierney said, half-whining and giving Dalton puppy dog eyes. "I wanna be done with therapy too."

"Didn't the therapy at Dunthorpe help?"

He sighed and admitted, "Yes."

"Just because you're a guy doesn't mean you have to think therapy is some kind of crutch."

"I don't think it's weak or unmasculine or anything," Tierney objected far too quickly.

Dalton needed a stronger argument. Grasping Tierney's shoulders in his hands, he pushed on them to emphasize his words. "Ian sees a therapist."

"I know." He nodded. "He told *you*?"

"My boss is one of those people who thinks that, if he's on the phone, no one can hear him even if he's standing in the middle of the office half shouting."

Tierney snorted. "True. I guess, if *Ian* sees one . . ."

"Exactly." Dalton kissed him. "Now, I have to get going."

"Me too." Tierney patted his butt as Dalton stood, but was obviously still preoccupied.

So was Dalton, after that. He spent his whole drive to work wondering how he could have forgotten about Ian. Or rather, about what Tierney might feel for Ian. In spite of telling himself to shut up multiple times, he also wondered how those feelings stacked up against whatever Tierney felt for *him*.

Since Tierney'd never been in a friends-with-benefits relationship before, he couldn't know whether what he had with Dalton was a typical one or not.

That was his story, and he was sticking to it.

Once he got to work, he *didn't* spend the morning pacing around his office, dwelling on whether it was normal for just friends to touch as much as they did, even when not having sex, or whether he'd want to spend all his free time with someone he only had lustful and/or platonic feelings for. Probably, in his case, it *was* normal because he had a lot of lost opportunities to catch up on. That was why he'd like to keep Dalton naked, someplace private for the next week, and why he'd broken his personal best record for coming in a twenty-four-hour period last night.

Except, he and lust were old friends, and what he felt for Dalton may have lust in the mix, but it went deeper. More substantial, something beyond the shell. Except this was what they'd warned him about at Dunthorpe—people who were emotionally needy tended to fool themselves into thinking that whatever they had was, like, *right*. *It*, whatever that was. Could that be what drove his feelings for Dalton now?

Was he willing to stop being friends with Dalton, just in case?

Don't wanna.

He stopped not thinking about their friendship when Gina appeared in his open office doorway and said, "You have the monthly quality care meeting in fifteen minutes, you know."

"Uh-huh," he nodded, pretending to be absorbed in something on his desktop. Until what she said sunk in. "Wait, what?" Fuck, he hadn't put it into his personal calendar—he never did, because it happened the same time every month. "Christ, I have a doctor's appointment at ten."

"You forget about it all the time." She lifted a superior eyebrow. "And I suppose you need me to reschedule your doctor's appointment while you prep for the meeting?"

He gave her his most winning smile. "If you schedule it, there's less chance of me screwing it up again."

She pursed her lips. "All right, give me this doctor's name and number." A few minutes later she called through his office door. "Dr. Palmer says she can see you the day after Thanksgiving at 11 a.m."

"Sounds good to me." It was only a few days' wait. Under normal circumstances, he might have taken any flimsy excuse to skip the appointment, but he'd really intended to go see the therapist. He had questions that needed answers. Except . . . this way he'd have a little longer to figure things out before he had to face any major decisions about Dalton.

Chapter 21

They fell into a pattern. Sometime in the evening, Tierney would call Dalton or text, and sooner or later one of them would suggest a sleepover—always at Tierney's place, because of the cat.

Truthfully, that was fine with Dalton. He liked the condo—the size and airiness of it. The furniture was ugly, but he could overlook that. He was mostly focused on the guy who owned it.

Thanksgiving morning, Tierney was still in bed, half-asleep when Dalton was out of the shower, dressed, and about to leave to meet his brother and sister. "It's nearly noon." He sat on the edge of the mattress.

"I'm being lazy." Tierney took Dalton's hand and tugged on it, trying to get him to lie down again. "Are you sure you have to go? If you blow off your family, I'll ignore mine." He grinned like a kid, the side of his face smashed into a pillow, and hair sticking out all over.

Scratching fingernails lightly down Tierney's back made his eyes shut, and elicited a sigh from him. "I have to meet them. They all take turns skipping holidays with our parents so I won't be alone. I can't really blow them off when they make that kind of sacrifice." Although, if it was left up to him, Dalton would ignore the existence of the holidays altogether. No matter how many times Andrea rolled her eyes and insisted, "It's not a sacrifice to avoid Mom's questions about my love life, and speculations on whether I'll die alone," he still felt guilty for taking them away from the rest of the family.

"Wish not being with my family on holidays was a sacrifice," Tierney muttered, then he pushed up onto his elbow and leaned close for a kiss. "See you tonight?"

"Yeah." At the club for Sam's Thanksgiving extravaganza and machination. As if he needed to machinate to get them together at this point, but Dalton hadn't told his friend just how much time he was spending with Tierney now. "You're sure you're up for that?" He didn't add the obvious comment about there being alcohol.

"If I can't hack it, I'll leave." He shrugged. "Besides, Ian will be there."

Ian again. Dalton stood, but was still tethered by Tierney's hand, fingers wrapped around his. "I should go, or I'll be late." Not true, he had plenty of time, but better to flee than to ask about Ian. He couldn't deal with Tierney's feelings for another guy right now, "just friends" or not.

"You okay?" Tierney's brow was folding into his confused V.

"Totally." Bending to give him a quick kiss, Dalton managed to free his hand when he straightened up again. "I'll see you later. Have a good day."

Tierney snorted. "With *my* family? Sure."

Even worried about how Tierney would handle the club, Dalton was more pleased than annoyed to be going out Thanksgiving night. It gave him his own thing to do for the holiday; something removed from his family, that didn't remind him his own mother and father would rather pretend he didn't exist.

Andrea and Luke were waiting out in front of the Kok Won Dim Sum Restaurant, along with a crowd of mostly Asian people. The place was cavernous and the decor reminded him of his high school cafeteria, but all the dim sum restaurants in the area had the same vibe.

"How long is the wait?" Dalton asked after hugging his brother and sister. Kok Won was always packed, and they usually had to hang out over an hour whenever they came here.

"Only a few more minutes," Luke responded, jerking his head at Andrea. "She got here really early and put our names on the list."

Andy smiled. "It's my Christmas present to you both. Don't expect any other gifts."

After they were seated and had picked out a dozen dishes from the various carts wandering the restaurant, Luke kept the family love rolling, turning to their sister. "So, when are you getting married?"

Her only response was to give him a narrow-eyed, down the nose, *you're so not funny* look.

Luke smirked. "I just thought I'd introduce a little taste of the holiday cheer at Mom and Dad's for you."

It was amusing, in a way, but . . . "So, Luke, when are you getting married?" Dalton smiled at his brother's horrified expression.

Andrea snorted laughter.

Unfortunately, Luke recovered fast. "The only one of the three of us that has a boyfriend is you."

"He's not my boyfriend." Oh, he'd said that far too quickly to be believed. But still. "I told you, we're just friends."

"Who is it?" Andy demanded, pointing her chopsticks at him.

"That's considered very rude in China," Dalton informed her, adjusting the napkin in his lap. Not that he actually knew, but it *seemed* rude.

She rolled her eyes but lowered the utensils. "How come I don't know about this but *Luke* does?"

Luke grinned evilly, in contrast to the fake innocence of his voice. "Oh, he didn't tell you about Tierney?"

"*Tierney*?" Andy shrieked, then clamped her lips shut as people turned to look at her. They didn't stay that way long, though. "You're still hanging around with him?" she hissed across the table.

"Yes." He shrugged, but it was difficult under the weight of both his brother's and his sister's scrutiny. "Really, we're only friends. And I told you, he's nothing like the way he used to act."

"'Used to act'? How do you know he won't go back to his old ways? What if *this* is the act, Dalton?"

"It's not. *That* was the act."

"A leopard can't change his spots."

"Exactly."

She glowered, and opened her mouth to say more. So Dalton threw his brother under the bus. "How long have you been looking for a boyfriend, Luke?"

"Wha'?" He goggled, *siu mai* poised in front of his open mouth. Then he dropped it and shook his head. "I'm not looking for a boyfriend."

"But you said, 'the only one of the three of us who has a boyfriend.'" Dalton returned his brother's earlier innocent voice and evil smile with his own versions.

"Ha," Luke muttered. "Funny."

Regardless, it distracted Andy. For a while.

"I'll see you tonight," she said when she kissed his cheek outside the restaurant as they were parting. "And Tierney too, I hear."

"You will?" Had Ian told her—

"At the club. Sam invited me."

Clearly the evil grin coupled with the innocent tone was in their DNA.

As soon as he got to his parents that evening, Tierney peeked into the formal dining room and groaned under his breath at all its crystal, silver-plate, and bone-china glory. The scene for the traditional Terrebonne family Thanksgiving was set. *Awesome.* But after trudging to the sitting room, he found it dark and deserted. Agatha hadn't said anything about them gathering someplace different when she answered the door, just pinched his cheeks and gushed.

"Huh."

"Darling, there you are," Mother called from behind him. When he turned, she was walking down the hall in the opposite direction, and saying over her shoulder, "I'm just going to check on the progress of dinner. Why don't you join everyone in the family room?"

"Sure." He nodded, watching her disappear around a corner. *Weird.* She'd normally be all over him, greeting him "properly" and telling him everything he was doing wrong.

"We have sparkling cider!" Sophie, his youngest niece, announced as soon as Tierney walked in and said hello. Father and Chase were standing by the grand piano, chatting, and Emily was over by the bar.

"Sweet." He held out his palm to her. "High five, small one."

She hugged his legs instead, which made him glow just a little inside. He didn't see her or her sister enough, did he?

"Hello, Uncle Tierney," Claire, his other niece, said then, sounding too proper for an eight-year-old. "Sophie and I are eating in the kitchen." She beamed, because she knew that meant they got all the treats Agatha had stashed away for them, and wouldn't have to eat anything yucky, like Brussels sprouts. So, not so proper.

"Cool," he nodded gravely. "You think if I start wearing dresses and playing with dolls, they'll let me eat in the kitchen with Agatha next year?"

"No. Sheesh." She rolled her eyes and went back to brushing her naked doll's hair. Well, naked except for all the "tattoos" she'd drawn on it over the years. Mother *hated* that thing.

Emily wandered up. "So, sparkling cider, tea, or mineral water?"

"Those are the nonalcoholic choices?"

She leaned closer to say quietly, "Those are the *only* choices. Everyone's on the wagon this year."

"Whose idea was that?"

"Your father's, believe it or not."

"Bet Mother hates it."

Emily raised her brows. "Yeah, she's gone to 'check on the progress of dinner' every ten minutes since we got here."

"Gotcha. So, while everyone else is teetotaling it, she's in the pantry chugging champagne."

Emily pursed her lips, but he couldn't tell whether it was a sign of disapproval or a way to suppress her amusement.

"Hello, son," Father called, and within seconds, coerced Tierney into walking across the room and joining him and Chase. They were talking business, of course. "How likely is Diablo to look favorably on a bid from us?" he asked as soon as Tierney was within a couple of feet of them.

Did they really have to discuss work now? "So, where are the aunties?" Grandfather's sisters were always here for holidays, since they had no other family. Those two were very traditional old-maid types, who drank copious amounts of sherry, and who Tierney suspected of wearing corsets and storing scented hankies in their cleavage. He'd never had the balls to ask about either of those things, though, not even when he was drunk. Well, not that he could remember.

"They aren't coming this year," Chase said, expression blank.

"They aren't? What're they gonna do, eat at the retirement home with the other lonely old goats?" Maybe they'd been unable to face a turkey without sherry.

Father cleared his throat. "They feel our branch of the family has impinged upon their honor."

"*Our* branch of the family? We're the whole trunk. They're, like, twigs. *Barren* twigs."

Behind him, he could hear Emily stifle a laugh, and he totally caught his brother smirking into his sparkling cider. Of course, then Chase had to be a dick. "They weren't very impressed by your toast at the wake."

"Oh." Tierney nodded, shoving his hands into the pockets of his slacks and rocking back on his heels. "I get it—*I* impinged on the family honor, so they won't show since I'm here." He snorted, adding in a mutter, "You should all thank me."

"Tierney," Father said. The tone was unclear, though; was he angry or tired? Or grateful?

Either way, it probably meant Tierney was supposed to shut up. *Right.* "Was it the gay thing?" He looked at his father in exaggerated interest. "Or maybe calling him a motherf—"

"Time for the girls to go into the kitchen," Emily interjected. "I'll check on Hyacinth while I'm there."

The three of them stood silently, eyeing each other until the door latched behind the girls and Chase said, "You're such a dumb-shit."

He'd heard those words before from the horse's ass, but they still made him sway with their force. "Thanks."

"Chase," Father said in that same ambiguous voice that he'd used on Tierney.

"I heard about that meeting, you know. The one last week. Jerry Brown told me."

"Golf-playing prick," Tierney said under his breath. Jerry and Chase had a standing tee time.

"What meeting?" Father tried to butt in.

Chase ignored him, staring at Tierney. "He said it was pretty rough."

That would almost sound like sympathy if not for the sneer. "It was."

Chase leaned closer, getting in Tierney's face. "It's your own fucking fault. You were practically begging to be treated like that, the way you came out."

"You fucker." Tierney's hands fisted in his pockets, but he kept his voice calm. "You don't have any right to judge me."

Father coughed in the throbbing silence. "Your mother doesn't like you using language like that—"

"I'm not judging you; I'm telling you facts." Chase narrowed his eyes. "Fact one is, this is all your doing, you asshole. If you hadn't done that at the wake, none of this would be happening. The aunties would be here—"

"You're blaming me for being gay?" Blood started pounding in his temples. "News flash, douche bag. It's *not a choice.* As hard as I fucking tried to deny it, do you really think I wouldn't have made another choice if I could have?"

"I don't have a problem with you being gay, I have a problem with your coming out!"

Saliva rained on Tierney's cheek, and that was good enough for him. Totally counted as throwing down.

"You've always done this shit—you always had to be the center of attention, but it was never enough, was it? You've done it now, though—you finally made such a spectacle of yourself that no one can talk about anything else, and you kno—"

Tierney punched the fucker.

Well, tried. Chase had been expecting it, and he blocked, but Tierney got him in a clinch, shoving him into Mother's grand piano with a *thud* and some discordant notes. "You wanted me to live in the closet for the rest of my life?" Tierney twisted his fingers in his brother's shirt and tried to hold the dude still, but Chase shoved him, and they both went down. "Faking it all the time and hating myself for it?"

"I just wanted you to not turn yourself into a fucking sideshow," Chase spit out, getting a knee in Tierney's stomach.

"Boys!" Father bellowed.

"No one asked you to stay in that closet all those years, you dumbass." Chase finally landed a punch, just below Tierney's eye, and through the disorientation of having his head knocked into the floor, Tierney heard him say, "If you'd told everyone when you first figured out you were gay, it wouldn't have been like this."

Mother shrieked just then, distracting Chase, and Tierney shoved his fist right in that mouth that wouldn't shut the fuck up. "What, you wanted me to stand on a table at the annual Christmas party twenty years ago and announce it?" Satisfaction dripped through him the same way blood dripped down Chase's chin. "I wasn't even invited to the fucking thing at fourteen."

Chase hollered and lunged, and then they were back to rolling around and flailing and trying to whale on each other. At one point Tierney came up hard against the angular leg of some piece of furniture, and the whole thing crashed to the floor, but he was pretty sure he tore off the pocket of Chase's shirt in revenge.

There was even hair pulling.

In the background, voices—mostly Emily's calmer one, interspersed with shrill tones from Mother and angry ones from Father—kept up some kind of commentary, but Tierney wasn't listening. All his effort went into trying to make his brother eat his words, every single one of them. Every insult and argument for the last thirty years, but most importantly, the ones spilling out of Chase as they fought.

"—don't fucking care if you're gay! I hate. The way. You. Came. Out." Maybe Chase had knocked his fillings around enough to tune him into the right frequency, but he suddenly *heard* his brother.

He doesn't care?

Tierney stopped swinging. Instead he swayed and panted, up on his knees and trying to blink his vision clearer. Across from him, Chase was doing pretty much the same thing, but he had blood on his chin and his lower lip was swelling.

"I hate how I came out too." Tierney swiped at the sweat on his forehead. "Total dick move."

"Uh-huh." Chase struggled up onto his feet, but then immediately bent over and planted his hands on his thighs, head hanging down.

"Do you two feel better?" Emily sounded somewhere between highly annoyed and relieved. Out of the corner of his eye, Tierney could see she had her fists on her hips.

"Yup." Tierney had to grab the back of a chair to do it, but he stood up and grinned at her.

She didn't grin back, but she wasn't glaring. Mother stood behind her, mouth agape and hand over her heart. Father slouched in a lounger, hair mussed up and forehead resting in his palm.

Chase's arm settled on his shoulders in the first brotherly gesture Tierney ever remembered from the dude. "When's dinner?" he asked.

Tierney started laughing. He hadn't had this much fun since he'd been a douche bag.

Chapter 22

Sam's Thanksgiving Extravaganza and Machination was crowded. The Monaco itself was crowded—packed dance floor, various lighting effects, thumping beat, guys in various states of undress, plenty of dark nooks—but the corner booth Sam had staked out for his "group" was overflowing with bodies. When Dalton got there, he found Andrea, Kendra the incident planning manager from the office, Ian's cousin Jurgen, and Jurgen's boyfriend Nik (who doubled as Sam's best friend) all seated with Sam and Ian, plus a couple of guys he didn't recognize standing next to the table, talking. He was pretty sure he'd recognize Miller, but none of the unknowns looked like him.

"Hey!" Andrea yelled in greeting, drowning out other "hellos." He could usually tell by the volume of his sister's voice how drunk she was. She appeared to still be at the giggly stage. Hopefully he could leave before she hit the "I'm going to die an old maid" stage. He'd borne the brunt of that too many times. And if she got to her vicious stage, well, he might need to bodily protect Tierney from the woman.

"Hi." Dalton pasted a smile on his face, and people started shifting, scooting closer together so he could squeeze into the booth too. Sitting next to Sam when there was room, he said, "I hope this place doesn't scare Tierney." It wasn't just that it was a drinking scene; it was also that it was a club scene. The man was a neophyte to this sort of place, at least as far as Dalton knew.

"If he even shows up," Sam responded, shoulders drooping. Ian noticed and leaned into Sam's other side, hand coming to grip the back of his neck, rubbing it. Dalton didn't hear what Ian said to him, but it made Sam's sappy smile appear, the one he only seemed to give to Ian.

They really were so cute.

Sam turned back to Dalton after a minute or two of nuzzling his boyfriend. "I invited some other people also, but it didn't work out." He pouted.

They'd need another booth if anyone else had shown up. "Did you invite Miller?"

Sipping his drink out of a tiny cocktail straw, Sam nodded. "He says he's not ready to go out in public."

"Have you seen him lately? How's he doing?"

Sam half shrugged, chewing on his straw for a second before dropping it to say, "Nik tells me he's doing pretty well. He's mostly healed. Physically."

There was no good response to that, so Dalton racked his brain for another topic, but there was no need. Ian had leaned against Sam's other side again, like a puppy dog who needed to be petted, which Sam appeared delighted to do.

Dalton gave up on them and tried to have a shouted conversation across the booth with his sister and Kendra. Thirty minutes later there was still no Tierney, and Dalton had hit the point where he *had* to text the man and check on him when his cell vibrated in his pocket. He knew somehow—maybe it was the tingle in his fingertips—that it would be Tierney.

Are you there?

Yes, Dalton texted back. *But you aren't. Are you going to bail?* They could meet up at his place.

On my way. Just a simple answer, but Dalton could feel the gritted-teeth determination in it.

"Was that T?" Sam spoke in his ear.

"Yeah. He'll be here soon." Tilting his head toward Andy, he took the opportunity to ask, "Why did you invite my sister? She hates him."

"Oh, yeah, but she needs to stop." Sam nodded. "I thought it would help if she saw you two together. You know, him being all attentive and responsive to you."

"You've never seen us together, how would you know what we're like?"

"Um, that *could* be a flaw in the plan, but I decided to sally forth on faith." Sam smiled brightly. "And since you brought it up? You haven't said anything about what's up with you two. If I didn't know I was your go-to guy for romantic advice, I'd think you were avoiding the subject."

Dalton picked up a stranded straw off the table and bent it into a little square. How much did he want to say? His relationship with Tierney had a quality of something fragile or precious, which would flourish best without a lot of attention focused on them. He didn't know how to define it, and he didn't want others doing it for them.

Or it was because, somewhere deep inside, he was still a little scared about repeating his past mistakes.

But Sam was staring at him, eyebrows up as high as he could make them go, except they kept dropping back down, because apparently he wasn't adept at expressing interest after a fruity drink or two.

Sigh. Dalton jumped right into the deep end of the pool. "I'm trying to not do anything stupid, like fall in love with him."

Sam dismissed the statement with a flick of his wrist. "Yeah, that never works."

"What?" Not at all the reaction he'd expected. "Thanks for the encouragement."

"I'm sorry." Sam shook his head, drunkenly regretful. "It's just, you know, that plotline never works."

Dalton pressed his back into the booth and gave his friend the squinty eye.

Using his glass to gesture with, Sam explained. "The lead character is always claiming he's only going to have a sexual relationship and not fall for someone, and then around the three-quarters mark he suddenly has this earth-shattering revelation that he's in love."

This had gone far enough. "Remember the discussion we've had about Tierney and I being actual people and not fictional characters?"

"I'm just saying, sometimes books have a line on the truth."

Dalton heaved a sigh. "*Anyway*. That's my plan." One he was failing miserably at following.

Sam fidgeted, swirling his straw around and around in his cocktail, like he could read the future in the patterns he made. "Okay, as your friend?" He swayed a little closer to Dalton. "I'm just telling you I think you need to come up with a backup plan also."

Oh thank God, some real advice. "Like what?"

"Well, like, if you do fall in love, make him fall in love with you too."

Or not. "Your plan seems to be lacking some details."

"Figuring out the details is up to you. This is your plotline."

Before Dalton could express just how unhelpful that was, Sam's eyes went big and he started bobbing his head, frantically. Then he said, "He's here," which was the first helpful thing to come out of his mouth all night.

Dalton turned just as Tierney appeared next to the table. All sound seemed to stop as everyone in their group froze and stared at him for a moment, then burst into exaggerated animation to cover up their reaction. It couldn't be more obvious that this whole outing was about him if they'd tried.

"Hi, Tierney," Sam called, much louder than he needed to.

"Hey, man, have a seat," Ian said, half-standing until the table stopped him from straightening further.

Nik and Jurgen said their hellos, while Andy and Kendra gave tight-lipped smiles, then started talking into each other's ears, casting glances in Tierney's general direction.

"Um, hey," Tierney said, pulling one hand out of his pocket and waving, before dropping it quickly. He wasn't really dressed right for the club, wearing a button-down shirt—sleeves rolled up and neck undone—with slacks. Not khakis or jeans, but dark slacks. Which fit his ass very nicely. It was probably what he'd worn to his parents'.

While the people in the booth were making room for him, Tierney shifted his weight, glance darting around until Dalton patted his leg and drew his attention to the newly available seat. Tierney's butt hitting the cushion was audible over the music.

"I don't know how long I'm going to last," he said, lips brushing Dalton's ear.

Goose bumps swept across Dalton's skin and down his neck, awakening bodily memories of other times Tierney had touched him. He almost turned for a kiss, but he could feel everyone watching them. At least, he thought he could, but he wasn't going to check.

Leaning just close enough to be heard, he said, "We don't have to stay."

Tierney took a deep slow breath in and then nodded. "I'll give it a try. At least I have some support."

Dalton rested his hand on Tierney's leg, squeezing, trying to communicate that he'd give all the support he possibly could. Glancing up, though, he found Tierney's eyes trained on Ian.

Oh. That kind of support.

Any contentment or joy Tierney felt over beating on his brother, then having a truly enjoyable (for the first time ever) Thanksgiving meal with his family faded as soon as he walked through the door of the Monaco and saw the crush of partially bared bodies and the darkness cut into varying patterns by every kind of light but natural. Then the overwhelming dance beat registered and his desire to flee nearly escalated into panic.

He'd forced himself to walk in, though, and then across the club, because Dalton was waiting for him.

Finally sitting with his friends, he began to relax. The constant reassurance of Dalton's thigh pressing against his helped. He didn't have to talk to anyone, just sit here and let others shout over the music while he soaked in the triumph of having successfully done a social thing without alcohol. The thump of the music was making his body buzz, getting him high on the atmosphere. This wasn't so bad after all. He could do this, have a decent time without a drink in his hand. The problem with habits—like, the addictive kind—was that they were triggered by things. He'd learned all about it at Dunthorpe. Smells and sounds and activities. He'd never been in a club like this, not a gay one at least, so it couldn't trigger much, could it?

It didn't take him long to figure out that wasn't the deal. It may be a gay club, but the smell of alcohol was the same as any other bar. And so was the party atmosphere. In other words, the vibe of Club Monaco was worming into him, tickling the part of him that liked its alcohol, waking it from its resting state. *I can do this.* He could hang on, right?

It was the damned Exposed Innerds song that pushed him over the edge. "She sits on the shelf all day and night . . ." it began in a wail, before the drums and bass crashed in and the story of the *Siren on the*

Shelf began. Tierney'd only heard the tune a couple of times, but he'd felt the words soul deep the first time he'd listened to them, because he knew that siren on the shelf, didn't he? *Bourbon.*

Or other alcohol would do, he'd never been *that* picky.

"Oh, I love this song," Sam shouted. "Let's dance." Then he bulldozed Dalton and Tierney out of the booth, dragging his boyfriend behind him, which was great, because Tierney felt the need to stand as the fucking song really got going. Stand and run . . . or get a drink. *This would be more fun if I were smashed.*

Getting drunk wasn't fun anymore, his higher brain reminded him.

"She thinks you're so gullible, her reality so plausible, you can't change your mind," the leader singer (whoever the hell that was) sang.

I so fucking can *change my mind.* "I gotta go," he said near Dalton's ear, then he fled. He shoved through the crowd, not focusing on anything but the floor and the next foot or two of his escape route. Stumbling, he pushed out the door of the club and through a bunch of guys trying to get past him to the inside. "Hey, chill, man," someone said.

"Tierney!" Dalton's voice.

He stopped in a pool of yellowish light in the middle of the sidewalk, relief over getting out of that atmosphere warring with disorientation over shifting from his nonsober persona. A hand grabbed his arm, long fingers gripping his biceps and pulling on him, spinning him around. Then Dalton clasped his other arm, gaze locking on his. "Are you okay?"

"Define okay." The feeling of disorientation started to drain away, though. Maybe Dalton was siphoning it off through touch.

Dalton searched his eyes for a second. "Did that bother you?" He stepped closer, letting his palms skim down and off Tierney's arms and lowering his voice. It was barely louder than the buzz of the streetlight. "Seeing Ian and Sam like that?"

Huh? "It was *everything*. Like, the smell and all the people in a party mood and the lights, but that fucking song was the last straw. I can't believe Sam *likes* it. I mean, the lyrics are so . . . I just, I got hit by a craving, and I had to bail." Craving was such a weak word for it.

"Oh." Dalton's nose wrinkled up in that cute, confused way he had. "So it wasn't because of them?"

Tierney leaned his shoulders against the brick wall of the club, the rough surface scraping him through his shirt. Taking a moment to wonder why Dalton thought Sam and Ian would make him want to fall off the wagon.

Because he thinks I'm in love with Ian.

Grabbing Dalton's wrist, Tierney pulled him closer, so they could talk more easily. So he could make what he had to say clear. Dalton's blue eyes were huge and totally focused on him. "Ian had nothing to do with why I left. I know I said before rehab that I was—"

"Dude!" Speak of the devil. Ian jogged up to them. "Are you all right?"

Tierney drew a deep breath, not letting go of Dalton, but having to look away from him, toward his buddy. "Fine, man. I'm okay."

Ian nodded, eyes flicking to where Tierney held Dalton's wrist.

Tierney slid his fingers down to interlace them with Dalton's.

"Just checking," Ian said. "Thought you might need some, uh, support." The corners of his mouth quivered, as if he was trying not to smile. Was that approval or amusement? *Who cares?*

"Thanks, dude. I really appreciate it, but crisis averted, you know? No help needed." Tierney forced out a social smile.

Ian tipped his head, turning back toward the club door. "Good to hear. I'll leave you guys to it, then?" But he didn't wait for an answer.

"I thought you wanted to hang out with Ian," Dalton said quietly.

Returning his attention to him, Tierney found Dalton's eyes just as big and magnetic as before. "You did?"

"This morning, when I said we didn't have to come here if it made you uncomfortable, you said you wanted to see him."

"I did?" He ran through what he remembered about that conversation. Not a lot of the words, mostly images. Like Dalton's bangs, still damp from his shower, hanging down and just skimming the arch of his brow, and the way his shirt fit his shoulders, and how much Tierney had wanted to undress him again. But, *oh, yeah.* "I think I meant he'd be here if I needed help or, like, an intervention."

Dalton gave him some more nose wrinkle.

"Because, you know, that whole thing about you being my lover means I should probably have someone else at my back in a situation like this." Didn't matter that he didn't *want* anyone else at his back, or his front.

Dalton untangled their fingers, and a second of alarm made Tierney's heart seize, but then Dalton's hands were cupping has face, and Dalton's lips were right below his. "This isn't an intervention. This is just me going home with you," he whispered before kissing Tierney.

It was a great kiss. A consuming one that drained away the last of Tierney's disorientation from the club and reminded him that there were reasons to go through life sober. Reasons like being naked in bed with this guy.

"Let's go home," he said as soon as his mouth was free. "Did you bring your car?"

"No, I took the bus." Dalton was frowning at him. "Is that a bruise on your cheek?" He passed his thumb over it, not lightly, and Tierney flinched.

"Forgot about that."

Dalton pursed his lips. "What happened?"

Chuckling at the memory, he took Dalton's hand again and started them walking toward his car. "Well, let me tell you about this year's Terrebonne family Thanksgiving . . ."

"You and fighting," Dalton said as they walked down the sidewalk. Tierney had let go of his hand and draped his arm around Dalton's shoulders. "When we met you'd just been in one with Ian, and now your brother? Not everything has to be solved that way."

"You didn't fight with your brothers?" Tierney asked, completely missing the point and steering Dalton toward a side street. Where had he parked?

"Of course I did, but I always *lost*."

"Which is why you don't understand the fine art of communicating with your fists." Tierney grinned, pulling him further along, down this narrower street with the single, sputtering light.

Dalton suppressed a shiver. A little bit of trepidation was normal, wasn't it? He'd witnessed an assault in an alley nearby. "You don't use your fists on me. We *talk*." God, if he'd had any idea that simply being in this neighborhood on a dark night would make him think of the bashing . . . He could tell Tierney it made him nervous; he knew he could. Tierney'd walk him back to the club and—

Tierney halted and turned to him, fingers gripping Dalton's shoulders. "I'd never use my fists on you; you know that, right? I mean, I can *talk* to you. Guys like Ian and Chase, they communicate more physically."

Dalton screened his eyes with his lashes, trying not to smile. "You and I don't communicate physically?"

Tierney grinned and tugged him closer. "That's a whooooole different type of physical communication," he said centimeters from Dalton's lips.

"Hey! Is that you?" Dalton jumped at the voice that came out of the darkness at the other end of the block, his blood racing, convinced of the necessity of communicating with fists in that heartbeat of time. "Tierney Terrebonne?"

Tierney jerked back, glancing around.

"Who is it?" Dalton whispered. Footsteps came closer, a few different sets, and Dalton couldn't help it—he grabbed the front of Tierney's shirt.

"I don't know," Tierney murmured. "I think it's okay, though."

Based on what? A band was cinching around Dalton's chest, making it harder for him to breathe.

"Are you remembering that night?" Tierney asked, focused on him and not any potential attackers.

Dalton managed a nod, peering into the shadows hard enough for both of them, since Tierney wasn't going to keep an eye out. He could see silhouettes now, multiple ones. He swallowed convulsively and tightened his grip. "Three of them."

"It's okay," Tierney said soothingly, running his hand up Dalton's back. "We can handle this." He squeezed him a little closer, angling them so they faced the oncoming threat, but were still touching. A unit.

"Hey, man, glad I ran into you," the unknown voice said, and then an innocuous, brown-haired guy came out of the shadows, another two men following along behind. "I was going to call you at the office, but since you're here . . ."

Not a bashing.

Of course not. What were the chances of being involved in two in one's lifetime?

The tension easing out of Tierney's body was what really reassured him, though. Slowly, he unearthed his fingernails from the man's chest. He missed a few seconds of whatever the other guy had to say, trying to get his adrenaline levels under control.

"Mark, nice to see you." Judging by Tierney's tone of voice and his smile, this was a business contact. He thrust his right arm toward the guy, not quite letting go of Dalton. "How's it going?"

In return, Tierney got the double-clasp handshake. *Totally wants something.* It was obvious in the man's smile and bright eyes. Well, unless he'd been drinking a lot. The guy looked at Dalton, eyebrows lifting expectantly.

"This is my friend Dalton Lehnart." Tierney's hand slid down to the small of Dalton's back. "He works in Ian Cully's department at the Health Division."

Ah. This was important enough to explain everyone's professional lineage. Dalton's more professional self began to take over, settling the last of his frazzled nerves.

"Dalton, this is Mark Sendecki, one of the commissioners of Marlyle County."

He couldn't be positive, but when Tierney caught his eye for just a second then, it seemed like his brow was trying to send some special message. But Dalton didn't need any signals; he caught the reference to Marlyle County immediately. When Tierney'd had his big meeting freak-out at the Interagency Disaster Relief office, he'd accused Sheriff Fowler of sleeping with one of the Marlyle County commissioners. A woman, so not this one.

"Oh, yeah, good guy. Cully's made some real changes, I hear," the commissioner was saying to Tierney. After that, he introduced his companions, then he and Tierney fell into chitchat that Dalton followed but didn't contribute to. Neither did Sendecki's friends.

Mark got to his point quickly. "So, I heard you had a few rough meetings," he said, grinning at Tierney.

Tierney ducked his head but was grinning too. "A couple, yeah." Hopefully only Dalton could tell how forced his smile was.

"Yeah, coming out isn't easy. Smart of you to do it so the whole world would know and you wouldn't have to keep telling people." It was fortunate Mark didn't seem to expect a response because Tierney looked a little knocked on his ass. "I've been meaning to reach out to you since then, make sure you know we'd still be open to a bid from Metropolitan Ambulance for the district one area service agreement."

"You would, huh?" Tierney had recovered. He was good, not sounding too excited, simply interested. Dalton knew this was major, though. Tierney'd told him enough to make it clear that losing the prospect of ambulance service in that region had been a blow.

Mark leaned closer, as if someone might overhear them on this deserted street. "Truth is, Crystal—the third commissioner," he bothered to explain, glance flickering toward Dalton for a second. "Crystal and I have been hoping for a way to do an end run around Sarah's plan to award it to American Ambulance—which is actually Fowler's plan. Guy's getting some kind of kickback, I'm sure." He waggled his fingers back and forth. "You know, just between us."

"Of course." Tierney nodded. "How about I give you a call Monday, and we talk?"

As Tierney wrapped up the conversation with just the right touch of joviality, Dalton totally saw how good his man was at the job, even when not being deceitful. Well, maybe this three-minute exchange wasn't really enough to judge, but he was still impressed.

Walking away afterward, holding hands, Tierney said quietly, "That fucking rocks."

"I know, right?" Dalton couldn't contain his smile.

"Thank you."

"For what? I didn't do anything."

Once again, Tierney halted, turning to him. "For just being there."

Oh God, the man was killing him. "Anytime." *Really. Anytime.*

Chapter 23

Waking up in the middle of the night, Dalton found Tierney watching him. Bluish moonlight streamed in the windows, and his expression was almost as readable as in the daytime.

"Hey." Dalton was probably smiling like a fool, but the man was too cute with the way his hair stuck up everywhere and those shadowed lines fanned out from his eyes.

"Hey, you," Tierney croaked, smiling back and lifting his hand to touch Dalton's face. Dalton took it as invitation to press on Tierney's shoulders until he rolled over and Dalton could lay himself out on top of him.

"I should brush my teeth," Tierney murmured between kisses.

"It's still dark." Dalton wasn't ready to let him up, not when Tierney was palming the small of his back like that, and his fingers were searching lower, tickling the skin of his ass. "Sex before sunrise doesn't require minty-fresh breath."

Tierney's grip tightened, and he turned them until he was on top, weighing Dalton down and taking over their kiss. Dalton let his tongue be the pursued instead of the pursuer, meanwhile working his hands along Tierney's sides until he could dig in and hold tight to Tierney's hips, guiding their motion. Not that Tierney needed the help, because they'd gotten so good at doing this together, rubbing off. Dicks slid, and ripples of aching want worked through him as they glided against each other. Pleasure—*oh God, such a romance novel word*—undulated through him with each of Tierney's thrusts, until Dalton was arching his back, waiting for the next wave of sensation.

"Stunning."

He opened his eyes at Tierney's whisper and got caught in his gaze, trapped there while Tierney ground against him. He was propping himself up on his arms but pinning Dalton down with the full weight of his pelvis, his cock alongside Dalton's. Wrapping his legs around Tierney's thighs, Dalton let him have control, and Tierney took it, grasping Dalton's wrists in his hands, then lowering his upper body onto Dalton's chest and compressing his lungs, which should be uncomfortable and frightening but was exciting. "Fuck me," Dalton whispered.

Tierney stilled.

"I want you to fuck me." So badly. He wanted to give himself to Tierney—something he'd read about in those books Sam recommended, but never fully *got* until now. "Please."

Tierney just stared, totally motionless.

Dalton's heart beat uncertainly, faltering with doubt. Had Tierney thought the other night was a one-time thing? "Don't you want to?" Too exposed and raw to pretend, he felt all the longing and questioning in his voice reverberate in his chest. But he trusted this man to not hurt him, didn't he? Not reject him. This was all about *his* needs, and he needed Tierney to want him.

Tierney shook himself. "I *really* want to." His grip on Dalton's wrists loosened, just a little, and he lowered his face until they were breathing the same few molecules of air. "But, um . . ."

Dalton's heart flat-out stopped for a split second, missing a beat.

"This is more than friends, isn't it?" Tierney asked very quietly. Somewhere below a whisper.

Yes. But Dalton took the coward's way out. "What do you think?"

Tierney was braver than him. He sucked in a breath before answering. "I think it is for me. Much more."

Thank God. "It is for me too."

Tierney's face relaxed, but then he tensed again. "I didn't finish telling you earlier— Shit, um, I'm not in love with Ian. I don't think I ever was, I mean, it was nothing like—" He snapped his mouth shut, eyes going wide.

Nothing like this. "Tierney, *please*. Fuck me."

"Christ," Tierney groaned so deeply Dalton felt it rumble through his groin. "Of *course* I'll fuck you."

It meant a condom and lube, but the whole time they were taking care of the mundane necessities Dalton's excitement was pumping through him, telling him this was *it*. What "it" was exactly, he couldn't say, but he was so eager that nothing seemed awkward or killed his yearning for Tierney. He offered himself up, ass in the air and head on the bed, not holding back his moans as Tierney slowly pushed into him, indulging in all his longings to be this man's slutty boy toy. He arched his back and spread his legs and begged for more of Tierney's cock like a porn star.

"Jerk yourself," Tierney said, words keeping time with his rhythm. "Are you doing it?"

"Yes," Dalton breathed.

"That special stroke?" he asked. "When your thumb glides up the underside and you tease that spot just under the head?"

"Yes." Moaning now.

"Don't stop." Tierney reared back, digging his fingers into Dalton's hips and working his own in fast, short strokes. Like he was pumping him up for a big explosion, one of those legendary "I shot forty feet" orgasms. Dalton fought against it, because he wanted this to last. If Tierney kept fucking him, nothing could ever go wrong. They'd be intimately locked together forever, doing this dance of thrust and receive.

But sex didn't work that way, and Dalton hit that tipping point where coming was more desirable than anything in the world—more than cotton candy or new shoes or the drag and glide of Tierney inside him—and he came in spite of himself, cum shooting onto the sheets like he was an air rifle and Tierney's cock was the priming mechanism. He shouted, possibly surprising some neighbors, but he cared so little right then, because his skin had erupted in chills, and his insides had spontaneously combusted and it was all so consuming he barely registered Tierney's moans and the way he dug his thumbs into Dalton's butt cheeks and held him motionless, in just that perfect position.

Afterward, settling onto the bed with Tierney's weight still securing him, Dalton had things to say, but he simply couldn't start tonight. There was so much to talk about and work out, and for now he just wanted to lie here in Tierney's arms and sleep, fully satisfied. So he didn't say anything, other than, "That was *so* good."

"So good," Tierney agreed, kissing Dalton's temple, then his cheek. He rolled over and worked his arm under Dalton's head, and they both slipped into unconsciousness.

Waking up again later, in full daylight, Dalton found himself alone in the bed with the condo silent around him. He quashed the immediate flare of apprehension under his breastbone. He was just being insecure; Tierney was around somewhere. He could even smell coffee. Was the anxiety even remotely justified?

Yes. Because in the middle of the night Tierney had come as close as any man ever had to saying he loved Dalton, and that changed everything. Now the relationship had blown past the benefits barrier, which could create problems for Tierney.

If he really cared about Tierney, would it be better to end this now? Make the sacrifice of his own happiness, just like he had after he'd left his parents' house? But that had been survival. This was different. This was soul-deep want.

Please, let me have this one thing. He didn't know who he was beseeching, because he was on the fence about God, but wasn't someone, somewhere keeping score? He'd lost his parents, and he'd wasted years with guys who didn't care about him, but then he'd been *good*. Supported himself and finished school and taken responsibly for himself. Hadn't he earned the chance at a real relationship with a man he was falling in love with?

He rolled onto his back and squeezed his eyes shut, covering his face with his hands and wishing with everything in him. *Let us work out.* Calling on any shooting stars he might have seen in his past and not taken full advantage of, any pennies he might have tossed into fountains and only halfheartedly thought about. He called in all those markers. Starting today, he'd haunt antique shops and rub likely-looking teapots and lamps, hunting for stray genies. If he'd believed in prayer, he might have done that too, but prayer had failed him too often in the past. So it had to be wishes or shirtless men in harem pants.

"—telling you, Sendecki's fucking *salivating* to have us bid," Tierney's voice floated through the doorway, and then the man himself followed it, cell phone held to his ear. He smiled at Dalton before rolling his eyes at the voice on the other end of the line. "No, for fuck's sake, don't set up a tee time. We can meet with him for lunch or something. Jesus."

He sounded so *normal.* So ordinary, like he was totally unaware Dalton had just freaked out after waking up alone. *Duh, because he is.* It made him self-conscious. The way he *should* be after overreacting and fighting off tears, then finding out everything was just fine.

"—I *got* this meeting with him because I'm gay, you dumbass. I never have to play golf again," he was saying, smiling hugely. He must be talking to his brother.

Moving carefully, still not quite in sync with reality, Dalton sat up, scooting to the edge of the mattress and resting his feet on the floor.

"Listen, man, I have to go. I have better shit to do than talk to you all day." Tierney's tone was joking, even affectionate. "Yeah, see you soon." Punching his brother really had cleared up years of animosity, hadn't it? Suddenly, Tierney's hand was on the back of Dalton's neck, and he stood just in front of him. He hung up the phone as Dalton met his smiling eyes. "Morning."

He tossed the cell on the bed and then urged Dalton to lie down again by looming over him until Dalton had to fall back or smash his face into Tierney's chest. As Tierney brought his body to rest on top of him, Dalton found the back hem of Tierney's T-shirt and slid his fingers inside, caressing naked skin and lifting his face so Tierney could kiss him.

Kissing stopped Dalton's brain, and he began to feel more normal. Maybe still worried, but only in the back of his mind.

"I wish I could stay in bed with you today," Tierney murmured, taking a break from their lazy make-out session.

"You have to be somewhere?" He wrapped his legs around Tierney's thighs, as if he might not let him go.

Tierney's lips grazed Dalton's ear, tickling him. "I have to meet with my new therapist."

That. The appointment to make up for the one he missed. Dalton swallowed as all his apprehension came rushing back. "Are you going to talk to her about us? Like, whether we—"

"It's going to work out." He pulled away enough to look into Dalton's eyes, and his own were determined, almost forcibly so. "At Dunthorpe they *recommended* we didn't start new relationships, but it's not like it's *forbidden*. Other people have to have done it successfully, right? I'll talk to Dr. Palmer about coping strategies or whatever."

Dalton traced the angles of Tierney's lips with his finger, thinking, until Tierney pressed a kiss on the tip. "Is something wrong?" he asked, then lifted up onto his arms, jaw tightening. "I mean, if, you know, what you said last night didn't mean what I thought it meant—"

"I want to have a real relationship with you. I want—" Dalton took a deep breath "—I want to be your boyfriend, not just your friend with benefits."

"Good," Tierney whispered, then kissed Dalton. "That's what I want too."

"Is that all right, though?" Dalton whispered back. "I mean, it's been less than a month since rehab—"

"I'm not giving up on you because things might go sour. I've cheated myself out of this before, and I'm not doing it again."

He couldn't say anything to that, because it too closely reflected the freak-out he'd had before. Tightening his arms around Tierney's shoulders, Dalton hauled himself up until his chest was smashed against Tierney's shirt, and he could feel both their hearts beating. He traced the shape of Tierney's lips again, but this time with his tongue. Tierney captured it, sucking it into his mouth and pressing Dalton back into the mattress.

Working his fingers under the waistband of Tierney's lounge pants, Dalton started tugging them off.

"I need to get ready to go," Tierney said, but he shifted enough for Dalton to get the sweats down to his thighs, baring his dick. "Gotta take a shower."

"Do it after." Dalton took Tierney's earlobe in his teeth and nibbled.

"After what?" He grinned.

Dalton smiled back. "After I make you come." He began to run his mouth down Tierney's neck, tonguing him, then he wound his fingers in Tierney's hair and kissed him, harder and more explicitly than earlier, grinding against Tierney's body. Shifting until their cocks lined up next to each other. Sharing pre-cum and friction and pushing away thoughts of them not working out.

Because they had to. He deserved this man.

Sam texted Dalton shortly after Tierney left. *We're going to visit my parents this weekend, so you wanna have lunch today, instead?*

Dalton leaped at the chance. He didn't want to pace around Tierney's condo for who knew how long, waiting for him to return, because now that he was alone again, his earlier uncertainty was back. So he set the condo alarm by following the instructions Tierney had left him, then took public transit to Simpson. It was a gray day, but not raining. One of those days where the clouds stretched uniformly across the sky like someone had built a roof over planet Earth and insulated it with dirty cotton.

He brought a book onto the bus with him—the one Tierney had given him—but instead of reading it he stared out the window at the buildings and went over and over things in his mind. Was he anxious about Tierney because he had no faith in himself? He'd never managed to pick a decent guy before now, so maybe he couldn't quite trust what was going on.

Trying to shore up his confidence, he made the mistake of playing the worst-case scenario game. It usually helped—he'd imagine the most horrible outcome to a situation, and it never seemed so bad once he'd studied it from all angles.

Until now. Because the worst thing that could happen was that their relationship would drive Tierney to drink, and he'd end up a penniless, toothless alcoholic living on the streets and dying by forty, and it would be all Dalton's fault.

Even the second-worst thing was pretty bad. It involved Tierney returning to his former asshole persona, and Dalton one day waking up to realize he was just another possession of a wealthy man again.

He truly believed Tierney had changed—he'd meant what he'd said to Andrea—but if Tierney fell off the wagon because of Dalton, couldn't his personality change back?

By the time he got to Murray's Bistro and found Sam standing out front, Dalton was desperate to talk to someone about it all. First, though, he hugged Sam very, very tightly.

"What happened?" Sam asked, voice rising in alarm.

Sigh. "I'll tell you after we order."

Once they'd been seated at their usual table—the host knew them by now—Dalton didn't even try to avoid telling Sam everything that had happened, even the parts he'd hidden up until now. All the important details about the night before, and the nights leading up to it. He skimmed over the really personal stuff, but Sam didn't press him for extra details—he seemed giddy with the amount of information Dalton was giving him, bouncing on his seat and clapping excitedly a couple of times. He even gasped when Dalton alluded to the near declaration of Tierney's feelings.

But it was when Dalton said, "Oh, and he bought me a gift," then pulled out *The Billionaire's Baby Daddy* that Sam had some kind of seizure and knocked half his french fries into his lap. He'd finished the burger already, fortunately.

"Ohmigod, Ian would *never* buy me something like this!" he squealed. "He'd buy *tampons* before being seen with a romance novel." Then he cocked his head and studied the cover more. "He'd probably role-play it with me, though. Except we'd need to get rid of the baby part."

So don't want to know about that. "If Tierney and I were a romance novel, what would you expect to happen next?" Today, Dalton needed some of that romance-novel logic to cling to.

Sam composed himself, holding up a single french fry. "Irrational fear. Something will happen and you'll both be confronted with whatever you're most afraid of, then break up for a while." Sam bit off the end of his fry

"Fear of what?" Not that he needed to ask; there were a million things to fear.

Sam flicked his wrist negligently. "Whatever. Fear is a big motivator in romance novels. It almost doesn't matter what it's fear of, but it's usually about commitment. One character thinks they aren't capable, or they got burned horribly in the past, or they're sure no one can love them because of the horrible disfigurement of their soul. Stuff like that." He wiggled his fingers in the air, illustrating. "Typically, the climax of the novel would come when he realizes he's madly in love with you, and has to come crawling back begging your forgiveness for being stupid."

"Tierney isn't really a crawler. He's more of a blurter-outer."

"Po-tay-to, po-tah-to." Sam seesawed his hand. "It's all about the big important man admitting he's wrong."

"But he's already admitted he's wrong. He announced to the whole world he was in the closet for most of his life."

"Yup," Sam said, then slurped pop through his straw. "Now comes the heart-wrenching climax."

Dalton toyed with his fork. "So, what you're saying is I have a lot of pain ahead of me?"

"I don't think so." When Dalton lifted his head, Sam was regarding him seriously. "The thing is, what happens in a book is *distilled* reality."

"Distilled reality." Repeating it didn't help him understand what Sam was saying.

Nodding vigorously, Sam leaned forward, speaking faster. "Because it's the written word, not a movie or anything, readers need, like, fortified reality in order to really *feel* the character's journey, so the author has to amp things up. Look at all the steps that go into making something happen and then only pick out the important ones, *then* she has to, like, give it steroids. Make it bigger than it would be in real life." He beamed. "But you guys? You've had more hardships than most couples have when they get together, so I think you're done with them. This? Is the beginning of your happily ever after."

Sam was so upbeat and positive about the future of Dalton's relationship with Tierney that Dalton left the restaurant with much less apprehension. It *could* work, and the thing about not getting into a relationship *was* only a suggestion. He'd support Tierney however the man needed, Dalton had no doubt about it—he'd spent most of his life in a supporting role. He was good at support. Even *liked* it.

He had to wait half an hour for the bus that would take him to his neighborhood, and right before it arrived, it began sprinkling. The shower wasn't worth digging out his umbrella for, but halfway home, the clouds really opened up and began dumping water. The rain was coming down in sheets, and even *with* an umbrella the two-block walk from his stop to his apartment left him damp from his knees to his toes. Dalton put his head down and hurried, just glancing up enough to navigate, around the next corner and then up the stairs to the little covered porch—

Where a man stood, waiting.

There was no split second of alarm over who it could be; Dalton knew that stance too well. It was Tierney, slouching against the wall, hands shoved into his pockets. Appearing as dejected as he had that first time he'd waited for Dalton in the parking garage.

All his apprehensions came back in a rush, but multiplied and stronger. He had to force himself to continue the last few steps. "Hey," he said, stopping in front of Tierney. "Um, what are you doing here?"

"We have to talk." Tierney didn't lift his chin, and his voice was barely louder than the rain hitting the ground.

Oh no. Dread washed through him, prickling down from his scalp to his toes. "Okay."

"I'm soaking," Tierney added when Dalton didn't move.

Dalton nodded, focusing on unlocking the door, then walking upstairs, Tierney behind him, to his apartment. The whole time, his heart was breaking because Sam had been wrong and all his fears had been right.

Maybe it's something else.

Except there *was* nothing else.

I can't have this. He couldn't have the relationship or the man, or anything. *Should've known.*

Once he'd entered his place, holding the door open as Tierney walked in, Dalton fell back on etiquette. "Can I get you anything? Maybe, um, a towel?" Tierney didn't answer, just stood in the entryway, dripping. A droplet per second, falling from the cuffs of his jacket onto Dalton's wood floor, hitting the ground with soft *plops*. Like a clock, counting the moments until Tierney ended what they had.

"I don't want to give you up," Dalton whispered, gripping the doorknob tighter. He should shut it, but he'd just have to open it again when Tierney left him.

"I don't . . ." The sound of Tierney swallowing made a weird counterpoint to the rhythm of water drops. "Me neither."

For a second, hope burned inside Dalton, strong enough to make him lift his head and meet Tierney's eyes. Then it died, because it was so obvious that *don't want to* was not the same as *don't have to*.

Plop. Dalton's attention was pulled back to the droplets. They were slowing down. More than a second between each one. *Ending*.

"Dr. Palmer said—" Tierney took a shuddering breath. "She pointed out . . . I have feelings for you, like, serious ones. Love ones."

"I have love feelings for you too." He had to say it, because if this was going to end, he wasn't going to hide from the pain. He wasn't an eighteen-year-old losing his parents. He was an adult losing the man he loved, and that had the potential to destroy him if he tried to outrun it.

"See, we're already in a relationship."

"Yes," Dalton agreed, then bit his lower lip, hard, trying to distract his heart from its pain. *Plop*. Another drop. Dalton watched, holding his breath, waiting for the next one to form and then fall.

"And that's . . ."

"Dangerous to your recovery."

"It's— I gotta take care of myself. I mean, what you said before, about not wanting to give this up, I don't either. I *don't*." His voice went ragged, like the sharp edges of life were slicing it to shreds. "But if it means drinking—"

"It's okay."

Tierney's hand fisted, and one of the rain droplets snaked down between his thumb and finger. "It's *not* okay. I don't want this, but I don't want you to be with the kind of guy I used to be."

Let me decide that. Except he couldn't say it, because Dalton himself couldn't be with that guy. Then he *would* be repeating his past.

"So," Tierney sighed, and opened his hand, hyperextending his fingers for a second, as if forcing them to relax.

One more drop trembled on the edge of his sleeve.

Plop.

"Meow."

Blue came meandering toward them, head lifted to Tierney. "Meow." Then he leaped into the air, hair standing up on his back, and Dalton thought things were about to get ugly. He stepped between his pet and his man to protect Tierney, but it was unnecessary. False alarm. Blue settled on his haunches and rapidly flicked one of his front paws, trying to get rid of the water he'd stepped in.

"How come he's not attacking me?" Tierney asked, tickling the fine hairs on Dalton's nape with his breath.

"I don't know." Dalton shook his head. "He's never not hissed at someone other than me." How completely, bitterly ironic that the person his cat had decided to accept was the one man Dalton couldn't have. Blue didn't care about that, though—he finished licking his damp fur, then he wandered off, tail waving lazily.

Tierney's cold fingers were suddenly on the back of his neck, making Dalton flinch, but he didn't pull away.

"I'm sorry." Tierney made a choking noise. "I really do, you know, love you." His lips brushed Dalton's ear, and his arms came around him, squeezing him, fingers digging into his side.

"I know." He placed his hands over Tierney's, as if it could steady his voice. "I love you too."

Tierney held him tighter, which was always what happened before someone let go, wasn't it?

They stood like that forever, or at least a minute, and the whole time Dalton had to fight not to turn around. He wanted to bury his head in Tierney's neck and let out the hurt inside him. But using the man as a crutch while he was trying to move beyond this part of his life just seemed cruel. They were doing this so he *wouldn't* hurt.

Even when Tierney's hold on him finally loosened, and he backed away, Dalton kept staring straight ahead. Into his apartment, where he'd live by himself for the foreseeable future, with just his cat to love.

"Bye," Tierney rasped, then the door clicked shut. When the footsteps had faded down the hallway, Dalton stopped keeping himself upright, slumping back against the wall and sliding down it until he could hug his legs to his chest and rest his head on his knees. He didn't move again until Blue came to demand attention.

Chapter 24

Tierney drove by the liquor store closest to his place three times before he finally pulled over in a gas station parking lot and called Ian. "Dude, are you— Can you come over?" He'd beg if he had to.

"Right now?" Ian's voice went up too high. "You want me to come to your place?"

"Yeah." Fuck, he needed to find one of those intuitive friends, who'd understand from his tone or something just how real shit was getting. "ASAP. I need, um, some help."

Another voice in the background came over the line, but Tierney could only tell that it was Sam's. Whatever the dude said, Ian changed his tune. "I'll be there as soon as I can. Hang on."

"I'm trying." After ending the call, he curled his fingers around the steering wheel and clung to it, taking Ian's words literally. Because that black hole he hadn't seen or heard from in so long was coming back, and if he didn't get a grip he might get sucked into the vacuum.

He didn't remember driving home, but he could remember the back of Dalton's neck and the feel of his skin when Tierney had kissed it for the last time. He realized he was back at the condo when he coasted into his parking spot and bumped the concrete wall in front of it. *Whatever*. That was why they called them bumpers, right? He didn't even bother to check for damage when he got out. He'd sustained enough damage himself already. Fuck the car, it was insured. More than he could say for his heart.

Once inside, he tried to sit on the couch and wait for Ian, but the ghost scent of Dalton's soap chased him away, in spite of knowing the smell couldn't possibly be hanging around. The guy's laugh might be, though. Maybe, that day Tierney had tickled him, some of his joy had fallen down between the cushions, and if Tierney put his butt in just the right spot, it would leap out and surprise him, like a squeaky toy.

He ended up at his dining room table. Had he ever sat here before? It was fucking monstrous, something his designer had picked out so he could host dinner parties. He'd never hosted a dinner party in his life, and he didn't plan on having one, ever. He could see Dalton doing it, if things had worked out and he'd moved in, but that was moot now, wasn't it? It didn't matter how easily Tierney could picture the guy living here, making dinner in the kitchen, or coming down the hall with a smile and a kiss when Tierney got home late some evening.

The sound of the intercom saved him from examining just how painful his thoughts were. He buzzed Ian in, but didn't wait for him in the hallway, because that was another place where reminders of Dalton lurked. Instead he just left the door ajar and went back to his stupid, ugly table and slouched in one of the frail-looking chairs, feet splayed out in front of him.

"Dude?" Ian called. Tierney could see the tips of his fingers, backlit from the light in the corridor, pushing carefully against the door. "You here, man?"

"Yeah." He must have said it loud enough, because Ian's whole body followed his hand, coming into Tierney's entry, then his living room.

"No lights? It's getting dark out." Ian flipped the wall switch he was standing next to, and the overhead fixture in the living room came on. "Nice place, T."

Huh. "You've never been here before?"

"Uh, no." Ian lifted a brow and tipped his chin in Tierney's direction. "I didn't even think you liked the place."

"I don't," he said. Except . . . "I kinda did, for a while, when— Never mind."

"Why am I here now?" Ian asked. "I'm guessing you aren't okay."

"I had to—" *Swallow.* He tried to ease the tightness in his throat. "Dalton."

Ian jerked his head back. "You *dumped* him? What are you, *stupid*?"

"What I am is a fucking recovering alcoholic," Tierney snapped, shooting out of his seat, ready to hit Ian, because, yes, he *was* stupid and someone should pay for that and Ian had made a pretty good punching bag in the past.

But the guy was already holding his hands palm out in front of him. "Sorry, man, I didn't mean to be insulting. Just, I'm shocked." Fuck, did he have to go being apologetic? "Why don't you tell me what happened?" Taking his coat off, Ian set it on the table behind the couch, then came around and stood in front of a chair, but he didn't sit until Tierney sighed and started heading his way.

"Actually, can you sit on the couch? I kinda, um, prefer that spot."

Ian didn't comment, he just moved. Maybe he had a sixth sense or something, but he didn't sit on the side Dalton usually did. Nice of him not to desecrate Tierney's shrine to a love that ended tragically.

"I could call Sam," Ian offered after they were both settled in, and the silence had stretched on for a couple of minutes. "He's better at this stuff than I am. I mean, you could tell him what happened and he'd have advice or whatever, probably better than what I can give you."

"No." Sam was Dalton's friend, and if Dalton needed someone to talk to . . . "You know anything about addiction?"

"Sorta. I looked into it because I think my dad has some problems, but he's not that interested in taking care of them, so." Ian shrugged.

Tierney rested his head on the back of the armchair and closed his eyes. Then he explained to Ian about recovering addicts being vulnerable, and how emotional triggers could push them into using, and the warnings about not doing anything major in the first year or so because that exponentially increased the psychological seesaw and blah, blah, blah.

Then came the difficult part. "Dalton and I talked last night, and we'd kinda decided to give it a try. Us. Stop the friends-with-benefits bullshit, because—" *Oh God* "—I have *feelings* for him, you know what I mean?"

"Yeah."

"And he said he did for me, and he wanted to go ahead and . . ." Shit, his throat was getting lumpy. Maybe it was a tumor. *Sure it is.*

"I getcha, it's cool."

Tierney squeezed his eyes tighter, because they were starting to ache, like there was too much pressure inside them. "I had an appointment today with my new therapist, and I was going to ask her about what we should do to make sure I don't, like, get into this relationship and then have things go haywire." His throat made a clicking sound as he swallowed.

Ian was silent, but Tierney could feel the dude's attention focused on him.

"So I went and explained to Dr. Palmer about Dalton, and she said we were already in a relationship, and my only option was to end it or I'd start drinking again." More silence, but this felt different. Confused. He finally lifted his head to see Ian. "If I start drinking again, I'll turn back into that guy I used to be. I can't be that douche bag with him. He'd try and hang on to the relationship even if the old Tierney did come back, I know he would and— *Fuck*." He hit the arm of the chair, but nothing changed. Hitting things usually helped, but not this time.

"But you came out," Ian said, face screwed up.

"I'm pretty sure if I'm drunk enough I can be just as much of a douche bag gay as I was straight. It's better for him if he doesn't have to put up with that shit from me."

"But wait." Ian shifted, straightening. "You're telling me— Just what did she actually say, dude?"

Had Ian always been this thick? Tierney rubbed his temples. "She said a lot of shit." Although he could only remember a couple of things. His head had begun ringing once she'd told him he had to end things with Dalton. "She said that every patient she'd seen who got into a relationship just after rehab had fallen off the wagon." He shoved out of his chair, pacing to the window, trying to loosen up his throat enough to speak. "In my 'immediate postrehab emotional state' I'm, um, fooling myself. Like, convincing myself he's the perfect guy for me, then down the road it ends badly and I'd—" He waved his hand in the air. "You know."

"Start drinking again?"

"Yeah." He didn't even go into the stuff she'd said about suicide. He wandered back to his chair and fell into it. "She gave me a scrip for antidepressants. Took away the best thing in my life and gave me some fucking pills to replace him." Lifting his butt, he dug the prescription out of his back pocket and set it on the arm of the chair, smoothing out the wrinkles with his thumb.

Ian huff-snorted, shaking his head. "If ending your relationship is supposed to keep you from drinking, why the fuck am I here making sure you don't?"

The guy may as well have whacked him in the head with a hammer, because the ringing in Tierney's ears started again. "Uhhh . . ."

"What the hell? Why are you letting this doctor tell you how to live?" Ian's expression was set, and dead serious.

Blurry vision joined the ringing in his ears, adding to his confusion. "Because she's my shrink?" Wasn't he supposed to trust her implicitly? "I mean, she's the authority." *Wasn't* she?

"So?" Ian scowled. "You know enough people in the medical community to know that not all doctors know their shit. Hell, most of them probably barely graduated."

"What, like, I'm just supposed to shop around until I find someone who tells me what I want to hear?" Didn't that defeat the purpose? Although it *was* a pretty good plan. And Marty *had* said something about finding the right fit . . . *She could be* wrong.

"If you go to five, and they all say the same thing, then you listen, but I'll tell you what. Janet, my therapist? She'd never bullshit me like that, telling me I was fooling myself like it's some fact she could absolutely *know*. If I felt like something was right and I wanted to do it, she'd never just tell me I couldn't, she'd help me figure out how."

Tierney blinked.

Ian leaned forward, planting his elbows on his knees. "T, you know how you told me your whole life was ruined because you believed it when your grandfather said you couldn't be gay?"

He had to work saliva into his mouth before he could reply. "Yeah?"

"So, now you're letting your whole life fall apart because someone else told you that you can't do something that feels right?"

He almost said, "It's not the same," except he couldn't, because it totally *was*. He could see it, literally, things were shifting and colliding in front of his eyes—Ian's frown and the cushion Dalton usually sat on. Rearranging to show him a different view. "Oh fuck, dude," he whispered. He got it now, and with the knowledge came anger, as usual, but this time it was all self-directed. "I fucked up so bad."

"This isn't even like you— You fight and question everything, but you roll over for these two people?" Ian seemed pissed enough to punch him now, and Tierney wanted the dude to—he'd punch himself if he could—and not just to stop the fucking reverberating ring in his head, but because someone as stupid as him *should* get whaled on.

"I'm afraid," he croaked like a frog, but he got it out. He had to or he'd keep it inside forever. "I just, I listened to her because—" He had to fist his hands and set his jaw in order to keep going. "I told Dalton I *had* to end it, dude, but I was lying to both of us. I used what that doctor told me as an excuse, then shoved the blame on her. Okay, I don't mean to sound like a psych text here—"

"It's cool," Ian assured him.

"I'm falling into the harmful coping strategies I used in the past," he parroted, something Marty had said, but it was the easiest way to explain and it was *true*. Ian totally understood the psychobabble, Tierney could see realization dawn on the guy's face.

"You mean, letting someone else tell you what to do?" Dude wasn't totally *un*confused.

"I kind of— *Christ.*" *Just say it. Have to say it.* As surely as he'd had to make that announcement at Grandfather's wake. But first, he had to shove up from the chair and stand, because his heart was jittering out the adrenaline and he couldn't just sit there anymore. "I used to think I was in love with you."

Ian went pale and completely still.

Oh fuck. "I'm not, dude," he rushed to explain. "Seriously. I never was."

Ian swallowed and nodded once. Taking a deep breath, Tierney tried to get his heart back into a normal rhythm before he told the dude the rest, but it didn't cooperate. "I just, see, that's what I did—what I'm *doing*. I, like, was afraid to be gay, so I *chose* to believe Grandfather when he said I couldn't be. Subconsciously. And I chose to believe I was in love you with you, but you weren't ready to be with me."

Color was returning to Ian's face. "T, man, I never meant to—"

"Yeah, no." Tierney threw up his palm to keep him from saying more. "I know you didn't, but, see, that's what I told myself, and I used it as an excuse to not come out even after I knew I couldn't fight the gay thing. Like . . ." He swallowed. "If the guy I thought I wanted wasn't gay, or wasn't out, there was no reason for me to be. I blamed you for all my, um . . . you know."

Ian still seemed a little dazed, but he said, "Okaaay. So, you're saying that now, you let this doctor tell you that you couldn't be with Dalton because you're scared . . . of what?"

"Fucking it up." Wow, he was just spewing out the confessions today. Puking them up. "Of being a prick again, maybe even when I'm sober, and—" *Oh yeah, totally nauseous.* "What if I stop giving him a reason to want to be with me?" He paced over to the windows and stared out at the growing twilight.

"And what, you think I'm not afraid of things going to hell with Sam?" Ian asked in that "what are you smoking?" tone of voice.

Uhhh . . . "Never thought about it," he admitted. Jesus he was stupid sometimes. Shoving his hands through his hair helped with the agitation. A little. "I gotta fix this. I mean, I have to try." He swallowed. "I just, I don't know what to say, because then we're back where we were before I saw Dr. Palmer, starting a relationship when I'm a bad risk." He whirled around to face Ian. "I can't just jump in, man. I gotta do this *right*." His eyes ached even more now, but his heartbeat was settling down. "I've leapt before looking too many times, and fucked too much up. I can't do that to him again." He shook his head, heading back to the chair, suddenly completely exhausted.

"You wanna talk to Janet?" Ian offered as Tierney flopped into his seat. "Or she could probably come up with some quality referrals."

"I can call my counselor from Dunthorpe, ask him what he thinks. I have his emergency number, and he said I could use it." He shoved out of the chair once more, but this time to find his briefcase and the notebook full of numbers he kept in it. "I'm calling Marty tonight. Far as I'm concerned, this is a fucking emergency."

"You ever thought we'd be sitting around doing this, dude?" Ian's voice was completely different, enough that Tierney forgot his mission for a second and turned back to him.

He was sort of smiling, mouth just turned up at the corners.

"Doing what?" Tierney asked him. "Talking about our boyfriends?"

Ian nodded, grinning now. "And our *therapists*."

"Yeah." Tierney shook his head. "No. Not in a million years. Now get outta here, man, I gotta call mine and then get my boyfriend back. I don't have time to be all angsty with you."

Ian laughed. Tierney walked the dude to the door. He had something serious to say to Ian, before he could call Marty. Something that was probably way overdue. "Thanks, man. For everything."

"No problem." Ian stared at him a second, then cleared his throat. "Um, what you said about your, you know, feelings for me—"

"Please." Tierney ran a hand down his face, dragging his looser flesh along, like he could wipe out some of his recent past that way. "Can we do the macho straight-dude thing and just pretend I never said it? Maybe let it hang awkwardly between us occasionally, but never talk about it again?"

"Works for me," Ian said, then gave him a bro-hug before leaving Tierney alone to call his lifeline.

But Marty didn't answer, so he had to leave a message. "This is Tierney. Terrebonne. Uh, I'm having some issues and the local therapist is kinda, well, bogus. I mean, *I* think she is. Anyway, I have a pretty majorly pressing situation and I need to get someone else's opinion on it. As soon as possible. Like, call me back at one in the morning if you get this then. Or two. Or whenever." He remembered to rattle off his number, then he settled his butt in his chair, placed the phone on the arm, and waited for it to ring.

Dalton didn't cry. He hurt too much to cry, like heartbreak had dehydrated his soul. He gave himself a headache, not crying. The pain forced him into bed early, where he lay awake all night, wishing Tierney was behind him, spooning him. Wishing for things to be different because then he could have what he most wanted. He *knew* Tierney wanted him in turn, but they'd *had* to do the responsible, adult thing and end it, so he couldn't even get angry or hate the man. Mostly, he just ached with wanting what was best for him.

That was such a *line*, one he'd read in Sam's books that sounded nice and altruistic, but he'd never experienced this—never felt that his own happiness was a reasonable sacrifice to make for someone else's. He'd gladly give it up if it meant Tierney didn't have to suffer.

It meant he had to lie here in the dark, trying not to puke, though. So, sick to his stomach, exhausted but wired, he waited for dawn. Eventually, wrung out, he drifted into one of those half-awake states that often followed tragedies of the heart.

That's when questions started percolating in his mind. As sluggish as bubbles in tar pits, he could watch them form in his thoughts.

Why hadn't they discussed the possibility of reconnecting when Tierney was on a more even keel?

If not seeing each other was supposed to make being sober easier, why had Tierney been so broken up about it?

Why had Dalton accepted it so easily? Because he hadn't truly believed he could have this? Because he was the one with the disfigured soul in Sam's romance novel scenario?

Because he was still afraid, deep down, of repeating his own past mistakes?

Well, duh. It was suddenly crystal clear. He'd had a freak-out at Tierney's place yesterday morning because some cautious part of himself was still afraid, but losing his man had woken up another part of him. A more mature, confident piece, with an intrinsic faith in the new Tierney. He could write the man off as a bad bet, or he could go with his gut and heart and believe.

I believe. Just, it was a little too late, wasn't it? And his belief didn't solve the main problem: Tierney was emotionally fragile right now, and a relationship could fuck up his recovery.

What am I going to do?

That last question was what finally dragged him out of bed. Because he was an adult, and adults got up in the morning and fed their cat. Especially when said cat had been yowling for a while.

"For the record, 11:45 is totally still morning," he said to Blue when he walked into the kitchen.

Blue meowed grumpily, then jumped up on the counter and sat on his haunches right over the drawer where the can opener lived. Dalton didn't care enough to put him back on the floor; he just opened the wet food while Blue watched, then mashed it into the dry and set it in front of him. The gulping and purring began immediately, and Dalton stood next to him, petting his fur, letting it soothe his hurt. Blue didn't really care about his feelings, or comforting him, but Dalton could pretend.

Tea sounded comforting, also. He could make himself a cup. If he had any around. Normally he drank coffee, but coffee was for days when he wasn't nursing a broken heart. Unfortunately, after ransacking all his cupboards, he confirmed his suspicion—he didn't have any tea.

"Should I go buy some?"

Blue ignored him and continued to lick one of his back legs, stretching it high into the air in front of him and running his tongue along the whole length.

Sigh. Getting dressed and going to the store was so much effort. He wandered into the living room and flopped into his chair, butt landing on something hard and about the size of a cell phone. He wasn't surprised to discover after he fished it out that's what it was. Waking it up, the first thing he saw was the little red circle above his message icon indicating he had a voice mail.

Tierney. He should've brought the phone to bed with him, then he wouldn't have missed the call.

Except it was only Andrea. Worse, it was Andy telling him that, after watching him and Tierney in the club on Thanksgiving, she could accept their relationship. "I still don't like him, but seeing how he looks at you and how he treats you . . ." She sighed before spitting out, "I guess it's possible he's changed." He cut it off and threw the phone onto the couch without listening to the rest. Once he told her what happened—and he'd *have* to tell her—his sister would probably hate Tierney again, regardless of why they'd ended things.

Whatever. Well, since he hadn't plugged his phone in last night, he probably should now. The battery didn't last that long anymore, and having a task would help him not dwell.

Standing, he picked it up, and as he turned, something on the floor in his entryway caught his eye. He had to get closer before he could figure out what it was.

A piece of paper. Folded in half, with his name written on it, lying a few inches in front of the door, as if someone had slipped it underneath.

He immediately thought of Tierney again—*of course*—and his heart did a somersault in spite of his reminder to it that he'd thought Andy's phone message might be from Tierney. Besides, would Tierney contact him this way?

Maybe . . .?

He stood staring at it a moment. Something about the handwriting was familiar. He couldn't recall having seen Tierney's, but, while this neatish, blocky penmanship didn't seem in keeping with Tierney's character, it *did* look familiar. Had he subconsciously noted Tierney's style? Was there some kind of omen in it being totally different than what Dalton expected? A sign he'd been looking at the whole person wrong? Thinking they could make things fit, when in reality Tierney's style was incompatible with his. *Look at his furniture.*

Except Tierney hadn't picked most of it out, and he'd told Dalton he thought it was ugly.

And Dalton had already decided to believe.

Squatting, he finally picked up the paper and unfolded it.

More of those blocky letters were inside.

We need to talk. I know I was in the wrong, and I want to make it up to you. Please meet me at Murray's, where you and your friend go, at 1 p.m. today.

—T

That was . . . weird. It didn't *sound* like Tierney, but he'd signed it. Sort of. It didn't matter, though; Dalton's hopes had already taken flight. He tried to tamp them down—being in the wrong didn't necessarily equate to them getting back together—but in the fifteen minutes he took to have a quick shower and get dressed, he grew progressively more excited. Maybe things really *could* work out. Maybe Tierney had figured out a way, or his therapist had offered another opinion.

Maybe Tierney didn't care, because he wanted to be with Dalton so much.

Maybe he'd realized that breaking it off was just *wrong*.

In the end, Dalton's hopes were so much stronger than his fears that he grabbed his backpack on the way out the door, just in case.

Tierney wasn't there yet when Dalton arrived at Murray's, so he got them a table and waited. It was in a different section than where he and Sam sat. Their typical spot was in the middle of the room screened by potted plants, while today he'd been shown to one against the mirror-paneled wall farthest from the entrance.

"Good afternoon, sir," the waiter said from his left side, startling him. "Will someone be joining you, or are you ready to order?" He glanced at the second menu the host had placed across from Dalton.

"I'm waiting for someone," he confirmed, then leaned forward to see the restaurant clock after the waiter nodded and turned away.

Was it a good sign or a bad sign that Tierney was late? Ten minutes wasn't that much, was it? Or could he have been seated already and Dalton missed him? It wasn't a huge restaurant, but there were so many potted plants and bamboo screen things that maybe there were dining areas he didn't even know to search? Trying not to be too obvious, Dalton craned his head and leaned various directions, searching. But nothing. He'd seen it all. Nothing by the side door, or the seating against the parti-wall next to the host's station, or the middle section where he and Sam usually sat. Although there was someone at their usual table now. Just one guy, who also seemed to be waiting. He had his elbows on the table and his mouth propped against his clasped hands, eyes darting around over the top of them, like he was inspecting the room and patrons, too.

Then he turned slightly, just enough to put his face in profile, and Dalton's heart palpitated. He *knew* that profile—he'd seen it the night of the bashing.

What the . . .? Oh God. *OhGodohGod*, the rhythm of his pulse echoed back to him. First the fruit basket, then the tickets, and now this? *Could* they all be related? Was he actually being *stalked*? *Don't get ahead of yourself.* Ducking down, he pretended he needed something from his backpack hanging on the back of the chair. As soon as he unzipped his bag and stuck his hand in, he grabbed the first thing he found.

The note from Tierney about how to set the condo alarm.

In Tierney's handwriting. Which was just as scribbly and jagged as Dalton had thought his handwriting should be.

But the note this morning was signed with a "T."

So?

The pulse pounding in his head had to be loud enough for the whole restaurant to hear. Fingers tingling with creeping numbness, he fished out his phone, keeping his chin tucked low and refusing to glance up. He turned fully sideways in the chair, hunching over.

I must look like a freak.

Whatever. He pulled up Tierney's name and texted him.

Did you want to meet for lunch?

It took a minute before Tierney texted back. *Yes, totally. I really need to talk to you. Where and when?*

Dalton's heart took off like a scared rabbit. He hit Tierney's name on contacts, and even the ring of Tierney's phone in his ear sounded like it was shaking with adrenaline.

"Dalton?"

"I'm at Murray's Bistro."

"Okay, tell me where it is, and I'll be there as soon as I can—"

Of course. Of course he wouldn't even know that's where Dalton and Sam met, because Dalton had never told him.

"—I need to tell you about stuff." Tierney swallowed, then went on. "I fucked up, coming over yesterday and saying we couldn't see each other, I mean, I talked to my Dunthorpe therapist and *he* said—"

"Tierney." He wanted to hear this, but he had more pressing concerns at the moment. "I got a note to meet you here so we could talk, at least I thought it was you, but it's not you, it's one of the bashers," Dalton rushed out. "I think. I think *he's* here to meet me." Risking a glance up, he nearly fell out of the chair with relief when he realized he was hidden from the basher's sight by a palm frond. He just needed to huddle here, and he was golden.

"Get out of there," Tierney nearly yelled in his ear.

"He's between me and the door." It would be hard for the guy to miss seeing him walk across the bistro, and he didn't want to take the chance of *not* being missed.

Tierney made a strangling noise. "Can he see you *now*?"

"No, I'm hiding." Leaning over slightly, he peeked past the palm frond, and the shock of recognition hit him again, like a glass of water in the face. "It's really him. I'm certain." *OhGodohGodohGodohGodohGod.*

Tierney groaned in his ear. "Please, just call 911. I'll be there as soon as I can. And *stay* hidden."

"I will."

"*Be careful*," Tierney said, voice shaking. "If you get offed before we have a chance to get back together, I'll never forgive myself."

"I will," Dalton promised, and in spite of the potential danger, hope infused his chest again, making it feel floaty.

But then Tierney hung up, and hope took a backseat to fear.

CHAPTER 25

The 911 dispatcher didn't seem to find the situation as urgent as Dalton did. He could hear it in her monotonous tone and the way she phrased her questions; as if she were reading them off a card labeled "Checklist for Potential Stalking Victims." She'd assured him a unit was responding, but Dalton was certain the officer coming was obeying all the traffic laws, and possibly stopping for a Big Gulp on the way. He wanted one of those cops who came screaming the wrong direction down the street, with lights whirling and sirens wailing. Luke may bitch about callers insisting things were an emergency and they needed a code three approach when they patently didn't, but right now Dalton would happily be one of the annoying crazies.

"Do you currently have a restraining order against the person of interest?" the dispatcher droned.

"No, but he's been instructed by a judge not to come within fifteen hundred feet of me." Maybe that would make her send the cops faster.

What it did was make her pause. He could all but hear puzzled interest in her silence.

"Um, I'm a witness in an assault case, and the judge who let him out on bail said he had to stay away from the victims and the witnesses."

"Okay," she said, in a much livelier voice. "You said you're in public, lots of people around?"

"Yes."

"And do you have any reason to believe this man is a physical threat to you?"

"Well, I did watch him beat up a gay guy for being gay, and I'm gay, so . . ."

"Please, stay on the line, sir, I'll be right with you." Dead air filled his ear for a few moments, then she was back. "The officer responding advises he's ten minutes from your location. You need to just sit tight and stay in a well-populated area. Have you told any of the staff what's going on?"

"No." He hadn't had a chance. His waiter had come close to the table a few moments ago, but then swerved away before Dalton could catch his eye.

As he answered the rest of her questions, he began to feel more secure. Safer. Tierney was on his way and so were the cops and he was in a public place. He unkinked his spine, sitting forward in his chair. Glancing quickly, he checked on his stalker.

OhGodohGodohGodohGodohGodohGod. "He's gone. The guy's not sitting where he was anymore."

Chimes were the only response he got. Familiar-sounding ones . . . the ones that told him his phone was shutting down due to a dying battery.

Fuck. He glared at the thing, wishing he could recharge it with brain waves, but then someone sat down across from him, and Dalton didn't even have to lift his head to know who it was. All the blood in his body rushed toward his belly, pooling there and causing a panic. *OhGodohGodohGodohGodohGodohGod.* Swallowing, he looked up and met the guy's eyes.

He'd known it was one of the bashers, but he still flinched when he recognized that face again.

"Hi there." The dude tipped his head in a weirdly friendly gesture of acknowledgment. "We haven't been, you know, properly introduced. Name's Robert." He held his hand across the table.

Dalton stared at it. Did one shake hands with someone who'd assaulted one's friend? He didn't think so.

The guy—Robert—pulled his arm back. "Sorry about lying to you on that note."

"Note?" The one telling him to come here?

"Signed it 'T,' 'cause I know that's what people call that guy you been hanging around with. You been spending a lot of time with him. Oughta be careful about that."

Careful? Dalton blinked at him. Had the guy been *watching* him? How else would he know about Tierney?

"Yeah, so guess I should get this over with." Robert took a moment, though. He huffed out a breath, blowing his cheeks up big and running his hand through his hair. "I'm here to apologize for my part in, you know, kicking your ass that night. It was one of those group things, herd mentality, you know. My brother Jimmy's always said I was a follower. Guess he was right. Anyway." He cleared his throat, shifting again.

Dalton shook his head, trying to get things to make sense. *Kicking* my *ass?*

The guy's lower lip poked out, just a little, and he frowned. "Doncha got anything to say about that?"

"Why are you apologizing to *me*?" burst out of Dalton before he thought better of it.

More of the shifting, as if Robert's seat was a bed of nails, or he had hemorrhoids or something. "Well, 'cause I feel guilty about what I did to you and Miller," he said while inspecting the floor next to his chair.

He thinks I'm Sam? Well, this was about the least-threatening confrontation Dalton could have imagined. As a matter of fact, he'd classify his current state as pissed off—he'd skipped right over annoyed. "You didn't *do* anything to me." Leaning back in his seat, he waited to see what would happen next. *Cannot* believe *this guy.*

Confused blinking happened next. "You're not Jurgen's cousin's boyfriend, Dalton?"

"Uh, *nooo*. Ian's boyfriend would be *Sam*."

When all he got in response was confused scowling, Dalton continued. "He's about eight inches taller than me? Much bigger nose?" He pointed to himself, tapping his sternum as he spoke. "*I* happen to be a witness in the case." Then he nearly said more. Words were rising up, crowding together in his throat. About how he'd seen the whole thing and he thought Robert and his friends were the worst excuse for humans he'd ever met. But this guy *was* one of those guys, and it seemed stupid to provoke him.

Robert whistled, of all things. "Well, shit. Guess that explains why you're spending so much time with that other guy. Say, you wouldn't happen to have Sam's number, would you?"

"What?" He had to grip the table to keep from reeling right out of his seat. "*Really*?"

Robert just kept looking at him expectantly.

Dalton leaned forward. "*Why* would I give you Sam's number?"

"So I can *apologize*," he answered, as if it were the most normal thing in the world.

"You *assaulted* him," Dalton hissed, trying to keep his voice from going strident like it wanted to. "You aren't supposed to contact him, or be in the same room as he is, or even *look* at him." Were flames shooting out his nose yet? He *felt* like he was breathing fire. "Same goes for me; didn't you hear me say I'm a witness?"

Holding up his hands, as if showing his palms would calm Dalton—*ha!*—Robert said, "Let's just hold on a second, I'm trying to make peace here. I was even gonna pay for your lunch. Been trying for a couple of weeks now—"

"Are you saying you *have* been stalking me? That fruit basket and those tickets were from *you*?"

"Now that was my brother Jimmy's idea. See, he was over in Afghanistan for a tour. When he made it home, he was mighty pissed off at me. Said he hadn't fought for the freedom of all Americans to have me trying to take someone's away."

"Wait." Dalton sliced his hand through the air. "So this isn't even a sincere apology? You're just doing it because your brother guilted you into it?"

"I wrote all the notes Jimmy delivered; those were *my* words and stuff." Robert poked the table with his forefinger, making his point. "He just did some recon, kept me apprised of your habits, and delivered the—"

"Okay, so *he's* stalking me. Still a crime."

Robert inhaled a very large lungful of air, the obvious kind people took when they wanted someone to know their anger was building. "Listen, we need to end this little chat, 'cause we're both getting hot under the collar. How about, if you won't give me Sam's number, you find it in your heart to apologize *for* me?"

A short, loud, totally unamused laugh escaped Dalton, and the heads of the diners nearest them turned. Murray's was always full of noise, but he and Robert were getting loud enough to start attracting a lot of attention. Did he care?

"No," he said, answering both their questions. Then he crossed his arms over his chest and lifted his brow.

Robert mirrored him, except he clearly wasn't conversant in the arrogant eyebrow thing. "I feel like I made all this here effort, and I'm not getting any return on my investment, as they say. That's just not right."

Un. Believable. Then the most obvious thing in the world occurred to him. "Did you apologize to Miller?"

"Well, now, that's different." Robert's jaw went hard. "See, Miller *lied* to us."

Dalton gaped. "Lied to you?" Parroting the guy was the most response he could manage.

"Sure did." Robert sat back with a satisfied nod, as if he'd done good. "All those years he pretended to be our friend, and he was gay the whole time."

People around them were beginning to murmur, but at this point, it didn't matter to Dalton if they were making a scene. He planted his elbows on the table and fake smiled, so angry he had to tense every muscle to keep from shaking. "Oh, and that's just the worst thing a guy can do to a bunch of repressed hicks, isn't it?" He was totally poking this bear, but he wasn't going to stop, because logic like that was just too fucking medieval to be withstood.

"Don't you judge me." Robert glared at him, eyes narrowing into slits. "Faggot."

The word sent an electric shock along Dalton's spine, making him sit up straight and meet Robert's stare. "Um," he said in that tone that implied being very sure about what one was about to say, "I think we're done here." He stood up. "I'm sure Detective Johnson will be very interested in what you've said to me today, and all the lovely gifts you and your brother gave me."

Robert stood also, blocking Dalton's way, nearly chest bumping him. Totally aggressive, and now they were really going to attract attention, but no, there was a ruckus near the door so no one was even looking their way. At least not from what he could see in his peripheral vision.

"Excuse me." He started to go around Robert, but the guy's hand shot out and shackled his left wrist, gripping too tightly. The touch catalyzed Dalton's anger, igniting it. Before, he'd been angry, but this new anger made him want to *do* things. Speaking very clearly, because he simply would *not* be misunderstood, he said, "Let go of me *now*, or you're going to regret it."

The sneer he got in return was exactly what he'd expected. "Yeah, who's going to make me?"

"Me."

"Hey!" Tierney's shout startled Robert into turning his head, which sucked because Dalton wanted to knock the guy's teeth into his groin, but his fist was already moving, rushing forward with all his anger giving it momentum and weight. In the final split second, Robert turned back and his nose caught the blow, and Dalton felt something snap. They both lost their balance, but he landed against Tierney's chest while Robert tripped over his chair, leading with the back of his head.

Dalton had turned into Tierney's arms before he heard Robert's thick skull smack into the ground.

Robert had a broken nose. Tierney'd kind of enjoyed confirming it was broken—before the police arrived, he was the only one around with advanced first aid training. At first he'd claimed he couldn't help because there was blood everywhere and he didn't have latex gloves, but the waitstaff found some, so he'd had to do *something*. What he did was order a dishtowel and then shove it—hard—against Robert's face to stop the bleeding.

After arriving just in time to watch the douche bag manhandle Dalton, it was the least Tierney could do.

The way Robert had carried on, you'd think he'd had his septum driven into his brain. He'd insisted on going to the hospital, which annoyed the hell out of the cops because it would mean an officer would have to go with him. They *could* choose not to place him under arrest, but that was clearly a nonstarter. He'd finally left in the ambulance a few minutes ago, with a squad car following behind.

Now Tierney and Dalton were waiting for Detective Johnson to finish up whatever needed his investigative touch and come talk to them. He'd let them into the backseat of his vehicle out in front of the restaurant. It was a little chilly, so Tierney had to keep his hands on Dalton. He didn't want his boyfriend getting cold; the guy was probably still in shock. Keeping all his body heat as near Dalton as possible was totally rendering first aid.

"How are your knuckles?" Lifting up an edge of the towel wrapped around Dalton's fingers, he checked the ice in the bag. "Too chilly?"

Dalton shook his head. "God, punching him felt *so* great," he repeated for the fourth time or so.

"And you looked hot doing it." Tierney tightened his arm around Dalton's shoulders and kissed his temple.

"I'm glad you came for me." Dalton had said *that* four or five times too.

"I never want to not come for you." Tierney nuzzled his boyfriend's hair with his whiskers. Until Dalton started giggle-snorting, and Tierney ran his words over in his head and laughter boiled out of him too. It was a great way to relieve the stress that the last few hours—like, twenty-four—had caused. Eventually he calmed down enough to add the important part. "I always want to be the first one you turn to when you need backup."

Dalton didn't ask what had changed between yesterday and now, just laid his head on Tierney's shoulder and nestled under his chin. "We can talk about all that later. Just tell me this relationship is really a go."

"This relationship is a go," Tierney murmured before kissing his hair. "But yeah, we have to talk."

"You're sure it's not going to endanger your recovery?" Dalton didn't move—in fact, he was too still.

"I thought we were going to talk about this later."

"Just answer the question. Please?"

"I don't think it will." He shifted around, so he could face Dalton, at least as much as being in the back of the car would let him, until he had Dalton's head resting half on his chest and their thighs were mashed against each other. "Telling you it was over nearly made me drink. Even if it's possible that I'd fall off the wagon if we split up, you're worth taking a risk on."

"Are you sure?" he whispered.

Tierney wrapped his other arm around Dalton, squeezing him into a tight hug. "One hundred percent certain."

Dalton kissed his neck, which Tierney took as acceptance. And since they had that worked out, sorta . . . "As soon as this is over, we're going back to my place where I can keep an eye on you."

"Are you feeling protective, now?" Dalton teased.

"Fuck yes. Jesus, you watch some dude who you know for a fact is a violent homophobic piece of shit grab your boyfriend and tell me *you* wouldn't be." With Dalton wrapped in his arms, Tierney couldn't miss how all of his muscles tensed up. "What?" Did he say something wrong?

"Are you officially my boyfriend?"

Shit. "Uh, unless you tell me otherwise, I am."

Reaching up and running his fingers along Tierney's jaw, Dalton relaxed again. "You are."

"And you're mine?"

"Of course." He said it with such certainty that Tierney actually believed it; actually *understood* the word. It was about caring for someone so much he'd sit in the back of a detective's car for hours with him, making sure he was warm enough and not stressed. Loving him so much that Tierney wouldn't say a word about how the guy's ice pack was freezing his genitals—well, not unless they were in danger of real damage. That was totally justifiable. Dalton would suffer too if Tierney's dick got frostbitten and the tip had to be amputated.

But short of that, he wasn't ever letting go of the dude again.

Maybe it was due to Dalton's leftover adrenaline, but it didn't seem like it took hours before Detective Johnson joined them in the back of his car. Well, Johnson was in front, looking through a sort of cage at them, frowning. "Why don't we go into the restaurant and sit down?" he suggested. "We'll all be more comfortable."

Climbing out of the car behind Tierney, Dalton was surprised to look up and see light-pink streaks of cloud were appearing in the sky. It was so similar to the evening he'd waited outside Club Monaco before the concert and this whole thing with Robert had started (even if he hadn't realized it at the time). He'd met Tierney that day too. Was that really just a little over a month ago?

When Tierney took his hand and asked, "You all right?" Dalton was pulled back into the present day. Over Tierney's shoulder, he could see the detective was almost at the door of Murray's.

"Yeah." When Tierney continued to frown at him, eyes flickering around his face, Dalton kissed him quickly. "I was just thinking about all the stuff that's happened in the last month."

That seemed to satisfy him. He tugged on Dalton's hand and they went to join Johnson, sitting next to each other and across from him at the table the officer had commandeered, in a totally different section than any Dalton had sat in before.

Weird how the police commandeered stuff, but other people claimed things.

Dalton liked Detective Johnson. He'd heard enough from his brothers to know not all detectives (or cops) were nice people, but Johnson clearly fell into the "nice" category. Or maybe it was because he was on Dalton's side. At any rate, as they had coffee, the detective made the interview seem more like a chat among friends.

"Bobinski was talking about cutting a deal with the DA before he even got in the ambulance," he said.

"Bobinski?" Dalton asked.

Johnson nodded while sipping his coffee, then said, "Your pal Robert's last name."

"His name is Robert Bobinski? I wonder if anyone ever calls him Bob?" Tierney was half-laughing as he said it, and Dalton got caught up in watching him. His eyes were sparkling greenish, and those little lines that fanned out from them were so sexy. The mark of a man who'd lived some. He squeezed Tierney's hand under the table, smiling when Tierney looked at him questioningly.

Johnson obviously didn't realize they were having a moment, and he interrupted it. "I still couldn't get an answer out of him about how he worked out you were Sam."

"You'd think a guy'd remember whose ass he kicked," Tierney said with a snort.

Dalton shook his head. "He didn't think I was *Sam*, he thought I was Ian's boyfriend." And that was another thing . . . "I think he was actually kind of *scolding* me for being with Tierney. Like he cared that I might be cheating on Ian?"

Tierney started muttering impolite things, but Johnson laughed, then shrugged. "I gotta go pick up the brother later and get his side. He's the one who made the original mistake, I'm thinking."

"That's what Robert said." Dalton wrinkled up his thinking nose. "I don't know how they knew Ian."

Tierney did, though. "Ian's cousin Jurgen is a state trooper stationed in Whitetail Rock."

"That's the town Miller's from," the detective explained, which was thoughtful because Dalton didn't know Whitetail Rock from a hole in the ground.

After that, they got down to business, and Dalton told Johnson everything that had happened, then answered his questions. Again, it didn't seem to take forever. Suddenly, the detective was standing, shaking their hands and saying he'd call if he needed anything more. "Or if I have information," he added before walking off.

Leaving Dalton and Tierney alone.

"Is this later enough?" Tierney asked him, turning in his seat to face Dalton. When Dalton turned toward him also, Tierney captured one of his knees between his own. "To talk, I mean?"

It was incredibly tempting to say, "Let's not and pretend we did." Except that wasn't even an option, not really. "We probably should, huh?"

Tierney held Dalton's hand palm up in his and traced the long lines on it. "Yeah."

Neither of them said anything for a few minutes. Dalton simply let Tierney tickle his skin and basked in the man's warmth and presence. "I love you." He'd always been a bit of a coward with Tierney, scared to direct anything that happened between them, or admit too much, but the words came out easily now. He was saying them before he knew he wanted to. But he definitely did want to.

Tierney swallowed, lifting his chin to meet Dalton's eyes. "I love you too. I told you yesterday and all—"

"I remember."

"—but that seems like it doesn't really count."

Dalton shook his head, then leaned forward and kissed Tierney, soft and sweet. "This counts."

"Totally counts." Tierney's fingers found their way into Dalton's hair and he returned Dalton's kiss, but his was a long, reassuring one. He didn't let go after it was over, either; instead he brought his forehead to rest against Dalton's. "I know it always seems like I, um, need you—"

"Tierney—"

"Just let me say this." Tierney pulled away, gazing into Dalton's eyes. "I need you, but I *want* you too. This isn't me reaching for the most reliable crutch I can find."

"I know." He nodded to prove it. "I want you too. Very much."

"Thank God." Tierney huffed out a relieved breath. "I know I'm a risk, but I'll never do what I did to you yesterday again. I let myself—" Shaking his head, he glanced at the ceiling, licking his lip before going on. "You know, I took my life back under my own control when Grandfather died. I mean, I wish I'd done it before he died, but regardless, I did it, and I'm not fucking letting someone else have that kind of influence over me again. I was using my old coping strategies—"

Dalton's finger over Tierney's lips shut him up. "I think we both believed it easily because it felt inevitable. A lot of people recommend you don't do this after rehab, so I think we both expected someone to tell you no."

"I guess." He ran his thumb along the center of Dalton's palm a few times, watching while he did it. "Breaking up doesn't feel like that to you now? Inevitable?"

"Being *with* you feels inevitable." He didn't even care how sappy that sounded. "I got up this morning, and it started to sink in that I'd expected it, and I gave you up without a fight. I didn't even ask you what she *said*."

Tierney shrugged. "It doesn't matter what Dr. Palmer said, because I talked to Marty—I'd just hung up with him when you texted—and he said it's not unusual for people just out of rehab to put too much faith in what other people tell them."

"That makes sense," Dalton assured him.

Tierney barely seemed to need it; the rest of what he'd been planning to say spilled out of him. "He said it's strongly recommended people don't start new relationships for a while, but that I was right—it's not, like, forbidden. And we're already in one, so . . ."

"So it's too late?"

Tierney missed the humor, or cared too much to play along. His fingers squeezed around Dalton's. "He said I needed to go with my gut but keep my eyes wide open. And my gut says we should be together. I'm determined to make this work, as long as it works for both of us." With his free hand, he combed Dalton's bangs back and tucked them behind his ear, looking intently into his eyes as he said, "I gotta tell you, it's really working for me."

"Me too. Really working." Dalton's smile felt as inevitable as they did. "I should probably be all cautious, huh? I just can't, not right now."

Tierney was still in serious mode. "It might not be easy. Marty had a list of things we need to watch out for, and he suggested that when I *do* find a local therapist I trust, you might need to come with me once or twice. Make sure we're on track."

"You know I'll go with you."

"I do now." Tierney gave him a single head nod. "He also said we have to be as honest as possible with each other."

Dalton turned the tables on him, pulling his hand out of Tierney's grasp and gripping his instead, squeezing hard enough that he could feel Tierney's knuckles shifting. "I *believe* in you. I'll do whatever it takes."

"Yeah?" His smile began to quirk at the corners of his lips, and now his eyes were sparking up again, lit from the inside. "Like move into my place?"

Maybe Dalton should have been expecting that, but he wasn't prepared for it at all. He swayed closer, and could only think to say, "I haven't even been in my new apartment a month." That place meant freedom for him.

"I'll pay off the lease."

Well, *that* helped bring him back to earth. Dalton tilted his head and gave Tierney his flattest, *you might want to rethink that* look.

"Sorry." Tierney grimaced. "I mean *you* can buy you out of the lease?"

"No, I can't." He knew Tierney didn't mean to bring up the specters of Dalton's past, but if honesty was going to be the basis of their relationship, he needed to begin now. "I may like to *play* kept boy," he said quietly, toying with a button on Tierney's shirt. "But I don't ever want to be one again." He lifted his head to catch the expression of regret on his boyfriend's face.

"I know, I'm sorry, I wasn't thinking. I mean, I want you there, I can't help it." He slumped. "I'm not good at delayed gratification, yet."

"We can't do it. You *know* that's pushing it too far too fast." Dalton forced himself to keep eye contact with Tierney. "I know you don't want to believe it, but there's still that possibility this won't work."

"Yeah, I've decided not to entertain that possibility. I'd like to encourage you to not entertain it, either."

Dalton sighed, but he was fighting a smile too. "How about: I don't entertain the possibility of us not working out, and you don't revisit the moving in thing until we're more solid."

"Like in a couple months?"

"You're supposed to wait a year."

"It's a *recommendation*." He was totally whining.

"Six months," Dalton offered.

Tierney studied him, probably trying to decide how negotiable this was. Then he nodded. "Six months." He grinned all at once, his eyes glowing and those sexy lines fanning out from them.

Dalton's stomach flipped over, like his roller coaster had just reached the peak of the first big hill and was now hurtling along. This was going to be an awesome ride. "Let's go home." He used that word deliberately, as a sort of promise to them both.

"Definitely," Tierney said, but then leaned forward to kiss him again rather than standing up. Just before their lips met, he added, "I hear make-up sex is really hot, and I want to test that theory out with you."

Epilogue

Tierney had planned operation *Trick Dalton into Living with Me* very carefully. Well, except for the part where he and Ian had broken the dining room table last week while scrimmaging in the condo. That had been sheer luck.

After climbing out of the wreckage, they'd stood around with Dalton and Sam, inspecting the damage in silence. Until it'd hit Tierney that he could use this to his advantage.

"Guess I should call the decorator and have her find a new one." *Nice*. He'd injected just the right amount of resignation in his tone.

"If you call her, you'll get another table just like it," Dalton had warned. "I'll help you find a new one."

"If you want." Tierney shrugged as if he didn't care.

Now, six months to the day since he'd agreed to Dalton's embargo on moving in together, he was driving over to pick up his boyfriend so they could go furniture shopping.

Little did Dalton know they were getting a lot more than a table.

Dalton had strong opinions on furniture design, and none of his opinions liked anything in Tierney's condo apart from the couch. Tierney was hoping, if he filled it with furniture his boyfriend *did* like, the dude would want to spend more time with the furniture. Like, *all* his time.

Tierney didn't see it so much as manipulating Dalton—it was more a case of ensuring they fulfilled the terms of the agreement they'd made to revisit the cohabitation question.

Pulling up to Dalton's apartment building, he found his boyfriend waiting for him out on the sidewalk, as stunning and hot as usual. He'd butched it up a little today, with a pair of tight skinny jeans, a black leather motorcycle jacket, and black ankle boots. As he walked toward the car, Tierney watched the flex of his thighs strain the denim in the sexiest way possible. It made his blood pump extra hard, and when Dalton opened the door, the curve of his ass as he sat in the bucket seat made it pump even more, but this time with a purpose.

"Hey," Dalton smiled, turning toward him.

"Hi, Roo." Tierney rested his elbow on the console between them, admiring his boyfriend and waiting for his hello kiss. Dalton had a T-shirt on under the jacket—a tight, clinging one. Two layers of clothes and he still looked so sexy Tierney wanted to throw him in the backseat, strip him down, and give him a full-body tongue bath.

How was that even possible?

Because I know how he looks under those clothes. Ungh. "Wanna go home first and take measurements?" He leaned closer to Dalton as he asked, close enough to smell the leather of his jacket. "Of my bed?" They were going to buy a new one while they were shopping for a dining room table, anyway. And hey, he'd delay the trip awhile for a good cause.

Dalton gave him a playfully suspicious squint. "Your bed needs to be measured?"

"Needs it so bad." He stretched across the console and kissed him. Lavishing his tongue on Dalton's lips the way he wished he could on the guy's body. His abs. Right now. He pulled back far enough to say, "My bed's *aching* to see you."

Dalton was tempted. Tierney could see it in his dilated pupils and the speed of his breath. His lips were still parted, as if he was waiting for Tierney to come back, or about to say, "And I'm aching to see your bed." But then he licked them, and somehow that made the haze of lust clear from his eyes, and muscles that had been slack rearrange themselves into something more pragmatic. "New table first. Then I'll 'measure your bed.'"

"C'mon," Tierney whined. "The table can wait. Let's go home."

"Your condo you mean?" Dalton asked with a small smile.

"Yeah, that." Tierney tried to look cute and boyishly pleading, still halfway on the passenger side of the car.

Moving, turning and pressing his torso snug against Tierney's, and wrapping his arms around Tierney's neck, Dalton said in his ear, "If we get the table first, I'll let you fuck me on it."

"Fuck me," Tierney whispered, then swallowed. "I mean, not literally, it's just an expression, you know, like 'oh my God' or something, because hell yes I want to fuck you on the new table." He pulled back just enough to see Dalton's blue eyes crinkle at the corners with amusement. "I have an idea. We'll go home and say good-bye to the old table before we say hello to the new one."

Dalton hitched himself closer again, kissing Tierney quickly, then running one hand down his chest.

Mmmm. Had he actually done it? Convinced him to go back to the condo? Maybe a little extra persuasion was in order. "It could use some more breaking. I don't think it's broken enough. Like, if we were to lay you out, naked, on the undamaged side—"

"The old one's broken because you insisted on playing rugby in the house." Dalton's hand found his dick, squeezing through his jeans, and Tierney sucked in a breath. "I think you and Ian both landing on it broke it enough." He gave him another quick kiss before adding against Tierney's mouth, "If you want to play ball with *me* on your new table? You need to take me shopping. Now." He tightened his fingers around Tierney's cock once more before letting go, then settled back in his seat.

Normally, Tierney would argue more, but the stakes were too high today. Besides, his brain was bathing in lust hormones, and not a lot of help right at the moment. He swallowed. "Okay. Let's get this done, but that means that later, you have to play ball with me on the table *and* measure the bed."

"Deal," Dalton said, then bit his lip, smiling.

Tierney focused on the steering wheel, trying to get his head back in the game enough to drive to the furniture store Dalton had picked out. Promising himself this would be the fastest shopping trip in history.

Tierney was so transparent. Did he really think Dalton would forget what today was? If nothing else, it was also the anniversary of the day he'd broken a man's nose, and *that* was something one remembered. The memory had resurfaced this past week, because the last of the bashers had made his deal with the district attorney. Dalton was somewhat relieved that he wouldn't have to testify, but not totally happy with the sentences each of the defendants had received.

Robert Bobinski had made the first deal with the DA. Apparently he'd gone straight to her office from the hospital to meet his waiting lawyer. Grady Fowler had made the next deal. Tierney had been especially unhappy when the guy had gotten away with no jail time, just probation and a whopping fine. "It's because his daddy pulled some strings," he'd bitched, pacing around the condo.

"And because they couldn't charge him with as many crimes since he didn't have the bat." Dalton had felt he should remind him of that, even if he was certain Sheriff Fowler had had something to do with the guy being let off so easily.

So, yes, that whole mess was near the forefront of his thoughts. Regardless, he was unlikely to forget that six months ago was also the day he and Tierney had made things officially boyfriend-like. *And* the day Tierney had asked him to move into the condo.

Tierney had hinted—heavily—since then, but never brought the subject up, exactly. Instead, he'd said things like, "Thank God we didn't listen to all that advice about not starting this relationship," then lead them into a conversation about their future together. Dalton sometimes let himself go there, imagine what they might be doing in two or three or ten years, because he couldn't imagine not being with Tierney, ever. It wasn't always easy—the second month after rehab had been particularly difficult, as Tierney'd adjusted to normal life even more. "What the hell do people *do* in the evenings to relax if they can't drink?" he'd whined.

Dalton had come up with one or two dozen ways to relax his man. He should get a medal for it, since Tierney wasn't an easy guy to relax. He had a ton of energy, and was always doing stuff like playing rugby in the condo with Ian. That second month they were together, when Dalton decided he was with the most hyper man alive, he'd accused him of being Tigger.

"Like from Winnie the Pooh?" he'd added when Tierney looked at him blankly, standing in the middle of the living room.

"Really?" He flopped down on the couch next to Dalton, nearly trampolining him off the cushion. "Why?"

"You remind me of him, when he bounces around on his tail." And drove the other characters insane.

"Tigger, huh?" Tierney bobbed his head from side to side, as if thinking it over, the whole sofa shaking with his motion. "I can live with that, but who does that make you?"

"I don't know. Do I have to be someone?"

Tierney squinted his eyes thoughtfully. "Let's see, who was Tigger's best friend? I don't think he had a boyfriend."

"I'm pretty sure he was in Christopher Robin's closet."

Tierney snorted a laugh, but wouldn't be knocked off track. "Was it Roo? I think it was; so I guess you must be Roo."

All Dalton could do was nod. "I guess so."

The name stuck, even after Tierney's abundance of nervous energy leveled out and Dalton had stopped accusing him of being weaned on Tigger blood. In truth, Dalton liked being Tierney's Roo. It was way better than being Ian's Squirrel, even Sam admitted that.

He also liked shopping for furniture, especially when it was so obvious what was really happening. The big tip-off was that Tierney insisted on going with him. The man hated shopping, of any kind. When he couldn't cajole Dalton into doing it for him, he paid his assistant to.

So, *duh*: Tierney wanted Dalton to pick out the new table because he wanted that table to also *be* Dalton's. It was ridiculously obvious. Apparently, though, Dalton wasn't as easy to read, because Tierney didn't seem to understand that by *agreeing* to pick out the table, Dalton was agreeing to part ownership of it.

At the giant warehouse-style store, Dalton watched from the modular storage section as Tierney stared at the talkative saleslady. You'd think she was speaking a foreign language—Tierney's mouth was even hanging open slightly. Dalton would have to step in if he started to drool.

He didn't though. Instead he shook himself out of his stupor and beckoned frantically. Dalton took his time wandering over.

"Um, what do you think of this one?" Tierney said as soon as he didn't have to shout. Much.

It's ugly. "Well, do *you* like it?" It was surprisingly similar to the old table, but the scrollwork legs were painted and the beading around the edge was even more intricate.

Tierney curled his lip at it. "No."

"We have quite a few other tables of this size," the saleslady reassured them, as if they couldn't see they were standing in two football fields' worth of dining room furnishings.

"Do you really need a table that's as big as the old one?" Dalton asked. "That thing's huge." He was now close enough that Tierney could touch him, and he did, just like always, taking Dalton's hand.

Tierney shrugged. "I dunno. I guess so."

Dalton squeezed his fingers. "So, you regularly have large dinner parties?"

Tierney's answer was to look at him is if he'd lost his mind.

"That's a no," Dalton said, pointing at him. "To both dinner parties and needing a big table. Do you see that changing in the future? The dinner parties?"

"Not unless you wanna have some."

Dalton ignored that, for now. "Maybe you could get a smaller table that has leaves to make it bigger?"

Tugging on Dalton to get him to move, Tierney towed him to the section with the smaller ones, the saleslady trailing behind. She kept watching them, sneaking glances at their clasped hands. Tierney refused to not take Dalton's hand in public, or kiss him if he wanted to. He'd said he'd hidden too many years to keep doing it now.

It always made Dalton melt a little when Tierney would blandly stare down someone who looked at them twice.

"This one's cool," Tierney said, halting in front of a small square table with simple lines and a pronounced wood grain.

"I really like it." Dalton picked up the hangtag to read the details.

"I don't know, are you sure it's big enough?"

Sigh. "It extends to seat ten."

"But it *looks* so small."

"It'll easily fit the two of us."

Tierney turned to him. "I don't know. Lay down on it and let's see."

"Tierney," Dalton admonished, trying not to laugh. But over Tierney's shoulder he saw how red the saleslady's cheeks had gone, and he couldn't stifle it. Fortunately, she giggled too, covering her mouth with her hand and tittering.

"Fine, you can lay on it at home and we'll return it if we have to." Tierney winked at him. "We'll take this one," he added to the woman helping them. Then he whirled back around and said excitedly, "If we get a smaller table, we'll have a ton of space, won't we? We could get shelves too, right? Sort of screen off the kitchen with them?"

In the end, they bought enough new furniture to fill a delivery truck. A small one, but still. They even picked out a new bed. And Dalton had to give his stamp of approval on each item, because Tierney refused to decide until he did. *So obvious.* And sweet.

Once the saleslady had left them, walking back to the store office to arrange for delivery of their purchases, probably adding up her commission in awe, Dalton finally dropped the bomb. "I know why you're doing this." He meandered one or two steps closer, until he was nearly in Tierney's arms, and their clasped hands bumped alternately against each of their thighs.

"What?" Tierney opened his eyes impossibly wide, which had made no one look innocent, ever, in the history of the world. "I'm not doing anything."

"You're making me pick out the furniture because you want me to like it so much I'll move into your place."

He dropped the act immediately. "Is it working?"

Dalton tilted his head and smiled before turning away to fake interest in some bookshelves.

"Okay, listen," Tierney said, untangling their fingers and splaying his on Dalton's lower back. "I know I'm supposed to wait a year, but it's been nearly seven months, and things are going great. I mean, you think so too, right?"

It was tempting to not answer again, but that would be cruel. "You know I do."

Tierney dropped a kiss on his temple. "And you said we could revisit it in six months, anyway."

"Has it really been that long?" Dalton asked airily.

"So, don't you want to be with me all the time? Your cat already lives at my place. Half your stuff is there too."

Reaching up, he carelessly patted Tierney's cheek. "I'll think about it." He had to pretend to be inspecting a very ugly vase to hide his smile.

Tierney didn't move for a few seconds, other than his fingers flexing on Dalton's back, then he leaned in and whispered. "I know what *you're* doing."

"What am I doing?" He couldn't keep the teasing out of his voice.

"You're messing with me, aren't you? Because you like it when I say it."

Dalton turned, so they were nearly chest to chest, holding this conversation within inches of each other because that's the kind it was. The special, *just between us* kind. "Say what?" He gave the innocent look a try, but it probably didn't work for him, either.

Tierney was grinning by now. He reached up and combed Dalton's bangs back, tucking the hair behind his ear, then rested his fingertips on Dalton's face. His cheek and the curve of his jaw and his chin. A small touch that told Dalton exactly how Tierney felt about him.

But still, it'd be nice to hear.

"You want me to say that I want you. Not just need you and love you, but want *you* in my life and my home and my bed."

Dalton bit his lip, like it might keep his internal explosion of happy from spilling all over the furniture store and making a spectacle of them. It didn't work, of course, because Tierney's hold on him tightened, and then Tierney's lips were over his own, coaxing him into a deeper kiss than was really appropriate in public, but right then who cared? This little moment was so big he couldn't contain it. He wrapped his arms around Tierney's waist and gave in.

"Is that a yes?" Tierney asked when they were done but still holding on to each other in their bubble of intimacy.

"Yes." He pressed one more short, clingy kiss on his man.

"I want to hear *you* say it," Tierney whispered, still smiling, but Dalton could hear that note of need in his boyfriend's voice.

So he gave him what they both wanted. "I want you, and I need you, and I love you. And yes, I'll live with you."

Tierney whooped, jumping back and grabbing Dalton's hand, then towing him along the aisle toward the door.

"Where are we going?" Like he didn't know.

"Where the hell are the people who work here?" Tierney shouted. "How'm I going to bribe some dudes to deliver this stuff today if I can't find anyone?"

Of course, the saleslady magically appeared from an office, and the whole time Tierney was paying her off and giving instructions about the delivery—"Give us at least an hour, because we have to break the old table more, first"—he wouldn't let go of Dalton.

As if he never intended to again.

Start at the beginning of the Romancelandia series at:
www.riptidepublishing.com/titles/too-stupid-live

Dear Reader,

Thank you for reading Anne Tenino's *Billionaire with Benefits*!

We know your time is precious and you have many, many entertainment options, so it means a lot that you've chosen to spend your time reading. We really hope you enjoyed it.

We'd be honored if you'd consider posting a review—good or bad—on sites like **Amazon, Barnes & Noble, Kobo, Goodreads, Twitter, Facebook, Tumblr,** and your blog or website. We'd also be honored if you told your friends and family about this book. Word of mouth is a book's lifeblood!

For more information on upcoming releases, author interviews, blog tours, contests, giveaways, and more, please sign up for our weekly, spam-free newsletter and visit us around the web:

Newsletter: tinyurl.com/RiptideSignup
Twitter: twitter.com/RiptideBooks
Facebook: facebook.com/RiptidePublishing
Goodreads: tinyurl.com/RiptideOnGoodreads
Tumblr: riptidepublishing.tumblr.com

Thank you so much for Reading the Rainbow!

RiptidePublishing.com

Acknowledgments

As usual, there are a million people to thank, and chances are good I'll forget one or two. (I'm sure they'll remind me.) I'd like to thank Stacey Heyworth from the Multnomah County District Attorney's office for putting up with my questions. Thanks to Tom for rugby tips, and Justin for sharing the glamor of working in a state office. Thanks to the Husband for giving Tierney things to bitch about. Beta readers! Andrea, Alec, MC, Thorny, Ellen, and Steve, this is your shout out. Finally, very great thanks to my editors, Chris, Caz and Alex.

Theta Alpha Gamma series
Frat Boy and Toppy
Love, Hypothetically
Sweet Young Thang
Good Boy
Poster Boy

Romancelandia series
Too Stupid to Live

Horny (in the My Haunted Blender's Gay Love Affair, and Other Twisted Tales collection)

Task Force Iota series
18% Gray
Turning Tricks
Happy Birthday to Me

Whitetail Rock
The Fix (Whitetail Rock, #2)

About The Author

Raised on a steady media diet of Monty Python, classical music, and the visual arts, Anne Tenino rocked the mental health world when she was the first patient diagnosed with Compulsive Romantic Disorder. Since that day, with her trusty psychiatrist by her side, Anne has taken on conquering the M/M world through therapeutic writing. Finding out who those guys having sex in her head are and what to do with them has been extremely liberating.

Anne's husband finds it liberating as well, although in a somewhat different way. He has accepted her need for "research," and looks forward to the benefits said research affords him. He thinks it's kind of cool she manages to write, as well. Her two daughters are mildly confused by Anne's need to twist Ken dolls into odd positions. They were raised to be open-minded children, however, and other than occasionally stealing Ken1's strap-on, they let Mom do her thing without interference.

Anne's thing is writing gay romance and erotica.

Wondering what Anne does in her spare time? Mostly she lies on the couch, eats bonbons and shirks housework.

Check out what Anne's up to now by visiting her site at AnneTenino.com.

Links:
Riptide: riptidepublishing.com/authors/anne-tenino
Chicks & Dicks Blog: chicksanddicksrainbow.com
Twitter: twitter.com/AnneTenino
Goodreads: goodreads.com/author/show/4831235.Anne_Tenino
Facebook: facebook.com/anne.tenino
Amazon: amazon.com/Anne-Tenino/e/B005FQZOHS

Enjoy this book?
Find more contemporary romance at RiptidePublishing.com!

Starstruck
ISBN: 978-1-62649-171-7

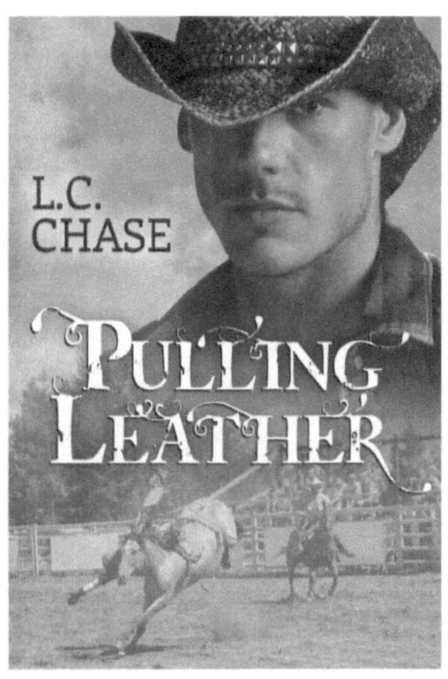

Pulling Leather
ISBN: 978-1-62649-162-5

Earn Bonus Bucks!

Earn 1 Bonus Buck for each dollar you spend. Find out how at RiptidePublishing.com/news/bonus-bucks.

Win Free Ebooks for a Year!

Pre-order coming soon titles directly through our site and you'll receive one entry into a drawing to win free books for a year! Get the details at RiptidePublishing.com/contests.